GREEN SUN

ALSO BY KENT ANDERSON

Sympathy for the Devil

Night Dogs

GREEN SUN

A NOVEL

KENT ANDERSON

MULHOLLAND BOOKS

Little, Brown and Company

New York Boston London

Copyright © 2018 by Kent Anderson

Mulholland Books / Little, Brown and Company
Hachette Book Group
1290 Avenue of the Americas, New York, NY 10104
mulhollandbooks.com

First Edition: February 2018

Mulholland Books is an imprint of Little, Brown and Company, a division of Hachette Book Group, Inc. The Mulholland Books name and logo are trademarks of Hachette Book Group, Inc.

ISBN 978-0-316-46680-6
LCCN 2017941369

10 9 8 7 6 5 4 3 2 1

LSC-C

Printed in the United States of America

For my sweet Elizabeth

CONTENTS

CONTENTS

GREEN SUN

CHAPTER ONE

WINTER — IDAHO

It's winter in Idaho, past midnight, and it should be dark, but the wind-driven snow crackles with lightning and shakes the clattering glassy branches of frozen trees. Green and blue curtains of aurora borealis flare and furl and curtsy across the northern horizon.

Hanson appears out of the hissing snow with a double armload of firewood, on his way to the cabin. An owl, back in the trees where the wind doesn't seem to touch him, watches with great yellow eyes as Hanson drops the wood onto the porch, opens the door, and goes inside, pushing the door closed against the wind. He hangs up his coat and feeds chunks of split locust into the cast-iron stove, watching the fire leap up before closing and latching the door. The only light in the cabin comes from the crazed mica window in the hinged stove door, flickering the cabin walls in and out like an old movie projector. It had seemed like April, spring on its way, when the storm blew down from the Hi-Line. He sits cross-legged in front of the fireplace, drinking tequila from the bottle, looking at his books stacked and shelved against the walls, the titles on their spines glittering in the firelight.

He'll be leaving in another six weeks, as soon as the quarter is over and he's turned in his grades. He'll miss his students—he knows that—and the cabin too, half a mile above Boise, where he walks the hills through all the seasons, watching the weather roll in from the northwest. But after three years as an assistant professor at the university in town, he's leaving. The English Department will be glad to see him go. He isn't anything like them and wonders how he ever thought he was. He's going back to the only work he could find after the war, a job where people understand pain better than rhetoric. So much for the life of the mind, he thinks, smiling—time to go back to what he was good at.

He reaches into the neck of his wool shirt and pulls out a compass the size of a dime that he wears on a cord. An army issue survival compass he's had since the war. The olive-drab enamel has chipped off the edge of the brass case, but the compass still works like it should, something he can trust if he thinks he's lost. He holds it level, watches the arrow turn, twitch, reverse itself, and steady up on north. Good old north, he thinks. You can depend on north, where it's always ice and howling wind and polar bears out there, white shadows deep in the blowing snow.

Finishing the last of the tequila, he stands and walks to one of the bookcases, considering the titles in the firelight, touching them, pulls out his Yeats, still warped to the shape of his leg from carrying it everywhere in Vietnam, wrapped in plastic, in a pocket of his tiger suit. He taps it with his knuckle, smiling, and slips it back into its place between *The Oxford Book of English Verse* and a King James Bible he picked up one night in a Motel 6 in Salt Lake City.

He's lived in isolated A-camps where he was always awake, even when he slept, in cities where he booby-trapped his apartment with trip wires, shotgun shells, and blasting caps behind the Sheetrock. And once, in a cabin by the Rio Costilla in the Sangre de Cristos in Northern New Mexico, seventy miles from the nearest supermarket, he had to make peace with ghosts. Their bodies had been buried on the property during the wars between the Spanish and the Ute Indians two hundred years before, and for the first week or so he slept outside by the river while they watched him, chanted, tore their own arms and legs off in display, and one night called an icy wind down from the mountains that uprooted three of the ancient cottonwood trees growing by the river. After that they left him alone—accepted him, he liked to think—and he was glad to have them out there at night, watching over the place.

Outside, the snow blows silently in the wind, rushes, spins, whirls away, and gone. The distant glow of lights in the town below.

In the partitioned end of the cabin that is the bedroom, he shucks off his jeans and long underwear, slips between crisp pale-green sheets and, with his hands clasped behind his head, studies the flickering shadows on the log-and-plank ceiling. His ears chitter and chirp and ring and whine with the tinnitus the VA doctors told him would never get better, only worse.

Death is in the cabin, on the other side of the wall. Hanson had heard him opening and closing the drawers of his desk, reading old mail. He's looking at the books, talking to them in his ancient language. When he begins to sing Hanson smiles, closing his eyes. Death is watching the fire. In the sky above the cabin, far beyond the storm and earth's concerns, the constellation Orion, huge and magnificent, is keeping time.

CHAPTER TWO

THE ACADEMY

Running third now, Hanson picked up his pace. He could talk to the pain. He could hurt the pain if he had to. He could step out of his body, watch himself run, and leave the pain behind. But Hanson trusted pain. It was real, not some abstraction or metaphor or clever analogy at a goddamn English Department cocktail party. On the street, whoever takes the most pain wins, simple as that, and Hanson could take as much as anybody wanted to serve up. So he was singing:

"Well, I had an old *dog* an' his name was *Blue*,

Had an old dog, an' his *name* was Blue,

Had an old dog…"

He jogged across the street, crossed back again. He couldn't see the runners ahead of him or, looking back, behind him. Well.

"Had an old dog, his name was *bluuuu,*

Betcha five dollars he's a *good* dog too…"

Come *on,* he told himself, *come on.* Run. He angled across Railroad Park, running parallel with a ten-foot hedge, its dusty leaves mutated with pollution. On the other side of the hedge a massive

6

steam locomotive—silver and gleaming black—seemed to move with him, picking up speed, flickering through the branches.

Third place, fine, he thought. Good. I *like* third place. Gimme third place, it is only running, after all. Who kills who is what it comes down to. It doesn't matter how fast you can run if you're dead. Nothing matters if you're dead—who you were or thought you were, what you believed, which gang you belonged to. That's all over. The good thing about death is that you no longer have to deal with your failures—the times when you were scared, uncertain, drunk, when your memory or social skills let you down, all the times you should have done better than you managed to do. That's all over too. When you're dead you can relax finally and get some sleep.

But he felt good today, running, good and mean. The harder he ran the better he felt, and when he felt really good he didn't want to dance or laugh or sing—he wanted to kick ass. He'd tried to explain that to normal people but couldn't even explain it to himself. The reason why didn't matter, not in combat or alone on the street with a badge and a gun. He was fine out there. "No problem, Your Honor, good as gold, sir, ready to meet the public," he announced, laughing, as he ran.

Just up ahead McCarty, who had been in second place, limped toward downtown, one hand on his hip. Hanson snarled and pushed a little harder, looking for Byron Fernandez, ahead in the lead somewhere. Fernandez was his only friend in the Academy. You'd think he was Hispanic with that name, but he was a middle-class black kid who'd grown up over in Alameda. He'd better catch up to Fernandez soon, though, because the high-rise Oakland Police Justice Center was in sight now, rising above the trees and traffic, blocking the sun.

A deputy chief had made the decision to accept Hanson's application and hire him unseen over the objections of Lieutenant

Garber in Training, the officer in charge of the Academy. He was, after all, a deputy chief, and subordinate officers like Lieutenant Garber needed to be reminded of that fact from time to time. Besides, Hanson had four years of previous police experience working the ghetto of Portland, Oregon, a city roughly the same size as Oakland, that like Oakland had brought in trainloads of black families from the South to work in the shipyards and defense factories of World War II. When the shipyards and factories shut down, they were stuck. In Portland he had received a number of citations for valor and innovation. He'd been a Special Forces sergeant in Vietnam, winning two Bronze Stars. He had a master's degree in English literature and was teaching English at Boise State University. True, he was thirty-eight years old, but many of the OPD's best officers were in that age group. Hanson, he had declared, would be an asset to the Department. The reasons this deputy chief had approved Hanson for the Academy were the reasons Lieutenant Garber didn't want Hanson. He'd learned the job in a different police department—he was too old—he wasn't going to be trainable.

By the time Hanson arrived in Oakland and discovered that he would be required to go through the five-month Police Academy, with twenty-one- and twenty-two-year-old recruits as classmates, the deputy chief was no longer with the Department.

Every Tuesday afternoon for several months prior to Hanson's arrival, the deputy chief had been meeting a woman named Brandi in a comped room at the Marriott Hotel. Brandi had been introduced to the deputy chief by a DEA mutual acquaintance, a crony of Lieutenant Garber. Under Lieutenant Garber's direction, surveillance was set. Video cameras were installed, and Lieutenant Garber, along with a sergeant from Vice, watched the crime-in-progress: accepting a gratuity, free use of the room at the Marriott. The deputy chief was not charged or arrested, but the week before Hanson arrived he resigned from the Oakland Police Department to take a job with the Detroit PD.

Hanson knew nothing of this, of course, but he had realized that signing up for the OPD was a mistake. He was not what they wanted, and they were not what he wanted, but he needed the job. They thought he had a bad attitude, and he did. Lieutenant Garber and the Training cadre had started in on him from his first day in the Academy, trying to coerce him into resigning, but good luck on that, he thought. He was tougher than they were.

At one of the first formal inspections, Sergeant White, a senior cadre, told Hanson that the hideaway pocket in his new wool pants wasn't deep enough to accommodate his "short wood," a ten-inch lead-filled billy club they'd been issued in addition to the longer nightstick—for close work. When Hanson said, "Yes, sir, I'll have it fixed," White reprimanded him for unnecessary talking in formation and put a memo of reprimand in his file. Most recently White had written a memo for Hanson's file about the last inspection, when he'd told Hanson to pull his uniform pants pockets inside out and pointed out a union label sewn into the bottom of the right pocket, a uniform violation. Hanson had to respond in writing, explaining how he'd been derelict in not removing the pocket label.

He'd made White look bad at the outdoor firing range when White had picked him to use as an example of how difficult it was to fire a handgun accurately after running thirty yards and back. Hanson had put all six rounds in the black, and all White could say was "*Normally* it's difficult to shoot accurately when you've been in a chase and are under pressure. Remember what I'm telling you, not Hanson's dumb luck. There's no luck out on the street." Hanson realized then that he should have blown a couple of shots, but when he started shooting he'd gone into point-and-shoot muscle memory, his body taking over, faster than thought, into survival mode.

He'd felt a little bad about making White look stupid at the firing range. Some days White started drinking after lunch, Hanson could smell it on him. White's life, he imagined, was difficult enough. But Hanson was getting weary of it, and he'd never had any such compassion for Lieutenant Garber.

Lieutenant Garber, several years younger than Hanson, had not done much time on the street, as was the case with most officers above the rank of sergeant, but had instead spent the years preparing for promotion exams and learning how to navigate the internal politics of the Department. His official objection to Hanson, voiced frequently to the Training cadre, was that Hanson was insubordinate. Hanson could be ironic sometimes when he shouldn't be and he asked too many questions in class just to stay interested and awake, but it wasn't insubordination. Hanson could follow orders and maintain a respectful demeanor.

It was late in the afternoon on a Friday, and Hanson, along with most of the class, was having trouble staying awake after the run that morning and a two-hour lecture on traffic law. Lieutenant Garber had come in at five to teach a class on writing search warrants for a test Monday morning, but he digressed into a rant about a recent probable cause ruling by the California Supreme Court and its "Communist" Chief Justice Rose Bird that had, once again, further eroded police powers.

The rest of the class leaned forward in their desks, listening intently, encouraging the lieutenant to go on so that the search warrant test might be postponed. Hanson sat back and listened too, skeptical as usual of Lieutenant Garber's politics, but telling himself to just listen and not ask any questions—this wasn't a college classroom. It hadn't been but a couple of weeks earlier when he'd suggested to a lecturer that police officers were basically armed social workers whose job was to interpret and enforce the social contract of the community they patrolled. Fernandez saw Hanson *thinking,* and when the lieutenant turned to close the hall door, he grinned and made a "slow down" gesture with his hand, warning Hanson not to comment. Hanson smiled back at Fernandez and shook his head: *Not today.*

The lieutenant was in uniform, beautifully tailored, and so wearing, of course, his OPD lieutenant's badge, a solid gold star. He stepped back up behind his podium, removed his hat, and looked the class over silently, in a manly, military manner, Hanson thought, establishing his excellent "command presence" as he went into more detail about the stupidity of the California Communist Supreme Court's latest assault on police powers.

A police officer, Lieutenant Garber told them, had stopped a black man walking in Beverly Hills at 11 p.m. because he was dressed inappropriately and was clearly not the type of individual who belonged in that neighborhood. The suspect claimed that he was a screenwriter, staying not far from where he'd been stopped. He had the odor of an alcoholic beverage on his breath, the officer testified, and based on the officer's past police experience, he believed the suspect was under the influence and asked him for some ID. The suspect responded to his request by saying, "Dream on, motherfucker, I'm going home," and began walking away, ignoring the officer's commands to stop. A cover car arrived and the officers now at the scene, observing the suspect's demeanor, his appearance, and his refusal to comply with the primary officer's commands, justifiably concerned that he might be armed, subdued the suspect and placed him under arrest. A resident, a somewhat elderly individual, who claimed to have observed the arrest—from his porch, almost a block away, under nighttime conditions—testified that the officers, brandishing their service revolvers, had assaulted the suspect for no apparent reason, slamming him repeatedly into the side of a patrol car while making racial slurs.

The suspect refused a plea bargain, and when the case went to trial, several Hollywood celebrities testified on his behalf and he was found not guilty of all charges, including possession of a quantity of cocaine the officers discovered in his shoe. The court had thrown that out along with all the other charges—assaulting a police officer, resisting arrest, public intoxication, and possession of cocaine—because, in their view, the police had no probable cause to stop him in the first place. He sued the Beverly Hills Police Department and was awarded 1.3 million dollars. The elements of a probable cause stop were going to be even more difficult to establish now, at least in California.

Jesus, Hanson thought, smiling, the fuckin' guy was lucky they didn't shoot him, in Beverly Hills, and that some rich liberal had seen what happened and was willing to testify. Christ, he…

The lieutenant had stopped talking and was just standing up there behind the podium looking at Hanson. So was the rest of the class.

"Yes, sir?" he said as mildly as he could. Fernandez was rolling his eyes.

"You seem to find this amusing. Do you have something that you'd like to share with the rest of us?" The lieutenant nodded for him to speak.

Fine, Hanson thought, okay.

"Sir. I'd blame the officers involved more than I'd blame Rose Bird."

Lieutenant Garber nodded for Hanson to go on.

"It was kind of dumb to…I mean, the primary officer…Sir, cops like this guy keep *inviting* the court to take police powers away."

Lieutenant Garber interrupted him by holding up one finger while looking out at the rest of the class. "Our constitutional scholar," he announced. "Thank you, Officer Hanson, for that insight. The officer in question, a seasoned officer calling on his hard-won expertise and knowledge of the streets, attempting to make an arrest of a suspect who was, in fact, in possession of a quantity of cocaine, is, in your opinion, 'dumb'?"

I'm dumb, Hanson thought, for saying anything at all.

"I'd call him an outstanding officer for making a legitimate arrest," Lieutenant Garber said. "*I'm* no scholar, but that's what I'd call him. Outstanding. But maybe you're aware of something here that I'm not privy to. Could you share that with the class?"

"Sir, you know, it's kind of a game sometimes, a—"

"A *game?* Is that what you think? The *game* of law enforcement? The *game* of protecting citizens from predators out there," he said, gesturing out the seventh floor window toward East Oakland, way in the distance. "I don't know anything about a game. And for the politically correct, I'm not just talking about Tyrone. This isn't about race, as it clearly is, obviously, to anybody honest enough to see it. It's about the law."

"Sir, I'm not trying to argue here, at all, but…why not just go up to the guy, the suspect, say 'How you doin',' talk to him, and see…"

Lieutenant Garber held up his hand and Hanson stopped talking.

"Class is dismissed till Monday morning. Hanson, you are not dismissed."

"Sir," one of the recruits began, "are we still gonna have the search warrant quiz on Monday, or…"

"I don't know, Parker. I don't *know. Study* for it."

Hanson got to his feet, stood beside his desk. The rest of the class left, looking straight ahead. Lieutenant Garber gripped the lectern he was standing behind.

"What are your intentions, Hanson?"

"Intentions? Sir?"

"Intentions," Lieutenant Garber almost shouted. "What are you

doing here? We don't get a lot of thirty-eight-year-old recruits with degrees in *literature*. You writing a book?"

"No, sir," Hanson said, keeping his expression neutral.

"Maybe a career in social work, then? To help the downtrodden? Or perhaps law school? You're not too old for that if you get started soon. Get a job with the ACLU."

Hanson didn't say anything, waiting Lieutenant Garber out.

"The reason I'm asking, Hanson, is because you don't seem to fit in very well here at the OPD. Your classroom work is satisfactory, more or less, but that's only a small part of preparing for the street, as a police officer, here in Oakland anyway. Sergeant Jackson, for instance, tells me that you and he have had some problems in the area of physical proficiency and self-defense, which I, for one, consider a very important part of your training."

Hanson nodded to show that he was listening.

"Very well, Hanson. You need to work harder then, to show us that you want to learn the kind of law enforcement we expect from our officers, and no one is going to make this training any easier for you. Think about it.

"You're dismissed."

"Yes, sir. Thank you, sir," Hanson said, and left the classroom.

On the way down the hall, he passed the open door of the Training cadre office, where Sergeant Jackson stood watching him from the doorway. Sergeant Jackson was the senior physical training cadre. He was a few years older than Hanson, and he'd been on the street for sixteen years. The word was that as a young officer recruited from somewhere in the South, he'd married a rich, beautiful, politically connected woman and didn't need the fifty thousand dollars a year the Department paid him. He came to work because he liked the job. He told lieutenants and captains when they were wrong and seemed to do whatever he wanted to on the street, no matter how brutal or outrageous.

Sergeant Jackson was tough and smart, fluid and fast. He had a temper but used it to his advantage. He fucked with Hanson every chance he got. "You," he'd say, when he needed a volunteer, pointing at Hanson as he sat cross-legged on the mats, taking a break with the rest of the class. Hanson would stand up, soaked with sweat, and walk up to Sergeant Jackson, who would jam his arm or wrist into a painful come-along hold or use him to demonstrate a take-down, faking a move in one direction, then pivoting to sweep Hanson's legs out from under him, all the while calmly and never out of breath explaining to the rest of the class what he was doing. Hanson never changed expression when Sergeant Jackson slammed him to the mat or levered a carotid choke hold on him till his vision closed down to black tunnels. Hanson was able to step outside himself and watch it happen, refusing to give Sergeant Jackson the satisfaction of any emotion at all. He couldn't afford to get angry.

The following Monday marked the beginning of the fourth month of the Academy. By then, half the class, the 106th Recruit School, had quit, dropped out with injuries, or been terminated for poor performance. Two were fired because of something their initial background checks had missed. Another resigned after being arrested for assault in a downtown bar. Trainees who'd gone through it together called the five-month Oakland Police Academy the OPD Street Combat Course. The cadre wrote out permission slips for the trainees—and a buddy to drive them— to go to the Alameda County Hospital emergency room. Broken finger, broken nose, cracked rib, and concussion were the most common excuses. Trainees limped to their cars after twelve- and fourteen-hour days of five-mile runs, nightstick katas, one-on-one choke holds, take-downs, handcuffing, and come-along drills. The recruits all wore Department-issued white T-shirts with an

Oakland PD badge printed on the front and a red, orange, and yellow woodpecker on the back. The woodpecker's beak curled into a snarl, and above him were the words TOUGH AS WOODPECKER LIPS. That afternoon they were sitting in a half circle on the floor of the gym, listening to Sergeant Jackson.

"Anybody who will fight a police officer will kill a police officer," Sergeant Jackson told the class. "Your badge and gun don't mean anything to him, because he doesn't have anything to lose. People. When you stop him on the street this type of individual will lie, interrupt, and argue. If you allow him to do these things, you are giving him permission to kill you, because he thinks you're weak. He will curse you and walk away if you tell him he's under arrest. When you reach out to handcuff him, he'll resist, fight back, and kill you—with your own gun if he doesn't already have one. Don't expect anybody out there to obey the law like we have to do. They live by the law of the jungle.

"He is not like you. Do not believe that liberal happy talk about how, down deep, we're all the same. He is a different kind of animal than you are. And when you find yourself in a fight on the street, you have no friends out there. You can't just give up, you can't quit, because if you do, he'll kill you. He damn sure—excuse me, ladies—he isn't going to simply subdue you, then go home to the wife and kids.

"Winning the fight is the only option you have, and that means the second he looks at you wrong, sasses you, back talks, or raises a hand, you knock him on his ass, hurt him, and keep hurting him till he stops trying to get up, then you arrest him and cuff him and think of something to charge him with later. If it goes bad and you think he's going to overpower you, then you shoot him and kill him. Do not hesitate to kill him if you have to. We are spread way too thin out there to hesitate. If Tyrone forces you to kill him to save your own life, the Department will back you up.

"In my years working the street, no officer who has had to kill a citizen in self-defense had to face anything worse than two weeks on administrative leave with pay. Oakland is the ex-con capital of California. These individuals do not fear the courts or prison. The courts are backed up two and three years with felony cases waiting to go to trial. The prisons are full. He knows this. If he has to go back to prison, he's at home there, anyway. That's his real home. He was born in prison. Prison was his home before he was born.

"He doesn't fear the law, the courts, or prison. So I'm here to tell you that he'd better fear you. You are the law out there on the street. You're real. You can hurt him *now*. Many of you grew up thinking it wasn't like that. Now you know."

After the class took a break, Hanson stood facing Sergeant Jackson on a brick-red foam mat for what was called a blocking drill. Sergeant Jackson wore padded red focus gloves on both hands, like stuffed catcher's mitts made of shiny plastic. Hanson stood with his hands at his sides, waiting for Sergeant Jackson to swing at his head. They were toe to toe, too close for Hanson to see both of Sergeant Jackson's hands in his peripheral vision, so he watched his eyes to predict when a blow was coming and from which side. He blocked blow after blow, even as they came faster and harder, until Sergeant Jackson, a little out of breath, said, "*Don't* look at my *eyes*. Watch my hands. Hands are what kill you. Not eyes."

They both knew he couldn't watch both hands. He blocked the next blow.

"*Don't* look at my *eyes*."

Still focused on his eyes, Hanson thought about breaking his nose, making him bleed, hurting him as much as he could before Sergeant Jackson kicked his ass, then got him fired. Or punching him in the throat and maybe killing him.

"Go ahead," Sergeant Jackson said. "Go for it."

Hanson needed the job. He looked down at Sergeant Jackson's right glove, watching it until Sergeant Jackson hit him in the side of the head with his left glove. Hanson turned his head to watch the left glove, keeping his arms at his sides, making no attempt to block the blow he knew was coming. Sergeant Jackson hit him with the right glove, harder this time, on the other side of his head, almost knocking him down, Hanson's eyes flaring with red and silver stars. He regained his balance and turned his head the other way.

"Take off," Sergeant Jackson said. "Get outta here while you still can. Take the rest of the day off."

Hanson walked past him, into his warbling tinnitus and through the rest of the class toward the two pairs of double doors he saw at the far end of the gym, hoping he could make it through whichever one was real before he puked. Something touched his shoulder, and when he heard Fernandez whisper "Fuck 'em," he smiled. He knew he could make it through the real door if he kept walking, through the Academy, unless they killed him, because that's what they'd have to do, he thought.

Down in the locker room, in the empty echoing shower room, breathing the steam, a rivulet of blood running from his nose. Seven more weeks and his class graduated from the Academy. November 19, 1982. He had the date circled on the Three Dragons Restaurant calendar thumbtacked to the water-stained Sheetrock in his kitchen.

CHAPTER THREE

MY GIRL

It was the winter solstice, December 21, the longest night of the year. Tomorrow the days would start getting longer. He'd be working through the holidays, a week that always kicked the annual murder rate into another ten digits before it dropped back to zero on New Year's Day. He couldn't find anywhere to eat in District Five, so after his last call he slipped off to the Junkyard Dog on Foothill for a Coke and a Gangsta Burger. He wasn't hungry—he'd had a protein powder milkshake for breakfast—but he knew he should eat something for the extra hours of overtime he'd be working. There weren't enough cops out there as it was, and this week anyone with any seniority at all would be out on vacation time. And others were just calling in sick. There were only two cars assigned to District Five, and half the calls they got dispatched to were off the district. Cover cars would be slow to nonexistent, worse than usual, but he was most comfortable working by himself anyway, and the holiday overtime was okay with him. Better working a patrol car than home alone or out in crowds of last-minute shoppers with supermarket Christmas music.

His semimonthly paycheck was more than twice what he could make doing anything else, even if he could find another job. He'd bought a sofa, a microwave, and another Crock-Pot he'd never use. He'd just put four new tires on his vehicle, a 1963 D1100 International Harvester Travelall, the four-door model, which he'd bought at a Forest Service auction in Missoula. It had gotten him from Boise to Oakland, but just barely. It was good enough to get him from his flat to the Justice Center. If it died on him completely, he could take a bus or walk. He'd have to get something else eventually, but that meant dealing with a car salesman, and he wanted to put that off as long as possible. Two more months and he'd be caught up on his bills and have money in the bank. What else would anybody hire him for? The next war hadn't started yet and he'd be too old to enlist when it did. He didn't think he could hack another two or three years in academia for a PhD, and if he could, then what? And he'd last about a day in some office job cubicle before he threw his boss out a window.

Once he got through roll call, away from the Justice Center, and out on the street, things weren't so bad. Out in East Oakland, by himself, with the life/death/life/death. And the way they shuffled him from beat to beat and district to district every night, there wasn't much in the way of any consistent supervision. He didn't have to look over his shoulder all the time for some sergeant showing up to second-guess him, expect him to handle things the OPD way. As long as he kept up his arrest quota, they seemed to pretty much leave him alone. The job might even work out, and he could retire and die in twenty-five years.

The Junkyard Dog was an old Airstream trailer painted wiener brown with a mustard stripe down its back. Mounted at the end nearest the street was a savage robot dog's head that had been welded and riveted and pounded out of a truck cab, its teeth and pointed ears fabricated from junked cars—grilles, bumpers, tail fins—its spotlight eyes glaring down Foothill day and night. The head sheltered the bulletproof service window like a carport. Hanson backed his patrol car into the parking space closest to the street, got out, and walked up to the window. The only other car in the lot was an older tricked-out gold Cadillac with a young woman in the passenger seat.

The driver of the Cadillac was already at the thick Plexiglas window that worked like a miniature revolving door. He'd put a bloody five-dollar bill down, but the chubby black kid in the Doggie Diner paper cap refused to turn the revolving door and take it. The name tag on his stained, too-small white tunic was JIMENEZ, but he didn't look Mexican. "We don't accept bloody money," Jimenez said, his voice muffled behind the bulletproof plastic. The blood was fresh, wet, gleaming through the paper fibers in the artificial light. Neither of them seemed to notice Hanson standing there, uniformed, armed, wearing his name tag, his PAC-set hissing and barking as Radio sent cars to and from calls.

"It's legal tender," the customer said, glancing back at the girl in his car. "Federal law say you gotta accept it." He was wearing a suit woven with iridescent threads that threw off a green-gold nimbus.

Jimenez just looked at him and shook his head.

"You think I'm just makin' this shit up? It's the law, my man. Nobody above the law."

Hanson hadn't asked Radio for permission to leave his district. He was glad the police union had opposed the Department's last proposal to put transponders on the patrol cars so they'd know where the cars were at all times. He'd never get anything to eat on duty when they finally pushed that through. The kid in the suit asked Hanson, "You gonna enforce the law, Officer?"

"You want me to arrest him or shoot him?" He looked at the kid behind the counter. "Jimenez..." he began.

"That's not my name, I just gotta *wear* this Mexican piece of shit all night."

"Give him a couple of napkins," Hanson said, speaking into the little microphone above the bulletproof window. "He can wipe it off real good, you roll it on in and take a corner that's not bloody—just two fingers, right?" He raised his hand over his head, pinching his thumb and forefinger together. "Then lay it in the cash register before we get into any complex legal debates."

Neither one of them said anything. They both looked pissed off.

"Think about it. Take my advice or argue after I leave, but right now I need a Coke and a Gangsta Burger. With cheese. Okay, Jimenez? *Por favor?*"

He turned to the kid in the suit. "I apologize for jumping ahead of you in line, but I've gotta get back on the street, and you guys might be here all night. Okay?" The customer only gave him a bad look. "Or," Hanson went on, his voice weary, "you can show me some ID right now. I think a bloody five-dollar bill is probable cause to run you for warrants and search your car. It's up to you."

"Give him his Coke," the kid in the suit told Jimenez, "and fuck you. I'll take my business somewhere else." He walked back to his car, carrying the bill between his thumb and forefinger. Hanson sipped his Coke, watching the Cadillac drive off, while Jimenez wrapped his burger.

"Thanks," he told Jimenez. *"Feliz Navidad."* He waited till he was only a few blocks from his district before he cleared from his last call.

Copy, 5Tac51 clear... and, 5Tac51, we've been holding this one for a while, a 245 Knife outside the Artistic Hair Haven at Sixty-sixth and Foothill.

"On the way," Hanson said, hanging up the mike, then pulling to the curb, where he flipped through his *Thomas Guide* and finished the cheeseburger in three swallows. He turned the *Thomas Guide* around, looked out at the street sign, and licked his fingers. He grunted, put the Coke between his legs, and accelerated up East 14th Street past a parking lot of dead-looking Christmas trees surrounded by concertina wire.

He had to arrest the owner of the Artistic Hair Haven, charging him with ADW, CCW, and ex-con in possession, but at least he didn't have to fight him to take him to jail. A lot of paperwork, though. Then he got a family fight where the husband had tried to set the Christmas tree on fire—his wife said—but he'd passed out before he could get it burning, and she'd thrown a pot of boiling water on him. He'd had to go to the emergency room with third-degree burns on the backs of his legs.

By 2 a.m. things were quiet and Hanson was driving the alleys out by 96th Avenue. A police helicopter clattered overhead and banked down toward the bay.

He had the seat belt unhooked and his holster pulled around toward his lap so he could draw his pistol quickly, imagining how stupid he'd look dead, shot to pieces behind the steering wheel, snugly seat-belted in against his holstered pistol. Lieutenant Garber and the boys would be rid of him. The constitutional scholar. The social worker. He smiled, imagining them laughing about it. He wondered if they'd have a bagpipe play "Amazing Grace" at his funeral.

A garbage can rattled up ahead, rolling across the asphalt, spilling beer cans, Christmas season fast-food trash, and a hairy silver-white possum who humped and waddled through the headlight beams toward the shadows, huge and awkward, a segmented tail, his face smeared with something white so he looked like a rodent mime.

Hanson drove slowly around the garbage can, leaning across

the seat, and called out the open passenger window in a strangled whisper, "Hey, Possum…"

5Tac51.

He stopped the car and peeled the mike off the dashboard, still watching the possum. "5Tac51."

5Tac51, we've got a report of twenty-five to thirty people, fighting now, at Eighty-second and Bancroft.

"Okay."

Car to cover?

"I'll take care of it," he said. Then to the possum, "Be careful out there, buddy. Merry Christmas." He laughed and sat up.

Car to cover, my ass, he thought, driving out of the alley. As if one would be available. As if one cover car driven by some cop he'd never even met would make any difference with that many people. Yeah, yeah, car to cover. If twenty-five to thirty people were still fighting when he got there, he'd have to call in an air strike to calm them down. Nobody could fight for fifteen minutes unless they were zombies. Who knew what was really the problem? What would he find? Could he handle it or would it kill him? It's what he liked about the job. He forgot all his problems, the doubts and mistakes and regrets he couldn't do anything about.

It was a sad little strip mall of failing and already closed businesses. Twelve or fourteen cars were parked in a lopsided circle, all of their radios tuned to the same station. Couples were dancing, drinking, and smoking marijuana. The red cherries of their cigarettes and joints glowed and arced and danced in the dark parking lot. They saw the patrol car turn into the lot, of course, but pretended they didn't. Hanson cut his headlights and pulled up a couple of car lengths from the outside of the circle. Donna Summer was singing, *"She works hard for the money."* He got out of the patrol car, watching them dance and listening to Donna Summer's song, which was about so many women, and men, in East Oakland.

It was a beautiful night. The best time of day, Hanson thought. He hopped up onto the hood of the patrol car, where it was harder for them to ignore him, but they managed until he waved both arms above his head and shouted, "Excuse me, you all. Excuse me," sweeping his arms up and back like a referee signaling a touchdown. "Excuse me, y'all, I need to tell you something." He was willing to look a little foolish if it would solve a problem. Not many cops were, so it usually got people's attention. Most cops would have stayed in their patrol car and given commands over the loudspeaker.

Finally, everyone was looking at him, poised on the hood of the car, no longer invisible. He looked back at them, not afraid, reasonable, making quick eye contact with many of them. If people see that you're afraid, they won't hear anything you say.

"Thanks," he shouted. "Thank you, ladies and gentlemen. Radio sent me out here, telling me that there were twenty-five to thirty people fighting...*Now*"—he paused, smiled—"I told 'em, okay, I'll take care of it." That got a few laughs and the tension began to drift away. A breeze coming in off the ocean was a little chilly at this hour, and the engine heat rising up from beneath his feet felt good. He thought he'd be able to write this up on an assignment card now, no major paperwork. It was just possible that somebody might shoot him, but not likely, and if they did, so what? "You're not fighting. You're just dancing and having a good time. But it is, you know," he said, looking at his watch, "two thirty, so somebody around here must be trying to get some sleep before they go to work tomorrow, and they figured a fight would get the cops here faster than saying it was a dance."

He shrugged, held up his hands: *What can I say?*

"Anyway, could you all do me a favor and go on home? I'm

sorry about that, but if you don't, they're just gonna send a whole lot more cops, and it'll be a mess then. You all know what I'm talking about."

Just then, the first six bass notes of "My Girl," the great Smokey Robinson song, rolled out of all the radios like a sign from God.

"Hey," Hanson said, smiling hugely, "'My Girl.'"

My girl, Hanson thought, singing along with it for a moment, the song happy—but sad too—out in East Oakland, where…Well, maybe you could find some happiness here when you were young and had a girlfriend and things didn't seem so bad yet. He looked out at the dancers.

"I'd be grateful, y'all, if you'd go on home."

And they looked at Hanson, looked at each other, and began walking to their cars, finishing their joints, drinking the last of their Olde English 800, their Night Train, some laughing, a few even waving an arm above their heads—*Bye-bye*—to Hanson as they walked away.

"Thank you all very much," Hanson yelled. "Thanks a lot. I appreciate it. You all have a good evening now. Good night. Hey, Merry Christmas too."

By the time he jumped back down from the hood, they were already starting their cars and turning on the headlights, which swung in arcs past and through each other, flashing off the storefront windows. Hanson watched as the cars pulled out of the two entrances, going in different directions, the bright headlights and red taillights passing each other, the radios fading.

He looked up at the stars, familiar as old friends from his time in Idaho, where he'd gotten to know them, respecting their elegant dependability, trusting the ancient protocols they observed in their turnings. Jupiter was up there tonight too, brighter than the brightest star, regal and steady in its orbit through the constellations. And mighty Orion—shaped like an enormous hourglass, lesser stars seeming to tumble through its belted waist into the starry nebula below. "Rigel," Hanson said, "Betelgeuse, Bellatrix, Saiph," paying his respects to its primary stars before getting into the patrol car.

When he turned his headlights on they flared off the curve of the huge chrome bumper of a car not quite hidden back in the alley at the end of the strip mall. He popped the magnetic shotgun lock while he drove, unlatching his door so he could kick it open and roll out with the shotgun if need be, stopping at the mouth of the alley, where he was protected by the front end of the patrol car, lighting up the gleaming midnight-blue Cadillac with his high beams, its windows tinted and dark. He did all these things easily, without dread or indecision, content for the moment with who he was, the past and the future dismissed. Maybe he felt whatever it was that normal people felt when they said they were happy.

The Cadillac's window slid down and the driver said, "Good evening, Officer. A beautiful night." He was about thirty, younger than Hanson, wearing a close-cropped beard and wire-rim glasses that slightly magnified his eyes. He looked almost like a young college professor in a thousand-dollar suit, except for the eyes.

"Good evening, sir," Hanson called out through his open passenger window, friendly but with his hand on the shotgun. "Are you waiting for someone?"

"Just leaving, Officer, thank you. Now that the music's over," he said, assured but not arrogant, polite, a voice you wanted to believe. "I admired the way you were able to disperse the crowd so smoothly."

He was up to something, and Hanson wondered who he was, but it was late, time to go in, and he felt certain that they'd see each other again. "Most people are reasonable if you give them the chance," Hanson declared, not believing a word of it.

"So true, Officer," he agreed. "That's always been my experience as well," which clearly it had not been.

"Of course," Hanson said, trying not to laugh. "Good night, sir. Drive carefully." The tinted window slid back up, and the Cadillac rolled silently out of the alley, made a complete stop at the street, turned right, and drove on. Hanson had gotten his pen out to jot down the license plate number, but it was obscured by some kind of plastic cover. He clicked the pen closed and watched the Cadillac turn at the next block and disappear.

Anyone who had been at the dance could have told Hanson that the man in the Cadillac was Felix Maxwell, drug lord of Oakland, homeboy out of the projects who had made his mark. No one could have told him, though, what was in the stars for the two of them.

CHAPTER FOUR

TEMPLE RABBIT

New Year's Eve and Hanson was parked at the south end of the Mormon Temple parking lot. The clouds had blown away, and far below, the bay gleamed like blued steel. The Temple was off his district but a straight shot down to the freeway if he got a late call, a good spot to finish up reports. He was glad he'd found it. He'd backed the patrol car up against a waist-high wall at a twelve-foot drop-off where no one could come up behind him while he was writing. The Temple filled the sky above the patrol car, its spotlighted marble buttresses and blazing golden spires rising from the Oakland Hills like the City of Oz. The enormous parking lot was empty, thousands of lighting globes—pastel blue and green—hovering above the asphalt like UFOs, massed and waiting.

It was cool and quiet there as he finished a domestic battery/ resist arrest report. His knee throbbed, but at least the ninety-dollar wool pants weren't torn. Tiny beads of blood had seeped through the material, but the dry cleaner could get it out.

While he wrote, he kept track of Radio traffic, voices out there on the radio. Most nights he never saw another patrol car until he pulled back into Transportation downtown at the end of his shift. When he'd been a cop in Portland, in the heart of North Precinct's ghetto, he'd had a partner. The same partner every night working the same beat, so they got to know the people who lived there, and the people got to know them. Nobody loved them, but they knew who they were and knew they could depend on them to be fair, or at least consistent—not just two more face-less white guys in uniforms.

Shuffled from beat to beat, the OPD street cops rarely got to know each other, much less the black citizens they were paid to protect and serve or, more realistically, to keep them contained behind the freeways, in East and West Oakland, and out of down-town and white districts. The cops lived in various IF YOU LIVED HERE YOU'D BE HOME NOW suburbs twenty to fifty miles outside the city limits, and coming to work in Oakland was like punching in at the meat-packing plant for their shift, then showering, leav-ing bloody work clothes in their lockers, and driving the freeway for an hour to a thirty-year mortgage. With almost no contact at work, and none off duty, they were mostly strangers to one an-other. If one of them needed cover, the closest car would go, of course.

When a cop got killed everything else pretty much stopped un-til the suspect was killed resisting arrest, had committed suicide, or, if the media got on the scene before it was cordoned off, was arrested, convicted, and sent to prison. And usually dead within a year—stabbed repeatedly, thrown off an upper tier, or set afire in his cell by unknown assailants—because people on the street had to know if they killed a cop, they would die too. It was business, not personal.

Oakland, with the highest proportion of ex-cons of any city in California, fielded one-man patrol cars, and there were never enough of them to cover the 35 beats in 5 districts and 360,000 people. Hanson didn't know it, but a lot of nights he was the only cop out there for 20,000 people.

He still was able to talk people into going to jail, like he had in Portland, but it was harder in Oakland. And some nights he could feel his mean streak growing. He had to be careful, he thought, or he might turn into what the OPD wanted before he realized what was happening. Every night it was life/death/life/death, but that's what he liked, that's when it seemed like all the bright lights came on for him.

He looked around the lot, leaned his head back, took a deep breath, held it, held it, then let it out slowly. Happy New Year. He'd been off the street for at least an hour on the call he was writing up, much of the time waiting in the Alameda County Hospital emergency room while an East Indian doctor stitched up the cut over his prisoner's eye and shoved packing up his broken nose so they'd accept him when Hanson took him to jail.

He looked over the report forms once more, made sure all the correct boxes were filled in, and signed them <u>Hanson / 7374P</u>. He checked the rearview mirror and looked down at the red and white lights rushing like rivers past each other on the freeway far below.

Everything between him and the freeway was the Heart of Darkness, where everybody was a suspect, even the victims. Even the cops were just another gang out there, as brutal—maybe more brutal—as any of them, so outnumbered they had to be in order to survive. In the end, organized and superior brutality was what allowed them to enforce the laws of another country.

In the side-view mirror a new shadow appeared, wedged between the wall and the asphalt lot, changing shape as it moved toward the patrol car. It seemed to have a solid core that elongated, shrank, sent out feelers then pulled them back, crabbing from side to side. When Hanson spotted the shadow it startled him, maybe even scared him for a moment before he slowed his heart, telling himself that it was probably just another trick of light, another illusion, omen, hallucination. Maybe a threat, maybe not. He put the flat of his hand against his pistol, shifting in the seat to be sure it would clear the holster against the seat back. He leaned toward the passenger window for a better look.

A jet-black floppy-eared rabbit bounded out from the wall into the open. It was real, the biggest rabbit Hanson had ever seen. It hopped closer to the car, stopped. Hopped closer. Stopped and turned its head, regarding Hanson with a pearly black eye—looking right at him—aglow from the Temple lights.

The Temple rabbit, Hanson thought. Of course. Like those monkeys that have the run of Hindu temples in India. The Indian doctor in the emergency room. Maybe some connection there?

"Hey," he called through the open window. "Hey, little buddy, is it true? You be the Temple rabbit?"

The eye stayed on Hanson.

"You speakeee English?"

Somebody's pet. Or raised for food in a backyard hutch. That's all. Nothing supernatural, but still, a black rabbit in East Oakland at night? It hopped closer, and Hanson had to put his head out the window and look down now to see it. The rabbit tilted his head, looking up at him. He was beat-up, like a tomcat, but healthy looking. A jagged streak of white fur ran from beneath one eye and down alongside his nose, as if a cut there had healed, the fur growing back white. Hanson slid back across the car seat, opened the door as quietly and fluidly as possible, and got out. He walked slowly around the back of the car. Looking casual, he thought, smiling, cool and smooth. The way he might walk up on a drug deal. He knelt slowly down, his knees popping.

"Hey, Rabbit," he said softly, duckwalking closer. "Freeze. Police officer," about to laugh, when the big rabbit sprang straight up in front of him, turned in the air, and vanished over the wall. Hanson fell backward, catching himself with both hands, his heart pounding. He jumped back up, hurried to the wall and looked down. Somebody's backyard twelve feet below. A shadow, the black rabbit, compressed the grass as it hopped, like the footsteps of an invisible giant, around the side of the house, then streaked across Lincoln Avenue and was gone. A black rabbit on New Year's Eve at the Mormon Temple. An omen far too complex to consider now.

Over the wall, from way down along the freeway in the flatlands of East Oakland, the whisper of celebratory gunfire. A distant crackling that Hanson could hear through his tinnitus. Hundreds of citizens down there welcoming in the New Year with pistols, rifles, and shotguns. Firing them into the night sky. Yellow and orange fire rising from yards and windows far below. Two people in Oakland would be wounded and one killed before dawn by spent bullets streaking back to earth. The first death of the New Year. He looked at his watch. Time to go in. Past time.

Hanson lived in Oakland, up above Grand Avenue. His flat was a few blocks from the border of Piedmont, a separate incorporated little town with its own police force and fire department. A little island of rich white people surrounded by the dark ocean of Oakland.

Just past the Safeway he turned off Grand, up Sunny Slope Avenue and left on Jean Street, where he drove past his house and parked a few houses away, on the opposite side of the street. There were no strange cars parked nearby, no one on the sidewalks yet. He got out of the Travelall, slung his bag over his right shoulder, slipped his hand inside, around the rubber Pachmayr grip of the Browning Hi Power and walked across the street to the flat he rented, the main floor of an elegant house built in 1907 after the San Francisco earthquake and fire—a real beauty back then, he imagined, long before the current owner chopped it into three apartments. Dust motes sparkled undisturbed in the entryway. He walked down the silent hall, checking windows and locks, to the kitchen, where he thumbed the safety on the Hi Power and put it in his hip pocket.

He poured three fingers of green tequila into a heavy, slab-sided jelly jar and tossed it back. It burned down his throat and blossomed in his stomach. Holding the thick glass up to the light, he considered the teardrop-shaped bubbles in the sides, air that had been trapped forty or fifty years ago. He had another, filled the glass again, and walked down the hall to the bedroom, where he took off his shoes and stretched out on the bed, his hands clasped behind his head, watching the ceiling, and fell asleep in his clothes.

Hanson is sleeping.

He doesn't mind so much going to sleep during the day, after working the street all night. The muted sounds of others leaving for day jobs—the open and close of their car doors, the engines when they start them and drive away—are reassuring. He feels safe and rarely dreams during the day, even waking up in the early afternoon sometimes without any sense of dread and no hangover at all. He doesn't care if he lives or dies. Most people see that in his eyes and reconsider, they hesitate, try to explain themselves. Those that don't, well, he survived so long when others haven't that his response to threat is instinctive, faster than thought, a life-force beyond his control. There are nights when he knows he can't be killed. He worries that he'll live forever.

CHAPTER FIVE

WEEGEE

It was Valentine's Day and Hanson didn't care. It was the beginning of his shift, he'd just turned north onto High Street when Radio gave him the hit and run call. They told Hanson they didn't have a traffic unit available. He took Foothill Boulevard back to Fruitvale, then north on Fruitvale a few blocks to the location. He was beginning to learn his way around a little. He hated doing traffic, though—a lot of paperwork.

Half a dozen people had called it in. The front end of a black van with dark-tinted windows and a Harley-Davidson decal on the rear window was embedded in the driver's door of an abandoned-looking green Oldsmobile. The radiator was still steaming when he got there, and the driver's side of the windshield was shattered, the safety glass still in one piece, but bulging out and covered with blood and long strands of black hair. Hanson checked the glove box and found a registration for the van in the name of Arlie Hollow Horn Bear. There was also a Baggie with a half-ounce rock of crank, street methamphetamine, but Hanson left it there, till he saw how things would go.

The sun was still well up, a nice afternoon, and half a dozen black kids were having a fine time riding their bikes around the wreck—down the street, jumping the curb to the sidewalk, then back to the street, pulling wheelies, watching Hanson to see what he was going to do. They were happy for the entertainment, ten or twelve years old, sleek and muscled, showing off.

"How are you young gentlemen today?" he asked, looking around, making eye contact with each of them.

"Doin' good."

"Fine as wine."

"How you, Officer?"

"Pretty good, so far. Any of you guys see this happen?" he said, nodding at the steaming van.

"I saw it."

"Me too."

"I saw it all."

"Did any of you all see where the driver went? I probably need to talk to him."

A couple of them laughed. Pulling fancy wheelies now, turning their handlebars left and right as they pedaled along on their rear wheels.

"Two of 'em. They went down Fruitvale. Both of 'em drunk."

"A big white guy an' a big Indian. Real big."

"I bet the Indian was driving."

"You got it, Jack."

"Exactly right, Officer. Busted his head all to hell."

"Weegee followed 'em. Down that way."

"Guess I better find Weegee then. I appreciate your help, young men."

"That's all right."

"We take care of business."

"You might want some backup. Both of 'em real big. Angels too."

"I'll see how it goes," Hanson said, sticking the registration in his shirt pocket and walking down the street. The bikes all peeled off on either side of him, some ahead, some behind, like an escort.

Another kid was pumping his bike toward them, uphill, gaining speed. He had a playing card attached by a clothespin to the bike so that one end of the card brushed each spinning wheel spoke, clattering like a tiny motor.

"Hey, Weegee. Where they go to?" one of the escorts yelled to him.

"Man, they in the Anchor." He looked at Hanson, sizing him up. "You better get you a couple more po-lice to go with you."

"Thanks, Weegee. I think I'll just go say hello to them. Ask what happened. See if they're okay."

"You the man. Do what you think."

"I think," Hanson said, turning around to locate his patrol car, "that I'd better take my car with me." He smiled at Weegee. "So I don't forget where it is in case I have to put a prisoner in the back. That almost always looks bad for the po-lice."

He double-parked in front of the Anchor Tavern, turning on just his amber rear flashers, and got out of the car. The Anchor was a small place, not a lot of room to use a nightstick, and he left that in the car. He stepped in the door and let his eyes adjust to the dim light.

The Indian had a weird, freaky laugh, a maniacal sort of stutter, a laugh to intimidate people. He looked to weigh about two forty. Fuck, Hanson thought, a drunk, speed-freak Indian. The white guy was maybe six foot six, wiry, and not so drunk. They were both wearing Hell's Angels colors, Oakland Chapter. The club-house was just a few blocks off Fruitvale.

"Mister Hollow Horn Bear," Hanson said, walking toward their table. The Indian turned around to look at him, then looked quickly away, as if he hadn't already responded to the sound of his name. Hanson walked to the table where they had heavy glass mugs, half full of beer. "Gentlemen," he said to them, picking up the mugs and putting them on another table. "I apologize for moving your beer, but those are big mugs."

The Indian watched Hanson, and the white guy leaned back in his chair, curious what would happen next. He looked out the window and saw all the kids with their bikes looking in.

"That's my posse," Hanson said.

"Where's the other cops?"

"Out doing good works, I hope," Hanson said, then, without breaking his rhythm, he casually pulled his PAC-set off his belt and asked Radio to send an ambulance by the Anchor Tavern. Radio told him it would be a while, and he put it back on his belt.

The Indian laughed, stopped abruptly and glared at Hanson. He had two deep gashes on his cheekbone, his nose looked freshly broken, and his hair was matted with blood. Hanson looked mildly back at him, trying to see into his eyes, but they were black stones, giving up nothing.

"You need to get sewed up," Hanson said. "Looks like you just about put your head through the windshield."

The Indian laughed, glared, laughed again, narrowed his eyes. "Me an' Pogo was just wrestling. Don't know nothin' about a windshield."

"I found this in the glove box of that black van," Hanson said, pulling the registration out of his shirt. "It's got your name on it. And all those kids said you were driving when it hit that Oldsmobile."

"Oldsmobile been abandoned six months."

"I don't think anybody's gonna complain about damage to that Olds, but I gotta get you to the emergency room and arrest you for DUI."

He laughed, stopped, glared. Hanson looked at the white guy. "Is he okay?"

"Yeah. You the only cop they sent?"

"Just me, Mister…?"

"I'm Pogo. You find anything else in the glove box?"

"You might want to get any valuables out before the tow truck gets here."

"I'll check it. Thanks."

Hanson nodded, looked back at the Indian.

"I'd appreciate it if you'd stand up so I can handcuff you. You know I gotta do that. We'll go to the emergency room, get you fixed up, then go downtown and take care of the DUI charge."

"Go on, Bear," Pogo said. "We'll bail you out."

Hanson nodded thanks to Pogo as the Indian stood up…and up.

"If you'd put your hands behind your back, *por favor*," Hanson said, reaching for his handcuffs, "I'll put these on, and double lock 'em so they don't tighten up on you."

The Indian looked at Pogo, just as a pair of OPD motorcycle cops pulled up and around Hanson's patrol car and onto the sidewalk, scattering the kids. The Indian took a step back and Pogo stood up, reaching over and snatching up one of the beer mugs, moving so fast that the beer that had been inside was suspended in the air stop-time, then splashed across the table and onto the floor. "Just you, huh?" he said to Hanson.

"I didn't ask for backup."

The two traffic cops gunned the engines of their big black and white bikes, turned them off, dropped their kickstands, and dismounted, both standing like sumo wrestlers for a moment before hanging their helmets on the bikes and walking to the door.

Inside the tavern they took a moment to stare the place down. Their leather gear creaked, and their sunglasses were blue mirrors. "If he's gonna be an asshole," Barnes, the taller one, said, looking at the big Indian, "then we'll treat him like one." His nightstick hissed out of its holder, and Pogo said, "Come on then, dickwad," gripping the beer mug.

"No," Hanson said, facing the two cops, pushing his open hand down in a gesture to Pogo.

Arlie Hollow Horn Bear charged Hanson. Hanson hit a table with his chest then hit the floor on his back, sliding feetfirst toward the bar, where customers were colliding as they hopped and fell off their stools. He twisted onto his side, pushed himself to his feet, stiff-armed a customer out of the way, and—as if he was walking underwater—trudged back to where the shorter motorcycle cop, his nightstick raised, backpedaled into the doorframe, the Indian closing on him like a city bus. A second police car, throwing shafts of red and blue lights into the afternoon sky, crabbed to a stop in front of the tavern. Hanson knew then that he'd been set up by the traffic cops, used as bait. They'd thought that if he was by himself, the two bikers, both of them drunk, would resist arrest and they'd have an excuse to come to Hanson's rescue and kick their asses. But that didn't matter now as he jumped up onto Arlie Hollow Horn Bear's broad back, locking his left forearm against the Indian's throat and pulling it back in a bar-arm choke hold. He hung on, his feet off the floor, cutting off Arlie's air and the blood to his brain while he spun and bucked and tried to elbow Hanson off his back, screeching the last of his air away and finally going down, hitting the floor like a fallen tree, unconscious, where Hanson handcuffed him in the few seconds before his lungs and brain began to work again. By then the other three cops had Pogo down, putting knees and elbows and short wood to him as still another patrol car screamed to a stop in front of the tavern.

When it was over the two motorcycle cops and the three day-shift patrolmen were out in front high-fiving each other. Pogo, his head bloody, was in the back of one of the patrol cars. He met

Hanson's eyes, then looked away and laid his head back against the seat. Knowing, Hanson thought, that I'm a liar and a punk, setting him up for a bullshit arrest.

"Hey," the tall motorcycle cop—Barnes—said. "You shoulda seen this guy choke that fucking Indian out."

"Yeah," the other one, whose name was Durham, said. "Fuckin' A. Tonto was about to do a war dance on my head when Hanson there choked that fucker to the ground."

Hanson just looked at him, his face hot, afraid he was going to be sick. His hand hurt, but he didn't want to look at it yet.

"Hey," Barnes said, forcing a laugh, "we're sorry about using you to set those two scumbags up, but it worked. They'll both be going to the joint behind all the charges we'll be putting on them. It was too good of an opportunity to pass up. What did you say to 'em, anyway."

"I said, 'Would you please stand up so I can handcuff you.'"

"Right. Good fuckin' luck," Durham said.

"I was handcuffing the Indian when you fucked up my arrest."

"Say what? Those two motherfuckers would have stomped your ass if we hadn't showed up. You still got a lot to learn in this neighborhood."

"I didn't need any backup."

"This guy just got out of the Academy," Durham said to the two beat cops. "He's thirty-eight. Can you believe that shit? By the time he's got as many years on as I have, I'll be retired."

"Fuck you," Hanson said softly. "I didn't ask for any backup." He stepped in closer.

Durham said, "Hold it right there, partner." Hanson could smell the cigarette smoke on his breath.

Barnes said, "Let him go, Dwayne. He's fuckin' fucked up. Let's get those prisoners transported."

"Fuck that," Durham said bristling.

"He's crazy, Dwayne, c'mon," Barnes said, wrapping his arm around him.

Yeah, yeah, hold me back boys, Hanson thought. "You're traffic enforcement and you made the arrests, so I'll let you do the reports on this," Hanson said, brushing past them and walking away, down the street to the far side of the wrecked van, where he finally looked down at his left hand.

The ring finger was dislocated, pulled out of the first knuckle, pointing backward toward some fifth dimension. Before he could change his mind or lose his nerve, he took hold of the finger, pulled it out, re-socketed it, and thought he was going to faint from the pain. He retched and vomited what was left of the cheese sandwich and lemon yogurt he'd forced himself to eat for lunch.

"Good thing you got some backup."

Weegee was standing by his bicycle.

"Weegee. How you doin'?"

"Doin' okay. How *you* doin', Officer Hanson?"

"Fine," Hanson said, dry mouthed. "Good."

Weegee looked at him. "You take it easy," he said.

"You too. Thanks for helping me out today."

"No problem. You did real good with those Angels, I thought, till the motorcycle po-lice got there."

"Well," Hanson said, "thanks, young man. I'm glad you thought so."

"Sure. See you later," Weegee said, lifting his bike into a wheelie and pedaling it halfway down the block, the playing-card motor clattering, before his front wheel hit the asphalt.

Hanson watched him ride off, surprised that a little kid's opinion of him seemed important. He smiled, then reached into the van, took the meth out of the glove box, crushed the rock to powder, and threw it into the breeze.

CHAPTER SIX

POST CERTIFICATE

March 21. The spring equinox. Two a.m. and Hanson was in his flat on the border of Oakland and Piedmont, polishing his leather with the sheer nude No Nonsense panty hose he'd bought the day before at Walgreens. He'd cut the panty hose off at knee level and put his hands in them where the feet would go, pulling them on like a pair of long gloves so he wouldn't leave fingerprints on what he was polishing.

The steel-toed ankle-high combat boots were not a problem, but there was no way to hold the other gear without leaving prints—pistol belt, keepers, Mace holder, handcuff case, and the smooth-leather clamshell holster.

Polishing leather and brass again, he thought. He should have stayed in Vietnam. Gone back to CCN. Gone to Project Phoenix, gone to Laos, the Plain of Jars, hooked up with the CIA. Stayed over there until they killed him. But he'd lost his mind—or his nerve—at the last minute and thought that it was somehow a good idea to go home while he was still alive.

He'd known that coming home had been a big mistake as soon as he stepped off the airliner back in North Carolina in his jump boots, wearing the green beret and the medals on his dress uniform. It had taken a little longer for him to realize that the war had been everything he'd ever wanted, but by then it was over, gone, and he was still alive. It was like losing the woman you loved, the one you'd never forget, your true love—having just walked away from her because you hadn't realized that you loved her, or even known what love *was*, and now anyone else would be a disappointment.

His best possibility now was to do a year on the street to get his POST certificate: Peace Officer Standards and Training. A license to be a cop in California, an attempt to "professionalize" the job, standardize cops, crank them out and deploy them as interchangeable cop units. To get the POST certificate, he had to make it through the eighteen-month probationary period, which included the five-month Academy. Nine months to go, he thought. He could do nine months.

With a POST certificate from Oakland, he could make a lateral transfer to a cop job anywhere in the state, trade in his East Oakland street-combat experience for a job in some little town down the coast. A place where he could become chief in a few years, where he'd *be* the law, an armed social worker enforcing the social contract of that particular jurisdiction. Where justice would be more important than the California Penal Code. If there was a problem, take care of it. By himself. Walk up to the house, the vehicle, the bar, the liquor store, the crowd, the parking lot. Go in, step up, announce himself, make a decision and resolve the problem right there. Enforce his own code his own way, and hell, do it without a gun. Fuck all of this by-the-numbers "officer safety" bullshit. He didn't need a gun, only morons needed a gun. Half the cops killed every year were shot with their own guns. If somebody wanted to shoot him, they'd have to bring their own gun: they couldn't use his. And they'd only get one chance.

The lights in his flat flickered, threatened to go off, then got brighter than usual before dimming back to normal. The wiring in the old house had been designed when no one used much electricity. It still had a fuse box instead of a circuit breaker, and he needed to buy some fuses. Then the lights flickered and something scurried out from the kitchen, down on the floor, hugging the wall, crossing behind Hanson at the edge of his peripheral vision, trying to get his attention. It looked sort of like a Day-Glo duck, and he decided to ignore it. "Some other time," he said aloud to the ceiling, just as the lights went off all over the house. He laid his leather gear down on the carpet, picked up his Hi Power, and walked through the dark house to the bedroom. He could finish up at dawn.

Hanson is sleeping, gone to where the war never ends. Where it's dusk now, up in Northern I Corps, with a five-man squad from the CRP, the Combat Recon Platoon, the twenty-five or thirty real killers they keep in camp. Psychos and drug addicts, war orphans, loners, haunted survivors, Vietnamese mercenaries paid in cash, U.S. dollars, CIA money that no one has to sign for.

It was getting dark in the mountains when they saw the enemy squad appear out of the brush along a stream far below and begin climbing the steep hillside to the east—eight or ten men, moving out at last light, unaware that they were being watched. Even in the fading light, at that distance, it was obvious they were local force VC, part-time fighters, probably on their way back to some half-hidden village and their families. They were out of rifle range. It might have been possible to wound one or two of them with half-spent M16 rounds, but not likely, and at the sound of the first shots they'd spread out as they began to run and be harder to hit, even dragging their wounded, over the hill and gone.

The CRP watched them silently, standing in a half circle

around Hanson, who was crouched in front of the PRC 25 radio, searching for the frequency of the big firebase off toward the coast. Hanson found it, keyed the handset, and said, "Fire mission." He identified himself with his call sign and, speaking softly as if the VC could hear him, said, "WP airbursts. We've got a squad in the open," giving them grid coordinates. They were well within range of the firebase's 155s and eight-inch artillery. Even if the squad made it over the hill, the big guns could blow them up on the other side. "We'll need those rounds on the way soon," he said into the handset, "before we lose them in the dark."

The firebase was Big Army, with a complex chain of command and security protocols, so they were slow. The CRP muttered, shook their heads, looked at the sky when he had to identify himself again and repeat the coordinates. The radio hissed with static.

Come on, Hanson thought, waiting, waiting, the radio hissing, all of them watching the VC squad work its way up the steep hillside. They'd be out of breath, their legs cramping, pulling themselves uphill through the shoulder-high elephant grass, cutting their palms and wrists on it. Hanson had done it plenty of times himself, his bleeding hands stinging with sweat. Come on, come on.

"Shot," a voice from the radio broke the static. Moments later two 155 rounds passed overhead, fluttering and snapping up there, the sound like huge flags in a gale. WP. White phosphorus, silver and white air bursts beyond the crest of the hill, lighting the dark horizon with boiling clouds, fiery swarms of WP arcing out of the smoke, each with its own fine white contrail. A speck of WP would burn through skin, muscle, and bone and out the other side. Water wouldn't put it out—it used the oxygen in water to burn hotter. If you could cover the wound with mud, cutting off the air, it might stop eating its way through you. Eventually. If you had some mud handy. You were fucked if it landed on you, the scariest shit there was.

"Drop three hundred," Hanson said into the handset, and two more rounds chuffed and snapped overhead, exploding down along the stream below the squad. Bracketed now, the VC were fucked and they knew it. The next rounds he called would be right on top of them. Nothing they could do, nowhere to hide, the hillside on fire. He couldn't see them through the smoke, but he knew they were running. The grass was on fire below them, flames marching up the hillside at their heels. They wouldn't be home for supper now, they would be dead.

He felt the CRP watching him and looked up into their eyes, their killers' eyes glittering silver and gold, reflecting the white phosphorus and fire. They talked with their eyes, and Hanson smiled, nodded, keyed the radio handset, and instead of asking for more WP, he said, "Cancel fire mission. Too bad—they got away."

They would wonder why they'd survived, that enemy squad. For as long as they lived now, they'd wonder about it but never guess that it had been Hanson with his CRP who had chosen to give them their lives, playing God up there in the mountains that night.

"Next time," Hanson said into the handset. "Good job. Thank you. Out."

One of the CRP passed a canteen around and they all drank, breathing in the cool evening air. It was time to set up their ambushes for the night. Overhead, stars began to show themselves up in the mountains of Northern I Corps, while in Oakland dawn is lighting the sky as Hanson sleeps.

CHAPTER SEVEN

THE ROCK SHOP

He was almost to the freeway when he saw it, on the corner of an unmarked intersection. A well-kept little house, its tiny yard like a Japanese garden, rocks and sand raked into overlapping arcs of blues, grays, and whites, like a quadrant of night sky. Slowing his Travelall at the stop sign, he saw stars and planets twinkle and spin across the yard—sunlight, he realized, flashing off bits of quartz, obsidian, and mica.

Through all the nights he'd patrolled the area he'd never noticed the place before. A louvered garage door was secured with steel rods and padlocks, a long black Lincoln from the forties gleaming in the driveway. Above the door next to the garage, stenciled in simple black letters, a sign with the words

REVEREND RAY'S ROCK SHOP

He drove across the intersection and pulled to the curb for a better look.

The neighborhood was deserted—no one on the street, no

48

cars, the houses boarded up. It was absolutely quiet. Even his tinnitus was muted now to quick bursts of static, faraway and close
at the same time, like rattlesnakes. The sunlight was pale as an
overcast winter afternoon, but the sky was clear bright blue. He
remembered a solar eclipse one Sunday when he was five years
old, home alone, the moon's shadow racing down the street.

Feeling a little dizzy, he looked at his eyes in the rearview mirror, thinking he should get more sleep and eat better. Not drink
so much. He had to take better care of himself or this job would
kill him before he finished his eighteen months and could resign
without looking like a quitter.

When he got out of his Travelall, walking toward the house,
he felt okay. An airliner whistled high overhead. Mourning doves
called from the trees. His ears chirped and whined like they
always did. The dizziness was gone. He heard music, though.
Someone singing maybe.

The Lincoln might have just been driven off a showroom floor
out of the past, its black paint reflecting Hanson like a dark carnival mirror, compressing and expanding him, walking him off the
ground, spreading him from bumper to bumper, then collapsing
him to a dwarf trapped down in the chrome hub of one of the wire
wheels. The wide whitewall tires were shiny new and the purple
plush upholstery was pristine.

It was a piano he'd heard, coming from the house. He closed his
eyes and felt the notes on his eyelids.

"It's Georgia…*always Georgia*…"

Sounded just like Ray Charles, singing "Georgia on my Mind,"
and it wasn't a radio. Maybe some kind of elaborate sound system.
He opened his eyes.

Why hadn't he noticed the rock shop before? He stopped at
rock shops off highways and county roads all the time. The owners were always unusual—eccentric, opinionated, obsessive,

manic, sullen, paranoid—idiot savants of one sort or another, in-bred geniuses, borderline psychotics who always received him as if he was a hallucination they'd been expecting. They'd take him back to their hidden storage sheds, show him the stuff in their basements, introduce him to their dogs. When he left they told him to be sure and come back soon and waved goodbye when he drove off as if he was leaving for another planet.

"Georgia on *my mind."*

The big door knocker—a brass lion with a ring in its teeth and blue-green opals for eyes—seemed to *consider* Hanson when he stepped up to the door. Beneath the lion, a smaller sign:

Cleave the Soil and You Will Find Me,
Part the Sea and I Am There
Open for Business

The singing stopped, but the piano cruised along. Hanson reached for the door knocker, and whoever had been singing laughed, trilled the piano, and called "Come on in, Officer."

Hanson opened the door.

He *looked* like Ray Charles: big dark glasses, smiling toward Hanson, but weaving his head as if hearing some other song. He was blind and sitting in a wheelchair at the piano, on the other side of a glass case of fist-size crystals that lit his face in patterns of blue and rose and diamond white. He played a few last notes of "Georgia," fading them out to silence.

"I knew you were on the way," he said.

"*I* didn't know I was on the way."

"You just didn't *realize* it. And you won't have no problems parked here. Nobody mess with *my* customers."

"Was that you singing?"

The blind man nodded.

"That was *wonderful*," Hanson said.

"Thank you, but that's Ray Charles's song, not mine."

"His song, maybe, but your voice."

"Just a trick," he said, slumping down oddly in his wheelchair, as if he didn't have any bones in his body.

"That's a great looking car you got out there," Hanson said, changing the subject. "Who…?"

"Just got it tuned up. Gotta keep your ride tuned and detailed."

"Who…?"

"I can see fine when I'm drivin' at night. Lights all around show you the way. My eyes is more sensitive at night, you see."

Black, blind, and crippled, Hanson thought, and crazy too.

"Ain't that the *blues?* Yes, sir, true enough."

He hit a note, another one, then began to sing. A somber, funereal march: *"Death don't have no mercy — in this land. I say* Death *don't have no* mercy, *in this* land…" He laughed and trilled the piano like Jerry Lee Lewis. "Been a while, hasn't it?"

"Since…uh?" Hanson said, trying to be polite.

"Since you saw me last. What brings you to Reverend Ray's Rock Shop?"

"I was over—"

"It's not a good location."

"I was on my way to—"

"Not for a rock shop. I know," he said, noodling the piano keys. "What you doin' out here on your day off? More to the point," he said, twisting his head around, looking up at Hanson with blind eyes through the dark glasses, "why you want to work out here at all? Where everybody hates you?

"I'll *tell* you why," Ray said, his blue-black dark glasses reflecting twin images of Hanson from below. "Hate is something you can depend on. Gives you something to live for. Better than love, an' that's a fact. Something you can believe in, little brother." He played a few chords on his piano, then the same chords again, only in a different key. "You got any friends around here?"

"Well…"

"Dead," Ray said, hitting a chord. "All the friends you had are dead. Why you suppose they already met with Death?"

Hanson thought about it.

"Well?"

"Bad luck."

"Say what? How's that?"

"They're so good at what they do, bad luck's about the only thing that can kill 'em. They get bored and take chances."

"Messin' with Death?"

"They're not afraid of dying."

"Everybody afraid of Death."

"Not everybody."

Ray played a few notes and sang, very softly, *"And then I go back home, and hear your* voice *again, but I'm alone.*

"Take a look around the shop," he said, gesturing like a ring-master. "I got the history of the world in this shop, little brother. Look here at my rocks, my gems, jewels, minerals, crystals. Precious, semiprecious, common, rare and priceless. I got fossils from the past and meteorites from *before* the past. I got it all here—life, death, gold and lead, love and war. Answers to questions nobody's asked yet, not in *this* lifetime.

"See that green glass over there? One shelf down, yes sir, you found it. *Sand* fused into *glass* by the first atomic bomb. Down in New Mexico at the Trinity site.

"See that *black* glass? One shelf over? They call it *weapons grade* obsidian," he said. "Uh-huh. For arrows and spears and what have you. Sharper than razors. Green glass, black glass, same old story, never changes. Whoever's got the weapons got the gold too. You know what I'm talking about. Don't matter if it's claws, teeth, daggers, or atom bombs. Weapons evolution is what you might call it. Evo-lu-tion. People talk about evolution like it's dependable though, logical. Forget *that*." He paused to smile and shake his head, trilling the piano. "You can't depend on evolution any more than anything else. Those dinosaurs ruled for millions of years, and they'd still be supreme, but there's always surprises." The piano rang like a church bell and he sang out, *"Meteor strike!"* laughing as the sound faded into the walls. "Didn't expect *that*. Forget about survival strategies and evolutionary status quo. It all starts over then."

Hanson clasped his hands behind his back so he wouldn't knock anything over and have to pay for it. He leaned down to look at some of the dusty stones piled up on wooden shelves.

"What you're looking at there's called dogtooth calcite. That piece came from Mexico, way down in a flooded cave full of water and all kind of blind sharks and rays and poisonous snakes. Some places even the rocks have teeth. Gots to, to survive.

"The diamond next to it? *That* one. Raw and uncut as the day it blew out of a pipe in the earth five million years ago. Go ahead and pick it up." Hanson picked up the diamond, turned it in his hands. It was the size of a billiard ball, heavy, gnarled and knotted, a frosted translucent white. He almost dropped it when Ray shouted, "And look at that, little brother! Down there, in that silver bowl, whole bowl of little meteorites, every one of 'em older than the sun, older than the solar system, all that's left of a star that burned out, blew up and went black four thousand hundred million years ago. They *rained* down in a meteor shower over Johnson City, Texas, out of the night sky, not but seven hundred years back. Wish you could have seen it. Put your hands in there and feel the weight, which is something you can appreciate, I know that. They burned down through the atmosphere into pure nickel-iron alloy etched with tiny hieroglyphics and green crystals no one's ever seen on earth, harder than diamonds and bright as flame. Look at that light!"

"How did…" Hanson began, reaching deep into the bowl of meteorites. He closed his hand on one and lifted it out. "Why don't they…Sir?" Hanson walked over to the piano, gem-crusted meteorite still in his hand. Reverend Ray was gone, an empty wheelchair behind the counter where he'd been sitting. Hanson looked out the window at the strange, deserted neighborhood. A pair of dust devils were racing each other up the street.

Something thumped on the floor behind him. He knew he should ignore it. Dismiss it, refuse to acknowledge it and walk out the door. It wasn't real anyway, in his opinion. But he turned around.

"Well, *what?*" he said. "What can I do for you?" He looked down at the jet-black big-eared rabbit, his ears scarred like a tomcat, pearly black eyes otherworldly and accusatory at the same time. A jagged streak of white fur alongside his nose. It was the same rabbit, the Temple rabbit. The meteorite was like a nail through his hand, throwing gold and green streaks of light across the ceilings and walls and floor. "What?"

The rabbit looked up at him, and Hanson saw prehistoric cave paintings and Renaissance angels in his eyes.

"Reverend Ray," he called. "Sir? Is this your rabbit?"

No one was there.

"Gotta go. Outta my way, punk," he told the rabbit, walked out and closed the door behind him.

CHAPTER EIGHT

FELIX MAXWELL

A hot wind was gusting in from Lodi or Tonopah, lifting plastic bags and fast-food trash into the darkened sky. It blew into Oakland two or three times a year, every spring, from the desert, hissing through the trees, shaking screen doors and rattling windows, trying to get in.

Dust glittered in the patrol car's headlights, and when Hanson turned south on High Street a pack of feral dogs broke cover, their yellow eyes flickering like pistol shots in his high beams. Radio whispered and snarled with calls for service, still backed up from the afternoon, some of them two and three hours old. Hanson had been going call to call across Districts Four and Five since the beginning of his shift, hungover and half sick from the brandy he'd passed out with the night before. He steered west on East 14th Street, microphone in one hand, poised to jump in between transmissions and clear from his last call, a drunken 245 involving a kitchen knife and a spray can of oven cleaner.

3L34, disregard that last call and cover 3L40.

3L34 copy . . . uh, the location again?

The horizon shuddered with silent heat lightning.

Yeah, yeah, Hanson thought, rubbing his eyes with the back of his microphone hand as Radio repeated the address for whoever was working 3L34. "Pay attention, dipshit. Come *on,*" his thumb on the push-to-talk button.

Car with the traffic stop?

4L14 at Sixty-Fifth and MacArthur.

Wait one, 4L14.

Up the block a pearly white Rolls-Royce Silver Shadow was double-parked out in front of Raylene's Discount Liquors. Glowing an otherworldly purple in the neon light from the barred windows of the liquor store, it had drawn a crowd, people surrounding the Rolls, out in the street. Hanson hung up the mike and pulled to the curb half a block away, turning on just his rear amber flashers, watching the crowd grow, his eyes bloodshot and the knuckle he'd fucked up at the last call throbbing like a pulse. He made a fist to hurt the pain.

Getting out of the patrol car he stuck his citation book in his back pocket and slammed the door shut with his hip, leaving his nightstick in the car. There wouldn't be enough room to use it in the middle of so many people. The amber flashers made a metallic *tonk-tonk, tonk-tonk,* and the radio PAC-set on his belt barked and hissed at him. He hitched the heavy gun belt up and turned off the PAC-set.

He tightened his fist on the jammed knuckle, looked down at it. Does that hurt? How about this? he thought, punching the fist into the palm of his other hand. He smiled at the pain, glad for the chance to get out of the patrol car, his back aching from the broken-down bench seat. And it was a relief to have the radio off, like shedding a headache he hadn't realized he had until it went away. Radio didn't know where he was, so if things went bad, he was on his own. Fine, he thought. Good.

The crowd wasn't hostile yet, but it wasn't friendly either. Not friendly, he thought, smiling at that. "My *friends,* may I have a word with you?" He laughed out loud, at the edge of the crowd now, and people who'd been acting like he wasn't there turned to look at him. He felt the muscles in his shoulders and chest on-call. His eyes were smiling now. It was his mean smile.

"Hi," he demanded, "how you *doin'?*" wading into the crowd.

Levon had been watching Hanson since he'd pulled the patrol car to the curb. From the backseat of the Rolls he could see two of him, one in each side mirror, coming their way through the crowd, bad smile on his face. It had been a while since he'd seen anyone move like that.

Felix and Tyree had driven up from LA that afternoon and picked up Levon just as it was getting dark. Felix had been in LA for three months and now he was back in town and wanted to drive around the neighborhood, get right back in touch.

Felix was working the crowd, up front in the passenger seat, window rolled down, talking to old Jessie Bacon, calling him *Uncle* Jessie, then palming a hundred-dollar bill into his hand to dismiss him.

Felix could think two moves ahead of everybody else — damn smart and a good politician when he felt like it. Other times, though — lately — even when it was important, he didn't want to go out at all, brooding back in that concrete bunker of his. Some days he was good as ever, taking care of business. Other times he'd take offense over nothing, suspect plots against him for no good reason. Tonight he was fine — a little full of himself, which was how he'd always been, had to be to get where he was. Maybe the time down in LA had been good for him.

Levon was getting to be an old man, sixty-one years old in October. Had more money than he'd need for the rest of his life.

Time to retire while he still could, somewhere nobody knew him and nobody could find him. Where it was warm and people were polite, but he couldn't quit on Felix now, not for a few months, anyway.

He looked at the cop again in the right side mirror.

Felix shook hands through the window with a young player who wouldn't live to see twenty.

"You do *now*," he said to the kid, laughing.

"A real honor, Mr. Maxwell," the kid said. "If I can ever be of help to you, please let me know."

The kid actually made a little bow, took a step backward, then joined back up with his posse.

Levon kept a hand on his army issue Colt 1911 till the kid turned and walked away. Too many goddamn people to watch at once. He didn't know why he'd brought that damn Uzi, it was worthless in a crowd like this. He must be getting old and stupid too.

"Felix," he said, "let's go."

"Noblesse oblige, Levon," Felix said. "I've known these people all my life. They expect to be able to speak to me."

"You've watched those *Godfather* movies too many times. You see that cop coming this way?"

"Since he parked his patrol car. I've met that officer, Levon."

"Take another look."

Hanson's jammed knuckle felt *good* now. His hangover was gone. A good-looking woman in a sequined halter top and hot pants pouted at him from the sidewalk, working her hips, shaking a finger at him like one of the Pointer Sisters. Hanson grinned at her, making eye contact.

"Great night, eh?" he asked, brushing past three guys who were trying to ignore him. When they didn't answer he stopped, turned, and looked back at them. "*Isn't* it?" he said, waiting for an answer, smiling, and looking at them with Shirley Temple eyes, wide-open-crazy, a trick he'd discovered years before. A look that was intimate and berserk, so unnatural no one had ever seen it before and didn't know how to react. It was easy too, and fun.

"Uh-huh."

"Yeah."

"Okay, then, and, hey, look at that *moon* comin' up," he said, pushing it, over the top now. "Moon, moon, moon," he crooned, turning away, parting the crowd. Heat lightning flared like a pane of glass out over the bay. He had the glow tonight, and nothing could touch him.

Levon saw Lemon Lee push his way through the crowd, angling in front of the cop. He laid his big arms across the roof of the Rolls, leaned down, his big buffalo head filling the window on the passenger side. "Felix, I got a bone to pick with you."

"Why don't you talk to *me*, Lemon," Levon said from the backseat.

"I want to hear from you, Levon, you'll know it right away. My problem's with your boy Felix."

Levon had known Lemon Lee since they were kids. Lemon was already an asshole in the third grade. He had been recruited right out of high school to play left field for the Kansas City Monarchs, black baseball's glamour franchise. Jackie Robinson and Satchel Paige had played for the Monarchs, before Jackie Robinson broke the color barrier. Lemon was the Monarchs' power hitter for two years, until the money and his own hostility ruined him, and the team let him out of his contract. He got by after that, working for different people, doing different things, most of them illegal. Levon couldn't understand why he hadn't been killed years before now. He was big, true enough, but an angry one-hundred-thirty-five-pound sixteen-year-old with a 9mm doesn't care how big you are.

Lemon would be happier dead, Levon thought. Maybe God was keeping him alive as punishment. He'd never seen much evidence for that kind of personal God, though, Levon thought, gripping the .45 and reaching for the door handle.

Hanson got through the crowd to the car just as a big man in his late fifties leaned down to speak to somebody in the Rolls, his tent-size yellow shirt pulled up, exposing his hairy black back. Hanson stepped up close behind him and said, "Excuse me," but the man ignored him. "Excuse me, please," Hanson said, touching his shoulder. He glanced around this time, to look at his shoulder, as if whoever had touched him had soiled the yellow shirt. "Get off me, motherfucker," he said, flipping his hand behind his back at Hanson, dismissing him, waving him off.

Time slowed down for Hanson then, all but stopped. Usually he kept his mean streak chained and triple-locked down, where he didn't hear it, but now its howls rose up with the whine and screech of his tinnitus.

He watched Lemon's huge hand floating toward him, flexing at the wrist and knuckles, easy to catch. He gripped the wrist with his left hand and the middle finger—big as a cigar—with his right. He pulled back on the wrist to keep Lemon off-balance and broke the finger. Lemon yelled, turning away from the car, Hanson twisting his wrist with both hands now for control and driving the side of his boot into Lemon's knee, dislocating the kneecap, on down the shin and *through* the arch of his foot, crushing that complex and delicate bundle of bones and tendons and nerves. He stepped away as Lemon fell to the street and found himself looking at Felix Maxwell, who looked back as if he was in on this joke, the guy with the eyes and wire-rim glasses who'd been in the midnight-blue Cadillac in the alley that night he talked the street dancers into going home.

Lemon was bellowing and flopping like a big yellow fish, and Hanson turned to the crowd. "Does anybody know this man? Heart attack. He needs an ambulance and my radio's not working."

Behind him Felix made a hand gesture to the crowd and some gang kid stepped out, him and his posse. A moment later they half carried, half dragged Lemon Lee away, heat lightning flaring overhead, stopping the moment like a camera flash.

"Good evening," Hanson said, absolutely happy, stepping up to the car.

"Good evening to you, Officer. A *heart attack* you think?"

Hanson glanced down, to keep from smiling now, shook his head, looked back up. "Who can say?"

"Maybe Satan struck him down."

"Satan's always out there," Hanson said, beaming.

Hanson nodded to the older gentleman in the backseat, then to the kid behind the steering wheel. "Looks like I should have approached from the other side of the ve-hickle. The steering wheel's way over there on the other side. Anyway," he said to the young driver, "since I'm here, could I see your driver's license, sir?"

"Did I break some law when I wasn't paying attention?"

"*Show* the officer your license," Felix said, reading Hanson's name tag. "My nephew," he told Hanson. "Sometimes he speaks before he thinks."

Hanson nodded.

"And may I introduce my mentor, Levon, always looking out for me."

Levon in the backseat was bigger than Felix. He'd have been a much rougher looking man but for his demeanor and well-cut clothes, his suit coat draped across the seat next to him not quite concealing the outline of a 9mm Uzi. Another cop probably wouldn't have noticed the outline or recognized what it was, but Hanson had trained with an Uzi years before. He nodded at the suit coat. "Starting to get warm. I'll be glad when they decide to switch us over to short-sleeve shirts."

"It's my car," Felix said. "The registration is in the glove box," waiting to open it until Hanson indicated that was okay. When Hanson nodded, he opened the bird's-eye maple glove box, took out the registration, and gave it to Hanson. "I bought it in LA last week. We're just out for a drive tonight. Tyree wanted to see how it handled."

Hanson looked over the registration and handed it back. The name on the registration was Felix Maxwell. He took the kid's driver's license, copied the information into his notebook: Tyree Raymond Stewart. "Thank you, Mr. Maxwell—and you, Mr. Stewart," he said, nodding to the driver as he handed back the driver's license. "It's a beautiful car. I'm worried, though, with you double-parked like this, if some drunk driver drove down this street, with all these people you've attracted."

Felix nodded. "We'll get out of the street here and on our way. If you don't need any more information. Thank you."

"Thank *you*, Mr. Maxwell," Hanson said, patting the hood of the Rolls, "for your help tonight with the crowd. I'm grateful. You too, sir," he said to the man in the backseat, ignoring the Uzi so completely that he might as well have been staring directly at it. The shiny cover of a new book, on the far side of the backseat, caught what little light there was: *Retire to Jamaica*. "Okay, Mr. Maxwell," Hanson said. "Be careful. This is a dangerous part of town."

"That's what I've heard," Felix said.

"I hope that large gentleman is feeling better and on his way to the doctor. Do you know him?"

"Never saw him before."

Hanson nodded, exchanging a smile with Felix, and walked away, the crowd making room for him this time.

The girl in the hot pants puckered her lips and blew Hanson a kiss. He gave her a two-fingered John Wayne salute and walked back to his beater patrol car as the Rolls pulled silently away.

There'd been no reason to bring up the Uzi. They were dope dealers and needed it for business. The only people they might shoot with it would be other dope dealers. If he'd called it in, there would have been a big deal for nothing. Maxwell would've bailed out of jail in an hour or two and he would've been doing paperwork till midmorning for the Feds at ATF, who would've been pissed about getting called out in the middle of the night. The OPD wouldn't have been happy about involving the Feds, and nothing would have come of it anyway. No rush. Maxwell and those gang kids had probably saved his ass with the crowd. He'd run into Maxwell again.

Radio sounded like two or three auctioneers talking at once. Districts Four and Five still hadn't caught up with the backlog of calls that always piled up before the beginning of the shift. Standing behind the open door of his patrol car, Hanson made some notes for himself about the Rolls and occupants, then he got in and slammed the door shut so it would latch. The car smelled of vomit and urine, cigarette smoke, fear, and salty blood. The sprung bench seat put him so low he could barely see over the steering wheel, as if he was too young to have a driver's license. He thought he might buy a seat cushion for work, smiled at that, and started the car.

In the Rolls, now turning down 69th Street, Felix looked out the window, studying the stars.

"He saw the Uzi," Tyree said. "I know he did. We're gonna be up to our asses in cops as soon as he calls it in."

Felix shook his head.

"He saw it, Uncle Fee."

"I know he saw it, Tyree," Felix said, tilting his head a little, still looking up at the stars. "But he's not gonna call it in." He settled back into the gray leather seat, the pearly white Rolls glowing like the moon, rushing past the wreckage of East Oakland, where Felix had grown up.

"Why wouldn't he?"

"He thought it was funny. He was fucking with Levon about it, fuckin' with all of us. He was all pumped up from walking through the crowd, like Moses parting the Red Sea. But if I'm wrong," he told Tyree, glancing back at Levon, "we'll just put it in your lap and say it's yours. So either way I'm not worried."

"What I *tell* you about that cop, the way he moved," Levon said, laughing a little. "He fucked Lemon *up*. Broke his finger, then come down on his foot."

Tyree looked at Felix. "I thought he had a heart attack or some kind of, you know, seizure or something like that."

"That *cop* seized his ass," Levon said. Then to Felix, "Lemon doesn't have a lot of friends, but the cop was walkin' on thin ice out there with that crowd. He was lucky you had that kid and his crew of thugs available to drag Lemon away."

"Now that kid's gonna want a job. A corner to work," Felix said. "Did you look in his eyes?"

"I wouldn't trust him either."

"As a short-term employee," Felix said, "we might be able to use him.

"I told you that I've seen that cop before," Felix went on. "He's the cop who stood on top of his patrol car and *asked* the crowd to leave. I've heard some things about him. New on the Department, but he's worked somewhere else. Nobody to fuck with but not an asshole. Not well liked on the Department."

"He's okay in my book," Levon said. "I thought I might have to kill Lemon back there, and go to jail for the night. I appreciate not being in jail."

"You see, Tyree? Be polite to police officers up here. Don't kiss their ass but be polite. And pay attention to everything—his eyes, the way he moves, not just the uniform. That's one reason they wear a uniform, so they look all the same. But they're not all the same."

"Let's go home," Felix said. "Officer say it be dangerous out here after dark."

The electric seat hummed as Felix tilted it back and closed his eyes for a moment, pulling something attached to a gold chain out from his shirt—a little hourglass carved out of clear quartz crystal, caged in gold, filled with tiny diamond chips instead of sand. He opened his eyes, held it up between thumb and forefinger, and tipped it over, watching the glittering chips sift through the neck and drift down to the bottom.

"No matter what happens," he said to himself, as if he was alone in the car, "it happens. But time always just keeps piling up."

CHAPTER NINE

WIND

And from the sixth hour there was darkness over all the land.

It was Good Friday, the day Christ was nailed to the cross. Also the first day of April—April Fool's Day. Hanson had put another week behind him on the way to getting his POST certificate and leaving the OPD.

The hot wind had been blowing a night and a day. It had followed Hanson home the night before, and woke him up in the morning. It rose and fell and then got worse as he drove across East Oakland, lifting whirlwinds in alleyways, throwing trash cans into parked cars, dust devils funneling down East 14th Street, sucking up bits of newspaper, yellow cheeseburger wrappers, parking tickets, bus transfers, liquor store receipts, and last year's posters of runaway children who were never found, their images so weathered now that they all looked alike. The wind made people irritable, touchy, more likely to argue and resist arrest. The fire department was busy with Dumpster fires and arson.

He'd pulled to the curb way out in District Five and was thumbing through his *Thomas Guide,* looking for the address Radio had given him, an Unknown Problem called in by someone who had refused to give a name. Radio had been holding the call since earlier in the day, and now he couldn't find the address. An Unknown Problem from an anonymous caller at an address he couldn't find.

The wind was blowing out of the past, shifting, gusting, full of voices, rocking the patrol car. He looked up and saw a kid on his bike coasting down from the next block, leaning to one side against the wind, trying to see through the windshield of the patrol car. It was Weegee, fluid and muscular from powering his bike, Hanson thought, every day, with no days off, across the bleak and dangerous districts of East Oakland. It wouldn't be long, he thought, before Weegee got his first 9mm, working as a lookout for some dope dealer in one of the projects, then got his own corner to deal from, when he'd be able to afford an Uzi. He was a good kid who'd work hard and probably die before his twentieth birthday. Maybe he'd make it to management or distribution or enforcement before he died. Hanson gave him a little salute through the windshield.

Weegee grinned, straightened up, and began to pedal, tucked into the wind now and building speed until Hanson thought he would pass the patrol car in a blur. At the last possible moment he braked, twisted the handlebars, and skidded sideways to a perfect stop, facing Hanson through the driver's window of the patrol car.

"Hey," he said, barely winded, "Officer Hanson. I thought it was you."

"We all look alike in our uniforms," Hanson said, not able to keep from grinning back at him. "How you doin', Weegee?"

"Doin' good."

"You live around here?"

"I get around. You know. What's up, Officer?"

"Lost again in East Oakland," Hanson said. "Maybe you can help me out." He picked up the *Thomas Guide*. "It's right here." He tapped a folded-back page of the ring-bound book of street maps. "Somewhere close, but I can't find it. Street called Bleeker Court."

Weegee looked over his shoulder, down the street, then back at Hanson. "You sure?"

"Yes, sir. Bleeker Court. Radio sent me."

"Why you gotta go…?" The wind slammed a trash can into an abandoned car across the street. "Why you gotta go there?"

Gotta Go… Marching cadence was gusting in from jump school years before. Hanson heard his own voice and the voices of people he hadn't thought about for a long time, most of them long dead. Gotta *Go,* Gotta *Be, Air*borne, *In*fantry…

"'Unknown Problem,'" he said.

"They want the po-lice there?"

"Somebody does."

Weegee looked down the street again. "This a funny part of town," he said, tilting his head slightly, as if he was listening to something.

"What…?" Hanson asked him.

"Oh, nothin', just…" He smiled. "Sound like somebody calling me, you know. *'Weegee… Weeee-geee.'*" He laughed. "Jus' that wind is all. I can take you," he said, pivoting his bike on the front wheel. "It's this way."

Hanson followed him in the patrol car down alleys and through open gates in chain-link fences across vacant lots, places he'd never seen before—streets with DEAD END signs that weren't dead ends, some kind of hobo jungle where fifty-five-gallon trash burners glowed red-hot and filled the air with sparks, down a sort of corridor walled off with stacked-up Dumpsters, past a junkyard where he saw three dog-sized pigs running stiff-legged, their short, twisted tails straight up, chasing each other through the blowing dust, squealing as they trotted over wrecked cars, refrigerators, and stoves laid out like coffins.

"Just *dogs*," Hanson told himself.

Weegee stopped at a real dead end, where a thicket of wrist-thick bamboo twenty feet high blocked the way. Hanson pulled up next to him, his tires crunching on the gravel turnaround.

"It's back there," Weegee said, pointing into the bamboo. "*I* can't find it sometimes."

"Sometimes?"

"Hard to explain," he said. "Buncha old ladies livin' there. All of 'em white too." He spun his bike around. "You see those three pigs?" He laughed. "I gotta go."

Weegee hopped on his bike, looked back at Hanson as if he was going to say something, but changed his mind and pedaled off. Hanson watched him ride away, then turned off the ignition and got out. He pulled out his survival compass, but the arrow wouldn't settle down. It just twitched back and forth. The bamboo rattled and whispered above him, and when he looked up a flock of orange-billed starlings tumbled and spun out from the leaves, then more of them, their speckled feathers iridescent green-black, squabbling and screeching, *daakdaakdaak*, then they were gone. Hanson tipped his head, listening, then parted the curtain of seg-mented glossy bamboo, followed a brick path through the thicket.

Twelve California bungalows, six of them on either side of a courtyard where a single tall date palm creaked in the wind, dead fronds rattling. Plants Hanson had never seen before in Oakland—or anywhere—grew rampant. Cat's-claw vines with yellow flowers and clawlike tendrils, prickly pear cactus with pur-ple pads. Passion vines all but covered the little bungalows and helped hold what was left of them together. Probably built after the 1906 earthquake, Hanson thought, when a lot of people who had lost their homes over in San Francisco moved to Oakland. A time long before the World War II influx of blacks to work in the shipyards, canneries, and automobile factories.

Old women, all of them white, living way out in the far south-east corner of East Oakland, their faded skirts and blouses and dresses too tight at the shoulders and hips, going in and out through the open door of unit 5. They would have all been young women, Hanson thought, when the place was new, the ferries, blazing with light on the foggy bay, making regular trips back and forth from San Francisco. He heard faraway dance music in the wind and saw them young again, with bobbed hair and beaded flapper dresses, iridescent like the starlings, dancing all night on the ferry, one of those glitter balls orbiting above them on the dance floor, dappling the walls with light.

He walked across the courtyard. High overhead the cloud of starlings swarmed into the shape of a snake, a shark, a pulsing jellyfish, then exploded and spun away to nothing. The wind whispered and sighed.

"Ladies," Hanson said as he took the sagging steps onto the porch of unit 5. "Good afternoon."

They ignored him as if he was somebody selling religion, coming out the door with magazines tucked beneath their arms, canned goods and paper towels and books cradled against their breasts, carrying shopping bags from stores that had long gone out of business.

"Ladies, excuse me."

An old woman pushed past him from behind and went on into the house, giving him a single angry glance, impatient. He had to step aside at the doorway for an old woman carrying a table lamp with a dented shade and another behind her with a cardboard box full of green and red ribbon, glitter stick-on bows, and already-used Christmas wrapping paper, the wind lifting some of it from the box before she could get her hand over it, bright paper flapping across the courtyard.

Inside, bundled newspapers, yellowed and flaking, were stacked up waist-high along the walls of the front room, on top of the furniture and the huge oak console TV set, a narrow walkway through the papers to the sofa, on past the dining nook, which was filled with *Oakland Tribune*s, chest high, up past the windowsills, years and decades of old bad news. The house smelled of burned food layered over with air freshener, and a faint rotten sweetness, like the breath of a drunk driver who tells you he hasn't been drinking.

"Who called the police?"

A loose window screen chattered in the wind.

In the kitchen an old woman in a bathrobe and a motel shower cap, barefoot, opened and slammed shut, one after another, already emptied kitchen cabinets.

"Ladies?"

They were looting the house.

Another old woman, her hair so thin her scalp showed, wearing only a dingy, flesh-beige slip, struggled to open a stuck kitchen drawer. As Hanson watched, it gave way and came completely out, the old woman stumbling backward into the far wall, a shoulder strap slipping off, exposing her breast. Cheap flatware clattered onto the buckling linoleum floor along with rubber-banded bundles of the plastic spoons and forks and knives that come with takeout food. She glanced at him and pulled the strap back up.

Lumpy black garbage bags were piled up at the far end of the kitchen, crushed cardboard wine-in-a-box containers spilling out. He closed the open refrigerator door as he walked past, through the door into what had once been a dining room, where a stocky woman in a flowered housecoat, her dead-looking brown hair gathered with a rubber band, nylon stockings rolled down beneath her knees, was rifling the drawers of a dark wood buffet. Her thin lips were lipsticked blood red and her eyebrows had been plucked, then penciled in as angry arcs.

A crash from the next room spun him around, and two more women hurried past as he walked into a bedroom, where the curtains were pulled shut and the overhead light was as subtle as a bus station, hundred-watt bulbs in the cheap ceiling fixture. Nobody had stolen them yet. Shards of a broken mirror that had fallen off the wall onto a dressing table splintered beneath his boots on the orange-and-blue shag rug—costume jewelry and face powder, coats and blouses and shoes, empty pint and quart vodka bottles. He looked at the body on the bed.

No wounds or signs of trauma that he could see, but he wasn't going to roll her over to check for exit wounds. It could have been anything—poison, suffocation, an ice pick through the ear—but she'd probably died, finally, of old age. She was on her back, naked, her knees up and apart, pushed open by gravity and death. One arm across her body, the other extended, palm up, her face was turned toward Hanson, eyes almost closed. Black blood had pooled in her buttocks and feet. The bedsheets, which had once been ivory, were shiny graphite black from years of being slept on, drunk, passed-out on, and never washed. Her dead face was not so much old now as ancient. Death had smoothed out all the laugh lines, frown lines, and worry lines, tightened the skin across her cheekbones and nose. She was ancient and anonymous, a death mask of any-woman. Aristocratic, ageless. He walked closer and stood over her, the sweet-rot smell of death would, he knew, stay in his hair and wool uniform tonight. Outside, the wind whined and chattered and snapped like gunshots.

He picked the bedspread up off the floor, empty vodka bottles clacking as they rolled off, and covered her. The scene had already been trampled and looted. He'd say he found her covered. When he walked back out into the kitchen no one was there. The house was empty, shuddering in the wind. A screen door somewhere squealed and slammed relentlessly. He closed and locked the back door, checked to see that all the windows in the house were locked, then went back to the bedroom and stood in the doorway for a moment.

"You'll be fine," he said, nodding at the corpse. "Everything's secured. You'll be okay now." Wind rattled the windows, trying to get in. "Okay," he said and went outside.

Out on the porch he took his PAC-set off his belt, keyed the mike, and gave his call sign. Static cut him off. The wind was blowing one direction up at a thousand feet and sheering off in another direction below that, ripping clouds apart. The wind was singing up there.

Radio told him: Wait one.

The cloud of starlings had corkscrewed itself into a glittering green-black funnel and was turning slowly overhead toward the San Leandro border.

Radio came back and told him to stand by.

He walked to the next bungalow, up the steps, and knocked on the door. He thought he heard someone talking inside, or maybe it was the TV, or just the wind muttering. He rapped on the door with his short wood, watching the birds, listening to the palm tree creak in the wind like a giant oar in an oarlock. No one came to the door, but the talking stopped.

Darkness rose from the trees like smoke, lifting with the wind and spreading into the clouds. Screen doors slammed and slammed through the blocks, and dogs howled at the sky.

5Tac51.

"5Tac51," Hanson repeated.

Uh, 5Tac51, disregard that assignment. You'll be 908.

"There's a dead body at this location."

5Tac51, do you copy, disregard. That location is not in our jurisdiction. You'll be 908.

"5Tac51, I'm going to need—"

5Tac51, it will be assigned to the county. I have an Alameda County case number for your records. Are you ready to copy?

Hanson copied the number into his notebook and put the PAC-set back on his belt. He looked back at unit 5. He began walking to his patrol car.

The black rabbit was almost hidden beneath the porch of unit 2. It looked like a shadow down there, a break in the concrete foundation. Hanson ignored it as he walked past the unit, wondering how he was going to find his way back to the district. It was getting dark, and he saw lightning shuddering on the horizon. The wind was bad enough without another fucking black rabbit. There were probably hundreds of black rabbits in East Oakland, breeding every night in the dark, famous all across the country, and he'd just never heard about them. An urban prey base for all the feral dogs. It was scuffling along behind him now, following him like a dog. He stopped, turned, and looked down at the rabbit. The wind ruffled its glossy fur into little black cowlicks, and its floppy ears twitched as it looked up at him. A jagged streak of white fur ran from beneath one eye and down alongside its nose. It was the rabbit from the Temple, yes. The Temple was miles away, mostly uphill, on the other side of two freeways. Same rabbit. It wasn't going to leave him alone.

"What?" Hanson said. The rabbit tipped its head and ate a few blades of grass, still looking up at Hanson with one eye.

Hanson shooed him with his hands, palms out, like he was splashing waist-high water. "Go on. Go on, now," but the rabbit didn't move and Hanson walked around it.

"Hey, Officer Hanson." It was Weegee, working his way toward him through the bamboo.

"Weegee. I'm glad to see you, young man. Whoa. I didn't know if I could find my way out of here. It really is a strange place."

"Yeah," Weegee said, looking at Hanson, then looking away and down. Shy, somehow, or maybe embarrassed that Hanson, a cop, kept getting lost. "I was thinking about that. An' I decided I should come back here and check."

It took a moment. Hanson understood that Weegee was afraid of the place himself, but he'd shown him how to get there, then come back. He bit his lip and looked up at the sky, but the sky was gone. Nothing now but black and gray clouds. "Let's *dee-dee* outta here, young man. If I can get through the fuckin' bamboo."

"What's that 'dee' stuff?"

"*Dee-dee mau.* Vietnamese. Means 'Let's get outta here.' "

Hanson put Weegee's bike in the trunk of the patrol car and drove away with Weegee. Weegee was excited to tell him about some local politician or drug dealer who was like Robin Hood. Hanson smiled and nodded but didn't really hear what he was saying, ignoring Radio too, listening to what the wind said. He took Weegee to the Junkyard Dog for a Gangsta Burger, then offered to drop him off at his house, but Weegee said he'd just ride his bike home, it wasn't far.

Later, Hanson looked at his beat map and saw that a tiny corner of Oakland, including Bleeker Court, was crosshatched out of the city limits.

CHAPTER TEN

FRIENDLY FIRE

Hanson is sleeping.

The City of Oakland is awake. An undercover narc named Sandler is chasing a fifteen-year-old black juvenile through backyards in District Four. Sandler and his two partners had spent several hours that night trying to set up a drug buy from people in West Oakland but had no luck. As Sandler was about to pull away from the curb in his unmarked car and call it a night, the fifteen-year-old drove past them, pissing Sandler off. The driver's head was all but hidden by the headrest—a small guy to be driving—so Sandler followed him and ran the license plate on the secret frequency undercover cops used. There were usually twenty or fifteen undercover cops on the street any given night, but the beat cops didn't know this, and they weren't aware of several classified Radio frequencies used by them and other special units. The Department, worried that the beat cops might expose the undercover and special unit cops, kept the frequencies a secret.

The license plate came back to a car that had been stolen that morning, so Sandler activated the red flashing lights hidden behind the grille of the bare-bones model dark blue Ford that almost anyone would realize was a police car.

The kid, whose name was Ezekiel, had been driving the car around most of the day, was almost out of gas, and was planning to dump it close enough to where he lived that he could walk home. When he saw the lights behind him, he took off, getting the car up to almost one hundred miles per hour on the Nimitz Freeway, the cop car right behind. It was a rush Ezekiel would never forget. He squealed up High Street, tried and failed to lose the cops near his neighborhood, skidded into a big blue mailbox, and bailed out of the car, running for home.

Sandler was really pissed by now and pumping adrenaline, so he spun his car out to a stop and jumped out, leaving his partners in the car, determined to kill or beat the shit out of Ezekiel.

Sandler realizes he is running parallel to the kid, so he arcs away from him and two blocks later is waiting when the kid, not in good shape, comes huffing out of the dark. Sandler knocks him down and holds the snub-nose .44 he carries to the kid's head.

Cover units had been dispatched to assist in apprehending a car thief. Two of them, both driven by young cops with less than six months on the street, catch Sandler in their headlights, leaning over a little kid, holding a pistol inches from his head, the kid screaming for mercy.

They've never met Sandler and, of course, don't know about the secret undercover cops, when they jump out of their patrol cars, pointing their service revolvers at Sandler, yelling, "Freeze! Freeze!" just as one of them accidentally pulls the trigger of his pistol, scaring the other new cop, who also starts shooting, and together they shoot Sandler nine times from the middle of the street.

Ezekiel is afraid to move and Sandler is dead.

There was nothing in the media the next day except a brief article that an Oakland police officer had been shot and killed by accident.

CHAPTER ELEVEN

STATS

Hanson's hangover was all but gone and the breeze off the bay smelled like the open sea. The first day of May, another month gone, no reason he couldn't make it through his eighteen-month probation. He remembered that his mom was the Queen of the May in her high school. He'd just keep marching.

He'd cleared from his first call of the day—attempted sodomy, 245 Knife, that's how Radio put it out—in a halfway house, resulting from an argument over whether Jesus was actually the Son of God or only a prophet. Both victims were also suspects, the alleged knife threat having been made against the alleged attempted sodomist. After Hanson managed to separate and calm them down, both seemed okay, except for being drunk and moderately psychotic.

It was almost the end of his monthly report period and he needed three more felony arrests and at least two misdemeanors to keep up with the rest of the squad on his arrest quota, to meet his stats. He could have arrested both of them for felonies, and he considered it. Even though the DA would never charge them, the two arrests would count toward his stats—two down and one to go. But processing them, the transportation and paperwork, would have taken two hours, so he wrote it up on an assignment card. <u>Problem solved upon departure. Hanson / 7374P.</u> Hanson tried to reduce most calls to assignment cards.

They'd promised to stay away from each other for the night, each of them alone in his own bleak room, and they both waved goodbye when he drove off. He raised his hand in response and caught himself hoping they'd be okay. What was he doing? They were drunk and psychotic black men in Oakland. They'd never be okay. They were fucked and doomed and beyond help.

He'd better come up with a few more arrests in the next couple of nights or Lieutenant Garber would have a reminder and an excuse to fuck with him. One of Fernandez's girlfriends, who worked up in Records, had told him that the lieutenant had them route all of Hanson's paperwork through his office. Working all this time out in Districts Four and Five, just a blip on the radar, he'd hoped the lieutenant had begun to forget he was there. He'd never seen anyone above the rank of sergeant out there, and not many of those. Except for shootings, ADWs, and quite a few armed robberies, it was mostly just domestic disputes, neighborhood disputes, property disputes, trespassing, threats and simple assaults, plus various 647s. So mostly he *was* a social worker. People in East Oakland only called the police after they'd threatened each other to a stalemate and it was either call the police or settle it with guns or knives or tire irons. Hanson could talk to people, calm them down, asking, suggesting, persuading, telling them what they should do, and not arresting them unless he had to. Which cut down on his paperwork but hurt his stats. Some nights, though, near the end of the report period, like now, he did his best to go by the book, do things the OPD way and solve problems by putting people in jail. He might feel bad about it when he got home at dawn, but he told himself that if it wasn't him out there doing it, he'd be replaced by someone who treated people a lot worse. And it was only for another—less than eight months. Then he'd be gone to a better department, where he could do some good once in a while. It was all a means to an end, and he shouldn't beat himself up.

Just up the street, in front of a falling-down Victorian house, a shirtless black male, early thirties, buffed-out prison build, was swinging a severed head by the hair. He'd begun slamming it against a tree by the time Hanson took his foot off the gas, the head breaking apart—nose, ears, then the jaw sloughing off. Hanson pumped the brake, turned in toward the curb, and, seeing that it wasn't a head but a dead potted plant, dried stalks and a root ball, put his foot back on the gas and straightened the steering wheel, wondering where he could pop a few felonies between Radio calls. He glanced in the rearview mirror at the guy, standing out in the street now, still gripping what was left of the dead plant and glaring at the patrol car, his eyes saying, *What the fuck* you *looking at, motherfucker?*

He needed some movers too, moving violations he could write some traffic tickets on. He'd find some movers, but if he didn't fill his arrest quota every month, he'd look like a mediocre cop, what they called a slug, and if you *looked* like a slug, you *were* a slug.

So what? That shouldn't bother him, his reputation with these fuckers, but it did. Day in and day out on a PD, reputation was everything. Who the other cops thought you were, before long, was who you began to worry you were. Once you began to *think* you were a slug cop and started losing your confidence, you couldn't handle the job and then you became what they thought you were. He missed having a partner just to *talk to* sometimes, but he was getting used to it.

There had been a lot of cops who didn't like him back in Portland, but his reputation there had been solid. He'd been a real hot dog cop out at North, the toughest precinct—ballsy and outrageous. He might have been weird, but he kicked in doors and was the first one through. He might have been a smart ass, a tree hugger, talked like a commie, but he didn't take any shit. They all thought he was a little crazier than they were, but that didn't take away from him being crazy brave.

But he wasn't brave, or even crazy, he just wasn't afraid, only angry sometimes. He was supposed to have died over there in the war. He worried sometimes that he might fuck up, get somebody else killed, do something careless and look *stupid* when he died. He didn't want that, and, of course, he hoped it wouldn't hurt too much or take too long when it happened. It was that simple, and he kept it a secret. Not a secret really—only something he knew he could never explain.

If he had a secret, it was his mean streak. He'd assumed it was something he was born with, but in the army and over there in that war he realized it wasn't just a character trait but more like a talent. If you practiced, you got better and better at it. He'd learned that if you're mean and don't care if you live or die, nobody messes with you. But he kept it under control now and had for a long time. He thought sometimes that, even under control, it looked out of his eyes at people, and when they saw that look, that's why they did what he asked them to do. Like a bad dog, it was still loyal, still protective, even though he kept it chained up. He'd had a partner in Portland for four years, until the partner got killed and Hanson chased down and executed the killer. Dana, his partner, had been a respected fourteen-year veteran of the ghetto known as "The Bear of the Avenue," fearless, almost a force of nature, who was a witness to Hanson on the job. The two of them had patrolled the same beat every night and worked with cops in two-man cars in adjacent beats who also saw Hanson at work.

Witnesses and word-of-mouth was how you got your reputation in Portland.

In Oakland a reputation was established with paperwork. Crime reports, arrest reports, property reports, witness statements, additional information reports, supplemental reports. A good cop had good stats, he made a lot of arrests that were recorded and filed. A good cop in Oakland usually had more than his share of citizen complaints, sometimes a lot more. Because he made more arrests, he was going to get more complaints, of course, but if you were a cop who used arrests as the first and primary way to deal with people out there, if you didn't try to talk first, and *listen*, you probably were going to get a lot of citizen complaints. The cops pronounced the word "citizen" exactly the way they spoke the word "asshole."

So many arrests were made, driven by the arrest quota, that only about one in ten complaints was ever charged by the DA, which was all the system could handle. Then it could be months, maybe a year before the case was looked at by a detective, and by then the suspect, witnesses, or victims might be in jail themselves—"Today's victim is tomorrow's suspect"—or dead, and the DA would be happy to toss the case out to get it off his workload.

The murder clearance rate was based on arrests—more stats—not on suspects found guilty. Guilty findings were mostly the result of confessions made after twenty-four or thirty-six hours of nonstop questioning. The confessions were recorded by detectives who didn't record the interrogations that led up to them. So sometimes, after two or three or four years in prison, the person who confessed was released when it came to light that he had been at work, or at someone's house or even in jail at the time of the crime, that there were videos or recordings or witnesses to prove that—and that the suspect had told this to the cops interrogating him until he finally confessed in order to get some sleep and avoid a death sentence they'd said he'd receive if he didn't confess.

The Department maintained the arrest quota like the army had kept a body count in Vietnam. It was the only way the Department could prove they were on the job when the crime rate kept going up every year. But the courts were so backed up with all the arrests that only cases virtually impossible to lose went to trial. Most of those arrested knew this, so they didn't plea bargain and were released to become stats another day.

Working a one-man car in East Oakland, Hanson rarely saw another police car all night. No one saw him at work except citizens, always strangers because Hanson worked a different beat every night like all the OPD cops. Every citizen contact with the police—if only a gesture, a glance or a half-heard comment—involved strangers who expected the worst of each other. Every single contact was potentially lethal.

It was early evening when Hanson backed into a row of parked cars where he could watch the Pioneer Chicken. The aluminum and glass building was spotlighted like a Salvation Army cathedral, outlined in flickering neon, steam rising like a cheap miracle from the kitchen in back. The massive Pioneer Chicken sign, ablaze with light, rotated and tilted through the dark sky like a ghetto space station—a cartoon covered-wagon, its neon wheels twitching *red, red, red,* while a pudgy white chef held aloft a cooked chicken the size of a motorcycle.

They'd had five or six takeover robberies in the past couple of months—the whole chain, Pioneer Chicken franchises all over town—and they had beefed up the lighting and hired minimum wage security guards who refused to work after dark.

On the other side of the street from where Hanson was parked, down at the intersection, a black man in his fifties, his left hand clenched in a fist, stood waiting for the light to change from WAIT to WALK. A heroin addict Hanson had first spotted back in January when he was working this beat. A few weeks before, he'd stopped him and written his name, address, and DOB in his notebook, like a mojo curse, keeping him in reserve for times he was low on arrests. He was usually on the street this time of evening, always alone and always wearing the same brown sport coat and slacks. Heroin was how he got through the days and nights, a way to get to sleep and a reason to wake up, only a misdemeanor but an easy one to write up.

As a trained police officer, Hanson could recognize the six signs of opiate addiction, so he had probable cause to stop him, search him for weapons, and inspect him for needle tracks, which were sufficient evidence that he was in violation of statute 11550 of the California Health and Safety Code: use of a controlled substance. The Narcotics Influence Report form was easy to fill out—not too many boxes to check off and, at the bottom, simple line drawings of a right and a left arm where the arresting officer could just sketch in the needle marks observed on a suspect.

Hanson got out of the patrol car and called, "Hey, Jonah."

Jonah looked up with a forced smile, his eyes deciding whether or not to run. He knew he was guilty of something but wasn't sure what it was. He held the smile, reviewing the past few days for a clue. The red WAIT sign was replaced by a green WALK sign.

"Come 'ere," Hanson said, and Jonah's smile began to fade. Too late to run, and where would he run to? He'd been to San Francisco a few times and down to LA once when he was in high school, but other than that, he'd spent his entire life in East Oakland.

Hanson gestured for him to walk over to the patrol car, and Jonah did, trying to put a little spring in his step and perk up his smile.

"What is it, Officer?" he said, still hoping against a lifetime of being stopped by police that he wouldn't be arrested.

"Come on."

"I was just going to get me some of that chicken," he said, gesturing with his almost-bald head toward Pioneer Chicken, then opening his fist to show Hanson the two dollar bills and change he had.

"I'm sure hungry," he went on, managing a smile.

"Roll up your sleeve."

"What now?"

"Roll it up."

"Sir. Officer, I was just gonna get my supper and go home."

"Roll it up."

He rolled the sleeve up and, his eyes on the revolving Pioneer Chicken sign, straightened his arm out to Hanson, his scarred, pocked, festering ruined arm.

"You carrying any weapons, Jonah?"

"No, sir."

"Anything in your pockets that—"

"No, sir."

"That are gonna cut me or poke me."

"No, sir. Sorry..."

"That's okay," Hanson said politely, before he could stop himself. "Step on over to the car." No fucking around here, no careless empathy, strictly business. Handcuffing somebody was where people got hurt. The suspect's last chance to run, to fight, to try and take your gun. Once those cuffs were on, though, it was a done deal.

"Lean over the hood and put your hands behind your back." A few people were watching from the Pioneer Chicken parking lot and Hanson glared at them, angry that Jonah was being humiliated. "Spread those legs out a little more," he told Jonah, kicking the run-down heels of Jonah's shoes with the toe of his steel-toed boot.

Once he had the handcuffs on, Jonah didn't say another word. He did what Hanson told him, without complaint, as if Hanson was nothing more than a gear or a lever in a familiar, relentless piece of machinery. Neither one spoke on the way to jail, but Hanson listened to Jonah's breathing behind the wire cage and considered what Jonah's evening would have been if he hadn't been arrested for 11550 H&S. Not much. A couple pieces of fried chicken, a glass of fortified wine maybe, and some heroin to soften the hard edges of his failed life. Then sleep.

Now, though, he'd spend the night, probably standing up, with a dozen drunks and sociopaths and bullies in a filthy holding cell where, before morning, he'd begin to go through withdrawal from the heroin. Then they'd chain him up to a ring bolt in the jail bus and take him out to Santa Rita, where he'd probably spend ninety days.

When he got out he'd have to scrounge up some money, find a place he could stay while he looked for a place to live, hope his drug connection wasn't in jail, and find a new one if he was. Get back to normal, essentially. He'd done it plenty of times before. No big deal. He probably wasn't even that pissed off about it. Just part of life.

Hanson got so drunk after work, passed out by 9 a.m., that he had to call in sick the next day, the phone shaking in his hand, the hangover was so bad. He used a couple of the bindles of cocaine he'd collected from the back of the patrol car when he didn't see any reason to write up and charge whoever had dumped them there, snorted them a little at a time while taking a long hot bath, listening to the water pipes gurgle in the walls of the old house.

He did his best not to think about Jonah, going through with-

drawal out in Santa Rita so Hanson could add one more misdemeanor arrest to his stats. To satisfy a sergeant whose name he
couldn't remember, an arrogant little-man lieutenant dedicated
to finding typos in report forms, and to gain the respect of other
patrolmen he mostly despised.

He wondered if he was getting used to that kind of thing and
if he'd start doing worse and not be ashamed of himself. He ran
through the usual arguments: If he didn't do it, someone—more of
an asshole than he was becoming—would. It was just a means to an
end, so he could do some good on another department. He only had
to do it for seven months now. Plus a couple of days. He was not a
quitter. Fuckin' A. Nobody could call him a quitter. It's not like he *believed* in the stupid laws he was supposed to enforce…And who gives
a shit anyway? It's only a job, a good-paying job in a bad economy,
and what else would he do? He was too old to start wearing a tie and
taking orders from some moron *citizen* he could kill with his bare
hands without breaking a sweat. Fuck yeah. He needed to start cutting himself a little slack once in a while.

Hanson was locked in the OPD jail sally port. The deputy had
been about to buzz him out when he had to run back and help
another deputy with the prisoner Hanson had brought in. The
prisoner had threatened Hanson all the way to jail, slamming his
forehead against the Plexiglas cage, yelling and spitting that he
was going to find out where Hanson lived and the next time Hanson saw him, motherfucker, would be the last time because he'd
have his shotgun with him.

Whenever he paused to catch his breath, Hanson would tell
him, never taking his eyes off the road, in a calm, reasonable voice,
that he was sorry the prisoner felt that way and that he really
shouldn't slam his head into the Plexiglas because he might injure
himself.

As soon as Hanson transferred him into jail custody and was buzzed back through the inner door of the steel mesh sally port, a deputy had called the prisoner a "shit bird," and the prisoner went berserk. Hanson couldn't see what was happening, but from the grunts and thuds, he imagined the deputies were struggling to get an arm around his throat to choke him out. The prisoners back there screamed at the deputies and urged the prisoner to keep fighting, though some of them were laughing.

Hanson smiled. He'd thought that the prisoner was just about primed and that the deputies might set him off.

The choke hold was illegal in most cities now. Once in a while, very rarely, a prisoner would die after it was used on him. His esophagus would swell up, he wouldn't be able to breathe, and unless someone did a tracheotomy on him, he'd die. Since the hold was used most often on black males—blacks making up a disproportionate number of arrestees—civil rights groups had managed to officially ban the hold. Mace didn't work on somebody pissed off or fucked up enough to fight the police, and usually you were too close to use a nightstick—the guy already had his hands on you. So if the prisoner was big and had decided to fight, often the only realistic alternative to the choke hold these days was to shoot him before he took your gun away and shot you with it. The civil rights ban on the choke hold had gotten a lot of suspects shot. A billboard just across the Berkeley border had recently been put up. A VOTE FOR THE CHOKE HOLD IS A VOTE FOR THE KU KLUX KLAN.

The sally port was a long hallway of steel mesh with an electrically locking door at each end. To enter the jail, Hanson had to put his revolver in a little locker and put the key in his pocket, and the deputy would buzz him into the outer door. He'd push that door closed, locking it again, walk the length of the sally port, and the deputy would then buzz him through the inner door. Only one door could be open at a time. It kept prisoners from slipping past an arresting officer or deputy and running out of the jail.

To his left was a holding tank for prisoners who hadn't yet been formally booked. As the struggle with Hanson's prisoner continued, he watched the people in the holding tank.

Two Mexicans in their late teens or early twenties. One was shirtless, and his chest, arms, and back were ridged with scores of red inch-long scars. They were from years of knife fights where the opponents held the blade so that only a couple of inches were exposed, and they'd slash with it, leaving shallow cuts that, Hanson decided, the Mexican had kept from healing by pulling the sides apart for a day or two so they'd be more dramatic. Not unlike Prussian dueling scars from a hundred years ago. This kid had been in a lot of knife fights.

The other Mexican kid, who seemed to be in charge, wore a gray striped train engineer's shirt with a very well-drafted pen-and-ink drawing on the back of a Chicano wearing a headband, a drooping bandito mustache, and mirror sunglasses, holding a sawed-off shotgun, the muzzles pointing directly at you, outsized and huge in perspective. Also in the tank were a drunk Indian who sat brooding in the corner where no one bothered him, a very drunk black guy in his late thirties who kept falling down, and a second black guy who was less drunk and arguing with the shirtless Mexican, who kept calling him his punk.

"You gonna be my punk. Soon as they turn off the lights you gonna suck my dick."

"I ain't your punk."

"You gonna be tonight, *ese.*"

The Mexican in the shirt told the scarred one to shut the fuck up.

Someone else deep in the jail began yelling, "Help me. Help me."

"Shut up!" the Mexican in the shirt yelled back. "All of you shut up!"

The deputy came back, blood on his uniform. "Fucker pissed his pants and we made him wipe it up with that fuckin' Hawaiian shirt." He looked up at a TV security monitor. "Hang on a second. I've gotta let her in," and he buzzed in a matron with a woman prisoner. An attractive black woman in her mid-twenties dressed like Little Bo Peep. As if she had come from a costume party. She wore silver eye shadow and red rouge on her cheeks. Her sky-blue dress flared out and up because of layers of petticoats she wore beneath it. She was wearing a corsage of red carnations and carrying a papier-mâché shepherd's staff wrapped with silver ribbon.

"You gonna suck my dick tonight."

"Shut up."

The matron asked Hanson to take the staff so she could escort Bo Peep upstairs to the women's jail. Hanson made eye contact through the silver eye shadow, and Bo Peep handed him the staff, curtsied in her petticoats, then, rising, said, "Girded with righteousness, I stand before the throne." Then she turned to the matron and followed her through a side door as the deputy buzzed it open, leaving Hanson with the silver-ribboned papier-mâché staff.

The Mexican in the shotgun shirt was smiling at him.

"Do you believe in the Devil?" he asked Hanson. "Do you? When the Devil comes I will laugh. I will laugh when he comes."

The others in the holding cell were watching Hanson. "What if we," he said, indicating the departed Bo Peep with a tilt of his staff, "were the last people on earth?"

"Then we would kill you," the Mexican said, stepping closer to the bars. "You think your badge makes you bad," he said to Hanson. "And your gun."

"And my staff," Hanson said, holding it before him.

"You ready to go?" the deputy said.

"Yeah. I'm ready."

The deputy buzzed the lock open, and Hanson pushed through the door with the staff in his hand.

"When the Devil comes, I will laugh. I will *laugh*."

Hanson propped the staff against the gun lockers, got his pistol out, checked to see if it was loaded like he did every time he re-holstered it, and walked toward the next door.

"When the Devil comes…"

Hanson pushed through the next door into the jail garage, considering the Devil.

Hanson was out in District Four, the patrol car backed up to the wall of a warehouse, glad it was almost time to head in so he could get drunk. The next two days were his weekend. He'd been seeing spider webs floating past streetlights since it had gotten dark—at least that's what they looked like, some seasonal phenomenon, he thought. As he was finishing a crime report, an old beater pickup rattled out of an alley, stopped at the street, drove across it, then continued on down the alley on the other side. The headlights were on, but it had no taillights. It was 3 a.m.

Hanson put down the report form, turned off the writing light and followed the truck down the alley another block with his lights off, giving Radio his location and the license number of the truck. At the next street he flipped on the overhead lights and the high-low headlights, the darkness opening and closing on the stopped truck, the driver placing both hands on the steering wheel.

He walked to the truck holding his flashlight at arm's length away from himself so that anyone who might shoot at him would shoot at the flashlight. He doubted that it made any difference. The only place people learned to shoot was by watching movies—it was all mostly luck, good or bad—and anyway, most shootings took place close enough to have been stabbings. There wasn't a lot of marksmanship involved.

He checked the bed of the truck as he walked past it. A flat spare tire, tow chain, a six-can case of empty oil cans, scraps of lumber, and a couple dozen empty beer cans.

Tall, pollution-mutant shrubbery brushed his shoulder and cheek with gray leaves that stunk of carbon monoxide, urine, and rancid exhaust from the Granny Goose potato chip plant twenty blocks away. The driver still had both hands on the wheel, and Hanson tapped on the roof with the flashlight.

"Sir..." he said, leaning back away from the door, alert and weary at the same time.

The driver of the truck was a white guy with dirty shoulder-length blond hair and bad teeth, wearing ragged jeans and a filthy I WANT MY MTV T-shirt. When he smiled Hanson knew he was an ex-con. It was in his eyes, that abused dog look, shiny with fear even as he pretended he was glad to see you. "Good evening, Officer," he said. "How are you this evening?"

"Hi, sir," Hanson said without enthusiasm. He hoped the dumb motherfucker didn't have any outstanding warrants. It was almost time to go home, and he didn't want to go into overtime taking him to jail. "Where you headed?"

"I'll tell you the truth, Officer, I'm on my way home," he said, "from my girlfriend's house." Hanson nodded at the lie. "June. She lives back there on Harvey Court." Sociopath jailhouse bullshit, and it just depressed Hanson. "I'll tell you, Officer...June's a great gal, you know? Officer?"

"Uh-huh," Hanson grunted. He lit up the inside of the cab with his flashlight, checking the floor, under the seat and dashboard, watching the driver's hands. The truck cab smelled like stale cigarette smoke and vomit, like the backseat of a police car.

"Could I see your driver's license, please." Radio came back and said that the subject did not have any wants or warrants but that he was currently on parole for 459C. The truck wasn't stolen.

It took him a while to find his driver's license, checking the glove box, his pockets, above the sun visor, a wallet stuffed with scraps of paper and old business cards, he finally managed to find it stuck behind the door armrest. "Here it is," he said, handing the limp, torn license to Hanson. "Have no idea why I put it there." He looked a lot younger in the photo on the license—more than younger, he looked okay, like he must have looked before he'd gone to prison.

"Mr. O'Donald," Hanson said, reading his name from the license. "This license expired three years ago." Everybody in Oakland was an ex-con, it seemed like some nights, or they soon would be.

"Is it that old one? The other one must be at home. That's why I couldn't find it."

Hanson pulled out his citation book and began writing.

"Officer, I'm almost home. I live over off High Street. I know I'm out pretty late, but my girl and I had a long talk. About the future, you know? I'd sure appreciate it if you could give me a break on this." His voice now had an edge of fear in it, and Hanson stepped back just a bit. "My parole officer...He's gonna be pissed."

"I have to write you up on this, sir. I've got no choice," Hanson said. But he did have a choice. He could just let the guy go. But why should he? The guy was scum.

"Officer, please. Couldn't you overlook it, give me a break this one time?"

"Can't do it, sir," Hanson said, writing the citation by the light of his flashlight, the red and blue patrol car lights sweeping relentlessly overhead, *raw, raw, raw,* alternating fans of color like carnival lights over the bleak little drama. "And both your tail-lights are out. I'm not even going to ask for the registration."

Hanson was way behind on traffic citations. He handed the citation through the window and asked him to sign it.

"Sixty-three dollars?" the driver said, reading the fine schedule, his eyes flashing blue, red, blue, red. "I don't have sixty-three dollars, Officer. I'm fucked if you write me up."

"You want to sign it or step out of the vehicle," Hanson said.

He signed it and handed it back to Hanson. "Can I go now?"

"Here's your copy," Hanson said, tearing it off and handing it to him, ready to kick his ass if he came out of the truck at him. But he only looked at Hanson, beaten but not surprised, a whipped dog. He stuffed the ticket in the neck of his T-shirt, started the truck, turned down the street.

Hanson watched the truck drive away, then got back into the patrol car, turned off the lights, and sat in the dark, his ears chirping like a plague of crickets. He felt like an asshole, even though, he thought, he hadn't done anything wrong. Hell, he'd let him skate on the registration. The white puke would have killed him if he'd had the balls and thought he could get away with it. And brag about it to his jailhouse buddies.

But *he* was an asshole, he thought. Didn't matter, just another asshole cop. Pretty soon he'd fit right in, one of the guys finally. If he'd start arresting everybody he could, pile up citations and kiss enough ass, he might make sergeant someday, or get on a special drug squad with the special assholes.

The little prick had been driving the alleys because he didn't want to get pulled over with no operator's license and God knows what else. He was probably out past his curfew, somewhere he wasn't supposed to be. Maybe he'd been "associating with known criminals." Who *else* would he associate with? Churchgoers and family men? Other losers maybe, guys with no heart left, who took their minimum wage checks, worked for their sullen week-end drunks.

His parole officer *would* be pissed. Probably violate him back to the joint. But, hell, he was doomed to go back to the joint anyway. Eventually. If Hanson didn't do it somebody else would. Anyway, fuck it. Time to go in for the night. He had two days off. He cleared from the traffic stop and told Radio he was on his way in.

He didn't know if he could make his eighteen months.

Once he got up to freeway speed, he fed the torn pieces of the citation out the window to the wind, watching them in the rearview mirror as they flickered pink in his taillights and vanished.

CHAPTER TWELVE

THE LIQUOR STORE

When he cleared for calls, Radio sent him as a cover car to the Black & White Liquor Store at 27th and Fruitvale. By the time he got there, more cars had been dispatched, one of them coming Code 3 up MacArthur, red and blue lights flaring through the darkening sky. He pulled partway up onto the curb, got out, locked the car, and then had to shoulder his way through the growing crowd, keeping his momentum, elbow tight against his holstered pistol, through the glass door and inside—the eye of the storm—hot, humid, the floor slippery with blood and alcohol, shards of broken bottles refracting the light. Outside, beyond the tinted windows, red and blue emergency lights strobed the yelling, fist-pumping crowd into fast slow motion.

Sergeant Jackson pulled into the lot and got out of his car, stiff-arming a Rasta man with dreadlocks out of his way, the Rasta man falling into the crowd, where they beat him to the pavement for bumping into them. Sergeant Jackson pushed past a fat teenage boy who was pumping both fists into the air, drove an elbow into his chest, dropping him to his knees, and just kept striding through the howling chaos to the front of the store where he turned and surveyed the crowd, taking charge of the other officers out front. As far as Hanson could tell, Sergeant Jackson only came out on the street to take over some situation that was going to shit or when he was in the mood to fuck with people—suspects, citizens, or other cops.

Inside the liquor store the light was bright and without shadow, chain-hung fluorescent fixtures humming overhead. Convex mirrors mounted at the end of each aisle distorted the scene from every perspective. The oscillating fan at the back of the store sucked up the stink of alcohol, blood, and gun smoke, dispersed it, then sucked it up again.

The failed and deceased holdup man seemed to float in an inch-deep pool of blood and alcohol, fresh blood still seeping from what remained of his face. He'd come through the door, the clerk told them, with a knife in his hand, "acting crazy." The clerk had pulled a .44 Special Bulldog snub-nose pistol from beneath the cash register—just going to point it at the man, he said, let the man see he was armed, you understand—but it went off accidentally beneath the counter. The 240-grain hollow-nose slug tore through the plywood countertop, mushrooming to twice its original size, before ripping through the suspect's neck from below, severing his carotid artery, all but severing his tongue on its way up and through the roof of his mouth and out his nose before lodging in the ceiling. He ran up and down the aisles, blood spraying from his neck and face, stumbling into the shelves and pyramid liquor displays until he fell.

"Just like a chicken with its head cut off," the clerk said.

One of the cops, the second so far, remarked in a John Wayne drawl on the folly of taking a knife to a gunfight.

"He won't be eating any more corn on the cob," a cop named Shannon said, looking down at him, one foot on either side of his head. The body suddenly arched, belched gore onto Shannon's boot and trouser leg and he jumped back into a display of Smirnoff vodka that had, until then, been undisturbed. "Well, shit," Shannon said, the display collapsing around him, its twenty or thirty bottles of vodka exploding, one after another, onto the floor, just as the windows began to shudder—music—a song from some popular movie or TV series, relentless, louder and faster, from cars jammed and trapped in the parking lot, their radios tuned to the same station.

"I wanna do it, do it, do it, do it, do it with you
You make me crazy…"

An EMS siren, way down East 14th, honked and warbled and brayed, getting louder, coming their way fast, the chained dogs for blocks around picking it up and howling along.

The crowd was growing, getting angry, one kid yelling at a Hispanic cop Hanson had never seen before. "Are you telling me I can't stand here on the sidewalk? Is that what you're telling me? I can't stand on a sidewalk? Is that what you're telling me?"

The cop had his nightstick out, holding it upside down, its length hidden behind his cocked forearm.

"This is a public fuckin' sidewalk, an' you're tellin' me—"

"I'm telling you to shut the fuck up, motherfucker, an' I'm tellin' you to get the fuck off my fuckin' sidewalk," the cop snarled, pivoting, snapping the stick out, slamming the kid expertly in the chest with it and knocking him on his back between two cars.

"I wanna do it, do it, I wanna do it with you
Let's go crazy…"

More police cars—too many—were pulling up, blocking the civilian cars in, doors slamming as the cops got out with nightsticks, shoving people out of their way, looking for a little stick time tonight. Time to go, Hanson thought, before somebody gets shot. A good two-man car—just a pair of cops who worked this neighborhood every night and knew the people—could have handled this, he thought, walking across the store, a slurry of alcohol and broken glass crunching beneath his boots.

A Kandy apple green Monte Carlo lowrider drove in from the street, over the curb, over the foot-high concrete parking lot borders, to the very front of the store, humping up and down on its hydraulic shocks, and Sergeant Jackson began slamming the car's hood with his Kel-Lite. The driver got out, ready to fight, and Sergeant Jackson pulled something from the back of his pistol belt that looked like a blue plastic camera. He'd been issued one of the first Tasers a month before. Hanson only realized what it was when Sergeant Jackson shot a pair of Taser darts through the front of the kid's silk shirt, a tracery of blue electricity throwing him against the open car door, slamming it shut. He slid to the asphalt beside the car, bewildered, then put one hand on the asphalt to push himself back up. Sergeant Jackson shouted down at him, "Have some more juice," turning the current back on.

Hanson worked his way through the crowd back to his patrol car. The OPD helicopter thundered overhead, and after it passed, one of the big liquor store windows shattered. Every cop in Oakland would be here soon, he thought, maneuvering his way through double-parked cars. Calls for service must already be backing up. It would be a busy night. If he hurried, Radio would keep him 908 at the liquor store long enough to drive over to District Three and get a couple of Junior Whoppers. It would be his only chance for something to eat tonight. He thought he saw that kid Weegee maneuvering his bike through double-parked cars and pedestrians but lost sight of him in the crowd.

Across the street a hunchback black man, a dwarf, his stunted legs bowed, seemed to be studying Hanson as he opened the door to his patrol car, but his smeared Coke-bottle-thick eyeglasses flashed red and blue, mirroring the emergency lights, hiding his eyes. He wore two wristwatches outside the right cuff of his buttoned-up long-sleeve shirt. In his left hand he held a quart bottle of Olde English 800 malt liquor. He watched till Hanson got into his patrol car and pulled away. Then he looked back at the angry crowd and began laughing, raised his deformed arms above his head, hopping from foot to foot, dancing as the piss-dark beer foamed out of the bottle, until the first gunshot snapped in the liquor store parking lot.

Dawn was just barely coloring the clouds in the east by the time Hanson finished his shift. "Rosy fingered dawn," he recited aloud, "child of morning." He checked the side mirror, managed to start the Travelall, and pulled away from the Justice Center, driving the deserted downtown streets past barred storefronts, stopping for red lights at empty intersections. He took Grand Avenue, turned onto Lakeshore, parked the Travelall and got out. Lake Merritt was gray and two-dimensional, a layer of fog hanging over the water.

He pulled a pair of handcuffs out of his back pocket and, eyes still on the lake, began ratcheting the cuffs, one, then the other, open and closed. Bits of dried blood, black and dark purple, flaked off and fluttered away like gnats. The clicking steel teeth were loud in the silence, so he closed them and put them in his back pocket. He'd have to use a toothbrush to clean the blood off with Simichrome paste. Putting his hands on people every night, most of them bleeding or drunk or dope sick, it was a miracle he hadn't gotten VD or hepatitis or who knew what else was out there. Like that new thing going around lately. Nobody knew what it was, but it seemed to be killing junkies and queers mostly. If he died from that, the OPD would claim he was both.

A horse-drawn tourist carriage turned onto the street, the slow *clop, clop* of hooves on the asphalt. A white horse in brass-studded black harness and blinders, taking her time. The driver, impeccable in a tuxedo and top hat, stopped next to the Travelall. Behind him, the lake began to glow as the sun rose.

"Late night, Officer?"

Hanson nodded. "Just going home to bed."

"Champagne and me, we're headed for the barn too," the driver said. "Comes out of the dark like magic, doesn't it?" The lake flickered silver now through the fog. He looked at Hanson's name tag. "Let me introduce myself, Officer Hanson. My name's Michael Townsend Landon. Everyone calls me Mickey, though."

They watched the lake color up.

"Best time of the day, eh, Champagne?"

Hearing her name, the white horse shouldered into the harness, the big spoked wheels moving forward, then back. Hanson put his palm on her shoulder, and she turned her head to look at him, her eyes dark behind the blinders.

"My big brother is in law enforcement, up in Lone Pine," Mickey said.

Hanson said. "A deputy?"

"Oh, no. He's the high sheriff himself. Inyo County. Has been for a long time now. Just about runs the place. He doesn't approve of what he calls my 'lifestyle,' says it probably costs him votes each time he comes up for reelection, but he always gets reelected. There's been Landons in Inyo County since the 1880s. My great-great-grandfather came from Indiana. He headed out for the Sierras in 1860, mined for gold in Bodie. Didn't fight in the Civil War."

"Mine fought for the Confederacy," Hanson said, "and all his brothers and cousins. Most of 'em got killed."

"My brother's looked after me since we were kids," Mickey

said. "All the family I've got left now. I tell him everything," he went on, for a moment almost as if he was talking to himself, "and he listens now. He's a Republican too. But he's still my big brother," he said, straightening his collar.

"Look at that," he said. "The lake sneaked up on us, right there, and it's all agleam now. We'd better be on our way," he said, reaching down to shake hands, wearing white gloves.

"It's a real pleasure to meet you," Hanson said, taking his hand. "Lovely."

Hanson said, "Champagne," touching her flank.

Mickey clucked to the horse, twitched the reins with his fingers, and drove on, Hanson watching them roll to a stop at the corner, the iron rims of the head-high wheels throwing sparks. They turned left, Mickey raising a gloved hand as they rolled out of sight.

Hanson looked back at the lake, gleaming now, a line of white pelicans, gliding only inches above it, their wingtips skimming the water—awkward-looking birds on land but graceful in the air—before they crash-landed, the way they always do, looking for fish. Somebody that summer had been trapping them, cutting their big bills off with a hacksaw, then setting them free to starve to death.

CHAPTER THIRTEEN

RUN PIEDMONT

Once or twice a week Hanson ran the blocks through Piedmont, an island of affluence with its own city government, built on a hilly plateau surrounded by the poverty and despair of Oakland. The streets were deserted, their huge houses, built after the San Francisco earthquake, looked empty, and Hanson imagined that if he walked into one of the houses he'd find partially eaten breakfasts still warm on tables and counters, the inhabitants vanished, never to be seen. The only people he saw were Mexican gardeners, the mailman sometimes, and an occasional patrol car from the Piedmont PD. The gardeners mostly pretended not to see him.

Jogging the blocks at random, he admired the houses, wide porches with Doric columns, bigger-than-life stone lions, solid oak front doors, faceted stained-glass windows, bay windows where the cats who sat behind the beveled plate glass followed him with their eyes. Hanson got to know the cats, pointing at them and shouting "Hey, buddy" as he ran past.

The Piedmont police were well-paid security guards, hired to keep outsiders out, but they were real cops, guys who'd done their time on the streets of Oakland and San Francisco, others from LA, Seattle, and back East, who wanted to live far from where they'd worked before, so they'd never run into people they'd arrested. They'd put in their years of street combat, and now they just had to be polite and friendly, charming colorful characters in their interactions with the citizens of Piedmont but also discreet when they kicked some outsider's ass if he was too stupid to leave when he was asked to.

The citizens of Piedmont wanted their town safe, but most were also good liberals, supporters of the ACLU, believers in human and civil rights, and they didn't want to see the cops thumping burglars, carjackers, and potential home invaders who'd been casing the streets, or have their children witness that kind of unpleasantness.

He turned the corner onto Nova Drive and saw a burglar up ahead who hadn't noticed him yet. Hanson slowed to a walk well behind him. A skinny junkie in his mid-twenties. Black jeans, the cuffs frayed where they dragged the street, black tennis shoes, and a faded olive-drab army fatigue shirt with dark stripes on the arms where a buck sergeant's stripes had been torn off. Dirty shoulder-length red hair and a half-ass reddish beard.

He was looking. Staying on the sidewalk but studying the houses he passed, the few parked cars, porches, mailboxes, checking out garage doors. Maybe something left out in the yard he could steal. Was anybody home, how young or old were they, what about alarms, did they have a dog? Hanson jogged up on him, quietly, close enough to put hands on him before he spun around.

"What's up, homeboy. You live around here?" Hanson said.

"Who the fuck are you," he croaked.

Hanson was wearing a sweatshirt with the arms torn off and a pair of cut-off Levi's. He laughed, delighted. "*Look* at me, homeboy," he whispered, his mean streak wide awake now. "Look at me, *Sarge*," he said, looking into his watery blue eyes. The junkie was going to need some more heroin by late afternoon, before it got dark. "You don't belong here. You're not allowed here. Head downhill, back to Oakland, where you belong," nodding his head at the way he'd come.

"I'm just taking a walk, man," he said, trying to keep his voice from squeaking. "It's a free country."

"No, it isn't. They just say it is."

The kid tried to say something, but he stuttered.

"We've met before, haven't we? Somewhere off Fruitvale one night. *Hey*. Didn't we?"

"Aw, shit, man. I dunno."

"Go home, Sarge. The war's over."

He stood there a moment, as if he'd forgotten who he was, then turned and walked away.

"Hey, dildo," Hanson said, stopping him with his voice. "If I see you here again, I'm gonna kick your ass, then have the cops arrest you for assaulting me. And the screwdriver in your pocket, that's a deadly weapon. Assault with a deadly weapon, Sarge. Plus whatever outstanding warrants I know you've got. That's how I see your future up here. Okay?"

"Yeah."

"Good. Bye-bye."

He walked away without looking back, doing that punk prison strut, tossing his long hair every few steps.

A free country, Hanson thought. Nothing free about it. It wasn't even a country anymore. If it ever had been. It was a corporation, and at his age he'd been lucky to get hired as a professional asshole by the OPD.

Clouds and a chilly breeze were pushing in from the ocean. It was going to be a cold, wet night. That kid still had a few hours to steal something, sell it, and score some heroin before dark. Or spend the night curled up behind a Dumpster, dope sick in the rain. He was doomed anyway, he told himself, running again, taking a left uphill, pushing it a little more. He'd been born doomed.

Half an hour later, sweating, half lost in Piedmont somewhere, he was walking with his hands on his hips, blowing, when he noticed the patrol car coming up behind him. He smiled. It was Knox, the Piedmont cop he'd gotten to know. He pulled to the curb alongside Hanson. "That runnin's gonna kill you, Hanson. Drop dead with a heart attack."

"Keeps me mean. Burns away my empathy. Makes me more cop-like."

"You need to put on some weight, Hanson, working in District Five. After dark."

Knox had gone to Vietnam early, been there and back before Hanson had even finished Special Forces training.

"Hey," Hanson said, "I been doing your job for you this morning," telling him about the burglar with red hair.

Knox rummaged through a shoe-box file of mug shots, pulled one out, and showed it to Hanson.

"That's him," Hanson said.

Knox nodded, thanked him, and tapped the mug shot back into its place in the shoe box.

"Hanson, you do *not* look like you belong here in the pleasant world of Piedmont. One of these days you'll fuck with some new guy on our Department who doesn't know you, and I'll have to bail you out of jail."

"Can I put my hands down now?"

"Just don't make any furtive movements."

Hanson laughed.

"Knock 'em down, kick 'em around. Tell me, Hanson," Knox said, "is it still scary out there after dark, down in the flatlands with Tyrone. I remember it used to be pretty scary after the sun went down."

"I fear nothing," Hanson said.

Knox had grown up in Boston, gotten drafted, and when he got back from Vietnam, took a job with the San Francisco PD and worked there for twelve years before taking a job with the Piedmont PD. He didn't talk about the war much, but he'd been in some shit, Hanson could tell.

"Hanson, you got some kind of death wish. You're too old to be doin' that shit."

"Not me," Hanson said. "I can't be killed."

Knox smiled at him, shook his head.

"Hanson," he began, put the patrol car in DRIVE, then looked back at him, "you be careful."

Hanson brought his heels together and gave him a crisp salute. It made him feel good to salute Knox. That's what a salute was for, to acknowledge your bond with people you respected—at least that's what it was supposed to be.

CHAPTER FOURTEEN

THE WEATHER'S CHANGING

To be detained, the party must be, in the opinion of
the officer, a danger to himself, a danger to others,
or gravely disabled.
—*California Welfare and Institutions Code 5150*

He looked familiar to Hanson the moment Hanson saw him, out
there in the water, the 5150 Radio had sent him to check on. Someone Hanson might have known years before, when they were both
a lot younger. He'd been walking around Lake Merritt all day, since
before dawn, a wino told Hanson, following the contours of the lake,
"like he was looking for something he lost." A white guy who
wouldn't respond to anyone who spoke to him. The people Hanson
talked to all remembered or told it a little differently.

"Man, he just ignore people 'cause they black. Nothin' new
about that in this town. Say hello to him, he just walk on away like
you not there, like you beneath his consideration. Can't be bothered. Even if he's crazy he's still a racist motherfucker."

"That individual? Something real wrong with him, you know
what I'm sayin'? Some kind of sick motherfucker, way he look at
you. Hu-uh, never seen him before."

"Pretty soon people goin' up to him, just to see, you know, say,
'How you doin?' 'What's up, man?' He just walk away. Then a cou-

ple of the brothers ast him did he think he was bad, 'cause he didn't look it. Say maybe he needed a ass kicking to straighten him out. No, didn't touch him, Officer. Just said it to the man, putting it out there for him to consider, you understand."

"Only reason he's out there in the water, his own damn fault."

He'd started angling into the muddy water, up to his knees, to get away from people, far enough out so they wouldn't want to ruin their shoes or get their pants wet.

Then they'd started throwing things at him, forcing him into deeper water, up to his chest, then his neck so that he'd had to paddle with his hands to keep his balance, tip-toe on the muddy bottom, then deeper, having to tread water to stay upright, broken tree limbs, beer and pop cans, balled-up milkshake cups bobbing in the water around him. It was a good thing there weren't many stones along the shore, Hanson thought, or the kid would have been stoned to death by the time Hanson had got there and pushed through the crowd.

"He was already out there in the water by the time I come by, so I don't know, Officer. But he's a lucky motherfucker you here an' takin' care of business, bringin' some order to the situation."

Even the birds were upset—seagulls, pelicans, the ducks, black cormorants, and geese were wheeling above the lake, screeching and keening—swooping down at him. Maybe it was just the strange weather they'd been having—the simplest explanation. The wind was gone, and it had been unseasonably warm all week. It was a beautiful day, and the forecast was for the good weather to continue through the rest of the week.

Hanson stood at the water's edge and waved the kid in. "Come on, man. Time for us to leave," he said, watching him paddle closer till he could touch bottom, then walk through the mud to shore and onto the grass. He was wearing a shapeless gray sweatshirt and jeans, no shoes or socks. Probably sucked off his feet by the mud. He looked surprised, just for a moment, when he seemed to recognize Hanson, then he put on that arrogant victim's look again.

"Lemme handcuff you," Hanson told him. "Just let me handcuff you because I've gotta do that. Okay?" he said.

He turned his back to Hanson and watched the lake while Hanson cuffed him.

"Got any ID?" He just looked at the lake or across the lake, and Hanson knew that he wasn't going to show up in any database. "You got any weapons," Hanson asked, "pocket knife, anything like that?

"You better look at me, man, so we can get this thing done." Then, in a softer voice, "Save us both a lot of trouble neither one of us needs…What's your name?" Hanson asked after he'd turned to face him. "What do you go by now?"

He just looked at Hanson.

"Fine," Hanson said. "Here's the deal. I'm gonna take you to the county hospital, and they can decide how crazy you are and what to do with you. Alameda County Hospital. I'm just your transportation. Now. Turn around real slow for me," Hanson said, moving his finger in a circle to indicate what he wanted, looking for any bulges in his wet Salvation Army clothes that might be a weapon. He wasn't going to pat him down. "You can stop now."

He didn't look like a kid, not anymore. Hanson's age, and had the same Scots-Irish Appalachian features, but they were softer, slacker, showed the years of drinking more. Hanson knew who he was.

"Come on, then," Hanson told him, and they walked up the slope to where the patrol car was parked on the grass. Hanson opened the back door. "Yeah," he said, gesturing for him to get in the car, pushing his head down to clear the top of the door. "They'll have some dry clothes at ACH. You doin' okay?" When he ignored him, Hanson slammed the door, got in the car, and drove out of the park, thinking about it.

It had been during the second week of basic training, really hot at Fort Bragg that day. One guy had let himself pass out, and immediately three or four others did the same thing. The DI was pissed about it and chose Hanson to fuck with, yelling in his ear that he wasn't standing at attention correctly, "in a military manner." The DI walking around him in a circle, adjusting the cant of Hanson's head, pulling his arm down.

He was feeling a little dizzy from the heat and decided that if the DI touched him one more time he was going to quit. Fuck them. He'd walk over to a pine tree he'd already picked out, sit down, and just go away in his head. Adios. They'd know he was pretending to be catatonic, but he could keep it up until they discharged him out of their fucking army and out of their fucking war. That's how he remembered thinking about it. But he hadn't done it.

Maybe the kid was just deaf and crazy, Hanson thought, and not another version of himself, split off from him that day in basic training and taken another road. Hanson was mostly deaf himself, his ears blown up in that war he went to, but he heard well enough, people mostly yelling at him on the streets, and as for crazy, he'd learned how to act like he wasn't most of the time.

He looked at the kid in the side-view mirrors, then in the rearview mirror, through the Plexiglas cage, the kid meeting his eyes, unimpressed, arrogant the way Hanson used to be. Finally, tiring of it, bored, he leaned back and looked out the window. "The weather's changing," he said.

Hanson pulled the car over, into an out-of-business Shell station. He got out and opened the back door.

"Get out," he told the kid, happy at the little bit of fear the kid's eyes betrayed. "Turn around."

He took off the cuffs.

"That's it. Don't even look back at me. If I see your eyes, I'll kick your ass."

When he didn't move, Hanson put his boot in the seat of his wet jeans and gave him a push. "Take off."

The kid adjusted the wet seat of his jeans and took a couple of steps, barefoot, his jeans still dripping water.

"Wait," Hanson said. He took out his wallet and pulled a twenty from it, paused and took the rest of the bills out, walked up behind the kid, jamming the bills in the pocket of the wet jeans. "Adios."

From the patrol car, he watched the kid walk down the street until he vanished around a corner, then he filled out an assignment card. <u>No complainant. Problem solved upon departure. Hanson / 7374P.</u>

He cleared from the call and was on the way to an Unknown Problem up on MacArthur Boulevard when the sunlight changed, faded or darkened, turning a dirty yellow. Sudden raindrops pocked the dusty windshield, and he looked out the passenger window. The storm was boiling up out of the bay, the sky black as Armageddon, trailing steely curtains of rain. Out at sea thunder drummed and boomed, an enormous armada of flaring thunderheads coiling over the horizon, pushing and pulling themselves inland.

He stopped the car and watched the storm sweep through the oil tanks and refineries, past the harbor cranes crouched like robot dogs, slapping down billboards and peeling the roofs off warehouses. It surged across the freeway, slowing then stopping traffic and flooding the streets of East Oakland. Power grids went black and transformers on phone poles exploded in sparks and the storm shook the patrol car on its suspension, hail battered the roof and sleet froze the windows opaque. Radio went silent.

Hours later, after dark, Hanson was on his way back out to District Four after transporting a prisoner, driving slowly through the flooded streets and fierce rain. Thinking over the day, he took some kind of wrong turn into a warehouse district. Mechanical bells began clanging. The red-and-white striped barrier arm of a railroad grade crossing dropped out of the dark through his head-light beams, and he skidded to a stop a foot from the barrier arm, where a red bull's-eye warning light tossed itself back and forth over the hood of the patrol car.

The train slammed down out of nowhere, out of the dark, thundering past and down the tracks, two stories high, like some Main Street in a tornado—boxcars, tank cars, flatcars, hopper cars, gondolas, rocking side to side through the rain out of Oakland—Erie Lackawanna, Santa Fe, Oregon Pacific, Pee Dee River, Kansas City, Illinois Central, Union Pacific—to some-where else, rain exploding into steam and colored smoke over the patrol car, the headlights of cars across the tracks like muzzle flashes between rail cars crashing and clattering past, rocking the patrol car. Hanson sat back in his rain-damp uniform and closed his eyes for a moment, exhausted.

He was wading the muddy Song Mai Loc, crossing that river again in monsoon season, the hottest part of the day, back in a war on the other side of the earth. According to the map he was us-ing, they were half a click from a village that had been called Mai Than before it was destroyed. Every village on the map was destroyed, (DESTROYED) printed beneath each village name, in parentheses. What had once been Mai Than, before it was de-stroyed, according to the map, lay on the other side of a rise, just beyond a blue line on the map that was the river they were cross-ing, the brown Song Mai Loc, the muddy Mai Loc River.

Warm as blood and barely moving, up to their waists halfway across—Hanson and five of the CRP, the Combat Recon Platoon, Vietnamese mercenaries, who were their best killers. They were into the third day of a five-day recon that Hanson had planned, to update information on the map.

They took a break on the other side of the river, in a dying stand of bamboo—to drink the hot, iodine-tasting water from their canteens, to have a handful of the dried little fish you could eat like popcorn, and to pull or burn the leeches off their ankles and groins where they'd attached themselves in the river.

Rau, the CRP platoon sergeant, hissed at Hanson and pointed. Four or five women driving water buffalo around the base of the rise toward them, already getting close, their high-pitched musical laughter floating through the rain. They hadn't seen them yet, and the buffalo hadn't smelled them because they were upwind, following a trail or road that wasn't on the map.

Mai Than must not be destroyed anymore—or not yet—and when the women saw them they'd send the village cadre, who would be main force VC, after them. Hanson knew that no friendlies had been in the area for over two years, and that's why he'd wanted to check it out on this operation. Good idea, he thought, smiling. They were way out of range of any firebase artillery fan, and no gunships or tac air from the 101st base in Quang Tri would be able to make it over the mountains in that weather. They were on their own. When the women walked up on them, what would he do then, say "Hi, only taking a break, gotta go"?

They could start running now, but the local VC would be right behind them, and they'd know the terrain a lot better than Hanson could read it off the map. Fine, Hanson thought, relaxing, they'd just stand and fight here, killing as many Viet Cong as they could before they were killed. Good.

"We must crokadow," Rau whispered to him, mimicking shooting a pistol, killing the women, shaking his head in a parody of regret: *Too bad.* He'd been killing other Vietnamese, of one political persuasion or another, since he was twelve years old. The only job he'd ever had. Back in camp, Rau sometimes shot up a mixture of opium and rice wine, but he knew his job.

Fuckin' monsters, Hanson thought, unbuckling a flap on his pack. All of us, he thought, pulling the plastic-wrapped High Standard .22 from his pack, then the suppressor.

He'd gotten too good at his job. After a while, if you survive long enough, the only thing that can kill you is bad luck, you're so good, and even if you step into bad luck, if you stay cool and do the next indicated thing, you'll walk out of it.

He carried the silenced .22 pistol on operations just in case they saw a lone VC or NVA to take prisoner, he'd shoot him so he wouldn't die right away, and take him. The pistol wasn't completely silent, but it was quiet. He had an extra ten-round magazine too. It was an accurate pistol, and he'd practiced back at camp until he was very good with it. He'd have no trouble putting a bullet in all five of them—there were five—in as many seconds. Head shots. What he liked about the war—what everybody liked about it if they liked it at all—was the simplicity. His job was to stay alive and keep the CRP with him alive.

After they killed the women, they'd run, pull the quick-release straps on their packs, drop everything but ammo and water, and they'd have a head start, back across the blue line where they knew the way now, back to hills and valleys where they could hide, where there weren't so many VC and, if they were lucky and ran hard enough, where he could call in artillery, where maybe they'd still be alive tomorrow. They could make it with a head start if they killed the women.

He wiped the pistol down with an oily rag he kept in the same bag, checked to see that he had a round chambered—a Boy Scout–size little .22 round—screwed the suppressor on, and thumbed the safety off. He exchanged looks with Rau and the other four CRP, and that's when the women began slapping the lumbering buffalo with their bamboo sticks and angled away around the hill, never suspecting they had been about to be slaughtered. Hanson stayed crouched, managing his breathing, while the CRP looked both relieved and disappointed.

The delicate laughter, the slap of bamboo against the horned buffalos' hides, the clank of bells on the buffalos' necks, growing fainter, then gone.

Everybody had been saved, and he was still sitting in the idling, stinking OPD patrol car in the rain, but the train had passed, down the track, silent, gone. The clang of the mechanical bell was only the ringing that was always in his ears, when he let himself listen to it. The striped crossing gate rose like an arm gesturing for him to continue his life. Cars were crossing now from the other direction, their headlights flashing in his eyes as they shuddered over the tracks. More cars were lined up and waiting, behind him, afraid to honk at a police car. He put the car in gear and drove on through the rain.

CHAPTER FIFTEEN

ELVIS HITLER

Another rainy night. The weather's changing. Radio traffic busy as always. Hanson drove past the address Radio had given him and pulled to the curb half a block down, his eyes on the house in the rearview mirror. Another 415F—Disturbance, Domestic—a family fight. People who needed someone with a club and a gun to make their decisions for them. The overheated engine dieseled out, pounding wipers stopped, rain hissed and steamed off the hood of the filthy patrol car. Radio went silent.

Closed up in a wall locker, his wool shirt and trousers didn't have time to dry out between shifts. They'd stayed damp, heavy and hot. He was hungover, with a headache and diarrhea, wishing he'd called in sick. He made a fist with his right hand—making it hurt—to put a little more edge into his attitude. It seemed to help, so he did it again, squeezing the festering blue puncture wound in his palm, which he'd gotten chasing a rapist over a chain-link fence two nights ago.

Reaching into the black leather pilot's case on the seat beside him, he pulled out a sixteen-ounce bottle of Pepto-Bismol and for a moment saw his dark reflection in the curved windshield as a brooding magician producing a pink rabbit. He slugged down the chalky antacid, tilted the bottle and squinted at it—already half empty—screwed the cap back on, and put it away. He licked his lips, checking them in the rearview mirror for pink residue, and his stomach cramped up again. Maybe, he thought, he should design a holster for the pink bottle, like the one he carried Mace in.

Channel three came back with his record check.

No outstanding wants or warrants on your subject. He is on probation for 245, 148 PC, and 11550 H&S. Be advised, he's been arrested twice for 242—by your complainant—in the past nine months. Charges dropped both times.

"904," Hanson said, switching back to channel two. He pulled on his left sap glove, eight ounces of powdered lead stitched into five pouches, one behind each finger, and a single, bigger pouch across the back of the hand. He kept the other glove tucked under his belt buckle—freeing his gun hand—the glove's cuff hanging out so he could snatch it out and swing it backhand, his best weapon by far for close quarters.

He got out of the car and quietly closed the door, stepping into a puddle of water dammed up with leaves and trash. The cold water poured over the ankles of his steel-toed boots, and when he walked up the street he felt one sock work its way down past his heel. He listened at the door for a moment, called out "Police officer," knocked three times with his short wood, then slipped it back into the little pocket along his leg when he heard the clatter of locks opening.

She opened the door the width of the night chain and looked out at him standing in the rain. Barefoot, wearing cutoffs, no bra under a black T-shirt with white letters across the front, EAT SHIT

AND DIE, she had a cigarette going between her swollen lips, the lower one split but scabbed over.

"Did you call the police," Hanson said, "or is this the wrong address?" She unhooked the night chain and stepped back just enough to let him squeeze in next to her out of the rain. She was a little heavy, her breasts filling up the T-shirt, the jeans cut off so high the pockets hung down along her chubby white thighs.

Hanson shrugged impatiently. "Okay?"

She opened the door wider so he could brush past her into the overheated, stinking house, where she looked at him as if she didn't know why he was there or why she'd let him in. She was out of shape, pale, and she looked tired. Her black eye was a couple of days old, and the bruises on her arm had turned blue-green and yellow. "What?" she said.

Hanson shook his head. "Nothing." He stepped around her, checking to see that no one was hidden behind the half-opened front door.

"I want him outta here," she mumbled, cigarette bobbing between her swollen lips. "I want the fucker outta here. Now! Right now!"

Yeah, yeah, Hanson thought, her voice exactly what he should have expected. "And what is the problem this evening?" he asked, his stomach seizing up again.

She took the cigarette out of her mouth, looked at Hanson, then shouted over her shoulder, "He's the problem. He's an asshole! And I want him out."

"And fuck you," a man yelled, his voice coming up through the floor.

How many times, Hanson thought, trying to will the cramps away, had he been in this movie before? With these same dumb motherfuckers?

He tried to breathe—a stress-reduction technique a

psychologist had taken an hour to explain one day in the Academy—and inhaled a lungful of her menthol cigarette smoke. It was just about impossible to know where a bathroom was in East Oakland, the way they moved you from beat to beat, and Radio too busy to give him time for a 908B, anyway. OPD had a number for everything.

Maybe he could take care of this quick, whip it out on an assignment card—Problem resolved upon departure—then use the bathroom before Radio sent him to another call.

His stomach calmed for a moment, and it was only then that it dawned on him why the house seemed even stranger than what he was used to. It was filled with Elvis memorabilia. More than a collection, it was a museum, an obsession, like some kind of celebrity death trip roadside attraction out in the desert. Visions and versions of Elvis through different countries, crafts, and art forms. The paintings on the walls were mostly done on black velvet, Elvis's features slightly Hispanic or Asian. Tijuana Elvis the matador. Saigon Elvis walking with a sad-eyed ghost soldier. Green Beret Elvis armed and deep in the jungle. Deer-Hunting Elvis in a Ford F-150 with a gun rack. Elvis with Che, with Mao, with Richard Nixon, and with Malcolm X. Preaching with Billy Graham, crossing the river with Dr. King, high in the clouds with the dead Kennedys, and kneeling alone beneath God's own light down in the garden of Gethsemane.

There were porcelain busts, hand-painted by machines, the red enamel on one not quite aligned with his pouting lips, the blue of his eyes slightly off-center in another, his nose, his smile, his sideburns—on all of them—unfocused, out of sync, so he seemed to be disassembling into other dimensions.

Molded rubber figurines—Barbie doll Elvises dressed in period doll clothes—many from the last Las Vegas period in the spangled white jumpsuit, boots and sunglasses. But there was

Hillbilly Elvis too. A GI Elvis. Elvis in a Hawaiian shirt and lei, from the movie *Blue Hawaii*. Karate Elvis in a black-belted gi, with cocked, deadly-weapon arms that rotated at the shoulders. The foot-high sheet-metal Elvis rode a wire strung from the kitchen door to the ceiling, ascending to Rock-&-Roll Heaven in a flowing-robe-like leisure suit, legs spread, bell-bottoms wide as wings, that lock of black hair over one eye, holding a glittering guitar at arm's length just below his crotch, rising to Glory.

Movie posters, collector's edition Elvis liquor decanters—filled now with colored water—behind a sad little plywood bar covered with red, white, and blue Naugahyde. Hanson looked at himself in the Elvis-profile etched mirror behind the bar. He looked awful, sick, and beat-up, worse than the woman.

The clang and boom of free weights in the basement shook the house like a minor quake.

"Could I please have your name, ma'am? And date of birth."

She stubbed out her Kool in an ELVIS ON TOUR ashtray from the Circus Circus hotel and took another from a musical cigarette box that plucked a few hesitant notes—maybe "Love Me Tender"—before the spring wound down.

"I'm the one who called the cops," she said, twitching the unlit cigarette between her fingers, her red nails chipped and chewed to the quick. "Why do you need my date of birth?"

"I need the complainant's information to complete my report. For the, uh, database…"

She stuck the cigarette in her mouth and rewound the cigarette box. It was "Love Me Tender," but now, spring-tight, it played at double speed, like music in a Chinese nightmare. Hanson was starting to twitch himself, flipping the ballpoint pen between his fingers. Elvis. Everywhere. Watching him. The bang of iron on concrete shook the house again.

"Can't you just tell him to leave? That's all I fuckin' want."

The clang of steel on steel rattled the Elvis dolls. Again. And again as he slammed more weight plates on each end of the bar. A lot of weight, Hanson thought.

"What's his name," he asked her. They studied each other as she gave him the information he needed.

His name was Paul. Her name was Racine and she was twenty-three years old. He would have guessed she was thirty. The underarms of the black T-shirt were wet with perspiration, and her smell, mixed with sweet perfume, rose up around him like a guilty memory, bringing him closer.

"He do this to you?" Hanson asked, reaching over, his voice a little hoarse, tracing the edge of the bruise around her eye.

"He got laid off at work," she said, looking up at Hanson. "At the door factory. He's been laid off three months."

"And this?" Hanson asked, closing his hand over the swelling on her arm, up where the bruises disappeared into the cotton shirt.

"Uh-huh."

"He using steroids?"

"Steroids?"

"I'm not a narc," he said. "I don't care if he uses steroids or not. Or if you smoke dope or whatever you do."

"Whatever?" she said.

"I just need to know what to expect from him."

She nodded, her hair brushing his chest. "Yeah," she told him, her lips against his breast pocket. "He likes to hurt me," she said, her leg touching the erection bobbing against his wet wool trousers.

"I'll go down and talk to him," he said and almost tripped turning away. Jesus Christ, stop it, he told himself. Stop. She's more trouble than that tattooed woman up in Missoula.

"You stay up here," he told her. "If you come down with me, it'll just start an argument. You can listen from the stairs."

Got fired from the door factory? The fuckin' door factory, he thought, walking to the basement stairs, the whine of power saws and planers in his ears, the *bang, bang, bang* of staple guns. He imagined waking up in bed every morning next to Racine as she lit her first cigarette of the day. Goin' to the door factory.

She was giving him that look. She wasn't bad, really. A little skanky, but skanky was okay. It was all, pretty much, okay. He was going to need all the help, all the diversion, all the going-away he could find to get through his probation period, still seven more months. Seven months and five days.

"Just don't talk," he told her. "Let me talk."

The stairway, constructed of warped, knotty, unpainted lumber and about forty pounds of bent nails, shuddered as they started down. She was right behind him.

Hanson wondered if the materials had come from the door factory, then realized of course they did.

The windowless, concrete basement was bleak as a torture chamber, blinding at first, ten thousand watts of warehouse guard lights hanging from the ceiling. They probably came from the door factory too, one at a time, every Friday after work, in the trunk of the car. Half the shit in Oakland is stolen, he thought, ducking his head to clear the overhang, a trickle-down, drug-trade economy.

The walls on either side of the weight bench were paneled with narrow Kmart door mirrors, dozens of them mounted edge to edge with black-tar flooring adhesive. A four-foot Nazi flag hung on the far wall, behind the weight bench. Weight, Hanson thought. Every house east of High Street came with a set of weights for staying in shape till the PO violated you back to the joint with a random 4 a.m. urine sample.

Paul was being cool, like he didn't even notice them, halfway through a set of bench presses, maybe two hundred fifty pounds on the bar. He raised it slowly, held it at arm's length without a quiver, lowered the bar, then lifted it again. Slowly. Impressing them. It was a lot of weight. He slammed the bar onto the rack, sat up, shiny with sweat, and studied them, thick blue veins wriggling like night crawlers along his arms.

Dark blue spandex shorts to the knee and a white tank top with Nazi SS lightning bolts bracketing the word BLITZKRIEG! Eighty-five IQ. Blue eyes. Blond. The crew-cut, and, of course, a Fu Manchu mustache. Maybe six foot one. Arms as big as Hanson's legs. Bat-hooded no-neck neck.

"Hi," Hanson said, his mouth dry, the stomach cramps back with a vengeance.

"'Hi'? Fuckin' 'Hi'?" Paul said, a little out of breath but trying not to show it. "'Hi' doesn't cut it. How about 'You got a warrant?' Dude."

"Don't need a warrant. Sir," Hanson said. "This isn't TV. Your wife called the police and let me in."

"Wife? That what she told you? I'm not married to the cunt."

"What's your name again, man?" Hanson said.

"Paul, okay? My name's Paul."

"Right. Paul. Paul. Your…uh…Racine called the police. Asked me inside. So I don't need a warrant…Paul. She wants you to leave," he said, stepping off the stairs onto the concrete. When his stomach seized up again, he clenched his tender, swollen hand into a fist, beating the cramps. The worst pain wins.

"I pay rent, dude. So fuck that," Paul said, lying back again, looking up, into the lights, doing three quick, angry presses.

"He hasn't paid rent in four months," Racine said from the stairs. "He sleeps mornings, hangs out with his buddies at the gym all afternoon, gets drunk, then, hey, it's time to come home and give me shit.

"I'm fuckin' through. Payin' the rent, fixing his special high-protein meals, walking on eggshells. Watching TV. Every night. Alone. While he's down here grunting. Ugh," she said. "Ugh. Watching himself in those cheap-ass mirrors like a faggot."

Paul sat up like he was spring-loaded.

"Fuck you, you dumb cunt. You're the faggot. Queer for Elvis. You must use him for a dildo. 'Cause that's the only way you're gonna get any. Look at yourself! I'm a queer?" he said, hitting himself on the chest. Like a bow-legged chimpanzee, Hanson thought. What was it called? Aggressive display. If they were outside he'd be throwing handfuls of dirt and leaves over his shoulder. "I'm hard. I'm bad. That's just how it is. Nobody gives me shit."

"Oh, Paulie," she said. "Not that I've—"

"Fuck you. And what did I tell you about the next time you called the fuckin' cops? Huh!" The sound came from deep in his chest, pumping up the anger. "Huh?" he said, pressing both hands, palms down, on the bench between his legs, lifting his body off the bench like a gymnast.

Hanson watched it in the mirrors like it was a movie. His uniform looked like shit, creases steamed out by the rain, the shirt hanging on him, baggy pants, like hand-me-downs from a big brother. With all the weight he carried—the pistol, nightstick, PAC-set, Mace, handcuffs, speedloaders, the short wood in its own little pocket. In this rain his sodden pants kept slipping over his hips, and he had to hitch them up, hooking his thumbs in the belt loops. Must be down to one forty-five, maybe less, he thought, burning adrenaline instead of food. Most of his calories came from Mickey's Big Mouth malt liquor, the flat little half-pint bottles of oily Popov vodka he sucked down after work, and the tequila he drank while watching dawn come up over the Oakland Hills before passing out in his bed.

"Huh?" Paul said again. "Huh!" working it, lifting and lowering his body—the alpha chimp, Hanson thought. Finally he pushed up and off the bench onto his feet, as if he was about to come up the stairs after her.

The stairs shuddered as Racine ran up and slammed the door. Paul sneered, spit on the floor. Very classy, Hanson thought.

"You call a cover car, dude?" he said, looking at Hanson, the tough guy again, the Fu Manchu mustache and the bunched jaw muscles. His Gold's Gym badass look.

Hanson opened his eyes wide, slightly unfocused, innocent—psycho innocent. His Shirley Temple eyes. "Say, you must be of German heritage," Hanson said, big eyes, nodding at the Nazi flag, the black swastika on a red background. Starting to have fun now. Deadly serious, life/death/life/death serious, not that phony workaday "Get serious now" bullshit. The hangover was gone, his stomach was okay. Because his body understood serious.

Paul hesitated, looked at the flag, back at Hanson.

"Deutschland. Jawohl," Hanson said. "Of course. I can see it in your physiognomy, the shape of your head." Surfing the wave now, the wave that could collapse beneath his feet and kill him if he lost his focus or his nerve. Just a moment of random bad luck could kill him now.

Paul held back, his eyes wary, then he ignored whatever warning had gone off in his head. He flexed his arms, shuffled like a boxer, to the left, the right, then toward Hanson. But Hanson only smiled.

"German. That's a fuckin' rodge, dude. Pure white Aryan. Both sides of the family. I asked you if you called a cover car. 'Cause after I kick your punk ass, I'll kick the shit outta him," he said.

"Not tonight," Hanson said. An addiction to curiosity is what it was. Betting everything on What'll happen if I do this? Curiosity will kill you like it killed that cat.

"Call one. Call two, dude. I'll take 'em as they come, one at a time. Like an assembly line, motherfucker, like poundin' fuckin' doorframes."

"No, Paul."

"No? No what?"

"No, you're not gonna kick anybody's ass."

Paul laughed. "Why is that?"

"Because you're gonna be dead," Hanson said as he pulled the sap glove from behind his belt buckle and backhanded Paul across the throat with it.

Paul froze, his eyes empty, huge, then full of fear when he realized he couldn't breathe. With an easy, casual, contemptuous wrist motion, Hanson flicked the leaded glove into Paul's face, dropping him—gagging, sobbing, whooping for air—to one knee.

He tucked the glove back behind his belt, wrapped his hand around the grip of the stainless steel .357, and popped the clamshell holster open. He owned this bleak little split second of time.

"I want to explain something," he said.

A bubble of blood swelled from Paul's nostril, then popped.

"And it's very important that you believe me, because I'm finished with verbal persuasion for tonight. If you see it in my eyes, maybe you'll understand. Right here," he said, "look here," pointing, his fingers in a V at his own eyes. Then, when Paul looked up, Hanson turned on his eyes, locking into Paul's.

"Turning them on." That's what he called it, but what he did was release them, let them go where they wanted to go—the way a compass needle sweeps north and holds—back to the eyes they'd become during the war, when Hanson was free to do anything he wished, already dead, with nothing to lose. Nothing had changed. They were still and always would be the same eyes, but he had to control them now, conceal them, contain them. But sometimes—those times when the world, when every-thing, seemed hopeless, and Hanson picked up his off-duty Hi Power 9mm, just to feel its cool weight in his hand, thinking it over—just once in a while, he'd let his eyes go free. Let them go to that place not many people ever visit, but once you do, it's always there, waiting for you. He'd look up from the pistol and the eyes would take him back there, to the walking-dead killer he would always be. Two, maybe three seconds was all he could risk, before they could—he knew—take him over. Where the eyes go, the body follows. He'd always made it back—holding, holding, then coming back—so far. And afterward he'd feel good, sane, for a few hours, like he was home.

Paul was looking up at him.

"I'm hungover, Paul. Sick. You know how that is, right?"

Paul nodded.

"I've got diarrhea, man. If I had to arrest you tonight, instead of just shooting you, if you forced me to arrest you, you know, I'd grab you, you'd grab me, yeah, yeah…" Hanson sighed. It was al-ways the same old dance. "I'd get you cuffed, but I'd shit my pants, my OPD uniform pants, and I'd never live it down. That's the only thing anybody would remember about me. Fifty years from now rookies would still hear the story. 'Hanson was so scared that he shit his pants.'

"So you gotta leave now and not come back till tomorrow morning, or I'm gonna shoot you. Six times. Kill you. Because you can't testify in court if you're dead. That's how it works. It's that simple. I'll say you came at me with a weight plate and I had to shoot you in self-defense. There'll be powder burns all over you. This thing," he said, glancing at the pistol, "might even set your shirt on fire. 'He was on me, man.' That's what I'll tell 'em. 'Didn't have any choice.' You weigh twice as much as me, all those big muscles you worked so hard for, steroids in your blood. Roid

Rage. And you're *white*. No problem with the black community. Nobody's gonna care how it happened. You're already bought and paid for.

"What do you think, Paul, do I have to shoot you?"

Paul shook his head.

"You got somewhere you can spend the night? Paul?"

"I can sleep down at the gym?"

"Good. And I think I can trust you to keep your word," Hanson said. "I think you're an honorable man." He looked at the Nazi flag. *"Meine Ehre heisst Treue."*

Paul looked at him—still working for every breath—respectfully.

"My honor is loyalty. Waffen-SS. The soldiers, not those fuckin' concentration camp guards. That was the creed they lived by. Some of the best soldiers in the world, and that stupid fuck Hitler," Hanson said, nodding toward the flag, "used 'em for cannon fodder there at the end. They were soldiers, man. So I'm gonna trust you not to come back till tomorrow. Not before noon. Can I do that, Paul?"

Paul nodded. "Right," he croaked. "Absolutely."

Hanson sat on the toilet, exhausted, the diarrhea gone for now. His pants hung down below his knees, the heavy pistol resting in the crotch of his trousers. He'd enjoyed breaking Paul down, disassembling the motherfucker. It had been a while since he'd done something like that. Since he'd had the opportunity and the excuse. He was pretty sure Paul would wait, at least till midmorning, before he came back and pounded on the door, told Racine to let him in, then beat the shit out of her again when she did. A nightlight glowed above the sink. A translucent bust of Elvis wearing a red-and-black-checked bandanna around his neck. Elvis was smiling.

"Okay," he said, back in the living room.

Racine looked at him, biting her lip. She was still barefoot.

"I've gotta get back on the street," he said. He knew he should get out the door right now, but his feet wouldn't move.

"I watched you and Paul-ee," she said, "through the floor vent in the kitchen."

His Kevlar vest was damp and heavy and interfered with his breathing. He must have pulled the straps too tight.

"He isn't coming back tonight." She looked at the bedroom door. "Anything you want," she said. "What do you want me to do? Come on. Tell me."

"I think," he began.

"This?" she asked him, pulling her shirt over her head, shaking her short bleach-blond hair out, the shirt in her hand. There were bruises on her ribs, beneath her breasts. "Or this," she said, popping the buttons on her cutoffs, one by one, her eyes on his. She let them slide down her legs to the floor, then stepped out of them.

"Come here," he said.

She pressed in against him, looked up, and he put his thumb against the split in her lip, softly, barely touching it but feeling the heat, the tiny pulse in there. She gradually increased the pressure, pushing her lip against his thumb, watching him, her pupils growing, until the lip cracked open and began to bleed.

"Gotta go," he said, stepping back, his voice hoarse. "Gotta clear from the call. Get back on the street."

"Give me your hand," she said, taking his wrist in her hand. "Relax, honey," she said, bringing the hand down on her breast. Blood collected on her lower lip into drops that fell, one by one. "Do you like…?"

"Here's my card," he said, fishing it out of his wallet with one hand. "Call me if you get in trouble."

"Come back later," she said.

"Lock the door behind me." He handed her the card with his bloody thumbprint on it. "Get some sleep. Don't let anyone in," he said, letting himself back out into the rain. Especially me, he thought, pulling the door shut, feeling her eyes on him as he went back down to the sidewalk.

The rain was coming down heavier than it had been and felt good, washing the sweat from his face and neck, cooling him off. He didn't have much longer before he went in for the night. He'd put on a clean uniform tomorrow. He could get the bathroom warm, hang the vest from the shower rod, and turn a fan on it. Should be dry overnight. He was lucky, he thought, glancing back at the house, to get out of there alive. He could commit suicide in a place like that. Another tattooed woman, he thought. And that's why he was still thinking about going back when he got off his shift.

He drove a few blocks, pulled to the curb, and filled out an assignment card. <u>Problem resolved upon departure</u>. When he cleared from the call Radio sent him to check for an ambulance, a man down by the Dumpster behind Carl's Country Market. Drunk and passed out, probably. They were passed out every-where you looked—sidewalks, gas station bathrooms, city parks, and front yards—sometimes in the middle of the street where they got run over by drunk drivers. A drunk in the street run over by a drunk in a car. There's a night's worth of paperwork.

We're getting reports of possible shots fired at that location. We've dispatched a 945, inbound from Highland Park.

"904," Hanson said. "Got it?"

Car to cover...

"I'll advise. On the ambulance too. I'm almost there. You are advised, though," Hanson said, looking at his watch, "that I'll be on overtime in fifteen minutes," he said, turning on his overhead lights. The driving rain and the water thrown up by the patrol car looked like a red and blue fireworks display moving through the dark at fifty miles an hour.

If the guy was DOA, maybe a 187, they'd try to send a beat car from graveyard shift, if there was one tonight, and he'd only have to fill out a supplemental report. The city wasn't handing out overtime if they could help it. They couldn't afford time and a half for a murder in East Oakland, not when they had one hundred twenty a year. If they did assign him as the primary officer, he already knew he'd have a hard time getting the OT money. He'd have to do all the paperwork for the call, then the paperwork for the OT and they'd find some way to deny the OT.

Behind him a pair of blinding headlights appeared out of nowhere, coming way too fast, the car bearing down on him in a nimbus of spray. He hit his brakes and skidded up over the curb, popping one of the patrol car's pie-plate hubcaps off before the wheels dug into a muddy front yard. The car flashed by through the rain, blazing, throwing spray, and in that frozen instant Hanson recognized the huge pristine old Lincoln from the rock shop, saw Reverend Ray clearly, no dark glasses tonight, smiling at him as the car flashed past and was gone, and Hanson knew for sure that an ambulance would be way too late to help that man down. It would take an ambulance ten minutes to get there, and Reverend Ray…he was there already.

5Tac51.

"Yeah…"

We've got two graveyard shift cars en route to the scene.

In his mirror he saw the overheads and high-low, high-low headlights of a patrol car coming up fast.

"Ten four. One of 'em just passed me. If you don't need me, I'll be 908…"

Copy, 5Tac51 is 908…

Hanson spun his tires in the mud, fishtailed around, back onto the street, and headed toward the freeway, glad he wouldn't be doing all the paperwork on a 187. And he would not be dropping by to see Racine. Not tonight. Maybe another time. Tonight he'd go home, get drunk watching the sun rise, and pass out in his own bed.

Angling toward the freeway, he thought about Racine and Paul. Paul down there in his mirrored Nazi basement. Elvis *Hitler*. There's a name. People would sure remember you with a name like that. *Gott Mit Uns*.

On the freeway, he heard one of the cars that had taken the man-down call request an ambulance, even though the victim was already dead.

CHAPTER SIXTEEN

GO ALONG TO GET ALONG

False alarms had been going off all over town, the rain pounding warehouse roofs, tripping disturbance devices, and interrupting electric eye beams. Hanson passed a block-long out-of-business body shop with the words SOUTH DAKOTA PRISON GUARDS LICK WETBACKS ASSHOLES painted in white, rust eating the words away, an old grudge. He was on his way to a meet requested by a sergeant he didn't know, which wasn't unusual because patrolmen *and* sergeants were moved regularly from district to district, often, literally, at the last minute because so many cops called in sick every day just before roll call. Morale was bad. On the Oakland PD a sergeant was expected to study for the lieutenant's test while catching patrolmen goofing off or fucking up. They weren't all bad guys, but the pressure was always on them, just like the pressure was always on patrolmen to fill their arrest quotas.

Hanson was working District Three that rainy night—the Department had pulled him out of the predominantly black districts to work closer to town and the white areas. One of the benefits of working out in Districts Four and Five was that sergeants were less likely to drive out there to catch you goofing off or fucking up. It wasn't so much that they were afraid for their safety, though some got that way, but too many situations out there could go bad and hurt their career. Things just *went* bad out there more often, and a sergeant didn't want to be in the area when it happened because then some of it could stick to him.

It was similar to the reason most patrolmen learned not to see very much on their way to calls Radio gave them. If they saw a problem no one had called in and stopped to deal with it, they had nothing to gain and everything to lose. No one would notice if they solved the problem except the citizens involved, whom they'd probably never see again, and if it went bad and got worse, it was their own fault for stopping. While the official problem Radio had given them was still waiting.

Hanson saw the sergeant's patrol car up ahead, through the rain, idling beneath a crumbling concrete overpass, white exhaust around the car like fog. The sergeant flicked his red and blue lights on and off, and Hanson pulled up next to him, facing the other way, driver's window to driver's window. Rain fell in sheets at both ends of the overpass like movie waterfalls.

His name was Sergeant Croix, a salesman, not a hard ass, with the easy manner of a guy at a car dealership. "I just wanted to officially welcome you to the squad," he said, though since Hanson usually worked a tactical car—a tac car—he was only in his squad for the night, but the sergeant was a hard worker and had decided it was worth his time to make the sale to Hanson, just in case.

"I've heard good things about you from Traver, and I was looking over the stat sheets here," he said, tapping his briefcase on the seat next to him, "and they tell me that you compare favorably in your activity with the rest of the squad."

Traver was a traffic cop Hanson had worked with a few times

early on, and they'd gotten along okay. Hanson had kept his mouth shut, nodding and listening to Traver's advice, which was solid, about writing up traffic accidents. Hanson hated doing traffic accidents, they involved measuring skid marks and then using plastic protractors and templates to draw the vehicles involved to scale on traffic forms. Traver could whip them out in no time, but Hanson was slow at it and drew his curves wrong a lot of the time, had to erase and redo them, and it looked bad on the form.

"Keep up the good work," Sergeant Croix said, lighting up another cigarette. "When anyone in my squad stops a drunk driver, I like to be called to witness the sobriety test. I want to see how you do it, and maybe I can help you out since you're still pretty new to this work."

Like a lot of the other cops on the Department, he didn't know that Hanson had been a cop before and wondered why anyone would decide to become a police officer at the age of thirty-eight.

He was probably about Hanson's age, but Hanson couldn't tell about cops his age and had mostly given up even trying to guess. They all seemed as if they'd grown up together in the same town, gone to high school together. Or maybe it just seemed like that to Hanson because they were all so different from him, able to do the job without ever really engaging it, offhand and detached. Back when they were twenty-one they'd gone to the Academy and signed a contract, made a deal with the Department, offering their services for a salary. Now they still showed up to put in their hours, and the Department still gave them their paycheck every two weeks in return. Not unlike, Hanson thought, a windbag college professor with tenure who uses the same syllabus semester after semester, giving out grades and degrees while teaching nothing. That's how it was done and it made sense. It's how most people in most jobs accommodated the work. But Hanson just wasn't able to do it. In the same way he was bad with money, with doing business. He expected people to tell him the truth and then they were his friends. If they lied to him, they were his enemies. But a car salesman, say, or a Realtor fell into a third category: neither friend nor enemy, who didn't tell the truth but didn't exactly *lie* either.

The cigarette smoke was getting more dense inside the sergeant's patrol car. The rain must act like a wall, Hanson thought, or maybe, because the humidity was way over one hundred percent, the air sort of rejected the smoke, couldn't absorb it, something like that.

"In-custody felonies and 11550 tests—I like my men to call me in on those too. Hell, I'll be out front about it. I like the court time. I made fifty-eight thousand last year, and I'm gonna try to break sixty this year, and I can do it, no problem, if you and the other guys in the squad keep me in mind. It's a good squad, Hanson."

Hanson nodded, even trying a smile—a normal smile so he'd look like he understood and agreed with whatever the sergeant was saying.

The sergeant exhaled more smoke, shooting the breeze now, cop to cop. "I've got to refinance my house and get a new rental property this year, and I'll need the overtime to do that," he said, shaking his head. "If you don't have some rental properties, the taxes will kill you. You'll see. I've been with the Department sixteen years now, almost seventeen, and that's one thing I've learned. I've got twenty deductions. Twenty. A lot of time and work, but with twenty deductions, you take home a pretty nice paycheck. You can live very well on our salary if you don't pay taxes."

He paused, yes, thinking about it, then nodded, timing it before going on. "I'd like a whole squad motivated by greed. Greed's as good a motivation as I know of to make quality arrests—that go to trial because some fuckin' DA can't kiss 'em off or plea bargain 'em away. They go to trial, we get the court time and put another asshole away.

"I happen to know that you always scored 'better than acceptable' in report writing in the Academy, and you can use that skill to your advantage when you write up the DUIs, 11550s, and felonies. It's the way you write 'em up that can turn a kiss-off into a quality arrest that goes to trial."

He looked at his watch, surprised, not having realized how much time had passed, because his conversation with Hanson had been so engrossing.

"Hell, I better get back out on the street. Good talking to you, Hanson. I'm sure we'll be seeing more of each other. Watch your ass out there," he said, putting his car into gear, smiling at Hanson one more time to close the deal and make the sale, then driving away through the curtain of rain falling from the overpass, his taillights streaking the street. Adios.

Without waiting for a sergeant to show up to witness the field sobriety tests, a DUI took a couple hours off the street to process. And anyway, who gave a shit about a drunk driver in East Oakland, everybody was drunk all the time.

Without waiting for a sergeant to arrive, an 11550 arrest took almost as long, after observing an individual who appeared to be under the influence of a controlled substance—usually an opiate, most of the time heroin—detaining and examining him for needle marks and constricted pupils. Needle marks were obvious if they were in the crook of the arm, but more difficult to find between the toes or in somebody's asshole or dick. In cases like those, comparing the diameter of the pupils, in millimeters, to the pupillometer on the cover of the 11550 pamphlet—a printed row of black dots that increased in size from left to right—was another way to ensure a quality arrest, make overtime by going to court, and put the suspect away, lock him up in an overcrowded prison, to punish him for using heroin instead of not using heroin.

If you've just made a felony arrest, maybe fought some guy to the street, handcuffed him in-custody, and the angry crowd is forming up to take your gun away and shoot you with it because his head is bleeding where you slammed it into the street, and he's yelling that the only reason you're arresting him is because he's black, and you probably shouldn't hang around waiting for the sergeant to come by, well, it would be better to just write his name on the report so he could still get the court overtime and be your pal if he caught you goofing off or fucking up.

Hanson cleared from the meet and was sent to cover 3L32 on a suspicious individual, possible 459 in progress, 3L34 was already on the way to cover. The address was in a strip mall not far away. Possible burglary possibly in progress. Hanson laughed out loud.

By the time he got there and out of his car, two cops had the possible burglar possibly cornered against the side of a closed True Value Hardware Store. The cops had assumed combat crouches, service revolvers pointed at the possible burglar, yelling, "Freeze. Freeze, motherfucker," sidestepping to stay even with him while maintaining a good sight picture even as he refused to look at them, duckwalking beneath the dark True Value window toward the alley.

Hanson realized that he too was sidestepping as he watched the three of them, pretty sure he hadn't made a good impression on Sergeant Croix and wondering why couldn't he just go along to get along occasionally. That's when he thought, Fuck this, and ran at the possible burglar, yelling "Don't shoot me" over his shoulder at the two cops, certain that what he was doing was not the correct OPD procedure. He should have driven there more slowly, giving the two cops time to possibly shoot the possible burglar, and stayed out of it. But it was too late for that. He was pissed off now, and wanted a little satisfaction. He dropped one shoulder and drove the possible burglar into an exterior wall, grabbed a double handful of his filthy shirt as he bounced back—"Come on, man, you want to freeze?"—in order to dance and slam him into the wall again. "Like on TV. Freeze, motherfucker." Then once more—"Come on, man. Can you do your fuckin' *part* here?"—before kicking his legs out from under him, then dropping his knee into the small of his back, out of breath but feeling the best he'd felt the whole fucking rainy night as he handcuffed him.

"Thank you. Very much," Hanson said, pulling him to his feet, enjoying the way the muscles in his shoulders and chest felt when he took hold of his arms and pulled. "I. Appreciate. Your. Cooperation," jerking him from side to side. "Fucker," stepping back so the two cops, guns holstered, could knock him down again.

Hanson traded handcuffs with one of the cops without a word and walked back to his car, wet and dirty but feeling real good. He didn't want anything to do with the paperwork. It was time to go in for the night.

CHAPTER SEVENTEEN

LIBYA

The rain had lifted when Hanson knocked on the door, but the horizon was dark with more on the way. Lightning spider-webbed the horizon as he watched, counting off the seconds until its electricity brushed his face in its passing, and he imagined himself disassembling into the storm. The door opened the width of the rattling night chain, and two small dogs stuck their heads through, wheezing, trying to wriggle out, one on top, then the other, ignoring Hanson until, against their will, they began sliding backward, back inside, and the door slammed shut. Hanson listened to the dogs throwing themselves against the door while a woman shouted, "Stop it. Stop! Stop that. Right now."

Half the night shift had called in sick that afternoon, the third day of rain. The sun was sinking fast behind the weather when the door opened. A stout black woman in her late fifties, all but filling the doorway, studied Hanson with disapproval. The two dogs leaned out from behind her, stiff legged, shivering with aggression.

"Yes?" she said.

Hanson looked down at his wet wool uniform shirt, silver

badge, gun belt, and muddy boots, as if to verify who he was, then back up. "Police officer?"

At the sound of his voice the dogs flattened against the floor, baring their teeth.

"You called the police?"

The woman considered him, then stepped aside, herding the quick little dogs back with her feet. With a nod of her head she indicated a white brocade couch, protected by clear plastic seat covers, as was all the furniture in the room. The white carpet was covered by clear plastic runners.

Hanson sat in the middle of the sofa, the plastic chirping against the seat of his damp wool trousers. The dogs positioned themselves at his ankles, coiled like springs, their little throats quivering, watching his eyes. One was black, the other a dark striped brindle, milky blind in one eye.

The woman looked down at him, her arms folded over her breasts. "Well?"

It must have been eighty degrees inside, the air heavy with wet-dog smell. Hanson smiled at the dogs with his eyes, but they only growled.

"Yes, ma'am, what's the problem?"

"I done told the police woman on the phone all about it."

"They didn't give me any details."

She clicked her teeth. "Next door," she said, cutting her eyes across the room. "That woman and the little boy calls her 'auntie.' Up at all hours, night and day, in and out, doors slamming to beat the band. Day and *night*." She was tapping her foot. "Live and let live is my watchword. That's what I was always taught. I don't complain, you won't find any complaints from me in all your complaint books, not from me. You hear what I'm sayin'?"

"Yes, ma'am."

"I know she says that my dogs poop in her yard, but they do

not, never have, never will, because I don't let them outside. Was some other dogs that did it, not my dogs, but if that's what she wants to think or tell people, it doesn't bother me. It's a free country. I've always bent over backwards to be a good neighbor, not to cause trouble or involve the police. And," she said, "I know that fireworks are against the law," looking at him for agreement.

He imagined they were. Just about everything they could think of in the State Capitol up in Sacramento was against the law in East Oakland.

"Uh-huh," she said, "called the police a hour ago an' you finally here. Did you see that mess out there?"

"No, ma'am."

"You must not be much of an investigator, then."

The dogs knew it too.

He nodded. "What happened?" he asked her.

"I'm here to tell you what happened," she said. "That boy over there, lord have mercy, can't stand still or be quiet, racing around on that bike of his, gets the dogs all worked up when they out there in the"—she looked down at the dogs—"in the yard," she said. "Uh-huh. Ain't that right?" she asked the guilty dogs. "I don't let 'em out, ever, but sometimes they *get* out if I'm not watchin' them every minute of the day is what I'm telling you. Those illegal firecrackers, I like to jump out of my skin sometimes they scare me so bad. Boom! Pow!"

The dogs leaped up in alarm and came down running in place, their claws clattering on the plastic carpet runner.

"Sounds about like one of those drive-bys that go on around here, police or no police doesn't make a bit of difference. But today, now, this morning, an' I don't pay attention to other people's business, I just happened to be looking out my window when that boy come out carrying a pumpkin—that's right, a big pumpkin. Set it down at the end of their sidewalk and put one of

143

those cherry bombs inside it, blew it up, pumpkin mess all over the place. Makes the neighborhood look bad. Scared the dogs to death. They come running and scratching on the back door for me to let 'em in, tore the screen up. I'll have to get it fixed."

The dogs were leaning against his legs. He could feel their hearts beating as she told the story.

"Have you ever heard of such a thing?"

Hanson shook his head then, to show he was concerned too.

Hanson said he'd go over and talk to the woman next door. He opened his notebook and she gave him, reluctantly, her name, but said her date of birth was her business. She hadn't done anything, and didn't want her name on a police report. Why would they want *her* name on the police report? She wasn't a criminal.

Hanson touched both dogs as he got up, just to let them know that he thought they were good dogs. The one-eyed brindle rolled over on his back with his legs in the air.

"Git," she snapped at the dogs, "git now," and they ran off together.

"You gonna *talk* to her? Is that what you get paid for, to *talk* to people? That what they payin' officers to do now?"

"No, ma'am." Hanson put his notebook in his pocket. "They mostly pay us to arrest as many as we can, handcuff 'em and take 'em to jail," he said, "but sometimes, well, I just talk to them, try to cut down on paperwork," he said, letting himself out of the house.

The glistening street was deserted, littered with budded tree branches that had been torn off by three days of storms. Silent blue lightning veined the thunderheads still lifting relentlessly from the bay, shuddering and booming like the faraway end of the world. From the sidewalk he could see the pumpkin shards glowing orange in the strange storm twilight. He kept walking toward the patrol car, not planning to bother anybody about the firecrackers, and then, one foot still in the air, stopped. He put his foot down carefully, turned on his flashlight, and with the beam of light followed the trail of blood from the street—stains and smears and spatters, gobs and strings of blood on the grass, gelled little pockets of it in the cracked concrete—to the little stoop-porch and the front door of the house.

"Police officer," he called, tapping the door with the flashlight. He didn't mind waiting, giving people a moment to organize their story or prepare to deny everything. No need to panic them into doing something crazy that he'd have to arrest them for and do the paperwork. At the same time he was poised to jump off the porch if someone came out the door with a knife, or to break their hand with the flashlight.

The chain lock rattled and the door was opened by a black woman in her late twenties wearing white shorts and a ribbed white tank top. Almost as tall as Hanson, she was sleekly muscled and barefoot, angry the moment she saw that it was a cop who'd knocked on her door.

"I didn't call the police."

She was a beautiful woman, he thought, who would be a real handful if he had to arrest her. The bridge of her perfect nose was swollen, as was her cheekbone, and her black eye—well, it made him a little dizzy.

"Wrong address," she said, moving to close the door.

"Radio sent me," he said, slipping his boot in to wedge the door open, watching her hands—gold and silver rings on all her fingers—"to check on a problem."

"No problems here."

"Blood," he said, shining the flashlight from the porch, using it as a pointer while watching her eyes follow the beam of light. "All the way out to the street."

"Is that a problem?"

Hanson smiled at that. Hard as she'd made her eyes, she

couldn't hide how smart she was and that she hated him on sight. She was deciding how much of it to tell him and how to tell it. She smelled funky and perfumed in the rain-washed air. Thunder broke over the house, shook them both. Lightning turned her eyes silver, stopped time, and burned their shadows through the floor. It began to rain again.

"Can I come in for a minute, out of the rain?" he said, stepping inside through the door, pushing it all the way back against the wall so he knew no one was back there.

"Who got cut?" he asked, closing the door behind him.

"If he dies, come back and arrest me. Good night."

"Looks like it was self-defense…"

"I'm not complaining. I didn't call the police. I don't need the police."

"Where did it happen?"

She glared at him, thinking it over. "In the kitchen."

"Show me."

"Why should I do that? I shouldn't have even let you in the door."

"Let's take a look."

She limped as she led him into the kitchen, where the floor was patterned with bloody waffle boot prints and her own whorled footprints. A bloody stainless steel potato peeler was in the sink.

"Where did you stab him?"

"What do you want? I couldn't get away from him."

"I don't think he lost enough blood to die or go to the hospital, but I want to be sure before I write it up. Show me where you stabbed him."

She touched the back of her own leg, just below the hem of her shorts.

"Where else?"

"Here," she said, her eyes on his, slipping two ringed fingers under the waistband of the white shorts. "I think I hit the bone, and he cut his fingers when he tried to take it away from me."

"Um," Hanson began, forgetting what it was he'd started to say.

"Are you going to arrest me?"

Hanson shook his head. "Are you okay?"

She just looked at him, her swollen black eye beautiful and erotic.

"I think he broke your nose a little bit."

"I'm okay," she said.

"And your foot?"

"Are you going to give me my rights?"

Hanson smiled at her. "I'd better take a look at that foot."

She didn't need him to help her hobble into the front room, holding onto his arm, they both knew that, but that's what they did. He put her into a nice overstuffed chair, and when he asked, she told him that the rubbing alcohol was under the sink in the bathroom.

While he was looking for the alcohol he called back to her that he wasn't looking for drugs, and she said that she didn't keep drugs in the bathroom.

He used two washcloths he'd put under hot water, cleaning the foot up, sitting on the floor below her chair, holding the foot in his lap.

"I don't think I'll tell any of my friends about this," she said, trying not to smile.

"Don't tell *anybody*," he said, reaching for the bottle of alcohol, "this was just a call about firecrackers." He cradled her foot, folded and pinched the washcloth into a tiny wingtip, and dipped it in the alcohol. "This is cold," he said, dry mouthed, "and it'll sting," he said, gently washing out the blood rimming her toenails. "When you paint your toenails, do you—"

The lights went off. He'd forgotten about the storm outside.

"Do you," Hanson began again, "um…"

"Maybe we…" she said.

It was too dark for them to see each other.

The storm crackled and lit them up, two seconds, three seconds, then it was dark again.

Hanson cupped his other hand on the arch of her foot.

In his notebook, he'd written her name, DOB, address, and phone number. Her name was Libya. He underlined it. Then he drew a circle around it. He stood by the door of his patrol car and considered the dark empty street. The lights were on across the freeway and, of course, up in the hills, but District Five was still without electricity.

He got in the car, started it, turned on the lights, and the instrument dials lit up. Radio snapped and buzzed and chattered with traffic. On the assignment card he wrote Complainant concerned about firecrackers, then he clicked his pen closed, folded the card twice, and stuck it in his pocket.

He drove a few blocks and pulled over at the High Street on-ramp, turned off the lights and got out of the car. Standing in the rain there he could see the freeway, the red and silver taillights and headlights streaming against and past each other. Maybe it was too late to quit now, maybe he was just too crazy to talk to anybody when he wasn't wearing his uniform. He got back into the patrol car and listened to the rain drumming on the roof, then pulled the mike from the dashboard, jumped into the radio traffic, and cleared from the call. He should go home, drink some tequila, and pass out.

Only a couple of cops were in the locker room when he came out of the tunnel from Transportation. He could hear them somewhere behind the banks of wall lockers, changing clothes. By the time he came out of the shower, they were gone, and he was alone in the empty locker room. As he put on his jeans, blue work shirt, blue-and-white running shoes, he felt as if he might be the last person alive on earth. He walked down the deserted hallway and out the push-bar steel door into the rain, two blocks more to where his van was parked, got in, locked the door, reached under the seat for the half pint of vodka with the red-and-white Popov label that he'd bought at the little Korean liquor store on the way to work. He drank the sweet, oily vodka down in four swallows, the warmth spreading in his stomach, then sat back and watched the rain cascade down the windshield, the side windows, watched the rear window through the rearview mirror, watched the shadows out on the street. The rain drummed on the roof of the car.

It seemed to Hanson as if it rained a lot, that May and June. He got used to the rain and even got to like it despite the damp wool uniform, wet steel-toed boots, raindrops puckering the orange crime report forms. The rain, blown in from the Pacific, from hundreds of miles out to sea, clattered softly in the rainspout outside his bedroom window at dawn when he went to sleep. It cleaned the oil and trash off the streets, mirrored streetlights and stoplights, murmured against the curbs, rushing and frothing down the clogged storm drains. The rain ran down his cheeks to his lips, where he licked it off, thinking how it had ridden the clouds in from the ocean.

He was done for the night.

Hanson is sleeping.

His books are all boxed up and stacked around the walls of his bedroom while he's miles away, sitting across the kitchen table from Libya, where they are talking with their eyes. His eyes have done more to keep him alive than any field manual or assault rifle or air strike, and now they're saving him again. He's articulate with hard eyes and crazy eyes, mean eyes, command eyes and ready-to-die calm eyes, but Libya is teaching him how to talk with soft eyes tonight during the storm, which will give up and be gone by morning. It's another language entirely, all new to him, but already he's dancing with her to the basic nouns and verbs and when he stumbles he has her to hold on to.

The rain has seeped down through the walls and across the ceiling of his bedroom, patterning the plaster into dark, cryptic icons—threats, bad memories, and ransom demands from the depths of Lake Merritt. Outside his window bushes whip in the wind, fanning shadows across the bedroom from the streetlight on the corner. Thunder explodes above the house. The storm pounds the walls and rattles the gutters, it rips a screen off the bedroom window, flings it cartwheeling away into the dark.

Hanson rolls over easily in his sleep.

CHAPTER EIGHTEEN

LAKE MERRITT

Hanson opened his eyes, clasped his hands behind his head, and listened to the house. It was quiet. The rain had gone away during the night. A good omen. He had two days off to deal with, putting off his first drink of the day for as long as possible.

He pulled on cutoff jeans, drank a beer to smooth out his hangover a little, and walked back to the sagging screened-in porch, barefoot and shirtless. Sparrows and house finches, gray and ragged as street people, flew off when they saw him, then circled right back to the feeder. A brazen rufous hummingbird streaked away, then, a moment later, just…*appeared*, his wings a blur, hovering just beyond the screen, watching Hanson. Goldfinches, tiny and impeccable, yellow, black, and white, clung sideways and upside down from the mesh bag of thistle seed Hanson had put out. Hanson smiled, delighted by all the activity, gone, out of himself for a moment. He went back in the house and put on a black tank top and electric-blue track shoes for a run around Lake Merritt.

Hungover, but he'd felt worse, he told himself, dodging

pedestrians, parking meters, and parked cars without losing his rhythm. He watched his reflection slide across the window of Tao Seafood, then he spun and sidestepped through the outdoor tables at Café Noir. Crossing Grand at an angle toward Walden Pond Books, he saluted Marshall, the owner, who was watching from the window.

Some kind of cramp, down low on his right side, had started throbbing with his heartbeat, eating up into his ribs. He picked up his pace beneath the marquee of the Grand Lake Theatre—PSYCHO II—ran the light at the intersection, past Blues Burger, where black girls wearing red-and-white uniforms and paper hats worked behind rotating bulletproof windows.

Farther down the block, through the glare on the plate-glass windows, he could see, in the lobby of the transient hotel, all the old men with no one to take them in, who sat there all day, waiting to die. He glanced at the upper windows, cornices, and ledges, imagining some young ex-con looking out the window toward the bay. Fresh out of San Quentin, out of money and behind on his rent, he'd be trying to think of someone he could call who might help him line up a score, already knowing he'd be back in the joint soon.

He stopped in front of the hotel and, his hands clasped behind his back, looked down through the glass at the jade plants, dozens of them on a shelf below the window. The soil in their pots was dry and cracked, the sun shining directly on them most of the day.

He walked through the door, a bell ringing as he opened it, all the old men looking up at him. The desk clerk was a fat white kid, and this was probably the best job he'd ever get. He was in a little nook set back almost out of sight from the front desk, leaning back in a folding metal chair, looking at a *Hustler* magazine. When Hanson walked up to the front desk and peered around at him, the kid pretended not to notice him. Hanson suddenly grinned, recognizing him from Portland. He hit the little silver bell with the heel of his hand. Nothing. He lay over the counter on his belly, legs dangling, and twisted his head to look up at the kid. "Hi. Young man. I must talk to you."

He didn't look up from the magazine.

In a peeling mirror behind the desk, Hanson saw the people in the lobby watching to see what this was about. What would happen? He tapped the bell softly, with one finger, repeatedly—*dingdingdingdingdingdingding*—not stopping till the kid looked at him. Hanson smiled, his eyes open wide, looking dorky, but also insane. His Shirley Temple eyes. The kid dropped the front legs of the chair on the floor, stood up, rolling the magazine in his hand, and walked to the other side of the counter from Hanson.

"What?" he said, and Hanson laughed, delighted at the kid's tough-guy act.

He batted his wide eyes at him, dorky crazy to the max. "I need to show you something," Hanson said. "Those jade plants by the windows."

"What?" the kid asked, more bewildered than surly this time.

"Look at me," Hanson said, closing down the Shirley Temple eyes. "It'll just take a few seconds. Let's walk over to the window."

"Are you a cop?"

"I'm going over there now, and I'm gonna wait for you. Okay?"

Hanson walked across the lobby in his cutoff Levi's and black tank top, sweeping his eyes across the lobby like searchlights. He stopped at the window, licked his thumb, and wiped a streak of dust off one of the jade plants. He dug his thumbnail into the dry, cracked dirt. Cigarette butts had been stubbed out in most of the pots. It pissed him off. The desk clerk was watching anxiously, still behind the desk. Hanson gestured to him with one hand and mouthed the words "Come 'ere."

The kid lifted the hinged end of the desk and walked over, his arms out from his sides as if he was so muscular that he couldn't bring them any closer to his body. He flipped his head to swing his hair out of his eyes. When he got to where Hanson was standing, he assumed a sort of sumo wrestler stance, his groin thrust out, arms hanging at his sides, utterly vulnerable.

"This is called Jade Plant. When was last time you watered him?" Hanson said in a Russian robot voice.

"I dunno. Ugly fuckers look the same as when I started working here."

"Hero plants. Still alive. Never watered. Still alive. Used for ashtrays. Still alive."

"Shit," the kid said, about to turn away.

Hanson stepped on his foot, and the kid glared at him, but only for a second. Hanson's scary-calm evangelist's look ate the anger, leaving the kid with fear in his eyes. "What is your name?"

"Marvin."

"What is *my* name? Marvin. Look at me," he said, reaching down and taking one of the kid's fat hands in both of his, not letting go. "You do not remember me? Lion of the Avenue. Fierce Tiger of North Precinct. The nice guy who wrote up not one, but two criminal complaints on you in such a way that the DA threw them away? Open your eyes."

"Hanson."

"Perfect. I'll see you in a couple of days. Start watering those plants, just a little at a time. Okay? Good to see you, Marvin." He walked out the door, the little bell ringing behind him, then looked through the window at Marvin as he shifted his weight from shoulder to shoulder like a boxer, grinning.

The pain down in his ribs was still there, insistent. He'd forgotten about it. He leaped the curb, dodged a cab turning left, and picked up his pace once more.

In front of the Chevron station, he jumped a brown patch of

sidewalk. One evening the week before, two black guys had pulled their car in front of a nineteen-year-old white junkie walking past the station. They got out of their car, each with a length of heavy chain, chain-whipped him until he was bloody and dead, got back in the car and drove off. That was the word, but there were no witnesses. Nobody saw it happen. OPD detectives had shown up the next afternoon, but had no suspects or motives. The owner of the gas station had hosed the blood off the next morning, but it had set overnight. The stain must be bad for business, Hanson thought, cutting back across Grand to the path around the lake.

Barely midmorning and Lake Merritt was steaming. The Chinese men and women in bright silk tunics and flowing black pants were out along the grassy bank, well into their tai chi routines—rising, turning, holding…sweeping into the next form. Gray-haired, slight in build, their serene detachment kept the thugs and drunks and lunatics who prowled the lake well away.

Out in the middle of the lake a gleaming white nineteenth-century whaleboat with bright blue trim moved smoothly away, rowed by eight women in their seventies, a ninth, the coxswain up front, leaning into her oar to bring the heavy boat around toward the opposite shore. The women wore white trousers, white middy blouses, white hats, and scarves that were the same shade of blue as the boat trim.

Seagulls waddled along the muddy shore, and at the far end of the lake, black cormorants dove, disappeared for ten or fifteen seconds, then popped back up in some different spot, tipping their heads back to swallow silver fish. A line of pelicans flew six feet above the water, banking, changing direction, and holding their altitude, big ponderous birds in unison alternating several wing flaps with a glide, as smoothly as a flight of heavy bombers. On the strip of grass between the lake and Lakeshore Drive, two young black dudes in their early twenties worked out with weights, a faint clang each time they added plates to their curl bar.

Hanson was bent over, elbows on his knees, catching his breath and wondering if the knife in his ribs was a heart attack, when a runner with a dog almost ran him over.

N/M, Hanson thought, cataloguing him. Negro Male. Six one, one eighty, dark complexion, shaved head, diamond studs in both ears.

He'd blown past never looking at Hanson, as if saying *I don't even see you, motherfucker,* a golf club in one hand and a studded leather leash in the other. His pit bull puppy ran ahead, tongue lolling out, crabbing to one side, then the other against the rhythm of the cast-iron weight plate hung from a chain around his neck. The dog looked happy.

Hanson watched them jog away, then tried walking the heart attack away down toward the weight lifters. He felt worse now than when he'd left home, sweating tequila, cursing the pain in his side. One of the weight lifters had walked off to talk to a couple of white girls in a BMW, and the other one, who Hanson thought he recognized now that he was closer, was sitting on a weight bench in the shade of a New Zealand tea tree, watching Hanson.

"Hey. Homeboy," he called to Hanson.

"Yes, sir," Hanson said.

"How about spotting me for a minute, Homey?" He was wearing baggy pleated khaki pants with running shoes, his shirt hanging from a tree branch. He was buffed and pumped up from the lifting he'd already done.

"Sure," Hanson said, walking over, surprising him. He looked more closely at Hanson, then swung around and lay beneath the weights. Hanson stood at the head of the bench, hands gripping the bar on the outside of the weights. They looked at each other, their faces upside down.

"Ready when you are, boss," Hanson said. "How many reps?"

"Twelve."

"Lotta weight," Hanson said, looking theatrically at one end of the bar, then the other.

"I got it." He did five reps, then paused, the weight straight up, looking at Hanson's eyes. "What's your name, man? I know you from somewhere."

"Hanson."

He grunted and pushed out more reps. "Where I know you from?"

"Raylene's Discount Liquors. You asked me if you'd broken some law when you weren't paying attention."

"Damn," he said, finishing his twelve reps without breaking a sweat.

"I look a lot different when I'm not wearing that uniform. You're Tyree, as I recall."

"Tyree," he said, setting the bar in the cradle.

The Tai Chi people moved as smooth as shadows on the lake, where the ladies, rowing their impeccable whaleboat, left an endless V behind them. The pelicans began landing, hitting the water like plane crashes, then gliding gracefully off.

The other guy, Tyree's partner, had come back from talking to the girls in the BMW and was standing ten feet away, watching Hanson. Tyree sat up and told him, "This is that cop I told you about, who stood on the hood of his patrol car and broke up that street dance. And stopped Uncle Fee just the other night."

His partner smiled.

"Show us what you can handle, po-lice," Tyree said, standing up and gesturing toward the weight bench. "I'll spot you."

Hanson looked at the bar. It weighed almost as much as he did.

"Unless you don't feel up to it."

Hanson straddled the bench, sat, then lay down flat. He

extended his arms, gripping the bar from below and Tyree helped him slip it out of the cradle and take the full weight, slowly let him have the full weight. Even without a hangover, it was too much weight for him, but he managed seven reps through all the blind will and pain he could muster. After lowering it to his chest for an eighth rep, he was able to raise it only partway, knew he couldn't do another rep, and lowered the bar to just above his chest, his arms still bent at the elbow. Without help, he'd have to try and tip the bar to one side, slide the end into the ground and crab out from beneath it or topple it onto the ground. If Tyree wanted to, he could shove the bar down into Hanson's ribs and claim that Hanson had dropped it on himself. At best Hanson would look clumsy and weak getting out from under the bar, and at worst, if Tyree shoved it down, he'd have broken ribs and maybe a punctured lung.

"Push that iron," Tyree said, looking down at him, cupping his hands around both ends of the bar. "Come on, po-lice. You can do it. Do it."

Hanson focused everything on the bar, his arms quivering, slowly raising it, slowly, raising it almost to the lip of the cradle, where Tyree took just enough of the weight himself so Hanson could roll it into the cradle. He looked up through the gnarled gray branches of the New Zealand tea tree, breathing hard, thinking it over, his arms feeling as if they might float out alongside him. "Thing is," he said. "About weight. How much. You can lift. Can't fake it. With iron. Either you can. Or can't."

"Did good…" Tyree began.

His partner said, "Yeah."

Tyree continued, "…raising that weight mostly with your mind. If you took better care of yourself, though, go into training, you could be *bad*."

Hanson laughed, exhausted, and sat up. "Thanks for the help."

"You know what I'm sayin'."

"I do," Hanson said.

"You off duty?"

"Officially? Off duty."

"You live around here?"

"Yeah."

"In Oakland?"

"Yeah."

"An' don't even have a piece with you?"

"Can't run for shit carrying one. Nowhere to hide it either. Worried somebody might see it. Blow me up. Say it was self-defense."

"Police say that all the time."

"I worry about them the most," Hanson said.

"Me," Tyree said, "I'm not packin'."

Hanson looked at his partner.

"That's my partner. I been knowin' him since I was five years old. We look out for each other. You need somebody watch your back in this world."

"I used to trust some people like that, but they're gone, mostly dead now."

"How'd that happen?"

"It just happens."

"You right about that."

"What's his name?" Hanson asked Tyree, then turned to face his partner. "Excuse my bad manners," he said. "I should ask *you*, if you don't mind."

"My name Quintus."

"A pleasure, Quintus. I appreciate you lookin' out for me and Tyree. Unarmed in the park, like we are," Hanson said, standing up.

"I been wondering something," Tyree said, "thought I'd aks you about. Since you're right here. If that's okay."

Hanson looked at him. "Sure."

"The other night at the liquor store, did you notice anything, you know, unusual, in the car, when you was talkin' to us?"

"You mean the Uzi the older gentleman in the backseat had under his coat?"

Tyree looked over at Quintus, then looked back at Hanson. "How come you didn't call it in?"

"Just a lot of trouble, for nothing. Extra paperwork for me. It was an accident I saw it, you all didn't *let* me see it, to see what I'd do. Disrespect me, test me. I'd have had to arrest you for that. We were all reasonable with each other, polite, no problem. I don't care if you got an Uzi as long as you don't try to shoot me with it, or if you don't"—he smiled—"use it responsibly. Uzis all over Oakland. Good seeing you again, Tyree," Hanson said. "Quintus," he said, nodding, "a pleasure. You all be careful now."

He was walking away, limping a little, when Tyree said, " *You* be careful. I hear it's some bad brothers out there where you work."

Hanson stopped and turned around. Tyree was holding his right hand up, brown palm out. Hanson smiled, put his heels together, and gave him a little salute. Then he walked on. He was feeling better now and began a slow jog back toward Grand Avenue.

He turned in a circle, running in place, taking in the Tai Chi people, the classy old women in the whale boat, Tyree and Quintus down there laughing about something—probably him—next to the weight bench.

Maybe he was doing okay out there on the job. Building a support base. For a moment he thought about going to see Libya. She sure beat a cop groupie at the bar across from the Justice Center, and he didn't have to spend time with drunk cops either. He hadn't imagined it, the way they couldn't stop looking at each other. They had eyes for each other. But that was insane, going to see her. He started running again, onto the sidewalk along Grand Avenue.

When he heard the *tick, tick, tick* of Weegee's card-in-the-spokes bicycle coming up behind him, he raised his hand and stopped running, catching his breath.

"Hi, Officer Hanson," Weegee said, coming to a stop beside him on the grass. "Liftin' weights with Tyree and Quintus," he said, smiling, shaking his head. "I never seen 'em talk to the police before. Never. They talkin' to you, though."

"Weegee, I think you know everybody in Oakland. Like the CIA. A one-man CIA on a bike."

"Well," Weegee said, modest, a little embarrassed, pleased, "I get around."

"It's always good to see you, young sir," Hanson said. "Keeping an eye on me, let me know how I'm doing." He *was* glad to see him. It wasn't just that Weegee was smart and funny. Hanson forgot about himself whenever he was around. "Why don't you pace me, ride along with me up to the Grand Lake Theatre and we'll get some ice cream if you want to. I'd sure like some."

"Okay," Weegee said, and Hanson began an easy jog, the pain in his side gone completely now. Weegee kept pace, rearing his bike up on its back wheel, making circles around Hanson. "The CIA, that's the Central Intelligence Agency. They're the spies. The C-I-A and the F-B-I. I know these things, Officer Hanson."

CHAPTER NINETEEN

FELIX AND LEVON

It was after six when Felix got back to the compound inside the San Antonio Village housing project, otherwise known as The Ville. Levon looked up at one of the security camera monitors as Felix was buzzed through the first electric gate—the same system used in jails. You go through the first gate, which swings back and locks again, trapping you in the corridor between gates until you're buzzed through the second one. At a glance, Levon saw how upset Felix was, waiting for the second gate to buzz open. The police frequency radio scanner in another room was barely audible.

As soon as Felix had started making money he'd moved five families to better housing, torn down the houses where they'd been living, and built a fenced, fortified compound in the middle of The Ville. He'd had to pay off two officials in the Oakland Housing Authority and an OPD police captain—through his lieutenant, actually giving the money to a patrolman—even though The Ville wasn't covered by the official police beat map, in a kind of limbo between the freeway and the bay.

Levon closed the book he'd been reading, a biography of

Theodore Roosevelt, using a dog-eared playing card—king of clubs—for a bookmark, when Felix came through the steel-sheathed front door wearing an off-white Italian suit.

"Everything down, fucked up," Felix said, "like you told me and worse besides."

Tyree and Quintus were in the other room, listening to calls on the police radio frequency, laughing and high-fiving each other.

Felix tilted his head toward a windowless hallway and said, "Let's go talk in the business room."

The business room was in the windowless reinforced-concrete bunker in the center of Felix's compound, surrounded by the project, deep inside East Oakland. No bigger than the waiting room outside a lawyer's office, it looked like a bomb shelter but one that was furnished with an expensive leather couch, a deluxe model La-Z-Boy recliner, a floor lamp, a bookcase, and, on the walls, framed black-and-white photographs of Martin Luther King, Malcolm X, and Felix's grandfather, Solomon Maxwell, taken when he was president of the Brotherhood of Sleeping Car Porters.

Felix lay down on the sofa, and Levon took his chair. A yellow legal pad lay on the floor next to the sofa. Felix reached inside his coat and pulled out a pair of octagonal rimless glasses, picked up the legal pad, and began to make some notes. "You see those lights in the sky last night?"

"What lights?"

"They out there every night. Look like stars, but they're not."

"Those glasses make you look more intelligent," Levon said, putting down his book.

Felix snorted, laid the tablet flat on his chest and the glasses on top of that. "Somebody's taking corners away from us, again, all along High Street. I got the feeling, whoever it is owns somebody, maybe a captain upstairs at the Justice Center. I got to stay home and pay better attention."

"The so-called Muslims are all over San Pablo and north of there. Beating up our people, taking their money and drugs, selling the drugs. The cops are fine with that, they say.

"I talked to my lieutenant downtown, and I don't believe a word he says. I *never* believe anything he says. And now I'm paying him five hundred dollars a month more than I used to. How smart is that? Maybe I should wear my glasses when I talk to him."

Levon looked up. "Tyree and Quintus ran into that cop today down at Lake Merritt."

Felix rolled his head over on the arm of the sofa and looked at Levon.

"The one who came up to the car because we were double-parked in front of the liquor store."

Felix studied the ceiling. "That's a real coincidence."

"He was running. Down at that lake. Tyree didn't recognize him at first. Asked him to spot him on the weight bench, just to mess with a white boy, but turns out he came over and was messing with Tyree. Wasn't carrying a gun. Said he lives in Oakland."

"I'll check with my lieutenant—did you know lieutenants wear solid gold badges—see what he says." He started to put his glasses back on, then said, "Maybe that's why nobody ever sees a lieutenant on the street out here. Maybe they're worried somebody will steal their badge. When he finally pisses me off enough so I kill him, I'm gonna remember to rip that badge off his white little chicken chest for a souvenir."

Felix wasn't a tough guy—he was a killer, though, and fearless. He thought of himself as already dead, and that's how he looked at everyone else too. He was ruthless and merciless in a brutal white man's world. He knew they'd kill him sooner or later. He'd written up a will and funeral arrangements, gave a copy to Levon each time he modified them.

CHAPTER TWENTY

WEEGEE'S BIRD BOOK

Other than his patrol car and his flat, the only place Hanson spent any time at all was in Walden Pond Books. The owner, Marshall, was an old-time East Coast radical-progressive who'd moved west in the early seventies. He was a soft-spoken, thoughtful intellectual with carefully considered opinions, but Hanson had seen him make friends with raving street radicals simply by listening politely. Hanson could feel himself relax whenever he walked into the shop. Marshall knew Hanson was a cop and they were both comfortable with that—it made no difference.

Marshall's assistant, Darrell, was in his late twenties, a UC Berkeley grad and self-proclaimed anarchist, who always seemed to be brooding, grumpy and suspicious to such a degree that it was funny, and he played it up. When it was just the three of them in the shop, Hanson felt like he was among friends.

Hanson had just finished a run around Lake Merritt and was catching his breath as he passed the bookstore. Marshall was just visible through the poster-covered window, stacking books shoulder-high on a window shelf. Hanson stopped and went inside. Marshall didn't even notice Hanson until he was standing by the cash register behind him, drumming his fingers on the glass counter.

"Marshall," Hanson said, "you know about stacking books so high in the window that the cops can't see in if you're getting robbed."

"Who's gonna rob this place?" Darrell said. "There's not nearly enough money."

"The take from a 7-Eleven isn't usually more than thirty or forty bucks. They'll shoot people for fifty."

"They?"

"The disenfranchised."

Marshall had been unboxing new books. *Milestones: The Music and Times of Miles Davis to 1960,* Miles playing his trumpet, holding it with both hands as if it might overpower him and escape, leaning into the music.

"Officer Hanson," Marshall said. "You looking for anything in particular today?"

"Birds."

"Well," Marshall said, laughing, "you know the store about as well as I do."

Walden Pond had once been an appliance showroom, the space was deeper than it was wide. All the new books, bestsellers, self-help, and coffee table art books were up front on display tables and display shelves. You could bring in coffee from the coffee shop next door and sit on a flower-print sofa or one of the overstuffed chairs.

The rest of the store was serious, rows of shelves Marshall had nailed together from one-inch pine boards. Hanson could tell at a glance when a book had been added or taken away from one of the pine shelves.

The books back there were twenty, thirty, forty years old—most out of print, forgotten, ignored—their mildew smell drifting between shelves. At night, Hanson imagined, when the store was dark and silent, back in the stacks, the books talked to each other. They talked in low voices until dawn, each of them telling the same stories over and over every night about what happened or didn't happen or might have happened, swapping different versions of the truth. All of them waiting through the days and nights for someone to pick them up, open and begin to read.

When he first started coming in the bookstore, Hanson would concentrate his attention on the War section, two bottom shelves in American History. The Vietnam War had its own subsection. He'd kneel down and, shuffling sideways, read the titles along the bottom shelves. *Dispatches.* Or a new history of the 5th Special Forces Group in Vietnam. Recently, however, he'd been focused on the bird books, reading about raptors: hawks, eagles. He walked down a narrow aisle between the stacks.

Falcons, hawks, and vultures—birds Hanson had gotten acquainted with in Idaho, missing them now sometimes. And California condors, a handful of them left, prehistoric birds who will soon be extinct and know it. Hanson used to look at them perched in their two-story aviaries in the World Center for Birds of Prey on a hilltop outside Boise. He'd make eye contact with them, hoping to learn what they knew. He found the "California condor" entry in volume one of *The Birds of California,* copyright 1923. Four volumes bound in green buckram. The condor was already in trouble in 1923. They were "extinct" or "very rare" in all areas north of San Francisco.

A dude in a black leather jacket came styling through the door, gold ring in one ear, Jheri curls pulled back with a green bandanna.

"How much the book 'bout Miles?" he said.

"Thirteen ninety-five plus tax," Marshall said.

"Awright, then," he said. "I be back and check it out. Miles, uh-huh."

Hanson put the bird book back into its place and wandered over to Erotica, a section where the new books and the second-hand books were not segregated. They were mostly too cerebral, too highbrow, to be a turn-on for Hanson. *Story of O.* Several editions of the Kama Sutra. A glossy coffee-table book of tantric sex. *The Marquis de Sade: The Complete Justine.* Phyllis and Eberhard Kronhausen's *The Complete Book of Erotic Art, Volumes 1 and 2.* Marshall kept Helmut Newton's *White Women* in Erotica. Hanson picked up *Chinese Foot Binding: The History of a Curious Erotic Custom* and started leafing through.

The nineteenth-century British author considered foot binding to be an example of human inventiveness in the art of pleasure. The woman's swollen feet, her hesitant gait, the heightened sensitivity of pain. The intensified pleasure for the man, as he holds captive the exquisite small silk shoes that encase the throbbing bound feet, positioning the submissive woman, fearful yet aroused, for his entry. Hanson caught himself thinking about Libya, her hurt foot in his hand as he bathed it. Libya's feet had high arches and she was not helpless.

Too bad, he thought. It had been a long time since he met a woman he thought was interesting.

"Hey, Hanson." Marshall was looking out the front window, over the books stacked chest high on the windowsill. "This kid on a bike outside. Been there since you came in the store. What's up with that? Cute kid."

He went out the door, taking Weegee by surprise.

"Officer Hanson," he said, "I was just riding by."

"Come on inside, Weegee."

"Can I bring my bike in there?"

"You bet. Come on in," he said, opening the door for him to

wheel the bike in, the playing card ticking slowly against the spokes. "Weegee, this is Marshall. It's his bookstore."

"Weegee. Welcome to my bookstore."

"And that guy over there, the grumpy-looking guy, that's Darrell. He was born in the basement of the University of California at Berkeley. He's really much nicer than he seems at first."

"Mr. Weegee, a pleasure."

"Weegee," Hanson said. "Let's go get a couple of All-American burgers…wait. I'm gonna give you a present, a gift. I saw it a few minutes ago, where it's been waiting for you on one of those shelves. It's lucky you came by. I'll be right back."

Hanson went back to the bird books and pulled out a barely used hardcover of the second edition of Peterson's *Western Birds*. Hanson had his own copy at home.

He gave Marshall a twenty-dollar bill, which Marshall pushed back to him. "My pleasure," he said.

"Thank you, Marshall. And if you'll let me borrow this pen for a moment," he said, opening the book to the title page. He looked out the window at Grand Avenue, looked at Weegee waiting with his bike, and wrote in the book, <u>For Weegee, my good friend in Oakland who saves me whenever I'm lost. With this book he can give names to all the birds</u>.

"Here you go, sir," Hanson said, handing it to him. "Thanks again, Marshall."

"Thank you, Marshall," Weegee said, a bit bewildered by it all. He opened the book to what Hanson had written, looked at it long enough to read it several times, not moving from in front of the counter.

Hanson said, "Let me put that in your pack, and we'll go eat."

"You didn't sign your name," Weegee said.

"You're right, young sir." Hanson took the book back. "Your Friend, Officer Hanson," he said as he signed with a flourish.

"Thank you very much, gentlemen," he said to Marshall and Darrell, and they went out the door into the afternoon crowd on Grand Avenue, walking toward All-American Burger up by the Grand Lake Theatre, Weegee at Hanson's side, pushing his bike.

They each got an All-American with cheese and split a large order of American fries. The girl behind the bulletproof Plexiglas didn't recognize Hanson but smiled at Weegee. Weegee introduced Hanson to her. "Darlene, meet Officer Hanson. He's off duty."

"Officer Hanson, always glad to meet a friend of Weegee's," she said.

Weegee got a Coke and Hanson drank water, two big cups of it, glad that his hangover wasn't as bad as it might be. The water helped, but he was still a little hot and jumpy, sitting at one of the grimy round tables, pedestrians all around them. Weegee devoured his burger and most of the fries, keeping an eye on Hanson and people on the street.

"You look a little worn out," Hanson said. "Where'd you stay last night?"

"Where'd I *stay?* I *live* with my auntie, Officer Hanson." Weegee sounded affronted. Then he laughed. "Course, could be I was out late. Summer vacation, you know. Riding my bike. Checking on things."

"Maybe we could try out your bird book one of these days while I'm off work. It has descriptions and drawings of all the birds we might see. Let me see that book. I'll show you something." Hanson showed him the black-crowned night heron. "Sometimes you can see one of those guys up in a tree at Lake Merritt."

"I like penguins," Weegee said.

"I haven't seen any of those at Lake Merritt."

"That's 'cause they all live down at the South Pole, on icebergs in the ocean. My auntie has a picture of penguins in her kitchen. They're my favorite bird," he said, getting out of his chair and pressing his arms to his sides, tilting his head up. "Walk around like this," he said, waddling back and forth like a penguin. "Hello," he said, nodding at an imaginary penguin. "How you today? 'Just fine, thank you.' They all know each other down at the South Pole on those icebergs, but they gotta look out for when those ice cliffs break off and fall in the water. You gonna finish up those fries?"

"No, sir," Hanson said, grinning. "I believe they must be yours."

Weegee sat back down and ate, asking Hanson, "How come Marshall didn't make you pay for the book?"

"He's a nice guy."

"You don't think it's because you're the police?"

Hanson laughed. "Like a payoff? So I won't run him in for selling books? Weegee, I buy a lot of books there. We're friends. And he liked you. Sometimes it just makes you feel good to give a present to somebody."

Weegee shook his head, smiling to himself at Officer Hanson's innocence. "How come you like birds so much? Mostly people shoot 'em with BB guns and slingshots."

"I used to do that too. Long time ago. Now, I like to watch them fly."

"Okay then. I better go," Weegee said. "Thanks for the All-American, and for the book too."

"You bet. Come on by my place any time. Let me give you my address," Hanson said, realizing he'd never said that to anyone else in Oakland. "We'll look at some birds." He wrote his address and his home telephone on the back of one of his "I'm a Police Officer" cards.

"Okay, Officer Hanson," Weegee said, getting out of his chair and hopping on the bike in one smooth motion. "Almost forgot. You remember that black rabbit we saw at where those witches live that day? I been seeing him all the time lately. Seem like he gets around as much as I do. See you later."

Hanson watched him ride away, thinking of all the times he'd gone on combat operations with twelve-year-old Montagnard kids, watched as their fathers and uncles and brothers helped them with their equipment, smiled and told them they'd be okay. And he'd seen them dead too, their wrists and ankles lashed together, slung on bamboo poles and carried back to camp, where the women bathed their wounds, clothed them, and laid their bodies in the red wooden coffins that the Americans kept out of sight most of the time. They were good soldiers, those little boys, their best killers, if they survived their first few operations.

CHAPTER TWENTY-ONE

SOLSTICE

By the time he got home that morning, after three hours of overtime, the sun was well up, enormous, pulling a hot wind in from the Nevada desert like an open furnace door. Even the mornings were hot now, and Hanson had trouble sleeping past dawn. The hottest time of the day was the beginning of his shift down in the flatlands of East Oakland, when the sun hovered above the bay, reflecting itself in storefronts and passing cars, cooking rainbows of crankcase oil off the streets. The plastic seat fabric was hot, the steering wheel was hot in his hands, his steel-toed boots never cooled off. He had pulled down the sun visor, pushed his sunglasses farther back on his nose and taken his Radio calls.

In the kitchen he tossed off three fingers of green tequila that burned away with no effect at all. Out the window finches and sparrows hopped and fluttered from the feeders to the clothesline, like musical notes. He'd been awake for twenty-one hours, wired on adrenaline and exhaustion, and he didn't want to sleep. He poured another drink, then looked at the Three Dragons calendar on the wall. It was the summer solstice, the day when "the sun stands still," it said on the calendar. The longest day of the year. Six months and he'd have his POST certificate. All he had to do, he told himself, was stay tough.

He set his drink down, walked to the back door, unlocked it, and took the rickety stairs to the basement.

The original coal-burning furnace, modified for fuel oil, stood cold and soot-streaked at one end of the basement, a massive firebox set in the concrete foundation. Jointed heat ducts branched out from it like the arms of a mechanical octopus, reaching overhead across the low ceiling and up again through the floor of the house.

Hanson's heavy workout bag hung from three chains hooked to a ringbolt under the stairs. He took the last step to the floor, spun and side-kicked the bag, cocked his forearm and slammed it again when it swung back at him. He leaned out of its way and picked up a white plastic kitchen timer from a shelf under the stairs, winding it while the bag swung squeaking past him in the ringbolt. He set the timer down, found the rhythm of the swinging bag, straightened up and began to punch, freckles of blood appearing on the dirty gray canvas. He hit the bag with his fists and forearms, kicked it, drove into it with his shoulders, grunting with effort, out of breath.

The timer dinged.

He leaned away, picked up the timer, his hands shaking, knuckles skinned, wound it again and went back to the bag.

When the timer dinged a second time he dropped his hands, sobbing for air, and slammed his forehead into the bag. He turned away, his legs quivering, walked to a weight bench and sat down, elbows on knees, head down, dropping sweat onto the concrete. Wind shrieked through the cracked caulking around a small window high in the opposite wall, just above ground level. The dirty glass was milky with age. A rosebush outside, caught by the wind, was scratching a message in the glass with its thorns.

Hanson stood and walked across the basement to look out the window, squeezing around behind the furnace where he stumbled over a pile of rotting black hose and brass coupling green with age. A face watched him from beneath the tangle of hose, a green face with no mouth or nose, a single rectangular eye protruding from the ridged forehead.

Squatting down, he saw that it was an ancient welder's mask made of Bakelite molded in layers of plastic and strips of fabric so that it looked like the mummified face of some de-evolved alien.

He reached into the hoses and a black widow spider scuttled out of her cottony web, rose straight up with febrile speed, past his hand, and disappeared into a crack in the wall. When he pulled the mask free a translucent flat centipede dropped out, twisting as it fell to the floor, where it vanished into the pile of hose.

The eye was a rectangle of thick green-black glass with a golden luster, slightly bigger than a business card, dark enough so that a welder could look through it directly at an electric arc as he welded steel. Hanson had read somewhere that you could use a welder's mask to look at the sun.

He took the mask upstairs to the kitchen and washed it out at the sink, sponging decades of dust off, using Windex to clean the eye. What was left of a decal inside the mask said that the glass was gold-mirrored. The face was hinged to a headband, and he worked it up and down, using soap as a lubricant, until it raised and lowered smoothly, locking into two positions, down over his own face or up, the green face looking at the kitchen ceiling. He slipped the still-damp leather headband on and tightened it with a Bakelite knob.

When he pulled it down all he could see were the worn knees of his jeans and his shoes. He tossed his head back and the mask flipped up on its own and locked with a *click*.

He imagined taking it on patrol, wearing it to family fights, coming through the door with a Cyclops eye and a robot voice.

"Obey my commands," he announced, "or death will take place here," striding across the kitchen, down the hall and out to the porch, where he nodded his head, dropping the green face down over his own. He looked up, blind in the mask, and located the sun by its heat.

A perfect sphere, floating in absolute darkness, green through the mask and seething, something most people have never seen and maybe aren't supposed to see. It was something most people don't want to see. The green sun. Up there every day, a terrible truth, like original sin. The sun was alive and it was watching him. Its angry face was infested and simmering with parasites, sunspots moving in pairs, coiled and rippling with cilia, burrowing beneath the flames across the face of the sun.

Hanson flipped the mask up, blinking in the glare, realizing how exposed and vulnerable he was on the porch when the mask was down and all he could see was the sun.

He pulled the Hi Power from his back pocket and held it against his leg, checking the empty street in both directions while the sun bore down on him. He flipped the mask back down for another look. The sun was waiting for him, steaming, boiling, looking down into the gold-mirrored eye. It began to turn, the side of its face blistering across the equator, splitting into a mouth and blowing gouts of fire.

A flare, a coronal mass ejection, Hanson thought, *and only two other people on earth saw it.* But the thoughts weren't his. He flipped the mask up. Sweat rolled down his face and stunned his eyes. He thumbed the safety off the pistol, stepped back, and told himself to slow down, be cool, don't think so much.

Only three people in the world—you, an astronomer in New Mexico looking through an X-ray telescope, and a third mate on a Maersk Line container ship in the Pacific Ocean, two days out from San Pedro.

Hanson watched the street, he looked back at the house. When the wind blew a garbage can rolling down the hill, he spun toward the clatter, the mask dropping back over his eyes, and that's when he saw him, floating in the blackness, green as the sun, wearing overalls, a company patch, DEL SOL over one pocket, the name DON over the other. He was looking at Hanson, his eyes a startling bronze, the only color other than green and black.

No sound of traffic down on Grand Avenue now, no aircraft, no shouts or horns. The wind was gone. Even his tinnitus was silent. Maybe he was finally dead, Hanson thought.

Not yet.

He recognized the voice he had heard as his own thoughts and put the gun away.

Why were you looking at the sun?

Hanson didn't know.

The flare you just saw will cause problems here.

Hanson wondered what kind of problems the flare would cause.

Darkness. A solar wind is on the way.

The eye went black. The wind picked up again. A siren warbled on the freeway, somewhere.

He raised the mask, his shadow beside him on the porch.

Most people only see Death once, he thought, and most of them try to pretend he isn't there.

He lifted the mask off and held it at arm's length, like a severed head, set it down on the porch.

In the kitchen he tossed back the drink he'd left there, poured another one and took it to the bedroom where he put it on the bedside table. He took off his clothes and got in bed. The sun, through the window, glittered in the glass of green tequila. Hanson listened to the hot wind howling around the house, rattling the warped window screens and keening beneath the eaves. He closed his eyes and went to sleep.

CHAPTER TWENTY-TWO

THE VILLE

It was dusk when Radio sent him to The Ville. He'd never been there and he'd never heard any patrol car dispatched down there, a strip of land wedged between East 14th Street and the bay. On the beat maps it wasn't clear whether The Ville was in the jurisdiction of the OPD, the Oakland Housing Authority Police, or no jurisdiction at all. The black marker pen used to draw the map boundaries cut a swath through the middle of The Ville, five or six blocks wide, along the southern border of District Four. It was another country.

All the beat maps were elusive, the way the boundary lines started and stopped, beats varying so much in size and shape, in the angles and panhandles and peninsulas. The beats were gerrymandered in or drawn at random, and always getting bigger the farther east into the ghetto they were, out in Districts Four and Five. At a glance, there appeared to be thirty-five beats, but there were only thirty-two. The numbers jumped from Beat Twenty-Eight in District Four to Beat Thirty-Two in District Five. There were no Beats Twenty-Nine to Thirty-One. The official beat map was drawn and numbered in such a confusing jigsaw pattern you wouldn't notice three missing beats unless you studied the map.

Radio told him they had a "neighborhood disturbance" down there, phoned in by several anonymous complainants, a call they'd been holding for a while. When they got more information they'd let him know.

"Okie-doke," Hanson said. "Got it. 5Tac51 be on the way."

Copy, 5Tac51.

The horizon was a band of gunmetal blue as Hanson angled down from MacArthur onto Seminary, his eyes relaxing from color into shades of gray. A bat streaked across Seminary just ahead of the patrol car, then banked away and vanished into the treetop and billboard clutter. Six or eight more caught his eye, gone in the instant he saw them, bats coming out now from attics and garages, chimneys, abandoned houses, out from under the freeway overpasses and bridges, fragile little mice with wings. In the time it took to drive two more blocks, the darkness closed over them, but they'd be up there all night.

"Call me in the darkness, I'll help you find your way…" Hanson sang softly, making up and filling in words from a song he and his dead partner, Dana, used to play on the jukebox whenever they ate at the Top Hat Café back when he was a cop in Portland. "Call me in the darkness, I'm waiting here for you."

His headlights surprised the first lookouts along the perimeter of The Ville. They spun and ducked into the shadows, calling out in their soprano little-boys' voices. "Rollers." "Rollers." "Rollers, Rollers." Their calls reminded Hanson of summer evenings when he was a little boy, the neighborhood children playing hide-and-seek. But these boys, ten and twelve years old, made three hundred dollars a week as lookouts, warning the project drug dealers when cops were in the area. They gave most of the money to their mothers, at first, anyway, if she was still alive and out of prison. Or to an auntie, a substitute mother in the neighborhood. But all of them saved up to buy a "nine," a 9mm pistol. Once they got a nine, they saved for an Uzi, because with an Uzi, they thought, nobody could fuck with them. If they survived long enough to take over a corner franchise to sell cocaine or heroin, the Uzi would keep the other motherfucker from taking it away from them. They were the smartest, most ambitious, hardest working children in the ghetto. They would do well in their world, but few of them would live to be twenty. They'd never grow up and they'd die like soldiers.

Hanson turned into the entrance to The Ville—there seemed to be one way in and one way out—and the calls of "Roller" were fewer and softer, following him like doves down the street, wondering what was he doing there in a one-man patrol car. They were accustomed to task force assaults by the OPD, DEA, FBI, DOJ—convoys of marked and unmarked cars, communication trucks, armored SWAT personnel carriers, and the helicopter overhead with its spotlight, issuing commands from the night sky.

The Ville was spread out, hundreds of row houses and little two-story duplexes on curving streets and cul-de-sacs. It was an old lowest-bid project, built at the beginning of Lyndon Johnson's Great Society, a self-contained ghetto within the larger ghetto of East Oakland, where the houses had begun falling apart the day they were finished.

An enormous full moon was rising. It dwarfed The Ville and, silhouetted against it, the weather-ravaged roofs and carports looked almost thatched, reminding Hanson of a Vietnamese village.

He didn't know what he was looking for as he slowly drove into the place, maneuvering through parked and junked and stripped cars on both sides of the already narrow streets. Street numbers above the doors had all been torn off long ago, and there were no street signs still standing, if there ever had been. Dead grass and bare dirt yards, the smell of trash fires, their smoke drifting across the face of the moon.

In the dark it would be impossible to catch someone running away if they had any kind of lead at all. Behind all the chain-link fencing, the project would be a labyrinth of ditches, dead hedges, discarded appliances and furniture, clotheslines, ankle-high trip wire strung through the weeds, foundation crawl spaces, culverts, and dark, abandoned apartments where the walls had been sledge-hammered through to other houses.

He found a space where he could angle-park the patrol car out of the street, pulling partly up over the curb, and told Radio he was there.

"Any name or address on a complainant?" Hanson asked.

Negative, 5Tac51.

"What *is* it you'd like me to do, then? Since I'm here and all."

Wait one.

He could hear a muffled exchange in the Radio room, urgent and curt, almost an argument, then Radio came back and she sounded like she was reading instructions word for word:

Surveil the area for a disturbance while displaying a police presence.

"Right," Hanson said, almost laughing. "I'll advise.

"Hello, moon," he said. "Moon, moon, moon," singing as he got out of the car, pulling a sap glove onto his left hand, flexing his fingers and tucking the right glove behind the heavy brass buckle of his gun belt. He snatched his nightstick from the driver's armrest and kicked the door shut. If the patrol car got trashed he'd be up past dawn doing paperwork, but he wasn't going to drive around, a doofus cop, waiting for something to happen. He'd rather move out on foot and make something happen.

He'd been in worse places at night. The darkness is your friend.

As he walked down the cracked and buckled sidewalk, shadows were tracking him, like children in Vietcong villages, just doing their jobs.

A kid on a big-wheeled bike came around the corner, leaning into the turn, surprising Hanson and himself, too late to stop or turn around, so he reared up into a wheelie, spinning the bike on the back tire, his eyes on Hanson, cutting them away and back again, like a twirling dancer.

"Whoa," Hanson said, startled but almost laughing, "how's it goin', young man? You seen any kind of problem for the po-lice?"

"*You* the problem," he said over his shoulder, dropping the front wheel and vanishing back the way he'd come.

Hanson walked on, deeper into The Ville, and picked a row house at random. The windows were dark, and the door was reinforced with sheet metal, with no doorknob or handle. The moon was behind him, his shadow growing to meet him as he walked up onto the concrete stoop. He rapped with his short wood on his shadow, listened, knocked again, heard the dead bolt turn, and stepped to the side, hand on his pistol. The door opened the width of a night chain.

"Good evening," Hanson said. The chain rattled off, the door opened wider, and the moon threw his shadow inside and past the hunchback dwarf who'd opened the door. He cocked his head back and looked up at Hanson through thick, smeared eyeglasses, one eye magnified more than the other. Squat and bow-legged, he was grinning like a primitive leprechaun with rotting teeth. Hanson recognized him. He'd been watching Hanson in the parking lot of the Black & White Liquor Store. He wore two watches outside the right cuff of his buttoned-up long-sleeve shirt.

"Yaw raw," he said, hitching his pants up. "Purloin," he said, bowing slightly and stepping aside, sweeping one hand down and out like a courtier. When Hanson stepped inside someone yelled down the stairs from the second floor, "What the fuck are you doing, Robert?"

"Nawp."

"Nothin' my ass. Close the goddamn door."

The dwarf hopped from foot to foot, rubbing his hands together, laughing silently to himself. "Kepler," he whispered to Hanson, "renoun."

"God damn it, Robert."

The dwarf put a finger to his lips, reached past Hanson, and quietly closed the door.

"Jesus," the voice upstairs said, speaking to someone else, but loud enough so the dwarf would hear him, "I should have smothered the dummy motherfucker with a pillow when he was a baby."

The dwarf gestured for Hanson to follow him, danced on his toes, then swaggered ahead, hitching his pants up again. He led Hanson through a curtained doorway into a room lit by a blue light bulb dangling from a ceiling fixture.

"Repart," the dwarf said, "Roger roo."

The walls were raw concrete, still patterned with the grain of wooden forms from twenty years before, the loops and whorls like giant fingerprints. The concrete floor was littered with fast-food trash, old newspapers, comic books and human feces. A three-foot machete hung from the wall by a nail over a bare mattress. The odor Hanson had noticed when he first walked in the front door was stronger here, nothing he'd ever smelled before.

"Yup. Roo," the dwarf said, gesturing grandly, clearly saying *All mine.* He turned and shouldered through another curtained-off doorway into a kitchen lit up like a bus station with one-hundred-watt bulbs—hell's gourmet kitchen. The stench made Hanson's eyes water, a stew of chemicals—Lysol, vomit, rotten food, and something so sour it tried to close his throat down. Tiny ziplock plastic bags shimmered like dying moths on the counters and floor. The dwarf took Hanson by the hand to the refrigerator and opened it, dancing from foot to foot, wringing his hands as if he was soaping them. Cheap frying pans covered the wire shelves, each of them crusted with an inch of something that looked like dirty plaster of Paris fudge. It was crack cocaine, the new drug from the East Coast.

The dwarf laughed and turned a circle on his toes, closed the refrigerator, pantomimed smoking a pipe, drawing hard on it, then threw his shoulders back, his face slack with theatrical stupor. Then he raised one hand, perked up, rubbing his thumb and forefinger together in the gesture meaning "money." "Mop, mop, mop," he said, giving Hanson a sly glance. Wheezing with laughter, he lowered his arm and studied the two watches on his wrist. "Bog. Ron," he said, and Hanson heard and felt the shudder of people coming down from upstairs.

"Bogron. Tawp," he said, cocking his head to look up at Hanson, grinning with delight.

"Tawp, bog," Hanson said, "retort."

The dwarf took his hand and shook it vigorously, nodding in agreement before opening the back door. "Rap, rap, retort," he said, unlatching the screenless screen door and pushing Hanson out.

The door closed behind him, and after the glare of the kitchen, Hanson stood there on the concrete stoop, blind in the moonlight. He hopped down, twisting his ankle in a tangle of wire and plastic, and stood close to the house, listening, until his vision returned. He thought that he knew where he was in relation to where the patrol car might be. He imagined the car destroyed, windows broken out, tires flat, in flames. He had no idea where he was. The moon filled the sky, rows and rows of back doors and concrete stoops glowing in its light.

When he stepped away from the house, dogs began to bark. Of

course, he thought, they must have been waiting their turn. He walked into the open, passing toppled and twisted swing sets, the ruins of a Great Society playground, thinking that he'd crossed the border to another country so illogical and dangerous that every decision is the wrong decision. Time slowed down, and he controlled his adrenaline like an IV drip—getting just what he needed but no more—feeling good.

When the three dogs came rocketing out at him from the dark he held an open palm out and they stopped, stiff legged and snarling at first, then quieting down, then coming closer, still on guard.

"Good evening, boys or girls," he said, kneeling, petting them with both hands when their eyes softened and they came to him, their tails wagging madly. "Thanks for showing up at this thing." They licked his hands and smiled their doggie smiles, as if Hanson was an old friend come back from the dead. They were night dogs, coyote-size urban survivors, ghetto dogs. "Lost my patrol car. Lost myself. Wearing the badge and uniform of the oppressor. Deep in the shit, down the rabbit hole, guys," Hanson said.

Tyree stepped out of the gloom and the dogs ran off.

"Your car's okay. It's being looked after. Fee said he would like to talk to you, if you have a moment."

"Fee?"

"Felix the Cat."

Hanson shook his head.

"You know," Tyree said, smiling, "Uncle Felix. Owns the Rolls."

"Why's he want to talk to me?"

"He's worried about you, walking around here like this."

"Well," Hanson said, "I'm glad my patrol car isn't on fire. But I always expect the worst, you know? Let's go, then. I'm ready to leave."

Tyree seemed to be leading him deeper into The Ville and

Hanson thought that the first person he'd shoot, if this was some kind of ambush, would be Tyree. And he liked Tyree. Then he'd kill as many of the others as he could before they killed him. Too bad.

Then they walked through a break in the row houses, and the patrol car was there, next to the Rolls. Felix was alone. It was three months since he and Hanson had spoken to each other, the night that Hanson fucked up Lemon.

"Officer Hanson," he said. "This *is* a bad neighborhood. I grew up here, so I know. You shouldn't be walking around here after dark, by yourself."

"Radio sent me."

"We heard that, but why would they send you here? The police never come down here, unless it's a whole lot of them, and I know ahead of time when they plan to arrive. That keeps things simple but interesting."

"Thank you for looking after my patrol car."

"I've heard that you are not well liked on the Department. Would you say that's true?"

Hanson nodded. "Three more days and six months till I get my POST certificate, then I'm gone."

"Where will you go?"

"I'm looking for a smaller department with a different perspective on enforcing the law."

"If you live that long. Since we first met, the Department has consistently sent you, by yourself, to extremely dangerous situations. I think someone on the Department is hoping you'll be killed."

"I can't be killed."

Felix smiled, not so much with amusement as something like affection. "Who can say? I'm more pessimistic about my own mortality but just as certain. What troubles me is the feeling that whoever sent you down here tonight hoped you'd be killed and then they'd put it on *me*. I've got a little cottage industry started. Creating jobs, as they say, in my old neighborhood. I'm telling you this in confidence. I hope I can depend on your discretion, because I know you walked through one of my employees' houses."

"Where's Levon?"

"Taking a nap. I picked him up at the airport this afternoon—he hates airplanes. He's been talking about retiring and was looking at some retirement property, far from here. But listen, I think you should work for me. I don't trust anybody I've got in the OPD anymore, and I'm still paying out a lot of money. I confess I've checked you out from before you came here and think we could—"

"You wouldn't trust me as soon as I went to work for you. Because then, as much as I don't like the Department, if I worked for both of you, I wouldn't be trust*worthy*. I couldn't do that, and besides, I'd get caught in no time. I'm no good at lying. I might as well wear a neon hat flashing guilty, guilty, guilty. I was stupid to get out of the patrol car. And again, I appreciate you looking after it. So I'll just go back to work now, no harm done one way or another. Fair enough?"

"Of course."

"Thank you, Tyree, for finding me wherever I was," Hanson said. "Good night."

Hanson got into his patrol car and started it up, keyed the microphone, told Radio, "5Tac51 will be 908. All problems solved upon departure."

Copy, 5Tac51—908.

Back at the Justice Center, the lieutenant who is on Felix's payroll stood looking out his office window on the seventh floor, listening to Hanson's voice on his police scanner.

*　　*　　*

Hanson is sleeping

He's back at The Ville, invisible this time, transparent as air, and alone in the deserted projects. He doesn't know why he's there or who sent him, but he assumes the worst. His senses are fine-tuned to threat as he moves silently from shadow to shadow. This is what his life is like when he sleeps—another full-time job. He's always working.

Water whispers through the corroded pipes in the wall next to his bed. The refrigerator clicks on down the hall in the kitchen, shudders, and begins to hum, heating up as it once again tries to pump a vacuum with a cracked compressor.

Across town, up in the regional park, Felix Maxwell and three of his men remove bodies from the back of a windowless van. They are wrapped in black plastic garbage bags and silver duct tape, heavy and limp and hard to carry. Rigor has come and gone and the bodies are beginning to bloat. Felix's men line them up on the hilltop and, one by one, try to roll them downhill like logs, but they bounce and twist and tumble into the brush, upending, sailing into the trees where the hillside drops off, branches breaking, tearing the bags, until the body wedges to a stop and it's quiet again. These men don't see the green and blue aurora curtains over the bay, swaying above the dark water until the charged solar wind rips them apart on its way to the North Bay electrical grid.

They've just launched the fourth bagged corpse down the hill when, far below, the flatlands of East Oakland—that dreary jigsaw pattern of light and dark—go black and disappear into the horizon. Downtown goes dark, the billboards and motel signs along the highway vanish. The darkness, like a tide, races up from East Oakland, across the freeway, and past, turning off all light in the hills above them.

CHAPTER TWENTY-THREE

CHINATOWN

Hanson took the underpass beneath 580, new graffiti—OAKLAND IS SOUTH AFRICA—spooling past, painted in turquoise blue on the bare concrete, and angled up onto the freeway, on his way in for the night, singing as loud as he could: "Gotta bop down the road, got a heavy load, bop, bop, pushing my truck," cool predawn air roaring through the windows as he pushed the junker patrol car to seventy, seventy-five, until it began to shimmy. "Gonna bop my baby, and I don't mean may-beee, bop, bop, I'm down on my luck..."

3L21, what is your 926? 3L21...

It was the third time Radio had called 3L21 in the past half hour. 3L21 was probably asleep in somebody's garage. Or dead. Hanson laughed.

"Bopping with my baby out in LA. She lives just off the freeway, gonna find her today."

His face was sunburned and stiff with dried sweat and grit from the wind that had finally gone away around 2 a.m. The patrol car began to crab to the right, and he slowed it down a little.

"Bee bop a lu bop, I'm down on my luck..."

He switched his Radio over to channel one just as 3L11 gave his location down in Chinatown, requesting another cover car and a supervisor.

3L11, I'm still trying to locate a supervisor. I'll assign another car as soon as I have one available...Do you want to declare a Code 33 emergency?

Negative at this time.

"I say bee bop a lu bop, yeah, yeah, yeah..."

The off-ramp to Chinatown, the last exit before Grove Street and the Justice Center, was coming up fast, just up ahead.

Car to cover 3L11 on shots fired? 3L21?

"Beepin' and a boppin', down on my luck," Hanson sang, taking the off-ramp on impulse, curious what 3L11 had, not telling Radio, knowing that it was probably a mistake.

Two patrol cars were angle-parked up the block from the address. He flipped his overheads on and off, so they'd know he was in the area and maybe not shoot him when he walked up to them, then continued around the corner where he pulled to the curb and got out of the car, gently clicking the door closed.

Chinatown at 4 a.m., the hot wind gone now, not even a breeze left, the pavement hot through his double-sole, steel-toed combat boots. Striding quietly—heel and toe, heel and toe—watching the street ahead, the doors and windows on both sides of the street, and the street behind, the barred windows of storefronts and the rear windows of parked cars.

He passed a phone booth, the armored cord—no receiver attached—dangling from the crowbarred coin box. A Christian fish symbol was drawn in Magic Marker on the wire-reinforced glass, JESUS LOVES YOU printed beneath. He'd been seeing them everywhere in Oakland the past few weeks, all three inches long, identical, done by a single person. He imagined the artist as a slightly chubby, fourteen-year-old black girl who believed if she drew enough of them they might make Oakland a better place. But then again, it might be a psychopath with a hatchet who'd gotten religion the last time he was in the joint, looking for people to Kill for Jesus when he wasn't drawing fish.

He turned the corner into the sweet-rot nimbus of a restaurant Dumpster, toward the static of police radios, never breaking step as he raised up on his toes to glance inside the Dumpster. Winos sometimes slept in them on pieces of cardboard. Died in them too, for the day shift to find. "Baby, baby, baby, an' I don't mean maybeeee, bop, bop, a lu bop…"

He was off OPD's clock now, doing this on his own time after twelve and a half hours going from call to call all across East Oakland, dealing with angry, frightened, insane people who always kept guns and knives close by. Some nights while he talked to them he saw their thoughts floating above their heads like cartoon captions. He'd had a protein powder milkshake and a candy bar that morning—yesterday morning—but he wasn't hungry now, wired and jacked up on adrenaline. He didn't need food. He didn't need sleep. He had the momentum and the glow.

Two graveyard shift guys in their mid-twenties crouched behind a patrol car, their revolvers braced on the roof, pointed at a shattered second-floor window across the street. Hanson had never seen either of them before. Both of them were wearing their hats, the gleaming gold hat badges like aiming stakes for the center of their foreheads. But they wouldn't get gigged for not wearing their hats if a sergeant ever showed up.

"Hey, what's up, Occifers?" he said. "Looks like an episode of *Adam-12* to me. You know, life imitating art."

"Get down," one of the cops hissed, keeping his stainless steel revolver aimed at the window.

"Grab some cover," the other one said, "before he shoots your ass."

"Wow. That's a serious felony. He shoot at you guys?"

They stared at the spotlighted blown-out window.

"He shoot anybody?"

"Not yet."

"He pumped some rounds through that window, and the door too."

"Chinatown, my Chinatown, when the lights are low," Hanson sang, pausing to make up the next line. "Chinamen with little feet, who knows where…they go…

"Is the shooter up there a person of the Chinese persuasion?"

"White guy."

Broken glass glittered in the street. Hanson walked out into the street, his pistol still holstered, keeping an eye on the window but holding his head so that he looked like he wasn't paying any attention to it. He crouched down and shined his Kel-Lite an inch or so above the asphalt.

Lead pellets the size of peppercorns glowed among the shards of glass. He turned off the flashlight, picked one up, and walked back, rolling it between his thumb and forefinger, singing softly, "You gotta bop, and keep bopping, do it till your luck turns around, just don't ever stop when you're riding the bop."

He popped the shot in his mouth and rolled it with his tongue, back and forth against his lower teeth, the sound reminding him of a girl back in Montana, when he was in graduate school. A barmaid at the Eastgate Liquor Store and Lounge, who had a steel stud in her tongue. The first one he'd ever seen. She'd come over to his table, picked up his long neck bottle of Coors, holding it like a cock, tilting it up against the light to see if he was ready for another.

"What's that thing in your tongue for?" he asked.

She just smiled at him, licked her upper lip with the studded pink tongue, and asked if he wanted another beer.

"Yes, ma'am," he'd said, "with a shot of Jameson's this time, please."

Before the night was over, he'd found out what the stud was for. He remembered how she used to run it clattering across her teeth when she was angry.

He tucked the shot under his lower lip and walked back to the car, leaning over the hood and looking at the two cops.

"You got a plan?"

"We've been waiting for a supervisor for half an hour."

Hanson spit the piece of bird shot out and laughed. "Fuck this guy," he said. "We look like dorks," reaching through the open window of the car to turn on the overheads.

"Hey," he said to them, "don't ever stop when you're ridin' the bop."

He sprung his clamshell holster open and walked across the street, pistol against his leg, almost invisible in the red and blue strobes that broke up his profile, seemingly carried across the street by the double sweep of lights, as if it was a colored wind.

The door to the narrow stairway to the second floor hung half open, splintered by the shotgun. The light up on the landing was still shining, even though the Sheetrock on both sides of the stairs was streaked and torn by shotgun pellets, powder burns, and black lubricant from the shot. The air was hazy with Sheetrock dust and the pepper smell of gun smoke, the white dust settling on his shirt and pants, puffing from beneath his boots with each step. He held his revolver two-handed, loaded with the illegal .357 hollow points all the cops carried, aimed at the closed door at the top of the stairs. The door was hinged to open inward, so in the time it would take the asshole to pull the door open and level his shotgun, Hanson could blow his heart out his back.

The landing was narrow, and kicking the door in would be awkward. He reached across his body with his left hand, tried the knob—not locked—backhanded the door open, and swung his pistol toward the double bed that filled half the room. A single room, sink in the corner, toilet down the hall, stinking of sweat, marijuana, and urine—decades of it. It seemed two-dimensional in the dispersed glare of the spotlight.

Three people lay on top of the dirty, bare mattress, the asshole on the far side, passed out, the shotgun, a Remington 870 pump, just like the po-lice carried, at his side in a sort of unconscious "shoulder arms." He was big, going to fat, wearing pink boxer shorts patterned with swollen red hearts. Closest to the door, lying stiffly, legs together, arms at her sides, was a pretty white woman in her thirties, and in between them, a girl not more than twelve years old, skinny, both naked, their eyes on Hanson as he stepped around the bed.

He lowered his pistol to the man's forehead, making quick eye contact with the two women, whispering hoarsely, "Get out," gesturing with his head at the open door. "Get out," his eyes now steady down the barrel of the pistol, holding it angled a few inches above the man's left eye.

The woman grabbed clothes from a dirty pile on the floor, yanked the girl up out of the bed. The wall above the bed, lit by the spotlight flaring off the ceiling, was covered with Polaroid photos, some new and glossy, others curling, the thin layer of black-and-white emulsion—the photo itself—crazed and peeling away from the backing. Hanson looked at them as the woman and child went out the door and pounded down the stairs. For-shit photos of the asshole in various sexual poses with the mother, the daughter, or both of them, and some of just the mother and daughter doing sexual things with tongues and fingers and a dildo that was veined, realistic in detail but oversize and a bright purple.

The asshole was white, as were the woman and girl. A white

guy. Bought and paid for. It would be a good shooting. Hanson would just say that the asshole raised the shotgun and he shot him in self-defense. He lifted the shotgun out of the man's fat, open hand and pushed the safety on with his thumb.

The flashes of red and blue coming through the slats of the blinds cycled faster now, more of them, car doors began slamming. When he heard boots pounding up the stairs, he yelled, "Police officer! Police officer! Code 4. Suspect is in custody." Now he wished he was wearing his stupid bus driver's hat with the badge on it so the cops wouldn't shoot him. "Police officer," he shouted, leaning the shotgun against the filthy sink and stepping out into the middle of the room, still watching the asshole but holding his pistol by his side.

Two cops came through the door, one with a shotgun, the other with his pistol drawn. They made eye contact with Hanson, who stepped farther back as the cops rushed around the bed, jerking the asshole up and off the bed by his arms and his hair, grabbing for pieces of him. They slammed him, face-first, against the wall and punched him in the kidneys, the smack of their fists leaving red blotches, dragged and threw him on the floor.

They called him motherfucker and handcuffed him, stood him up like a log and hit him some more.

Hanson handed the shotgun to the next cop who came through the door, who, surprised, took it, and Hanson said "Good job" as he squeezed past him and down the stairs and outside, where the air didn't smell as bad, and crossed the street past three empty patrol cars silently sweeping the street and store windows with red and blue lights, slipped past the Dumpster, and vanished.

He drove the few blocks to the Transportation lot at the Justice Center, telling Radio, "5Tac51 is 908."

Copy, 5Tac51—908.

The locker room was empty, between shifts, and his boots

echoed as he walked past a wall locker painted Mary Kay pink, a pair of pink satin high-heel pumps side by side in front of it. A sign on the locker door read FOR OPD'S FIRST FAGGOT COP. San Francisco was hiring them, but not Oakland. Not knowingly, anyway.

He took a shower and changed into jeans, running shoes, and a black T-shirt, threw a bag over his shoulder, slammed the locker shut and locked it, and walked the three deserted blocks to where his Travelall was parked. He got in, wrenched the door shut, and reached beneath the bench seat for the flat little half pint of Popov.

He drank it down in four swallows, the vodka blooming in his stomach as he studied the massive sweep of concrete spiraling up to the already busy freeway above him. His eyes relaxed, his shoulders relaxed, he slumped into the seat listening to the *thump, thump-thump* of cars and trucks on the metal expansion ridges in the freeway overhead.

With any luck, no one would mention him in the paperwork. He wasn't there. The Department wouldn't want to pay the overtime, the other cops would want the credit, and they could write it up as if it had been done by the book. Correct procedures had been followed, the suspect taken, professionally, into custody. An excellent felony arrest that a dozen officers could add to their monthly arrest quotas.

As usual, Hanson was behind on his arrest stats for the month, but he could scoop up a few junkies for track marks before the end of the report period. Or he could always talk a citizen into taking a swing at him. He never had to say anything he couldn't repeat in court. It was what Hanson said with his eyes when he smiled at the citizen and violated his personal space. It was easy to pick out someone who wanted to hit him, then insult him into taking a swing. He could see the punch coming with plenty of time to avoid it, kick the guy's legs out from under him, drop a knee into his neck, handcuff and arrest him. It was more work and riskier than an 11550 H&S narcotics arrest, but assault on a police officer was a solid felony stat, and it left him feeling better than he did after popping a junkie for needle tracks. A little better, once the rush of the fight wore off. Most of the people he talked into swinging on him were drunk or just stupid, but too bad. Arresting people for being addicted to drugs, or insulting and bullying someone into taking a swing at you, was just part of filling up your stat sheet. And he knew, of course, that he could have been the asshole with the shotgun on the bed, and the asshole could have been him in a police uniform, and it wouldn't make any difference at all.

He took Grand Avenue, turned onto Lakeshore, parked the Travelall, and got out. Lake Merritt was silver and gray blue in the dawn.

A horse-drawn carriage turned onto the street, the slow *clop, clop* of hooves on the asphalt. It was Champagne, in brass-studded black harness and blinders, taking her time. Mickey, impeccable in tuxedo and top hat, stopped next to the Travelall, reins loose in his hands.

"Hey there, little girl," Hanson said, his shoulders and arms relaxing, the whine and chirp of his tinnitus softer, further away. "I've got something for you. In my off-duty vehicle. Been carrying it around for days now."

He walked over, reached through the open window of the Travelall, and took out a plastic Baggie—a dozen sugar cubes he'd picked up at All-American Burger earlier in the week.

"Okay if I give these to her, Mickey?"

"Of course," Mickey said from the high seat of the carriage.

Hanson held out the cubes, one at a time, in his open palm.

"Late night, Officer Hanson?"

"One late call, in Chinatown, my own fault. Hoped I'd see you two here on the way in. I met this woman, out in East Oakland, got 'involved' with her, I guess you could say. She's real good-looking and smart too. I like her and, well, we're hot for each other too. I am, anyway, and I think it's the same for her.

"Listen, I'm laying this on you because I trust you and I don't know who else to ask about it. I apologize, so…"

"Just keep talking. We're interested, and you know, I'm just a fool for romance myself, Officer."

"Sometimes I just ache for her. And I don't know if I can, or at least if I want to, keep hacking this job and life in general out here by myself anymore." It was the first time Hanson had said anything to anyone about Libya.

"So what's the problem with you and her?"

"She's black and I'm a white cop and it seems stupid to even consider it."

Mickey laughed. "It's all stupid. With anybody. If you're worried about getting fired by the OPD that you so enjoy working for, that's one thing, but otherwise what have you got to lose? I'd recommend a direct course of action to see what's possible and what's not. Right or wrong, that's my view on matters such as this. You gotta be prepared for consequences, but that's nothing I have to tell you about. If I was you, the job you have, I'd sure give it a try. You're not very happy, if you'll allow me, and she might be great for you. Or not. Give it a try."

Hanson nodded. A direct course of action was the best way to deal with anything.

"I have news too," Mickey said. "We're moving up to Lone Pine in a few days. Retiring. Both of us. We'll be there for Fourth of July."

Hanson fed Champagne another sugar cube and tried to take it in. He'd gotten used to seeing them once or twice a week, on his way home, by the lake. It made him feel less crazy, talking life over with a decent guy who was a queer carriage driver from San Francisco. "Well," Hanson said, "you never mentioned that before."

"I built a cabin and a barn up there twenty years ago, on land I inherited from my grandfather…came into a little money." He leaned down toward Hanson. "One lucky bet, on a horse. Couldn't afford to build anything up there what it would cost now. Have to live in a tent." He clucked at Champagne. "Champagne, you'd be in a corral—no warm place for you when the snow comes."

"I'll miss seeing you here at the lake. But I'm glad you'll be in a good, safe place."

"Ah, the lake is lovely, isn't it? Like that Yeats poem you're so fond of. 'The Lake Isle of Innisfree.' Hanson," he said, "I've told my brother about you. I told him you'd make a fine deputy sheriff. *We* told him, didn't we, Champagne? He'd find a job for you. A Peace Officer certificate would be superfluous. He can hire who he wants."

"I've never been to Lone Pine. Only seen it in the movies," Hanson said. "It's a fairy tale to me."

"I was thirteen, fourteen maybe, when they filmed *High Sierra* on the Whitney Portal Road. My brother got Humphrey Bogart's autograph," Mickey said, "and my first lover was a gaffer with the movie crew." Mickey hadn't talked about Lone Pine before. Mostly they'd talked about poetry and Mickey had told him stories about the gay scene in San Francisco.

"Lone Pine is real to us. It's our home I think, eh, girl," he said, turning to Champagne, the reins light in his hands as he raised them, both he and the horse straightening their shoulders, their posture perfect, prepared to go. Then he reached down to Hanson.

"It's been a real pleasure," Hanson said, taking his hand. "Good luck to both of you."

"The pleasure's been ours, Officer Hanson. You come and visit us. Any time. You're always welcome."

"Who knows? Maybe I will."

"In the meantime, you be careful. This is no place for you, if you don't mind my saying so, since I've said it before. Champagne thinks your talents are wasted here too."

"Lone Pine. Maybe I'll visit," Hanson said, but he knew he'd never go. Maybe he would. Who knew? "Champagne," he said, touching her again, then stepping back, checking for traffic.

Mickey clucked to the horse, twitched the reins with his fingers, and started to drive on. Then he checked Champagne and said to Hanson, who hadn't moved. "Direct course of action, Officer Hanson. Why not?"

Lone Pine was halfway between Death Valley and Mount Whitney, the tallest peak in the lower forty-eight. When he finally got his POST certificate maybe he should go for a visit, see Mickey and Champagne and introduce himself to the high sheriff. He was really going to miss Mickey and Champagne.

He got in the Travelall and was halfway through an illegal U-turn when he stopped in the middle of the street. Weegee was walking his bike on the other side of the lake. It looked like Weegee. It was Weegee, and he was with Libya.

He drove on, up Grand to the other side of the lake, where he pulled up over the curb, got out of the Travelall and jogged over to where he'd seen them on the walkway in the trees—or thought he had. He couldn't find them. Just another hallucination.

Hanson is sleeping.

Across town, in East Oakland, Weegee and Libya are eating pancakes after getting back from Lake Merritt.

"We're going to need a nap after getting up so early," Libya said, "but it was worth it, to see the lake at dawn like that."

"Yes, ma'am," Weegee said, finishing his milk. "Before the sun came up, I felt like I was invisible."

"The lake," she said, as they walked to the bedroom, "and that beautiful white horse. It was like a fairy tale. So quiet."

"We haven't heard the neighbor lady's dogs lately," Weegee said. "Why they so quiet?"

"They left town. Packed their little dog suitcases. Stole a car and drove to Texas," she said, plumping her pillow and looking at the clock. Weegee lay next to her, his hands behind his head, looking at the ceiling, thinking.

"Why they want to go to Texas?"

"They have a cousin in Dallas. He's a real bad dog, named Red Spot, who robs banks and liquor stores, sells dope, everything you can imagine. The Law Dogs are always after him, but he's too smart for a bunch of Texas cracker Law Dogs. The dogs next door wrote him a letter telling him that they wanted to be gangstas, and Red Spot's momma, Arlene Pit Bull, said he had to help 'em out.

"Red Spot said, 'But, Momma, what I'm gonna do with those spoiled little indoor dogs? All they know how to do is jump up on the sofa, poop on the carpet, and bark, bark, bark. How they gonna be gangstas?'"

Weegee laughed. "That's what I'd say."

"She's a tough old pit bull, Weegee. She just told him, 'Son, they family, that's all that matters.'

"'But they from Uncle Barko's sorry-dog family down in Mississippi,' Red Spot said, 'an' the best they could do was steal an old worn-out Chevy Monte Carlo with slick tires.'

"'Red Spot,' his momma say, 'I know you'll find 'em something.' And that was the end of the conversation."

"What the names of those dogs? That went to Texas. I never did know."

"LeRon and JJ."

"What's that ole Red Spot gonna do with LeRon and JJ? They so high-strung all the time and make so much noise the po-lice would catch 'em right away."

"I don't know, but he's gonna have to find 'em some kind of gangsta work. That's all I know about it now, so let's close our eyes and take a little nap."

Weegee fell silent. He had the look he got when he wanted to tell her something serious. Weegee went everywhere and he kept his eyes open.

"How come you never say anything about Fee?" Weegee said. "Everyone knows him but you never even say his name."

"Fee? You talking about Felix Maxwell?"

"Yes, ma'am."

"I knew him a long time ago," she said, "when we were both real young. He was different then."

"Don't you like him anymore?"

"Baby, he was different, a nice man sometimes. I got real sick once—from some of the stuff he sells now—and he helped me get well. But now, honey, it's dangerous even to be around him. You know it would break my heart if you got hurt because of him."

"Naw," he said. "I'm too fast to get hurt. 'Faster than a bullet' is what Fee says."

Her eyes got hard, but she softened them, collecting herself. "Honey, you should stay away from him."

"I see him all the time," Weegee told her, "all the time. He's a hero. He gives money to people who live in The Ville. Buys all the poor people Christmas dinners. Everybody cheer when he drives by in his beautiful Rolls-Royce car, say he's like Robin Hood, who was a gangsta in the olden times. He takes from the rich white people and gives to the poor black people. Just like old Robin Hood."

"He's not Robin Hood. He's—well—he's a bad man now," she said, more sad than angry. "Now he sells that bad stuff to his own people. Takes their money and keeps it for himself. He kills people, Weegee."

"He *has* to," Weegee said, "or they'd kill *him*. He's brave and smart, and he's always real nice to me, talks to me like I'm grown-up and says when I get a little older he'll give me a job and you won't have to worry about money because I'll take care of you."

"Oh baby," she said. "I love you so much that I think I'd die if you got hurt. Come over here and give me a big hug and let's go to sleep and dream about that beautiful white horse and how we could ride him away from Oakland, to a place where everything is beautiful and nice—where it's safe all the time."

CHAPTER TWENTY-FOUR

DEVILS & ANGELS

"The only, uh—All I can do if I, uh, if I get mad at some, uh, asshoe. Fu-fu-fuckin' asshoe. If I get mad, uh, all I can do is bump, *bump* 'em with my wheelchair."

"They send me out here again I'm gonna have to arrest you and your wheelchair. Load you both up and haul you to jail. They'll cut you loose in the morning, but you'll have to spend the night *locked up* with assholes. There's no handicap facilities down there. You'll be sittin' in your own piss when the sun comes up. So why don't you just go home and save us both a lot of grief? I don't need the paperwork."

"Fu-fuhkin' asshoes," he stuttered, spraying spit on his sunken chest. "What I'm ssssposed-supposed to do some asshoe fuh, uh, fuh, you know, if he…fucksss with me?"

"You're the one who fucks with people."

"Buh, ah, buh shit! If you wash, *you* was in this fuh, fuhkin' wheechair…"

5Tac51, can you go?

"Wait one," Hanson said to him, holding a hand up and taking his PAC-set off his belt. "What you got?"

A problem with some bikers at the Lone Butte Tavern, fifty-four hundred Foothill. It's off your district, but you're all we've got, and the barmaid just called for the third time.

"Yeah. I can go."

Be advised that you'll be Code 6....

"Fine. From Seventy-sixth and Holly."

"What I'm sssspisss...sup-osed to, if all, you know, all I, all I can..."

"If all you can do is bump 'em with your wheelchair?"

"Uh, uh..."

"Save your money. Buy a gun. Somebody fucks with you, shoot 'em."

"But, but, uh, buu..."

"*Steal* some money if you have to. Or else stay out of bars. But don't get me called back here tonight."

"A guuu, you think, I, uh, a guu..."

Hanson nodded. "Yeah. A revolver. Something you can hide in the wheelchair that won't go off by accident. I gotta go. I don't want to have to come back and arrest you. Get some money. Buy a gun. But go home tonight. Please. Okay?"

"Oh-kay, Offi-Officer, buu..."

"Thank you," Hanson said. "I appreciate it. Get some sleep. It's a fucked up world." Hanson walked around the patrol car and opened the driver's door. "You know that better than I do."

The Man in the Moon's doughy face was lopsided, swollen, as if he'd taken a beating, bobbing through high, thin clouds.

Hanson looked at him over the roof of the patrol car. "But don't shoot *me*."

"Uh, uh, I, uh."

"I gave you my best advice. Is that fair?"

"Oh, I, uh, yeah…"

"Okay, then. Good night. Go home. Go get some sleep."

"Guh-good, uh, okay…"

Hanson got in the patrol car, shut the door, made a U-turn, and drove west on East 14th. In his rearview mirror he saw a flash of chrome from the wheelchair. Up ahead, the dark windows of abandoned businesses threw his headlights back at him.

A blur of movement.

Up at the next corner, across the street between the car wash and a burned-out storefront. He punched the gas, jumped the curb and bailed out of the car, running, but whatever it was was gone. He caught his breath next to a car wash wall with SANTANA FUCKED IVONE IN THE CAR WASH spray-painted on it.

He walked down the street and found two parked cars with the passenger windows smashed, glove boxes rifled, and a tape deck torn out of one of them. He'd let the owners call the police in the morning, but he followed the fresh footprints in the dust, leading away from the cars, down into a stand of brush and spindly trees fed by runoff water from the car wash, where he listened, studied the trees in his peripheral vision, looked at the stars. He skidded ten or twelve feet farther downhill, reached up, grabbed a tree branch, and bent it down until a pistol dropped into his other hand. The weather was warmer. People were washing their cars more often. The trees were greening up and were a popular place to ditch weapons.

It was an old top-break Harrington & Richardson .38, which had been dangling from the trigger guard, a six-shot revolver loaded with four mismatched rounds. The chrome plating was blistered with rust, the barrel and cylinders caked with oil and dirt, the grips gone and replaced with wraps and wads of black electrical tape. A gun that might not shoot at all, might go off by accident, or might explode in your hand. But it never hurt to have an extra throw-down gun.

He turned off his lights half a block away from the Lone Butte and pulled to the curb, where he got out of the patrol car and walked the quiet street toward the tavern. His OPD star and a pair of silver wings over his left pocket glowed in the streetlight. That morning he'd found his silver army jump wings in a dresser drawer. He'd polished them up and, after roll call, pinned them on his uniform shirt just above his silver OPD badge.

The Butte was a couple of blocks from the Hell's Angels club-house. It was their turf, and they usually took care of their own problems, putting them in the hospital without bothering the police. Two dozen chopped and customized bikes were angle-parked in front of the place.

There wasn't a butte within two hundred miles of Oakland. A warped wooden shipping pallet suspended on chains above the door of the bar creaked in the breeze. It had been painted with someone's idea of a butte. It looked more like a rogue wave or a volcano, but it was real enough. It contained its own correct-ness. In some other world, certainly, there were buttes like that one, a desolate dark landscape, seen or remembered by whoever painted it, through an alcoholic blackout or seizure, in a skid row flop where the windows were nailed shut and the ceiling covered with chicken wire.

Something—*thump…thump…thump*—was pounding the heavy windowless door from the inside, like someone slamming a victim repeatedly, expertly, and rhythmically, against it. Hanson could feel it too, an almost sexual ache, in his arms and shoulders. It had been a while since he'd gotten to pound somebody that way. He pulled the door open and felt himself free-falling through a thun-derstorm of sound and light.

We're kickin' ass and takin' names,
Down and dirty, ain't playin' no games

A vintage jukebox was pulled out from the wall, its swollen plastic pipes and bubble windows throbbing with retro neon, turned up so loud Hanson imagined it torquing with bass notes, like a cartoon, side to side, across the floor.

Gonna hunt you down, kick in your door,
Biker soldiers goin' to war—All right!

Guitars and keyboard pounding, buzzing, snarling and honking with feedback, chattering, ringing like bagpipes taking you out of the trenches and over the top and into massed machine-gun fire but who gave a fuck? Not Hanson. Everybody dies sooner or later. Hanson could taste his own blood. He grinned. Radio had sent him to the kind of place where he belonged. But the bikers in the Lone Butte weren't Angels, they were Road Devils, some dipshit third tier membership from Sacramento that Hanson had never heard of. Reading their colors he saw they were a subsidiary club to the Angels who relied on the Angels' protection for their survival.

Kickin' ass and takin' names…

The barmaid was in her early thirties, overweight, wearing a BUD LIGHT T-shirt. When he walked toward the bar, she looked past him to the door, expecting more cops. Too bad, lady, Hanson thought, just me tonight.

I said kickin' ass and takin' some names—Yeah!

"Hi," he yelled over the music. "What can I do for you tonight?"

She sucked on the cigarette, looked again at the door. She leaned over the bar, cigarette held down at her side, and yelled into Hanson's ear, "I was supposed to close almost an hour ago. We got hours posted over there on the door."

"You asked 'em to leave?"

"Hell yeah," she said, taking a drag on her cigarette.

"Who'd you talk to?"

"The big asshole with the blue beard," she said, pointing to a huge biker wearing his vest and colors with no shirt, his gut hanging over his belt, heavy rings on all his fingers. The wraparound blue-mirror sunglasses plus the blue beard helped him look like a giant bloated insect. He had a pool cue in his hand.

Hanson smiled, nodding his head to the music.

"I told him *twice*," she shouted. "Told him I had to close up. He *laughed* at me. I got a teenage girl at home."

"I'll go talk to him"—turning and walking into the noise, past bikers and their old ladies, moving his head and shoulders to the music, as if he'd been invited to the party, his silver badge and jump wings gleaming, flashing. On the other side of a pool table, one of the Devils smashed a beer bottle over his own head, laughing as beer and fresh blood foamed from his rat's-nest hair down his neck.

Out on the road an' in the wind,
Where it ain't no law, ain't no sin

A woman in a leather bra pursed her lips in a kiss as Hanson walked by, and another pulled her tits out of a tank top, squeezing them so that delicate blue veins showed through the skin, offering them to Hanson. He took a long look, then met her bloodshot cracker-blue, dilated eyes.

Kickin' ass and takin' names…Kickin' ass and takin' names…

The chapter president, with the blue beard, was leaning on his pool cue, watching another Devil shoot. On the far side of the pool table a kid in his teens sat watching, propping a beer up to his lips. He didn't have to worry about his legs getting in the way because he had flippers instead of arms and legs, like a seal.

Kickin' ass and takin' names…Kickin' ass and takin' names…

Just as the president leaned in for a closer look, Hanson stepped up behind him. "Excuse me," he shouted. "*Excuse* me,"

Hanson yelled over the music, tapping him on the shoulder while the young man sitting on the pool table, holding his beer mug with flippers looked on with interest.

The president spun around and looked down at Hanson.

"The *lady* over there," Hanson said, gesturing toward the barmaid, "wants you to *leave* so she can *close up.*"

"People in *hell* want ice water too," the president said, turning away.

Hanson tapped him again.

"Goddammit, *what?*"

Another Devil walked over to watch.

"If you don't *leave,*" Hanson shouted, absolutely happy, "you'll be in *violation.* Of the *law,* sir. Trespassing. Then I'd have to *arrest* you. I'd appreciate it—be *grateful,* sir—if you'd take your *people* and go somewhere *else.*"

He looked at Hanson, looked at the door of the tavern. Looked at the other biker, who shrugged and shouted, "Just *him.*"

Somebody pulled the plug on the jukebox. In the silence the president's voice boomed. "You fuckin' guys. How stupid do you think we are? They send you in here by yourself, then when we start kicking your ass, the rest of the precinct comes through the door. Maybe if they sent a couple of big guys in here, throwing their weight around. A couple of motorcycle pigs. We might fall for it. Or three or four. I'll tell you fuckin' *what,* though…"

That's when Hanson saw Pogo, the Angel Barnes and Durham had set him up to arrest that time at the Anchor Tavern. He'd been watching from the foyer to the men's room. He walked over, gestured to Hanson—*Just a second*—and said something to the president of the Devils. The president looked at Hanson, shook his head.

"Let's go," he announced, circling his hand above his head. "Let's get in the fuckin' wind."

"You'd *better* move your asses out of here," the barmaid yelled, holding a phone aloft. "I called the police, a *lot* of—"

One of the bikers stiff-armed her into the wall behind the bar.

Hanson and Pogo followed the Devils outside and watched them start their bikes and thunder off, the kid with flippers holding on, behind the president, on the pussy pad.

"I better go, Occifer," Pogo said. "Nobody's blaming you for that shit back in the Anchor Tavern. It was those two biker cop assholes set it up." He got on his bike, about to kick-start it. "And you're something for luck, man. If I hadn't been there, what did you think you were gonna do?"

"Watch 'em leave or arrest 'em, sir," Hanson said, grinning, purely elated, the way he'd felt every time he'd survived a firefight. "They didn't leave me no selection on that."

"Shit," Pogo said, grinning himself, showing all his meth-rotted teeth. "I could see that you were a standup motherfucker right away, back at the Anchor Tavern," he said, kicking his bike to life. "Take care of yourself out here at night, Hanson." He laughed, gestured *Fuck 'em!* with his fist and forearm, and was gone as sirens wailed, getting closer, from all directions—one, then two patrol cars coming around the corner with their overhead lights flaring, the first one Sergeant Jackson's car.

CHAPTER TWENTY-FIVE

DIRECT COURSE OF ACTION

Over the years, a lot of people had promised Hanson that they would find out where he lived and one night, when he came home, they'd be waiting for him with a shotgun. So he always drove past his flat and parked a couple of houses down, on the opposite side of the street if possible, and looked for anything that was out of place or just felt wrong. Something he'd know when he saw it. He didn't even think about it anymore. As he walked he watched doors and windows and backyards, listening and smelling the air. It was like looking both ways before crossing a street. One of the reasons most cops lived in the suburbs was so they'd be more difficult to find.

He unlocked the heavy, beveled-glass front door and the piece of toothpick he'd broken off between the door and the doorframe—a little burglar alarm—fell out. He stepped inside, shrugged the bag to the floor and listened to the house, pistol in hand. Nothing looked out of place. Eighty years old, the house had an odor of pitch, mildew, soap, plaster, and varnish. If anyone else was in the house, he'd smell him. Still, he looked in the bedrooms and closets, glanced under the beds, tried the knob on the door to the basement, walked the hallway to the bathroom, where the shower curtain was still open the way he'd left it—all places he'd found burglars and fugitives and the insane hiding in other people's houses. Then into the kitchen and back to the sagging sunporch—*clear.* He thumbed the safety of the Browning back on and slipped it into the hip pocket of his jeans.

He poured himself three fingers of green tequila and took it out to the front porch, where the sun was just pushing up out of the hills, huge against the horizon, blowing wind and long shadows down the street, pulling free from power lines, radio towers, the barbed limbs of distant trees, its skin fragile and tremulous through the atmosphere as if it might tear and flood the hills, turning the flatlands of East Oakland into an ocean of fire. He looked away a moment too late, the sun blinding him with light so that he had to feel his way back to the door inside where something or someone, aflame with the colors of the sun—a burning man in the hallway—blew past him and out the door, vanishing into the glare. He poured himself another drink and decided it was time to go see Libya.

At 10 a.m. he was standing on her front porch, his bag slung over his shoulder, wearing fresh jeans and a sage-green dress shirt he'd ironed on the flip-down built-in little ironing board in his kitchen. He wasn't drunk yet or hungover, but he was nervous in that neighborhood out of uniform, keeping track of passing cars. A block over somebody was setting off Fourth of July firecrackers a week late. The basketball hoop on the small frame garage at the back of the house looked new. Direct course of action, he thought, laughing at himself.

He pushed the doorbell button again and heard the *ding-dong* inside. It was in working order. He counted ten seconds to verify his sense of passing time. Maybe she wasn't at home. Maybe she wasn't alone. Maybe she'd seen him and wasn't going to open the door. He was stupid to show up at her door without calling first, he told himself, but he'd left his notebook with her phone number in his police locker. He told himself to expect the best, for a change. A pimped-out green Pontiac slowed to look him over, and he wondered if it might be the guy who'd beaten her up and maybe that's what she liked. Before he'd left his house he'd been having erotic daydreams about her, but now—time's up, he thought, relieved, when she opened the door.

Be positive, he thought.

"Officer Hanson. What a surprise. Did Radio send you?"

"It's my day off."

Her lips, her throat, the fine collarbones, and the swell of her breasts beneath the man's flannel shirt she was wearing, the shirt-tail knotted high on her stomach—he hadn't just imagined his reaction to her.

"I wanted to see if you were okay," he said.

She made a fluid gesture, delineating with both hands the lines of her body. "All okay." She was wearing red leather clogs with wooden soles that made her as tall as he was.

"How's your foot?"

She smiled finally but didn't laugh. "Healed by your touch," she said, running ringed fingers into her hair, the tendons flexing on the back of her hand. "Why don't you come inside? That woman next door is probably peeking at us through her blinds."

"Okay," he said, stupidly, thinking that all the neighbors were probably watching them.

By day the house was light and airy, books in the bookcases, mirrors throwing light from the walls. Most of his days, he thought, were nights—headlights and streetlights—and shadows. The kitchen was pleasant too, a 1950s Formica table with tubular chrome legs and a white enamel stove and a cute fat little refrigerator, where all he remembered from that night were the bloody footprints on the floor and the bloody potato peeler in the sink. And there in the sunlight, on the wall behind the kitchen table, was the picture Weegee had told him about the day when they were at All-American Burgers, after Hanson had bought him the bird book. It was an oil painting on a piece of fiberboard, battered and smudged by rough handling, then left and forgotten at some thrift store, the face of a glacier dominating the background, bluer than blue, more massive than the Justice Center, frozen in time by the painter at the moment it had sheared off and was about to plunge into an ocean of icebergs populated by penguins who seemed not to notice or care about the falling cliff of ice and the monster wave it would create.

"You're Weegee's auntie," Hanson said, seeing Libya suddenly illuminated. "He told me he lived with his auntie."

"You're *the* Officer Hanson, aren't you?" she said. "I never made the connection," she said wonderingly.

"Penguins are his favorite bird," Hanson told her.

"He loves this book," she said, taking Peterson's *Western Birds*—Weegee's bird book, the book that Hanson had signed—from a stack of cookbooks on the refrigerator. "I never made the connection," she said again. "He's my little brother. My half brother."

"Where's Weegee now?" Hanson asked.

"On a field trip to Golden Gate Park. I've got him signed up this week with the Boys and Girls Club."

They sat in the living room, Hanson in an armchair, sitting forward in the seat, Libya on the velvet couch, barefoot, her long legs curled under her, a low table between them. Beeswax candle scent mingled with the smell of honeysuckle floating in from outside.

She rose up and looked out the front window. "Where's your car? What do you drive besides a patrol car?"

He'd parked a block down the street, he told her, a habit from the job. His International Harvester Travelall. He bought it right before he went to graduate school and he paid four hundred dollars. The guy he bought it from worked on the transmission by digging a hole in the ground and driving the Travelall over it, then sliding down in the hole to work on it.

"*Graduate* school?"

"Well, yeah…"

"In what? Criminal *justice?*" she said.

"Nineteenth-century British literature, actually."

She just looked at him.

"A long story," he said.

"Not that it matters," she said. "That's what you do now. Get paid to enforce the law whether it's good or bad. Or right. Dog on a chain. *Their* dog on a chain."

"You've never had a white boyfriend, have you?"

"No, it always seemed pointless if not just stupid."

"Where's your boyfriend that beat you up? The guy you stabbed with the potato peeler."

"I have no idea."

Hanson looked at her, angry now, nodding his head, *Yeah, yeah, yeah.*

"You need to go," she said, standing up. "Weegee will be home soon. I don't want him to know."

"Know what?" he said. "There's nothing to know. Thanks, see you later. Bye-bye." And he let himself out the door.

CHAPTER TWENTY-SIX

DOWNTOWN

MEXICAN WINO

Hanson was working downtown, filling in because the weather was nice and a lot of cops were taking vacation time. Others, who'd used up their vacation time and were scheduled to work, were calling in sick at the last minute. As soon as he cleared from Transportation, Radio told him to check for a 647F in the 2200 block of Broadway.

He drove the few blocks to I. Magnin and saw the Mexican passed out, sitting propped up beneath the display windows. Mannequins in fresh summer clothes postured in the windows above him while pedestrians and shoppers coming out the revolving door pretended he wasn't there. The sun seemed to have scorched his shadow into the wall.

Hanson double-parked in front of the store, got out of the car, and stood looking at the wino for a moment, studying his ravaged, filthy, sunbaked face. He had once been handsome.

Hanson pulled on the black leather gloves he used for handling winos, gripped his shoulder, and shook him. "Sir," he said. *"Por favor."* But the Mexican's head just flopped from one shoulder to the other. Hanson made a fist and ran his middle knuckles up and down the Mexican's breastbone as if it was a washboard. It was painful enough to wake him up.

"You have to come with me."

"Ah. Of course," he said. Hanson helped him to his feet and walked him to the patrol car, where he'd already opened the back door. The Mexican knew the routine, a wino lifer, putting his hands behind his back so Hanson could cuff him, then, as drunk as he was, and handcuffed, slid into the car almost gracefully, from years of practice.

He gave his name, age, and military serial number as soon as Hanson got back in the car. Hanson wrote them down in his notebook, glad that he'd volunteered the information. Hanson didn't like asking the winos their age for the box on the arrest form. He felt their humiliation when they'd say "Forty-nine" or "Fifty-one," embarrassed because they knew how much older they looked—not old men yet, by normal standards, but finished, all but dead. All hope gone for anything more than their next mickey of wine. A lot of cops humiliated them out of irritation or just for entertainment. They had no reason to expect kindness from anyone, but for some reason they would often talk to Hanson on the way to jail about the lives they'd had, or believed they'd had, and he would listen to them.

The Mexican had fought in Korea, he said, seen a lot of combat. In spite of the handcuffs, he unbuttoned the sleeve of his long-sleeve shirt, managed to pull it up to his elbow, then twisted in the backseat so Hanson could see the puckered scars. "I thought I had found a home in the Marines," he said. Hanson listened but didn't say anything. He was only a little surprised when the Mexican asked him, "Why didn't *you* stay in?"

"That war was over. I'm not a good peacetime soldier."

"Of course. So you are a soldier on the street now." Even drunk, he still spoke with impeccable formality. "I wonder...May I ask you something, Officer?"

"Go ahead."

But the Mexican didn't speak again until they'd reached the back entrance to the jail. Hanson picked up the mike and asked Radio to have the jail open the door. He hung up the mike, and the louvered steel door began clattering open. "What was the question, Mister Sanchez?"

"Ah...it was not important," he said, "but..." The bottom of the door rose above the windshield, moving faster now, the hinged steel panels ratcheting up until the door boomed and locked open. "You still see Death sometimes, I think."

MERLE&EARL

Whenever he worked downtown the 5150s spotted him right away. They were afraid of the other cops, but when they saw Hanson they wanted to confide in him, give witness, confess everything. They'd jaywalk through heavy traffic to describe highly developed civilizations beneath the jail, tell him about devices the VA had installed in their heads that read their thoughts, stole their ideas, and gave them instructions.

Merle&Earl, though, waited for the WALK sign, looked both ways before stepping off the curb, and kept looking both ways, back and forth, as he crossed San Pablo where Hanson was parked in a loading zone, finishing an arrest report on a shoplifter he'd transported to jail from Cost Plus. He pretended not to see Merle&Earl, knowing that just a glance would bring him immediately, hoping he'd walk away. By the time he came up to the patrol car, Hanson had his pistol in hand, just out of sight below the window. Still though, Hanson pretended not to notice him there, shifting his weight nervously from foot to foot, clearly not planning to give up.

"Could I have a word with you, Officer?"

Finally Hanson looked over at him, keeping his face as neutral and detached as he could manage, to discourage conversation.

"Just a moment. In confidence, of course."

A man Hanson's age, intelligent eyes, a winning smile, he was wearing a white plastic Alameda County Hospital bracelet that looked new.

"I've been hoping we'd have a chance to talk while you're working downtown."

Hanson had never seen him before. Merle&Earl must have seen the irritation in his eyes or the set of his mouth.

"I'll get right to it, then."

His name was Earl and he was in transit, he said, and couldn't reveal his permanent address but could tell him that he lived in the western U.S., though he was no longer with his wife after someone in the Department of Defense decided that it would be better for the country if he lived alone. A few months after his wife left, he had a stroke, or so the VA told him, and while he was in the hospital the DOD put the transmitter in his head.

"Now he tries to tell me what to do. Bad things. Always bad things, and when I saw you I wondered if you might…"

Who? Hanson said. "Who tells you?" regretting it immediately. If they irritate you into responding, it takes that much longer to get rid of them.

"My Siamese twin, Merle. He's been telling me to commit suicide lately."

Hanson just looked at him.

"See, I wrote this book, *Laugh a Minute.* It's a comedy, and I sold it to Doubleday, but Merle stole it, and the Department of Defense published it."

He snapped his head around, looking down at his shoulder as he spoke. "*I* wrote the book," he said, in a different, harsher voice. "The title is *I Gotta Go.* Sure, it's a comedy, but it's a lot more than that. It's a book about how to leave if you're with people and you want to go. It's about how to leave *gracefully.*"

"What's wrong with you," the voice continued. "We shouldn't be talking to the cops. He'll just put us back in the lockdown ward."

Earl stuttered, "Fu-fuck you, Merle." He strained to bring his head back upright, and once he had, he relaxed. "You see what I mean, Officer Hanson? He's a thief and a liar and I can't get rid of him. I haven't slept the last two nights."

"Doesn't he get tired?"

"Eventually, but I'm the one who has to carry him around and feed us and every other thing."

"Why's he such an asshole?"

"He's still furious that I left Elaine. After all this time. He was in love with her."

"Are you taking your medication, Earl?"

Earl avoided Hanson's eyes, then set his jaw and looked at him. "No. They just make *me* weaker and *him* stronger."

"You're the one who should know, I guess," Hanson said. "The shrinks don't know as much as they think they do."

"They don't. None of them," Earl said, relieved.

"I've gotta go, Earl," Hanson said, then smiled. "Look, I shouldn't do this, so don't tell *anyone* or I'll be in deep shit."

Earl looked at him hopefully but didn't speak.

"Okay?"

"No one," Earl said.

Hanson pulled one of his speedloaders from its holder on his belt, removed one round, and put the speedloader back. "Keep this," he said. "It'll give you extra strength, a .357 magnum, a powerful round. It should even things up between you and Merle. But you and Merle have to work things out. It's not your fault that you had to leave Elaine. It's too bad but not your fault. And he needs to keep in mind that he's dependent on you for almost everything. If you get sick, he gets sick. If you get locked up, he's stuck in there with you. So you have to forgive each other and work together," Hanson said, starting the patrol car.

"Thank you, Officer Hanson. I'll guard this," Earl said, gripping the bullet in his fist, "with my life. And don't worry, no one but Merle will know you gave it to me."

"Okay," Hanson said, putting the car into gear. "Good luck to both of you."

"Wait," Earl said, with that other voice.

Hanson looked at him, his foot on the brake.

"Come on, Merle. Let's get a move on," Earl said in his own voice, and they limped and lurched their way back across the street.

Hanson imagined himself wandering in the wind, able to feel the ground beneath his feet but unable to see it, wondering where he was and how he'd gotten there.

2L2...

2L2...

Hanson picked up the mike. That was his call sign today. "2L2..."

Can you go...?

I'M A BLEEDER

He was back at the Hotel California, up on the sixth floor looking for a pre-op transvestite whore who called himself Black Velvet. Down in the hotel bar and grill he'd beaten a trick bloody with a catsup bottle. The bartender had called it in. It was happy hour.

It was getting dark by the time he'd tracked him to the sixth floor. Another transvestite, his hair up, wearing a teal-and-mauve patchwork satin kimono open to his navel, watched Hanson coming down the hall. Standing just inside the door to his room, he had one hand on his hip and the other, holding a lit cigarette, high up on the doorframe, revealing most of his augmented and very attractive breasts.

In a smoky voice he said, "You looking for that Vel-vet bitch, honey?"

"I am, indeed," Hanson said.

He tilted his cigarette, pointing languidly down the narrow hallway.

"Ah," Hanson said, nodding, "thank you very much." He started back down the hall, stopped, looked back at him, and said, "That is a beautiful robe, by the way," then walked on, the whore saying, "Why, thank you, baby."

Other residents, in bras and panties, fishnet body stockings, and tight vinyl, pouting in their doorways, their eyes on Hanson, all pointed toward an open window. The hallway carpet runner, frayed and bare and stained, a dead gray flesh color, ended at the window.

Hanson climbed out onto a fire escape landing. It was dusk, and just below him the buzzing hotel marquee flashed CALIFORNIA in bursts of gold neon. He went halfway up the next section of steel ladder, stopped, and looked down through the grid work between his feet at traffic passing six stories below. A man stood looking up at him from the sidewalk, illuminated by the yellow light. He was wearing a shiny blue warm-up jacket, the words TOKYO JAPAN embroidered in silver across the back, spelled out by the undulating body of a grinning dragon. Hanson recognized Death immediately and wondered, What am I doing out here?

He shook his head, smiling ruefully at Death, and backed carefully down to the fire escape landing, the ladder gonging like doom with each step he took. He slipped back inside and Death walked on to the corner, turned, and was gone.

Hanson didn't find Black Velvet, but his victim, a doe-eyed ex-con who'd been born in Oaxaca—not much more than five feet tall—was hiding in the bathroom at the other end of the hall. Everybody downtown was an ex-con, it seemed, but he had gotten out of San Quentin, fifteen miles to the north, across the San Rafael Bridge, just the day before. He didn't want to get involved in his own assault. There *was* no assault. *He* didn't call the cops.

"I'm fine," he said. "Is no problem here." His black hair was matted with blood, and though he had wiped most of it off his face with paper towels, he hadn't gotten it all out of his eyelashes. They wanted to stick to his cheeks when he blinked, holding themselves closed for a moment before popping open again. It was a little disorienting to Hanson, as time…stopped…held…started again each time he blinked his eyes.

He was glad to be off that fucking fire escape, though.

"You're bleeding pretty good," Hanson said.

"Is okay, Officer. I'm a bleeder. You know? I bleed easy." He was moderately drunk, doing his best to be cheerful.

"Okay," Hanson said. "Why don't you get your stuff, and I'll walk you out."

"But I paid for the room, Officer. In advance."

"If I leave you here, you're not gonna cause a problem so I have to come back, are you?"

He shook his bloody head, smiling up at Hanson.

"That's gonna piss me off if you do."

"No problem, Officer. I swear."

Hanson wrote it off on an incident card. <u>No complainant on arrival. Returned to service.</u> He'd written the guy's name and DOB in his notebook, just in case. If he decided to find the whore and stab him, with any luck, Hanson thought, he'd be off duty or tied up with another call.

No problem, Officer.

CHAPTER TWENTY-SEVEN

LOST CAR

It had taken Hanson an hour and a half to process a shoplifter named Gerald McPhee, a twenty-one-year-old junkie, who had tried and failed to steal a leather-look jacket. The old and overweight security guard holding him had, while waiting for the police, finally decided to handcuff him but had managed to cuff only one wrist when McPhee had pulled away and ran for it, out the door and down the hall toward the exit, just as Hanson stepped out of the elevator in front of him. McPhee had swung the open, ratchet-toothed cuff at Hanson's face but it was a spastic try and Hanson grabbed the cuff chain with one hand and McPhee's long dirty hair with the other. He waltzed him across the hall, hip-butted him off balance, and smashed his face into the wall, breaking his nose. When McPhee bounced off the wall Hanson kicked his legs out from under him, slamming him to the floor, then drove his knee into McPhee's shoulder, dislocating it. The paperwork was overwhelming: shoplifting, resisting arrest and assaulting an officer. No assignment card with <u>Problem solved upon departure.</u> Hanson did decide to overlook the needle marks on

McPhee's forearms and save himself from having to write up an 11550 H&S report.

The heat was at its worst, the sun low in the sky, hurtling in flames toward the deep water beyond the bay. Radio sent him to talk to a man who said his car had been stolen. He'd be waiting outside the Exxon station on Broadway, all the way across town.

"2L2, copy," Hanson said.

Hanson had heard Radio give the same call to 2L4 when he was driving McPhee, his arm in a sling, from ACH to the jail. 2L4 had cleared from the call after a few minutes. Some kind of bogus stolen car, it sounded like, an insurance deal, or maybe the guy's wife or girlfriend had left him, taken the car, and he was reporting it stolen so she'd be picked up. Nothing Hanson wanted to waste much time on. He was behind in his stats, with the end of the report period coming up. And he was way behind on his paperwork. 2L4 had kissed the call off, and now Radio was giving it to him secondhand.

The inside lights had been turned off in the Exxon station, and the mechanic was about to close, pulling the steel shutters down over the service bays by the time he got there. Two old men stood out front, both in their late seventies or early eighties, wearing ties and wool suits that had been fashionable thirty years ago, tailored to fit them before old age had left them frail. They stood side by side in the hot late afternoon, their hands clasped behind their backs like a preacher and his deacon. They didn't look bogus.

He pulled up to the front of the station, got out of the car, and asked, "Are you the gentlemen who called about the stolen car?"

"I did. I called the police. Solomon Maxwell. My good friend Mr. Freely," he said, indicating the other man, who made no effort to hide his exhaustion and anxiety.

"It's been three hours," Mr. Freely said, wiping sweat from his face with a damp linen handkerchief. "The other officer thought we'd forgotten where we'd parked it, and at this point..."

"You're the second officer I've had to explain this to. My car was stolen."

2L2, are you still at that Exxon station call?

"2L2, still here. I'll advise," Hanson said. Two old men who lost their car, he thought. Both of them had sweated through their shirt collars.

"Why don't we go inside, gentlemen? It's cooler in there and we can sit down to do the paperwork." He glanced at the mechanic cleaning up one of the bays, who nodded impatiently and looked at the clock. Hanson, who was roasting in his wool uniform, considered him. Uh-huh, he thought.

"We'll be fine out here, Officer," Mr. Maxwell said. "The proprietor is about to close for the day."

"Accommodate me, gentlemen," Hanson said, ushering them into the air-conditioned waiting room that smelled of old cigarette smoke, Juicy Fruit gum, and motor oil. The concrete block walls needed a coat of white paint, and the plastic chairs were dirty and cracked. There were stacks of old *Motor Trend* and *Sports Illustrated* on a counter next to a cracked coffee maker. When the two old men were seated, Hanson asked them, "Do you recall where you parked the car, sir?"

"I do, indeed. A 1982 dark blue Cadillac Seville. It was within a block of this filling station, but it's gone now."

"Was it uptown, do you think," Hanson said, indicating the direction with a nod of his head, "or down there?"

"I can't be certain. I was busy watching the traffic," Mr. Maxwell began.

"We're lucky to be alive in this traffic," Mr. Freely said. "I remember when the trolley was still running and people were civil to one another."

"We parked less than a block away. I'm certain of that," Mr. Maxwell said. "It took us nearly an hour to find a public phone in working order to call the police after we discovered the car was stolen…"

"None of the shops," Mr. Freely said, "would let us use their phone. They refused to let us in the door."

"Well," Mr. Maxwell said.

"They refused to let you in the door?"

"A couple of desperados is how they perceived us, I'm afraid," Mr. Maxwell said.

"They refused to let you in the *door?*" Hanson said again. He was outraged. Two formal old men sweating in their suits and the fuckers wouldn't let them in to call the police.

2L2, are you clear? We're backed up down here today.

"2L2, negative. I'm still on this stolen vehicle call," Hanson said, seeing the relief in the old men's faces at "stolen vehicle." "I'll be out here for a while, but I *will* advise you when I'm clear."

"I'd hoped to find someone who could fix the clasp on my watch," Mr. Maxwell said, "but the jewelers we managed to speak to told us they didn't do that kind of work."

"We're gonna close up now, Officer," the mechanic said, opening the glass door to the service bays, letting in the hot air, holding it open and waiting for them to stand up.

"We'll be needing the room for a little longer."

"We've got to close up."

Hanson stood up and looked at him. "Until I'm done."

The mechanic said, "Yeah. Okay. Sure, Officer."

Both men looked exhausted, and Mr. Freely was appealing to Hanson with his eyes. Fuck the stats, Hanson thought. He asked them if they'd mind waiting for just five minutes, ten at the most, while he made the check of the area required before he could take a stolen vehicle report.

"I'm sorry to make you wait like this," Hanson said, "but I'll be back very shortly."

Mr. Maxwell told Hanson they'd be glad to wait if that was necessary.

They watched him drive off, and he hoped they'd stay put. He should have told the fucking mechanic to watch them. He didn't want to have to go looking for them. He put out a description of the car so downtown cars could be watching for it and began circling the blocks, driving slowly, his amber flashers on. He could drive as slow as he wanted to, holding up traffic, and he did. If he didn't find the car, he wondered how he could get them home, hoped they had the phone number of a friend or one of their children who could come down for them. If not, he'd drive them himself. The relief sergeant, whoever he was today, could kiss his ass. This was a priority call as far as he was concerned.

After checking several blocks around the Exxon station, on the way back to see if he could arrange a ride home for them, he saw the Cadillac Seville. It was less than a block away from the station, if the station had been three blocks to the east.

When Hanson told them he thought he'd found the car, they both looked so exhausted he offered to drive them in the patrol car, though he was embarrassed about putting them in the backseat like prisoners. Mr. Maxwell saw the Cadillac as soon as they turned the corner of the block it was on.

"I apologize for your trouble, Officer. I believe that now I recall parking here."

From the PAC-set, Radio asked if he was 909 from the S/C stolen vehicle.

"Almost done."

"Thank you very much for your assistance, Officer Hanson. I'm only sorry my absentmindedness put you to so much trouble," Mr. Maxwell said.

"No trouble at all, gentlemen," he said, nodding to acknowledge Mr. Freely. "It's easy enough to misplace your vehicle in downtown Oakland, especially if you haven't been down here for a while. There's a new building going up or down, it seems like, every day. Sometimes I'm surprised I don't lose my patrol car."

"Do you have a card, Officer?" Mr. Maxwell asked.

"Of course," Hanson said, finding one in his wallet. "I should have thought to give it to you earlier. Drive carefully. I'm sorry Oakland put you to so much trouble this afternoon."

They all shook hands, and Hanson stood in the street, blocking traffic, until the Cadillac pulled from the curb and pulled away. Hanson waved goodbye. He hadn't asked for a driver's license or registration, which he should have, to put on his report, but he was afraid the license would be expired. The report would come back to him with the empty boxes circled in red ink, and he'd have to respond with an "incomplete report" form, acknowledging his carelessness, but it was worth it.

The sun had disappeared beneath the ocean, but the distant line of clouds far out on the horizon was in flames.

CHAPTER TWENTY-EIGHT

NEIGHBORHOOD BEEF

It was still early in the shift, mid-August. Hanson was back working the tactical car out in District Five.

5Tac51, we're getting complaints about a neighborhood dispute in the eight hundred block of Havenscourt.

"5Tac51 copy. On the way."

We'll kick a cover car loose as soon as one becomes available.

"I'll take a look. Do you have an address on a complainant?"

Negative, 5Tac51.

"Copy. I'm almost there. I'll advise on the cover car."

He turned north onto Monroe and saw the problem two blocks up: six or eight people on either side of the street, yelling, gesturing, leaning forward and motherfucking each other. Another cop wouldn't make any difference except to provoke the situation.

The street was lined with parked cars, so he turned on the overhead amber flashers, double-parked, and got out of the car without his nightstick. A nightstick wouldn't solve the problem or save his ass for long with this many people, and he'd look stupid with it dangling at his side. If things got serious enough for a nightstick, they'd be serious enough for him to shoot a couple of people when they tried to take his gun.

They were all acting like he wasn't there, that the patrol car with flashing orange lights wasn't in the middle of the street. So far on this call he was invisible, but he smiled like an extra in a crowd scene and waved at the people on the other side of the patrol car to indicate that he'd be over to talk to them too. They ignored him as he trudged up the weedy embankment on the corner while they shouted insults across the street and over the patrol car. "Ho."

"You *momma* done *that.*"

"Goin' fuck you *up,* bitch."

If they wanted to pretend they didn't notice him, he'd pretend not to see a problem, a crazy white man in an OPD uniform wearing a .357 magnum. He stopped in front of the biggest, loudest guy on his side of the street and smiled at him. "How you doin', sir?"

He wasn't in charge and not very smart, but he was big and glared at Hanson, trying to mad-dog him away. He wasn't afraid, even though he knew an Oakland cop could get away with shooting him, but he was confused when Hanson kept smiling, with eyes as calm as midnight, then nodded and said, "Yeah," agreeing with him maybe, about something he thought but hadn't said yet.

Hanson glanced up at the sky. "I think it's just gonna get hotter. The sun comes closer every day now. Did you know that?" he asked, shaking his head. "I read that it's gonna start setting the trees on fire in a couple more years."

The shouting began to falter.

"Anyway," Hanson went on, "nothing we can do about it. Heat."

The people across the street had gotten quiet, wondering what the cop was doing. He turned to a stocky guy in his early thirties who was walking his way. He'd noticed him standing with a younger woman when he'd walked up the hill and he'd picked out the woman as the problem.

"Hi, sir," he said. "They sent me to check on a neighborhood problem, and this must be it. What's the problem about?"

"I'll *tell* you what the problem's about."

"Good. Deal. What's your name, sir?" Hanson said, taking out his notebook. "I hope we can solve this, then I can be on my way."

"Don't tell him shit," the woman he'd been with said.

"Fred," he told Hanson, giving her a look, then back to Hanson. "My name's Fred, okay?"

"Yes, sir. Thanks," Hanson said, jotting it in his notebook. "What's everybody so pissed off about?"

The people across the street had begun shouting again. One or two on Hanson's side shouted back, but a look from Fred shut them down.

"Thank you, very much," Hanson told him.

"See the fat one over there," he said, "the one in the big orange, what do they call 'em?"

"Muumuu?"

"Yeah. Moo-moo."

The woman who'd told him not to say shit hissed at Hanson. Fred looked at her, then said, "Alvin, will you look after Louise for me?"

The big guy Hanson had talked to about the sun nodded and walked over to her, putting her in shadow. Hanson felt like he was on the way to solving the problem when up the street an almost-new but stripped down economy black Ford sedan rolled to a stop and four Black Muslims got out wearing the usual black suits, white shirts, and black bow ties. They crossed their arms and stood there looking at Hanson.

The local so-called Muslims had just lately started showing up at situations in East Oakland the way they used to back in Portland when Hanson worked there in the seventies, following police calls on a scanner, difficult and dangerous, but they'd been righteous back then, prepared to die if necessary for their beliefs and Hanson had respected and even admired them. But these new Oakland Muslims were mostly just criminals who dressed up like Muslims, thugs in cheap suits, stealing the authority of those originals, and he didn't want them to start hanging around at his calls.

Hanson didn't read the paper, watch TV or talk to many other cops, so he was all but clueless about how the businessmen and politicians who controlled the city chose to support the Black Muslims on the backs of all the other black citizens of Oakland, thinking that if they did, they wouldn't look like the racists they were, and because they were more afraid of the organized Black Muslims in North Oakland than they were of the unorganized black citizens in East and West Oakland. The city council gave the Black Muslim elders interest-free loans and awarded development grants, even when the money evaporated, loans were never paid back, and nothing had been developed.

"Are those guys friends of yours?" Hanson asked Fred.

"Not anybody I know."

"Could you excuse me for just a minute? I'll be right back."

"Go ahead," he said.

"I appreciate your help," Hanson said. "Be right back."

Hanson was tuned as tight as a steel guitar, walking toward the Muslims, feeling good, perfect, walking that fine line where he couldn't fuck up unless he started thinking about fucking up. He didn't like breaking his momentum with Fred and the neighborhood dispute, but they were curious, watching to see what he'd do now, cooling off. He was singing softly to himself: "Po-lice officers, how can it be, you arrest everybody but cruel Stagger Lee, that *bad* man, *bad* man, *cruel* ole Stagger Lee...

"Good afternoon, my Muslim brothers," he said, aggressively cheerful. "Have you come to restore peace to the neighborhood? Help me out here?" he said, gesturing with an open hand toward the people watching from their yards. "I hope so. There's four of you and only one of me. Even though I *do* have my official badge." He tapped his chest. "I left my special hat in the patrol car."

They watched him with practiced impassive badass stares, as if they could see through him.

"What do you say?"

None of them said anything, so he began looking them over like a drill instructor, grumbling and snapping about their imperfectly shined shoes, their haircuts, ill-fitting suit coats, and dirty fingernails. They acted just like recruits should, eyes straight ahead, hands behind their backs, taking the criticism of an inspection, as they'd been trained to do by somebody, while he made them look bad. And what else could they do with most of the neighborhood watching? Grab him, beat him up, kill him? The real Muslims might have, but not these guys, they weren't prepared to die this afternoon.

Hanson walked back to the front of their car and looked them over as a group. "Not gonna help me out today?" he said. "Then why don't you get back in your car and go bake some bread down at the bakery?"

"We're here to monitor police interaction with the community," the one in charge said, part of a speech he'd memorized.

"Have at it, my brother. But stay out of my way."

"We do whatever is necessary."

"At your fucking *peril*," Hanson said. He turned on his heel and walked away, listening, listening through his tinnitus for the sound of a shoe on the street, the flapping of a lapel, any sense that they were rushing him. They could shoot him in the back of the head, and the joke would be on him then, but they'd missed their chance, and anyway, he didn't give much of a fuck if they shot him. He'd finally get some real sleep.

The two arguing groups showed more interest in him now. Hanson once again waved at the group across the street. "Be right with ya'll," he said. "Thanks for being so patient.

"The Muslims are going to monitor my interaction with the black community," he told Fred. "I hope you can help me out here. I want to look good for them." The woman was gone, and so was the big guy named Alvin. "What's this problem all about?"

It was about a parking place. Someone on their side of the street had driven to the liquor store, and when they got back, a few minutes later, their parking place had been taken. But it was more complicated than that. He heard Fred out and asked the others there how they saw it.

He walked across the street, around the patrol car, and talked to the woman in the orange muumuu, one of those huge black women who control entire blocks in East Oakland. He was polite to her, listened, called her ma'am, thanked her, and made eye contact with all the others on that side of the street. "Okay. Yes, ma'am," he said, then went back to talk to Fred.

In not much more than five minutes of walking back and forth across the street, mediating the problem, he persuaded both groups to go back inside, for just a little while, or maybe go on home if they were visiting and didn't mind doing that, thanking them all for helping him out. He ignored the Muslims and got back in the patrol car. "Thanks, now. I appreciate it."

He made a slow, careful U-turn in the street and, a few blocks away, pulled over and filled out an assignment card. <u>Disagreement over parking place. Problem resolved upon departure</u>. He dropped the card into his briefcase and cleared from the call, pleased with his negotiating abilities.

CHAPTER TWENTY-NINE

FELIX THANKS HANSON

Hanson hung the mike up and pulled into the lot of an out-of-business gas station, the pumps gone and every window of the office and garage broken. He got out of the patrol car to look for the man with a gun. A breeze had come up from the bay, and he was glad for the chance to walk for a while. Over the years he'd been sent to a lot of man-with-a-gun calls, but he'd only found three. He didn't expect to find one that afternoon, but he wouldn't be surprised either.

The storefront Church of Jesus' Grace United had its doors open, and Hanson looked in at the band rehearsing—drums, guitar, and keyboard.

He looked inside, through the door into the foyer, prepared to see the man with the gun up there singing. Instead, he met a heavyset handsome black woman, all dressed up. She was wearing electric-blue eye shadow that matched her sequined blue dress.

"Good evening, ma'am. How are you this evening?"

"Just fine, Officer. Getting ready for Sunday morning. How good of you to take the time to check in on us."

"Glad to do it. My pleasure."

The three-piece band began playing "You Gotta Move" with a singer who was more Motown than gospel, a little slick, but he was good.

You may be high, you may be low,
You may be rich, you may be po'…

"You should come to one of our services, Officer Hanson," the church woman said, reading his name tag.

"Maybe I'll come one of these Sundays," Hanson said, wanting to believe that he might.

"It's wonderful," she began, looking past him for a moment, over his shoulder, then back at him, "to see you taking an interest in us."

You may run, can't be caught,
You may hide, cannot be found.

"Glad I could stop by," he said, turning to look too, across the street, just as all the neon signs in the liquor store window began blinking and bubbling on in the fading afternoon light. "Has there been any problem right around here in the past twenty minutes or so?" he asked, hating to spoil their easy, empty exchange.

"I wouldn't know, Officer. I've been working with the music director for the past hour."

"Someone called in about a man with a gun right around here."

"Lord knows there are a lot of them these days."

"Thanks," Hanson said. "Guess I'll take a look across the street."

But when God, when He come around,
You gotta move.

Everything was closed down there except for the church and the liquor store. Drunks sat with their heads down, backs against the liquor store wall. One was sprawled, passed out, on the sidewalk. The OPD rarely showed up at that corner, and when they did it was usually two or three of them—never good news for anybody.

They all seemed to see him at once, like a school of fish. Four of them got to their feet, drunk but wary, swaying, trying to focus their eyes individually. The others put their bottles behind them where they sat, looking straight ahead, away from Hanson. He wasn't there if they couldn't see him. One guy came out from behind the store, zipping up his filthy, too-short chartreuse pants, wearing a brown vinyl coat with no shirt. Surprised to see Hanson there, he did his best to glare at him. Hanson smiled back.

"Good evening, gentlemen," he said, imagining himself as one of them instead of a soldier of Oakland's army of occupation. "Nice night." He walked through them to the liquor store entrance. Looking at the sidewalk, they said "Uh-huh" and "Awright" as he passed.

The liquor store owner, stocky, dark skinned, with a shaved head, looked to be in his early fifties, mustache, a gray scar on his neck—someone who had managed to get out of whatever life he'd been in when he was younger before it killed him, with enough money to buy this store. He looked blandly over his shoulder at Hanson when he walked in, then went back to arranging bottles on the shelves behind the cash register, standing on a step stool.

"Good evening," Hanson said, checking the convex mirrors tilted on their stalks, reflecting each empty aisle like funhouse tunnels.

"Uh-huh," he said, his back still to Hanson, turning a couple of the bottles around so the labels were centered.

"How's it going?"

"Slow," he said, the bottles clinking as he lined them up again. "Goin' real slow since you parked that police car across the street."

241

"Somebody called in about a problem on this corner."

"No problems I know about."

"Radio sent me. A man with a gun."

The owner reached down for a feather duster and began dusting the bottles off. He leaned back, looked at them, dusted some more. "Lotta people got guns. You got a gun."

"Yes, sir," Hanson said, "but I think they meant that this guy was, you know, brandishing it."

"You mean like, waving it around."

"Yes, sir," Hanson said, glancing out the windows, checking the mirrors, figuring the owner kept his gun under the cash register.

"See a lot of that too, you spend much time around here. Good way to get yourself shot by some other man with a gun. Pull out a gun, you better use it, is what I say."

"Yes, sir. I agree. Sorry I'm costing you money tonight, but I had to look around," he said, thinking that he sounded like a TV cop.

"Could be somebody dropped a dime on the man. Caught him messing with his woman, call the po-lice," he said, drawing out the word. "Or his woman caught *him* messing around. Call the po-lice and get somebody like you down here to put him in jail for CCW, or shoot him."

Hanson didn't say anything.

"You need to arrest somebody," he said, finally turning around, gesturing with the feather duster, "you could arrest one of those fools out front. Drinkin' on the street's against the law, isn't it?"

"I don't need to arrest anybody. I'm just doing my job. Same as you are, Mister…?"

"Johnson. Norris Johnson. I own this place. You want my date of birth? Check and see if I got any warrants? Maybe you could arrest *me*."

"No need, Mr. Johnson. I'm sure you're okay."

"Damn right I am."

"Could I have some of that spearmint chewing gum," Hanson said, "please," nodding at the display of cigarettes and gum.

Norris Johnson got down from his step stool, reached under the glass counter, picked up a green pack of gum, and slapped it down on top of the scratched glass between them. "That's twenty-five cents."

Hanson put a quarter on the counter, which Norris Johnson ignored.

"You need anything else?"

"No, sir," Hanson said, watching the street outside reflected in the bottles and advertising mirrors behind the owner. "Sometimes I think the only way to find a man with a gun is to drive to the location, get out of the car, and announce, 'Here I am,' see if somebody tries to shoot me."

"They teach you that in the Police Academy?"

"I thought of it myself."

"Does it work?"

"Hasn't yet. It's just a theory."

"Theory like that might get you killed."

"No," Hanson said, peeling the foil off a piece of gum. He folded the gum into his mouth and looked at Norris Johnson. "I can't be killed."

"That right, Officer?"

"Good night, Mr. Johnson. It's been a real pleasure," Hanson said.

He walked out the door just as Felix's Rolls came to a stop across East 14th Street, then rolled across the intersection and pulled to the curb in front of Hanson. Felix was driving and alone in the car. He stepped out onto the sidewalk just in front of Hanson, smiling and wearing a gorgeous pale gray suit with a cream-colored silk shirt and a black tie.

"Officer Hanson," he said, "I was hoping I'd find you down here this evening."

"Good to see you, Mr. Maxwell," Hanson said. *"Bon chance."*

Felix looked at him, thinking it over, then said, "The truth is that I heard you take this call on the police scanner. I drove over because I wanted to see you."

"What can I do for you?" Hanson asked him. He'd always felt comfortable with genuine badasses. It didn't matter what side they were on. It was a quality that pretty much simplified things between people. As long as they weren't so crazy that Hanson had to worry about them turning on him.

"Officer Hanson," Felix said, shaking Hanson's hand and putting his other hand on Hanson's shoulder. "My friend. I've been looking for you."

Hanson nodded, prepared for anything.

"To thank you for helping my grandfather the other evening."

Hanson thought for a moment, shook his head. "Forgive me, but I don't—"

"Downtown. The old gentleman down there to get his watch fixed."

"Solomon," Hanson said, smiling now, "with his friend Mr. Freely. Solomon Maxwell."

"My grandfather..." Felix said, interrupting Hanson without meaning to, then nodding for Hanson to continue.

"That was your grandfather? Well, no wonder. Dying from the heat in that wool suit, lost his car, and after they'd been turned away from... The fuckers down there wouldn't let them in out of the heat."

"Because they were black and old."

"I'm sorry, Felix."

"Just how it is, Officer."

"It shouldn't be."

"He told me how the first cop they talked to just blew him off, dismissed him as not worth the trouble, and," Felix said, "the way you looked at the gas station manager when he said he had to close up."

"I didn't think he noticed," Hanson said, looking down, nodding, then smiling at the memory. "I was glad to help. Your grandfather told me that they must have looked like desperados."

"He was president of the Brotherhood of Sleeping Car Porters," Felix said. "It's a long story. I gave him that car, but he isn't supposed to drive down there by himself. He knew I'd take him, or somebody would, but he refuses to ask me any favors. I look after him, but I try not to let him know. I'm not always available."

People were coming out of the church and congregating on the sidewalk.

"I'll let you get back to work," Felix said.

"You bet," Hanson said. "Give my best to your grandfather."

Felix stopped and turned around. "Something else. About you and those Muslims. Inspecting them. Everybody's heard about that. How you made them look stupid. Watch your back. Those people will kill you. Believe me. They have an understanding with the city and the OPD. Be careful," he said, getting back into the Rolls and driving off.

"You all have a nice evening," Hanson said to the drunks before walking back across the street, smiling at the now very friendly church people, excusing himself as he maneuvered through them to the abandoned gas station.

At his patrol car he paused for a moment, listening to the gospel music coming from the church. Maybe he would drive over on a Sunday morning one of these days, just to take a look. See what happened. Who knows? He drove a few blocks to a parking lot where he could see in all directions and filled out an assignment card. <u>No suspect, no complainant. Checked area on foot with negative results. Hanson / 7374P.</u> It was getting dark enough so that he had to turn on his headlights.

CHAPTER THIRTY

NARC CAR STOP

It was a nice Saturday evening out in District Five, the sun low in the sky. Hanson drove over to the newly opened Burger King in District Four without clearing from his last call, hoping a sergeant wouldn't drive by and spot his car while he waited in line for two Junior Whoppers and two milks, his PAC-set hissing and barking, everyone else in line pretending not to see him. It was a gamble to open a Burger King in District Four, too many holdups and they'd pull it out. Hanson wanted to use it as often as possible before it was shut down.

He'd finished one Junior Whopper with cheese and a milk by the time he crossed High Street back into District Five, where he cleared from the disturbance call. Radio came back right away, sending him Code 2 on an "unwanted son with a gun," in the area of 82nd and East 14th Street. He tossed the other burger and milk out the window, turned on the overhead lights, and angled down toward East 14th. He was only a few blocks from the location when the dispatcher was interrupted midsentence by the high-low electronic yodel announcing another armed robbery.

The channel went silent for a moment, then the dispatcher read out the mostly useless details.

Pioneer Chicken 211, downtown, involving a 187. Two N/Ms, both mid-twenties, approximately five ten, medium build, short afros, and dark clothing. Suspect one with a handgun. Suspect two, sawed-off shotgun. Suspects herded the employees and three customers into the cooler, locked them all in. Both suspects raped a cashier, then shot her. She died en route to ACH. Possible suspect vehicle a light blue over dark blue Lincoln with tinted windows and possible wire wheels. No license plate or further details.

For a moment he saw the ring-bound *Thomas Guide* open on the seat next to him as a collection of fourteenth-century maps. END OF THE KNOWN WORLD. Every page was blank except for a tiny sea serpent coiling across the parchment.

He pulled the mike off the dashboard, his thumb on the push-to-talk button, waiting for an opening to tell Radio he'd arrived at his location.

AC Transit driver has parked the bus at this time and is watching from the sidewalk. He says the subject is under the influence or possibly 5150...walking up and down the bus, screaming at passenger.

. . ..

Car calling, say again...Unit calling, your PAC-set is garbled. You'll have to use the radio in your vehicle...

. . ..

Fifth and Foothill...

Little gold letters spelled out MOTOROLA across the top of the mike, its perforated once-beige face was rubbed to bare metal by years of use.

Negative, the driver does not know if the subject is a male or female. The subject is brandishing a knife at this time, we understand...I have 3L13 covering...Unit with the car stop, go ahead...

At Fifth and Foothill on a black LTD, John Frank Mary one zero two.
Unit with the car, stop. Repeat your call number only.

People up and down the block were patrolling their yards with baseball bats, frying pans, golf clubs. Inside the house, the complainant was draped in a red muumuu and must have weighed four hundred pounds—a whale with tiny human hands and feet. She reclined enormously on a beige vinyl sofa bed on wheels, propped up on pillows, smoking hungrily. She must have lived on that couch and slept there at night. Hanson saw no way she could be moved.

The house had its own microclimate, humid and rank—a bucket of dirty diapers, food left burning then forgotten on the stove, unwashed dishes used as ashtrays, shoulder-high piles of garbage bags. Children wandered through the kitchen, regarding Hanson with a kind of dull anticipation on their way out the door. The complainant used the children as messengers, to fetch her things and to deliver notes she wrote on a lined notepad with a picture of Michael Jackson on the cover.

She was drunk and had changed her mind about involving the police. "You like Michael?" she asked, holding up the notebook.

Hanson gave her a noncommittal smile and held out his hands, palms up.

"That's all right. Lotta people don't like him. He's not like anybody else." She dropped the notebook on the floor. "You ever arrest my son? He's the one got everybody scared out there."

Hanson asked what her son's name was.

"You'd know it if you knew him," she said, dismissing him.

Hanson thanked her and found his way out of the house. It was a big, high-ceilinged place, with people in every room, children and adults who seemed to be just passing through, startled when they saw him, then acting like he wasn't there.

Outside, across the street, a woman in a tiger-stripe slip was screaming down at a man from her front steps, a pair of silver scissors in her hand, holding them like a dagger. When the man saw Hanson he tried to smile, backed away from the porch, said something—Hanson could read his lips: "No problem here, Officer."

Walking to his patrol car, Hanson noticed Death, up on the corner. He was wearing a reflective vest and a hard hat, holding a traffic sign that said SLOW on one side and STOP on the other, directing traffic around some repair work. Hanson wished they could take a walk together, talk some, go back to the war where Hanson always knew who he was and was always sure of what he was doing, but Radio sent him in the other direction.

He was stopped at a red light at 82nd and Bancroft singing, "I got sunshine, on a cloudy day..." when a light blue over dark blue Lincoln Continental—the description of the Pioneer Chicken suspect vehicle—crossed the intersection in front of him. Through the tinted windows he saw the shadows of a driver and a passenger, saw them look his way, the Lincoln continuing on down Bancroft, its wire wheels flickering, the yellow-orange streetlights sliding one by one up the long hood, over the windshield, across the roof, down the back window and off the trunk, vanishing into the past at the speed of light.

Relaxed and wide awake, his pupils dilating, he turned through the intersection behind the Lincoln so smoothly, following it so perfectly, that it felt like he'd been preparing for this all his life. The streetlights glowed brighter and warmer, painting the failed and wretched ghetto street with subtle color and crisp detail. Time, he noticed, was unfurling a little more slowly and reliably than it had been.

He lifted the mike off the dashboard to give Radio his location, the license number of the car, and go through the motions of re-questing a cover car, which he knew wouldn't be available, but Radio traffic was so heavy that he wedged the mike back into its holder.

When he closed up on the Lincoln and turned on the overhead lights, it swerved across the centerline, almost hit a parked car, sped up. They hadn't noticed he was behind them till he turned on the lights. Now, he imagined, they were arguing over what they should do—ignore him and hope he'd disappear, speed off, run him off the road, bail out of the car and run, pull over and kill him, pull over and surrender, pull over and pretend to surrender, then kill him. He bleeped the siren and felt his waist to be sure he didn't have the seat belt on.

He hit the siren again. The Lincoln cut its lights, continued on for another block, then turned down a driveway and around behind a five-story U-shaped apartment building, where it was hidden from the street. Hanson followed, his blue and red strobes spinning out and back through the courtyard lot like a Tilt-A-Whirl at a ghetto carnival—snatching windows, walls, stairwells, doorways, Dumpsters, out of the dark, flinging them away, bringing them back again. Hanson threw the patrol car into PARK, pulled the shotgun from the dashboard lock, and stepped out into the V of the open patrol car door. If they bailed out and ran in different directions he'd be able to shoot them both. He tipped up the worn old Remington 870 with one hand and rattled it like a blued-steel snake, comfortable when he was holding a shotgun, jacking a buckshot round into the chamber.

The steel *clack-clack* of the shotgun echoed off the buildings. Hanson's voice: "In the car. Police officer. Do not move unless I tell you to."

He watched himself from the other side of the patrol car—that

Hanson watching him, the one with the shotgun—switching places, back and forth, out of body in the overhead lights.

"Driver. Turn off the car and drop the keys out the window." He waited, wondering if they were too stupid or scared to follow instructions. He wished he could just kill them both and be done with it. "Lower your window."

The electric window, reflecting the lights from the patrol car, slid smoothly into the door. Hanson saw that the driver had both hands on the steering wheel. He was a kid, nineteen or twenty, wearing a top hat.

"Turn off the car. Turn it off."

The exhaust from the car stopped rippling the spotlighted air.

"Drop the keys out the window."

He shouldered the shotgun and stepped away from the protection of the patrol car and put the front sight on the driver's window.

"Do not look at me. Drop the keys out the window."

Hanson held the steel bead of the front sight steady, just below the driver's jaw, as if the gun weighed nothing, looking down the length of the blued-steel barrel as the keys glittered down to the pavement.

"If I see a weapon, I'll kill you both." His voice shook the dark buildings. "Driver. Open your door from the outside. Keep both hands where I can see 'em. If I can't see both empty hands, I will shoot you. Passenger. Stay in the car."

The driver pulled the outside door handle with his left hand, keeping his right hand extended through the window.

"Push the door open with your knees and—don't look at me—get out of the car." The driver swung the door open, his top hat falling off, both hands extended as if he was blind. "Behind your head. Lace your fingers. Step sideways away from the car until I tell you to stop."

He took two sideways steps, and Hanson said, "Stop. Get down on your knees."

The driver squatted, put one knee down, then the other.

"Passenger. Stay in the car.

"Driver. Take your hands off your head and hold them way out away from you and lay down on your stomach. Your head turned toward the car. Don't fuck this up."

Hanson's finger tightened on the trigger as the driver put one forearm down, but then he lay all the way down on his stomach.

"Spread your arms way out to the side, like Jesus on the cross. Good. Spread your legs. Way apart. Farther.

"Passenger. Open your door and put your hands up where I can see them, above the roof of the car. Don't look at me. Now step out."

"Don't shoot," the passenger shouted. He was older than the driver, in his thirties, wearing expensive clothes. These weren't the holdup guys.

"Now. Walk backward."

"Don't shoot."

"Keep walking till I tell you to stop."

"Don't shoot."

"Do what I tell you to do." Hanson walked him backward, then sidestepped him to the left, had him kneel, then lay down behind the driver. They weren't the holdup guys, but why didn't they stop right away? Why did they pull in here?

Sirens wailed in the distance, closing in as Hanson stepped around into the flashing high-low beams of the patrol car, stepping carefully, aiming the shotgun at the two suspects, one eye still on the car. More headlights and overheads flashed and spun in the lot, the yelping of sirens going suddenly silent. The sound of boots on the asphalt. He raised the shotgun as two cops he'd never seen before stepped in with handcuffs, then he pushed on the safety, walked backward to the patrol car, and locked the shotgun inside.

Two special unit narcotics guys walked past him. The one in the leather vest, with his badass Fu Manchu mustache and long hair, said, giving him orders, "We'll take it from here."

"You'll what?"

They ignored him. Uniformed cops were lifting the prisoners up by the cuffs. He didn't care if they wanted to take charge of the prisoners and do the paperwork—that was fine with him. He'd still get credit for the arrests on his stat sheet. But the guy in the vest had pissed him off.

"What?" Hanson said, crossing in front of the narcs and standing between them and the prisoners. "What are you talking about?"

"We'll take it from here."

Suddenly Hanson was unanchored in the urgent rush of all the mindless emergency lights. The arrest had gone so smoothly that maybe he was still waiting to explode. Maybe, after planning but failing to kill the two suspects, because what the detective had said made no sense, he was afraid that he was losing his mind. Whatever the reason, he was in the narc's face, chest-to-chest, saying, "Why don't you 'take it' and fuck yourself?" This was the fucker he should have a license to kill. Who the fuck did he think he was talking to, and what was he talking about?

Then Sergeant Jackson was there. "Let them take the prisoner," he said, his voice low, calming, trustworthy, the tone of voice Hanson used to settle disputes without making an arrest. "I'll explain."

There had been seven police cars and a fire department ambulance crowded into the lot behind the apartment building with a police helicopter circling overhead. An emergency vehicle traffic jam, pulsing with light, radio loudspeakers barking and squealing, clicking on and off. Yellow plastic tape, printed endlessly with POLICE POLICE POLICE, kept reporters and other citizens away, but people who lived in the apartments watched from above, leaning over wrought-iron railings, drinking and smoking dope, trading rumors. Two lieutenants had come and gone.

Sergeant Jackson was still there with Hanson. Their cars were the last two in the lot, with only their parking lights on. The passenger in the suspect car, Sergeant Jackson told him, was a confidential informant working for narcotics, a paid undercover OPD snitch.

"Foolishness," Sergeant Jackson said, "but it's officially above my pay grade. Nonetheless, Officer Hanson, you should have put out your location on the stop. There are people who already think you must have some kind of death wish, the way you take calls by yourself."

"I…" Hanson began. "Radio was…" He didn't finish the sentence.

"The good news is that there won't be much paperwork on this," Sergeant Jackson told Hanson.

Hanson nodded. "Yes, sir," he said.

"All right, then. Excellent." Sergeant Jackson opened the door of his patrol car, about to leave, then turned back to Hanson. "No," he said, "the good news is that you didn't kill both of them."

He smiled at Hanson then and drove off.

CHAPTER THIRTY-ONE

I'LL GO BACK ANYWAY

It was so seldom that Hanson saw a cop on the street in Oakland he knew—much less wanted to talk to—that when he got the call to cover for Morris, a young kid he'd been in the Academy with and liked, he volunteered. Morris needed someone to watch his prisoner, and Hanson was glad for the chance to say hello, the first time since they'd graduated.

The neighborhood houses were old, built back before East Oakland was all black, but the owners were taking care of them. Sometimes out there one street would be falling apart, burned down, trash-blown, drug and gun and gang territory, while the next block over was green and well-maintained.

The suspect was handcuffed in the back of Morris's patrol car when Hanson pulled up behind it. Morris was interviewing the woman and her husband out on the front lawn, and trying to keep an eye on the suspect at the same time. Hanson stood at the rear of the car to watch the suspect after getting the story from Morris.

The woman had called it in. Her husband was holding him at gunpoint, the would-be rapist.

She'd been up in the bedroom, she said, when somebody came in the front door and started up the stairs. She'd thought it was her husband, who'd left for his shift at Discount Tire half an hour earlier and must have come back to pick up something he'd forgotten. Then the suspect appeared in the bedroom doorway. He told her not to scream and he wouldn't hurt her. Told her to take off her clothes. It was a miracle her husband had come home when he did.

The husband told Morris that he'd called when he got to work, just to say hello and maybe cheer her up—she'd been feeling down for a couple of days—and no one answered the phone. That had worried him enough to drive home, and when he got home he let himself in and called her name, and she'd come running down the stairs, screaming, wrapped in a sheet. The suspect was still upstairs trying to get the bedroom window open. The husband had held his pistol on him, making him lie on the floor while his wife called the police.

The suspect hadn't been out of prison two weeks, after doing almost four years of a six-year sentence for possession for sale, assaulting a police officer, aggravated assault, resisting arrest, and public intoxication. All one incident, the only time he'd been arrested except for a couple of juvenile charges years before. He must have pissed the arresting cops off, Hanson thought.

A nice couple, the woman pretty, in her early twenties, crying now. Her husband was fifteen years older, shaved head, a mustache, the kind of guy who's worked hard all his life. He was angry with her because it had scared him, and he wasn't the kind of guy who got scared very often. "*How* could you forget to lock the door when I was gone?" Hanson heard him ask her—probably not the first time he'd asked that—before they went inside to finish the interview with Morris.

"I thought I'd locked it," she managed, sobbing.

"I'm sorry, baby," her husband said.

Hanson stayed with the prisoner, who stared straight ahead, refusing to look at him. He wasn't much older than Morris, good looking, buff, Jheri-curled hair, tough from dealing drugs on the street and four years of prison.

Hanson looked at the house, then stooped down and looked at the suspect again. He didn't look like the kind of stoned moron burglar who'd walk into an unfamiliar dwelling in the middle of the day, then decide to rape a screaming woman. Steel security bars over all the windows and doors. And he hadn't touched her. *Told* her to take off her clothes. Something wasn't right.

Hanson opened the patrol car door, read him his rights from a card—which, he knew, would piss off the detectives who got the case because they'd want to get all the voluntary incriminating statements they could before Mirandizing him, but fuck them.

"Do you understand what I just told you about your rights?"

"Yeah," he said, looking through the cage and out the windshield at the house.

"Anything you want to tell me about what happened?"

He hunched up and leaned forward to take the pressure off the handcuffs.

"Let me double-lock those for you," Hanson said, "so they don't tighten up. I'm willing to write down your version of things. What really happened?"

"Just like she said."

"Do you know her?" Hanson asked, finishing the cuffs, putting the keys back in his belt.

"It doesn't matter," he said. He looked back and up at Hanson. "What are *you* doing out here?"

"It's my job."

"Uh-huh." The sweat-and-vomit miasma of the patrol car wafted over Hanson. The stink that collected on his uniform and in his hair every night.

"I knew her," he said, settling into the backseat. "A long time ago I knew her. I thought about her a lot when I was locked up. I called her two days ago and she told me to come over. Just got out of the joint, living with my mother. Can't find a job, ex-con, you know. Fucked. I rode the bus and walked the rest of the way. She came to the door. She let me in. When I walked inside, I thought, 'What if this was *my* house.' You know? If *I* lived there, if *we* lived there, me and her. She locked the door. I followed her upstairs, thinking about that.

"When her old man showed up she started screaming. What else could she do?"

"Why don't I write this up, man," Hanson said. "You'll be fine."

"I won't be *fine*. Do I look like I'm gonna be *fine*? I'll be going back anyway. Why fuck up her life? He's taking good care of her. Better than I could do."

"You sure? I'd do a good job writing this up. Why go back for something you didn't do?"

He looked down at the floorboard. "What you think I went in the first time for?" He looked at Hanson. "You work here? I'm guilty. Write that up." Then he said, "I'm glad I came to see her. It was worth it."

Maybe he was lying. Maybe she'd planned the whole thing after he called for some reason. Or maybe he wasn't lying, and she hadn't planned anything, and they just wanted to see each other. Maybe they used to be in love. That stopped him. He'd never imagined anybody ever was in love out here. Now, wasn't that a thought? That would make his job just about impossible. And he thought about it all that night. He'd never considered it one way or the other.

And when had *he* ever been in love?

CHAPTER THIRTY-TWO

THINKING ABOUT LIBYA

Hanson was out of liquor. He'd thought he had another fifth of tequila but hadn't been able to find it, going through drawers and cabinets and looking under furniture, room by room. He did find a stethoscope behind a bookcase, which he draped around his neck while he continued looking for the tequila. One night, months before, he'd picked it up off the floor of an emergency room hallway, taken it home and forgotten about it.

He gave up on the tequila, got a beer out of the refrigerator, and took it back to the sagging sunporch, where he could see an arc of the MacArthur Freeway just visible in the distance where it curved around the east wing of ACH, the place he took the wounded and insane on nights he was working. As always traffic was heavy in both lanes, streaks of red and white light suspended in the black sky. When he reached down for his beer the stethoscope tapped him on the chest, reminding him it was there, and he took it from around his neck and studied it in the dim light from the kitchen. He put the rubber ear tips in his ears, pressed the black diaphragm against his chest and stood very still, searching for his heart.

The sound was distant, as if from the bottom of a faraway ocean where it had been waiting, calling to him all his life. A fluid double pulse, tireless, fearless, unmistakable, speaking to him in a long-forgotten language that, if he could only remember it, would explain everything.

He looked over at the phone. She'd told him that it was foolish for them to see each other. Bad for everybody, especially Weegee. They hardly knew each other, and anyway, she was black and he was a white cop. Hanson knew she was right, but he was in love with her. He'd been in love before, but nothing like this. He couldn't stop thinking about her. He thought about her all the time. He thought about her when he was at work. He thought about her after work when he got drunk in the kitchen. All in the world he wanted anymore was to be with her, look at her, hear her voice, and keep her safe. He thought about her every night when he went to sleep and woke up thinking about her. Almost forty years old and a fool in love. Maybe, he thought, if the lights hadn't gone out that night when he had been cradling her foot in his hand, her graceful perfect foot. Who knew? Now, though, he wanted to hold her foot again, press his face against it, smell it, kiss it, wash the blood off with hot compresses, then gently clean it with cold, stinging alcohol.

What if he went to see her now, off duty, and she was with some other guy, some black guy? Would he be sensible enough to walk away, sensible and reasonable and gutless enough to leave? And if the other guy decided not to make it easy for him to leave, well, then he'd have to fuck the guy up and go to prison. For what? Fuckin' A, he was stupid. He knew why and what for.

It was dark out there, late, time was passing. He imagined her naked in her bed, the sheets across her shoulders, or thrown off onto the floor. Lying on her side. On her stomach. Time was relentless. He imagined her lying on her back, alone in the bed. He imagined himself naked next to her, his arm across her breasts, smelling her, putting his mouth on hers, what they would do. And her hands, the gold and silver rings on her fingers, her hands on him.

He pulled the stethoscope from his ears, crossed the room for his wallet, stuck the Hi Power in the small of his back and left the house. She'd be alone. Weegee was gone for ten days to Camp Mendocino. Hanson had had a conversation with Weegee the week before, when Weegee was standing by his bike at the east end of Lake Merritt watching the cormorants dive for minnows. Weegee had been to Camp Mendocino before. They had canoes and everyone slept in tepees.

Hanson parked directly in front of her house and tried not to run up the walk to her door. A light showed in her window, the only light in the dark block, a candle flickering behind the drawn curtains, tendrils of smoke drifting through the light. A Sam Cooke record was playing in there. He rapped on the door with his knuckles, feeling as if he was in a different time zone, where the woman with the little dogs next door would see him, all the badass neighborhood brothers would see him, everybody would see him there. The OPD would nail him for sure, arrest him, fire him, put him in jail. He didn't care.

The door opened, and as soon as he stepped inside she closed and locked it behind him. "I knew you'd come tonight," she said. It was 3 a.m. and she was smoking marijuana, holding the joint delicately with her fingertips. She smiled at him, moving with the light and shade of the candle, across the walls of the room, away and back, the joint glowing as she inhaled, unbuttoning her white cotton blouse.

"I've been thinking about you," she said, turning with the light.

"Here, baby," she said, taking the joint from her lips, hissing smoke and holding it out to him. "I won't tell." She ran the fingers of one hand through her hair while he watched her, the joint hot between his fingers. "Or have you come to arrest me finally?" she said, pulling her blouse open, peeling it off one arm and flinging it to the floor from the other.

The last time he'd smoked dope had been after an academic cocktail party, with a chubby assistant professor who taught something in the Art Department, whose husband, she'd told him, was on leave in Prague, documenting prewar deco architecture there.

"No, ma'am," he said, sucking in smoke, feeling like he'd stepped into a miracle. "I'm off duty tonight. Two criminals," he said, taking another drag, "beyond the law." It was the happiest he'd felt since—well, he couldn't remember. "Though it may be necessary," he began, his chest so tight he wondered how he was still able to breathe, forgetting what he'd planned to say as, looking at him, she reached back with both hands and let her bra drop.

CHAPTER THIRTY-THREE

COUNTERFEIT STARS

Hanson is sleeping, watching the birds in his backyard at dawn with Weegee.

They're looking through the bird book to decide if it's a black-chinned hummingbird out there or an Allen's hummingbird. Weegee holds up the bird book. "The book says you can't tell the difference between the females."

Hanson smiles at him. "Might be the same species."

Across town in San Antonio Village—another country—Felix watches the night sky where a counterfeit star hovers above the bay, blinking and flashing out there, as if it is twinkling, in and out of position. Counterfeit stars. They put at least four of them up every night, at least four, sometimes more than that. High-altitude aircraft—he calls them star throwers—drop the stars off at dusk, synchronized with the aircraft strobe lights, to settle into position, where they go dark, then light back up when the aircraft have gone. It's obvious what they're doing, but no one has reported on it or written about them. How do they keep it a secret? The air traffic controllers have to know.

Most people never look up at the night sky, and the stars are masked by light pollution, but still, thousands of people must notice and don't say anything. Afraid they'll sound crazy.

Felix tries not to bring it up anymore, even to Levon. He can see in their eyes what they're thinking when he does, smiling and agreeing with anything he says, like he's crazy.

He can't afford to get angry about it. That's what the stars are hoping he'll do. He can't get angry.

The counterfeit stars know that he's aware of them, what they're doing. They're listening to him think it right now. They don't care if he knows. Because what can he do about it? Report it to the authorities?

He laughs. It's almost 4 a.m.

Some strike force or task force is collecting intelligence on him, all the agencies—OPD, DEA, FBI, ATF, CIA. The DOJ's in on it too—they own the judges. Others. Every night, without warrants or probable cause, with nothing. All illegal. They make the laws up and change them as they go. Tap his phone, bug his house. IRS in the banks counting his money. Informants everywhere. Snitches watching him day and night, recording every word he says, then splicing them into whatever they need him to say so he's guilty. And the stars up there every night.

When they can't catch him in something, they just make it up. Things that never happened. Classify them out of the public record, "Law Enforcement Only," then reference them in a couple of bulletins or quarterly reports, and pretty soon they're true. "Common knowledge, Your Honor," and none of his lawyers will have access to dispute them. But they'll still want their fuckin' money.

Nothing to do about it now, he thinks, but go to bed. Try to sleep. It's getting cold.

CHAPTER THIRTY-FOUR

SECOND TIME

Hanson and Libya are in bed together, comfortable now. Out on the Nimitz somewhere a fire truck honks and yodels, the neighborhood dogs howling along. A police helicopter clatters up out of the bay and thunders overhead, its spotlight slashing the windows.

"Tell me something you've never told anyone before," Libya said.

He told her about the Vietnamese women with the water buffalo. How he would have killed them. What he was like back then.

"I almost died from shooting heroin," she told him, her eyes glittering with the memory. "I was twenty," she said, throwing one naked leg over his, arching her back.

"How…" Hanson began, looking at her, forgetting what he'd started to say, forgetting who he was now, all of it.

"Too late," he said, "to call this off."

"It was too late the first time I let you in the door."

*   *   *

An hour later, still in bed, they'd been passing a joint back and forth, when Hanson said, "Something else I've never told anybody—I don't think I have, not for twenty years, anyway, because I'd forgotten it myself all these years, till now. It's not a secret, though, or a confession."

"Let me get comfortable first," Libya said, moving herself closer, "before you tell the story."

"My junior year in high school I got a part-time evening job at the Holiday Inn in Greensboro. All the hotels and motels, restaurants, movie theatres, bathrooms, everything, was segregated, by law. But when I worked there—I don't know why or who decided it—the Holiday Inn was where the black singing groups stayed, and the Holiday Inn was the nicest motel in town. It was a secret. If it had become common knowledge, white people would stop coming there. They'd have gone out of business. My mom had gone to high school with the manager, and that's how I got the job. I was sixteen and looked like I was about twelve years old.

"My job there was mostly being the room service waiter, and, of course the groups ordered room service because the restaurants in town were segregated and mostly white anyway. After my high school classes, I'd go to the Holiday Inn, put on one of those white waiter smocks, and pretty soon the room service requests started coming in. These groups, Libya, were huge, Motown, people you heard on the radio every day, Top 40 artists: the Shirelles, the Marvelettes, the Chiffons, Patti LaBelle and the Bluebells, the best there were. They were stuck there before and after their shows, sort of sequestered there in the Holiday Inn, bored.

"I'd bring them five-dollar shrimp cocktails on those big phony silver platters with a big bell-shaped cover over them.

Hamburgers. I'd bring them egg sandwiches on that huge platter that I rolled down the halls on a cart.

"I'd knock on the door, 'room service.' They'd kind of sing, 'Come in,' or the next time, 'Come on in here, honey. We been waiting for you,' and they'd be sitting on the edge of one of the twin beds, maybe four on a bed, in matching stage outfits, the whole group smiling at me as I came through the door. They teased me and made me blush. They were wonderful.

"The men who were on tour—these were the real guys too: Gary U.S. Bonds, the Isley Brothers, Junior Walker and the All Stars—I knew their music, sang their songs when I was alone. They were the best in the world. The guys would pay for the women's setups—ice and mixer for the bottles they'd bought at a government-run Alcoholic Beverage Store, pay me from big rubber-banded flash rolls, twenties on top and one dollar bills mostly beneath.

"I remember I'd tell the women's groups—they're sitting on the edge of their bed—tell them how great they were, how I loved their music, them drinking straight rum from paper Dixie cups, and they'd say, 'Thank you, baby.'"

Hanson laughed at the memory, happy in it, spread his hand out over Libya's ribs, held her breast, lowered his head to hers and looked in her eyes and said, "'Thank you, baby.'"

CHAPTER THIRTY-FIVE

OVERTIME

She's strutting now, the dispatcher, down in the windowless radio room in the basement of the Justice Center, tethered to the electricity by a coiled black cord. Assigning one-man cars to complaints and calls for service, responding to traffic stops, record checks, requests for backup—sending the cars out and bringing them back on line, good to go again. The 911 operators handle the phones, process the backed up calls, all the requests, complaints, and accusations, write them in shorthand on punch cards and hand them to her when she passes. Robbery, rape, burglary, battery, domestic violence. Shots fired, missing persons, suspicious persons, DUIs, trespassers, wife beaters, lewd and lascivious acts. Drunks, barking dogs, the insane, screaming, hissing, talking in tongues, passed out, down on the street, dead. It's always night in the radio room, always late, down there in the basement where the twenty-four-hour clock glows like the moon.

Hanson cleared from the call and angled down toward the freeway. His ankle ached from falling off a chain-link fence, his left hand was bleeding on the steering wheel, and he was two hours into overtime. He pulled over on a quiet street just north of the freeway and shined the flashlight on his hand. Two puncture marks like a snakebite at the base of his thumb. He must have done it when he lost his hold and fell off the fence. He was wiping the blood off onto his sock when he heard a car wreck—an explosion of metal and glass—looked up and out the windshield at a rising cloud of steam glowing silver white in his headlights half a block away.

"5Tac51. I've got a collision in the seven hundred block of Hamilton Street. Are there any graveyard shift cars available to take it while I check for an ambulance and stand by?"

Negative, 5Tac51.

"I'll be at this location, then," Hanson said.

Maybe it's not as bad as it sounded, he thought. Then he smiled at himself. Nothing he was going to be able to kiss off on an assignment card and go home.

He turned on his brights and overheads. A cherried-out '63 Chevy, a Kandy apple red Super Sport with wire wheels, the front end destroyed, floated in the steam. As he watched, the Chevy backed away from the parked Buick it had hit, pulling the Buick's door off, dropping it in the street, then, trailing debris, thumped past Hanson's patrol car on flat tires, the radiator fan clattering, fan belt squealing.

"Well, shit," Hanson said aloud, turning around to follow it, lights and siren on now, adding to the noise. He stayed behind the Chevy at twenty-five miles an hour and gave Radio a description and license number. A DUI arrest might get somebody on graveyard shift to swing by to get his name on the report, and maybe he could kiss the paperwork off on him. A moment later the smashed-in left front fender of the red Chevy peeled the tire off the wheel, and the rim, throwing sparks, pivoted it into two more parked cars. The horn started blaring, lights began coming on all over the neighborhood. A lot of paperwork.

He pulled in behind the Chevy, blocking it from backing up again, his overhead lights flashing, and ran up to the driver's door, standing just behind it so the driver couldn't slam it open into him. She looked like she was fifteen. "Get out of the car," he yelled over the horn. She ignored him, grinding the starter. Steam from the crushed radiator blew on him, a hot fog, stinking of burned rubber, soaking his wool shirt. "Get outta the car."

"Fuck you," she said, blood bubbling from her nose, turning the key on/off/on/off.

She was under the influence of more than just the liquor Hanson could smell. She looked back at him, spit blood, her teeth pink, and he saw it in her eyes. Shit, she was dusted.

The grinding starter lurched the Chevy backward. Hanson reared back out of the way as the driver kicked the door open and the ankle he'd twisted gave way. He fell to the street and she ran off into the dark. Hanson limped after her, pain shooting up from his ankle like electricity, his holstered pistol slapping his thigh. He reached to his belt for the PAC-set to call for assistance, then remembered it had stopped working. He'd lose her if he went back to the patrol car to use the car radio.

She wasn't running very well, and she wasn't very big, but if he was right about the angel dust he'd have a hard time handcuffing her by himself. In addition to killing pain, it made a person superhumanly strong. It also made them crazy.

Hanson cut her off at the front yard of the corner lot, grabbed her arm, and she pulled it free. He grabbed her other arm and hung on. She clawed his face. She tore his name tag off. When she tried to bite him, Hanson stepped back and jerked her off her feet, which put them both on the ground because Hanson's ankle gave way again.

"Eeeeee," she screamed. "Eeeeeee. Help! Eeeeeeee."

As he got to his feet, she lunged for him, but he threw her back on the ground.

From the screened porch of the corner house, a woman yelled, "Leave her alone. I got a gun and I will shoot you."

"Ma'am," Hanson began, as the girl got to her feet. He kicked her legs out from under her.

"Help!" she screamed. "*Chinga tu madre!* Help meeee!"

The voice from the porch yelled, "I got a shotgun. Go on now. Let that child alone or I'll shoot."

"I'm a police officer."

"Then why you beatin' up on a little girl like that? You ain't no policeman. You just a street thug and a rapist."

The girl spit at him, *"Puto,"* and got to her knees, then up like a runner in the starting blocks, just as a flashlight beam from the porch hit him in the face. "I *will* shoot you!" The girl sprinted away.

"Shoot me, then, lady. Go ahead the fuck and shoot everybody," he yelled back. "And shoot the people whose cars she ran into, why don't you," he went on, hobbling after her.

He heard sirens. Red and blue lights began flickering through the tops of the trees. The flashlight beam went out.

Two patrol cars, coming from different directions, had her caught in their headlights. He limped toward them as two cops got out of the cars and grabbed the girl, slammed her to the street, and fought to twist her arms behind her. Hanson stood on the curb and watched as she pulled loose.

They knocked her down again, on her stomach, one of them put one knee on her neck, the other on her upper arm, grabbed a handful of hair and twisted her head, while the other cop dropped a knee in the small of her back, got one wrist handcuffed, then, with the help of the first cop, brought the other arm around and cuffed it too. When she tried to get to her feet, the second cop stuck his nightstick between her cuffed wrists—handle above one wrist, the tip below the other—and twisted her arms till she stayed down. A good job.

"Thanks for the help," one of them told Hanson.

Hanson laughed. "No," he said, "*I* thank *you*."

"You're on overtime, aren't you?"

"Absolutely."

"You might as well transport her. Since you're going in anyway."

"Of course. You guys probably need to go back to sleep. But who's gonna do the paperwork on this shit?"

The two other cops looked at each other. They'd been on the street for maybe fifteen years.

"*You're* the primary officer."

"You guys made the arrest."

"What's your problem, man?" the other cop asked him. "We're just here to help you out."

"It's been a long night, Officer. Yeah, I'll transport her. You two gonna help me load her ass into my car?"

"Yeah. Yeah. We can do that."

They cuffed her legs while she spit and tried to bite them. Hanson brought his car down, and they lifted her by the handcuff chains, ankles and wrists, flopping like a fish, and tossed her in the back of Hanson's car and slammed the door.

"Don't forget to put our names into the report. We'd *appreciate it*, okay? We need the court time. You know, we all gotta cover each other's asses out here."

"You bet," Hanson said.

"Singer and Neal," the cop said. He was giving Hanson their badge numbers when the girl kicked the side window out of the patrol car with her bare feet. The three of them pulled her out of the car again and used Hanson's belt to strap both handcuff chains together, hog-tying her and throwing her back in.

"I'm taking her on to jail," Hanson said. "I don't want her dying in my patrol car while I'm making sketches of the damage. I'll put you guys in the report if you'll write up the damaged vehicles."

"We'll do it on a continuation form," Singer said, "and turn it in at the end of our shift. Both of us used to work traffic. Just put our names in the report."

"Thank you," Hanson said. He gave Singer the report number and drove on to the freeway.

Even with the cuffs locked down tight, the angel dust made her strong and pain-resistant enough to pull her left hand out, slamming the Plexiglas shield with the freed handcuff, banging her head against it, screeching at Hanson how her boyfriend's crew was gonna fuck him *up* for touching her. "He don' let *nobody* touch me but *him*, mother*fucker*. They gonna cap you' skinny white ass, *pendejo*."

Once he had pulled into the jail parking area and they'd lowered the clattering steel doors, he sat on a concrete ramp and watched as four jailers fought her out of the car.

He washed his hands and forearms twice, his face and neck, though it was probably too late by then to keep her blood from getting into his own. He limped upstairs to the front office, found a desk with an IBM Selectric typewriter, and began typing like a demon, trying to finish the reports before a civilian clerk showed up for work and wanted his desk back. His blue wool shirt was bloody, and it was torn where the name tag had been ripped off. His pants were muddy and grass stained, and one knee was torn. He'd probably have to replace both of them, shirt and pants, at eighty dollars each. The swollen heel of his thumb was hot and throbbing, and he thought for a moment about getting a tetanus shot, but all he wanted was to get home, drink some tequila, and go to bed. He ignored his aching ankle, the scratches on his cheek and neck that stung with sweat, and kept typing. He always typed better when he was exhausted. He'd had a typewriter just like this one that he'd bought with money he'd won in an essay contest back in graduate school. After a few minutes he was almost enjoying himself, the words taking him away.

An hour later he'd finished—it would have taken him twice as long, three times as long, to write the narratives if he'd done them by hand. He pulled the last form out of the humming IBM, stacked it on top of the pile of finished forms, and sat back in the office chair. All he had left to do was the overtime-worked requisition form.

He pulled one out of his briefcase and looked at it. One-third the size of a piece of typing paper, the top two inches was taken up with boxes printed FOR AUDITORS USE ONLY. The bottom half a row of signature/approval boxes to be signed by the shift sergeant, watch commander, division commander, and bureau commander. That left him a two-by-six-inch box to summarize the calls he'd just finished typing up. There was no way he could have squeezed it in with a pen—black ink only, blue ink voided any OPD form—so it would be legible enough to be approved, and if any of what he wrote was outside the lines of the box, it would be disapproved. If the form was approved it was kept for six years, probably to build a case against someone for excessive claims for overtime—who knew? If it wasn't approved, again, per the phone-book-thick *Manual of Rules*, it would be "destroyed."

The three hours of overtime he'd just put in on top of his ten and a half hour shift was almost enough to pay for a new uniform, which would take him all morning to have tailored, on his own time. Destroyed, he thought. Fuck you. Destroy *this!*

He rifled through the desk drawers and found a smaller

typeface ball for the IBM, locked the machine so that it squeezed the letters closer together, and, single-spacing the sentences in, managed, on his second try, to fit in a very abridged but acceptable version of the calls he was claiming overtime for. They'd probably find a way to disapprove it or lose it, and he needed a supervisor's key to turn on the Xerox machine.

He heard them before they came through the door, and pulled on a sap glove, but he didn't look up as Barnes and Durham came laughing into the office.

"Well, look here," Durham said, standing with his hands on his pistol butt and nightstick. "Must be a new secretary."

"Did you get promoted?" Barnes said. "This is the job you should have had in the first place. You don't belong out on the street."

"You guys are so manly in your leathers, it's enough to bring out the queer in me," Hanson said, swishing his right hand. "Where you been, trolling down South of Market?"

Durham slammed his helmet down on a desk and said, "Come on, you little dick, let's see who's the faggot. Come on, *come on.*"

Hanson smiled, tired but happy now, leaning back in his chair.

"Come on, man," Barnes said, taking Durham by his jacket. "He's not worth all the paperwork."

"Bye-bye," Hanson said.

"The DA's gonna be calling you about that Anchor Tavern deal with the bikers. It goes to court next week," Barnes said. "You *be* there."

"If I'm there, I won't be a friendly witness."

"What the fuck does that mean?" Barnes said, still hanging on to Durham.

"It means that if I testify I'm gonna say it was bullshit, everything but the DUI. I had that Indian arrested when you showed up and started the fight. Maybe they'll sue you for aggravated assault. I hear that the Angels have a big legal fund."

Barnes grabbed Durham with both hands. "Come on," he said, pulling Durham toward the elevators, then, over his shoulder to Hanson, "You're in deeper shit than you know."

On the way home Hanson thought about the time he watched *Yellow Submarine* in Vietnam.

CHAPTER THIRTY-SIX

LIBYA TELLS WEEGEE
A STORY

It is midmorning, Libya and Weegee are sitting at the kitchen table. Weegee is painting a birdhouse that Libya helped him build, using plans in a book he got out of the library. Libya is looking at his bird book.

"Tell me about those dogs who went to Texas, LeRon and JJ," Weegee said, applying green paint to the roof of the birdhouse.

"LeRon and JJ? They got stopped by the Highway Patrol."

"What happened?"

"LeRon was speeding. JJ said he should slow down, but LeRon thought he was already a bad dog gangsta. He told JJ, 'Relax, you'll live longer.' And that's when a Highway Patrol car pulled them over."

"It's a stolen car! You shouldn't drive fast in a stolen car!" Weegee said.

She nodded. "LeRon doesn't know anything but his front yard and watching TV. He just about peed on the seat covers when a big dumb highway patrolman walked up to the driver's window—his hand on his gun, ready to shoot somebody like they always are—and told him, 'Would you please step out of your veh-hickle. Sir.'"

"Oh no," Weegee said, putting down the paintbrush.

"LeRon was so scared he almost jumped out the other window and ran off into a bunch of skinny pine trees."

"He would of got shot for sure if he ran," Weegee said, "and the highway patrolman would have said he saw him reach for a gun, then dropped a gun next to him."

"But JJ growled at LeRon, real quiet, to shut him up, and *bit his ear* so quick that cop didn't even see it, to calm him down. Then JJ says to that highway patrolman, real polite, but like he was scared too, 'Officer, we sure glad to see you.'

"That highway patrolman looked at him like he was crazy and told him to put his paws on the dashboard where he could see them, and JJ did, right away, but he kept talking too, said, 'Officer, my friend Spot here, he was driving fast because he was scared.'

"'He'd better step out of the vehicle and do it *now*,' the highway patrolman said.

"'Officer,' JJ said, 'we just a couple of old working dogs, go to work every day and obey the law. And respect police officers too. Back at that last rest stop, we were in the *pet area*, when a man, I mean two men—I'm so scared I can't hardly even talk—came out of the men's room, and they both had guns. When they saw us doing our business in the designated pet area they laughed, and the one with the shotgun said to the other one, 'Hey, *ese*, check out these mariposa little *perros*,' then he laughed in a real bad way and yelled, 'You ugly little *perritos* better find another place to pee.' They both had gang tattoos all around their necks and down their arms, crosses and daggers and skulls.'

"'And teardrop tattoos under their eyes,' LeRon managed to add, 'and the Virgin of Guadalupe on their chests.'

"JJ kicked him when he said that.

"'The one with the shotgun had a pistol and holster just like yours, Officer. On his belt. I forgot to tell you,' JJ said, making himself shiver, 'they scared me so bad. And before they saw us the one with the pistol said something in Spanish and the other one said, 'Fuck a bunch of cops. We already killed one cop,' and slapped his hand on that pistol, just like yours, like the police carry to protect us, and said, 'So a couple of *perros* won't make any difference,' and he pulled his gun and said, 'You better run faster than that cop did.'

"LeRon got so excited at JJ's story that he started barking," Libya told Weegee, who started laughing too.

"'And we got in our car and Spot here drove away as fast as he could. And that's why we were speeding, Officer.'

"'Back at that Red Rock Rest Stop?' the highway patrolman growled at them.

"'Yes, sir,' JJ said, 'and they might still be there.'

"So that highway patrolman ran back to his car, drove across a ditch, breaking off his muffler, and went roaring and backfiring the other way, lights and siren and everything else turned on, headed for the rest stop."

"And JJ just made it all up!" Weegee said.

"He's an ugly dog with those pop eyes and scrunched up little face, but he's smart," she said. "Then he told LeRon to head for Nevada, but *drive the speed limit*, and before long they were in Reno playing the nickel slot machines."

CHAPTER THIRTY-SEVEN

CONCUSSION

Hanson was working downtown again when he got a call to cover 2L23 on a neighborhood problem up in North Oakland. He pulled over and checked his *Thomas Guide* by the light of a lopsided full moon to locate the address, near Your Black Muslim Bakery, where calls for service were rare. The OPD allowed the neighborhood to police itself with Black Muslim enforcers. The police brass didn't like it but followed orders and did their best to pretend they weren't the city council's stooges.

When Hanson finally found McClure Street, 2L23's car was pulled to the curb in front of the address Radio had given, and a new blue-over-blue Cadillac was parked crossways in the middle of the street two houses up the block. Three of its four doors were wide open, the headlights and interior lights were on.

Whoever was working 2L23 that night—the primary officer on the call—didn't notice Hanson's arrival. He was just inside the doorway of the complainant's house, his head down, taking notes, talking to a woman wrapped in an elaborate blue Muslim gown and head scarf.

Hanson rolled closer to the car in the middle of the street.

When he flicked his bright lights on/off and blipped the loud-speaker, a Muslim in a black suit and bow tie, wearing a narrow-brimmed black hat, bolted from behind the open driver's door, running away down the street. Hanson punched the gas, keeping him in his headlights, closing on him before he sprinted down a tree-lined sidewalk and Hanson hit the curb. He threw the patrol car in PARK—the transmission jolting it to a stop—pulled the keys, kicked the door open, and ran after him in his steel-toed boots.

He had no idea why the Muslim in the hat had bolted from the car, but it didn't matter. He was a suspect, for something, because he was running. It didn't matter what it was or if he'd done it or not, because he was *guilty* of running. Fucker, he thought, his lungs already aching, working inside the hot cinched-down Kevlar vest. The suspect was running from *him,* not from the OPD, or from some drug law or subsection of the California Penal Code.

In spite of his equipment slapping and pulling his pants down, his drinking, poor diet, and chronic lack of sleep, not many suspects ever outran him. The few that had were teenagers in basketball shoes, sprinting into one of the projects where they knew every hole in the chain-link fences, all the shortcuts, crawl spaces, bad dogs, clotheslines, ditches, and the houses where someone would pull them inside and turn off the lights. If someone ran from a cop, when you caught him, especially if he tried to resist the handcuffs, especially if it meant you had to get your uniform dry-cleaned from rolling in the dirt with him, most cops, Hanson included, would probably slam his face into the dirt or asphalt, repeatedly, while telling him, out of breath, "Don't. Ever run. From the police."

The suspect was more than half a block ahead of Hanson, but

Hanson was gaining on him, and every time the suspect glanced back it cost him an instant in momentum and morale. Hanson kept his breathing even.

The streetlights overhead threw their shadows, Hanson's and the suspect's, onto the sidewalk, where the shadows lengthened, shortened, faded into the next patch of light, from streetlight to streetlight. The suspect's narrow-brimmed black hat lifted off his head, hit the ground, and rolled on its brim until it toppled over the curb onto the street. He glanced back, hesitated, made a decision, slid and skidded to a stop, spun around, and began running *at* Hanson, who dropped his shoulder as they collided, the suspect going over him, his knee slamming Hanson's head back, both of them going down.

The suspect started to get up, and Hanson, still on his back, willing himself to stay conscious, threw his arm back, grabbed the suspect's pant leg, and pulled him back, facedown. Hanson crawled up his back, pulling himself hand over hand, while the suspect struggled and got on all fours beneath him. Hanson took a handful of hair and pulled his head back, gripped his throat and focused what was left of his strength into digging his thumb and fingers around the ball of cartilage, his esophagus, till he saw two more cops running toward them, their gold hat badges glinting in the streetlights. Then unconsciousness took him like a leopard dropping from a tree.

He woke up three hours later, strapped to a gurney, hot and sick.

"Take it easy," a voice said.

"*You* take it easy."

"What's your name?"

Hanson opened his eyes and pulled himself up against the straps to demand, "What's *your* name," but the pain took his breath away. He'd have vomited, but he hadn't eaten anything for a day

and a half. He gently put his head back down and closed his eyes
again.

"Can you tell me your name?"

Hanson slowed his breathing, apologized to the pain for disrespecting it, and waited politely for the next question.

"Do you know who you are?"

"Yes." His head boomed, and he added, "Hanson. 7374P."

The doctor told him he'd tried to fight his way out of the
ambulance.

"I'm sorry."

If they unstrapped him would he act right now?

"Yes, sir."

Someone unbuckled the restraints.

Did he have someone at home who could wake him up, check
on him every couple of hours?

"No."

Did he have an alarm clock he could set to wake himself up every two hours?

"What for?" he asked, annoyed, and the pain narrowed its eyes
at him. "Why?" he asked, softly.

He had a concussion and if he didn't wake up every couple of
hours, just to be sure he was okay, he might sleep himself into a
coma and never wake up.

"Fine," he said. "Sure." He wasn't going to set a fucking alarm
clock.

Hanson is sleeping.

He's been asleep for fifteen hours. The sodium vapor streetlight, up at the corner of Jean Street and Santa Clara, has constructed a circuit board on the window shade. It glows and fades,
cycles on and off, flickers, the polarity reversing itself sixty times
a second. He sees the electricity through red webs of capillaries

in his eyelids, hears it crackling off the window shade, filling the room till it's a roar, and now he's strapped into one of those tiny old space capsules, like the one he saw at the Smithsonian before the war. It hadn't been designed to hold a human, but they'd wedged him into a slanted seat to test him, to see if his heart and lungs, his brain, the pockets and coils of internal organs, could survive whatever is out there.

He is not afraid of dying, but he is alone and far away, lost now for a long time in a wrong life. Belted and buckled into the rivet-studded capsule, he feels the heat building. Sweat stings his eyes, his ears ache and pop. The capsule shudders, picks up speed, pushes him deeper into endless sleep as the walls begin to glow cherry red. He feels his face distorting. He can barely breathe. He can't breathe. The heat shield is boiling away in clots of fiery ceramic slag and magma and black honeycomb.

Suddenly the capsule lurches and rocks beneath him, slowing as the drogue parachute deploys, rocking the capsule, and he's weightless, the pressure on his chest lifting. The capsule hisses into the ocean, bounces, bobs side to side in the waves, and wakes Hanson up in his bed in Oakland, the window shade snapping open to blue sky and sunlight. He lies there sweating, alive. The mattress bounces beneath him again, and the black rabbit hits the floor and hops away.

CHAPTER THIRTY-EIGHT

WEEGEE VISITS

Pain takes us to places we cannot anticipate, to events we have managed to completely forget, returns us to worlds we hadn't known we ever visited. Pain bends our attention to what we would ignore. Hanson used to smile and say that pain was his friend.

He lay there after the black rabbit had gone, studying the pattern of cracks in the plaster ceiling. It was hot, and he was naked on top of the sheets. Still alive, saved this time by a New Year's Eve hallucination that wouldn't be ignored or dismissed. The black rabbit had awakened him from the coma dream that would have killed him if he'd slept any longer.

His head was pounding, and he knew it was going to get worse. The last time something had hit him hard enough to knock him out for more than a few seconds, he'd been drunk, driving home from the Portland police club at 3 a.m. in a snowstorm, almost home, when he hit black ice and drove his VW van into a phone pole—it had gotten a lot worse the next day. Assaulted that time by a known phone pole, though, no question about it.

Whoever he was, the man who'd run out from under his own

hat had scheduled Hanson for an appointment with pain. It was already in the house, just looking around, he supposed, to see how Hanson had changed since the last time, reckoning who he was now so it would know the answers to the questions it would be asking him.

He should have gotten some pills from the emergency room doctor, but it was too late for that now. He didn't have anyone to call, and anyway, the phone was way out in the kitchen. He hoped it wouldn't ring. He hated the phone.

His eyes followed the cracks in the plaster above the bed, tracing the rivers and tributaries and deltas across the ceiling, imagining himself on his way out to sea, the water changing color beneath him from brown to green and finally to a blue as pale and clear as the sky, doing his best not to think of what would be coming soon to see him, sailing into the horizon. He eased a pillow beneath his head and went to sleep.

The house was dark when the pain woke him up and began punching him behind his eyes. The questions were easy at first, the pain exploratory, tentative, patient. Hanson denied everything: What? How should he know? No. He wasn't there.

Soon though, the interrogation began in earnest, questions coming faster, one after the other, and the punishment for each evasion, denial, or excuse was worse each time, in different, surprising ways until Hanson had to recite to himself the tricks he'd learned:

Stay relaxed, like you do at the dentist, think of it like that, for as long as you can. Don't anticipate the drill. Just let it happen.

Answer a question with a question—but not smart-ass. Try that a couple of times, two or three times, but spread them out. Don't be disrespectful, but don't show fear or weakness. Interrupt them while you still can. Ask them to repeat the question.

"Wait!" Tell them you're not the person they want. As if it just occurred to you that a mistake, an honest mistake, has been made. Who knows how. No one's fault, it's built into the system somewhere.

Sincerity will buy time. When that stops working, move on to bewilderment. It's going to be a long night, so accept it.

As it gets worse, visualize yourself on another planet—a different self, the *real* you, on a dark planet light years into the future, watching the false you being questioned. Say to yourself, softly, "I'm not me. Again, I'm not me, I'm not me…"

Relax your eyes and imagine the future. Pretend that it looks hopeful.

If you can make yourself sleep…No. They'll wake you up and make you pay for that. Disregard. Forget that one. Do not try sleep unless it's worked for you in the past.

Never get angry, and do not deceive yourself into believing you can win. You deserve whatever you get. You're guilty. Confess and apologize for trying to deny it.

Do not think you can make friends with the pain. If you do, it will be perceived as the desperate, stupid trick that it is. Do not attempt to be clever or ironic, and never, ever patronize the pain.

Dawn is on the way. Do not shoot yourself in the head. Don't allow yourself to think about the gun, don't look at it and *do not* touch it.

Consider the situation from other perspectives.

He was better at dawn. He thought the phone had been ringing during the night, but since most of the phone calls he received were prerecorded messages, he usually ignored the phone anyway, the mindless ringing.

By afternoon he was half-asleep, trying not to think about the night coming up because the pain was already bad. The bird feeder was empty, the birdbath dried up by now. So what? Fuck the fuckin' birds. No. That's wrong thinking and it will come back on you. You'll pay for that. The birds are good. He wished them well and accepted his guilt for the empty feeder.

The doorbell rang. He thought it had, but no one ever came to the house. It rang again, *ding-dong…ding-dong,* and he knew it wasn't just a burglar or a Seventh Day Adventist. It was someone who'd found out where he lived, who wouldn't go away, waiting for him to open the door.

He sat up, his head gonging, slowly pulled on his jeans, and stood up. The Hi Power was cocked and locked on the floor, a round in the chamber and the safety on. He was sure there was a round in the chamber but decided that he didn't care because he wasn't going to take it with him. It would hurt too much to lower his head far enough to pick it up. Whoever was at the door could kill him, and that would be fine.

He walked slowly and as softly as he could, his head down, eyes on the floor three feet ahead, a posture that seemed to hurt the least. His downcast eyes got a glimpse of a spoked bicycle wheel—that's what it looked like—behind the lace curtain over the beveled green glass. When he got to the door he turned the dead bolt, pulled the door open, and carefully raised his head.

"Hi, Officer Hanson. I hope I didn't wake you up. And I hope it's okay for me to come by your house like this. I haven't seen you for a while so…But maybe I should just go. Are you okay?"

"Weegee," Hanson said, the pain loosening its grip, letting go, stepping back. "Weegee," Hanson said, smiling at him, "come in."

"Is it okay if I bring my bike in too?"

"You bet," Hanson said, the pain walking away, gone, waiting till next time. "Let me put on a shirt."

Weegee leaned the bike against the wall in the living room, and they walked back to the kitchen.

"Good to see you, Weegee," Hanson said, opening the refrigerator door. "I don't…I've got water. Got *ice* water. How about some ice water?"

"Thank you," Weegee said. "You okay?"

"Sure," Hanson said, busting open a plastic tray of ice cubes. "Never better," he said, laughing at that, filling the glass. "Let's go out on the porch."

"Birds," Weegee said. There were still a few seeds left in the feeder and scattered on the ground beneath it.

"Here," Hanson said, putting the glass of ice water on the little table on the back porch. "I'd better get them some water too," he said, filling a pot with water from the faucet, enjoying the way the sound changed as the water got deeper, fuller, as the pot filled. "Bring that bag there," he told Weegee, "and follow me."

They went out the side door, walked down past the collapsed garage to the grass and trees on the slope beneath the screened-in porch. Hanson took down the feeder and filled it, let Weegee fill the birdbath. Went back in the house.

"Birds," Weegee said, finishing off a second glass of ice water, holding it up to the light and clinking the ice cubes against the side of the glass. "You know where The Ville is?" Weegee asked.

"San Antonio Village?"

Weegee nodded. "You ever go there?"

"Just once."

A neon-orange blur appeared—as if out of nowhere—just beyond the porch screen, buzzing, juking side to side.

"What kind of hummingbird is *that?*" Weegee said.

"Rufous."

"I never seen one of them before."

"They don't live here all year round. They migrate from Mexico, up the Pacific Coast, they raise their babies, then the whole family flies back down the other side of the Sierra Nevada to Mexico."

"My auntie has a book about the Aztecs. There's pictures of them with war helmets shaped like hummingbirds."

Hanson thought how it would have been nice if Libya had visited him, along with Weegee. They could sit on the porch and watch the hummingbirds.

CHAPTER THIRTY-NINE

FLINT'S RIBS

The sun was bruised and swollen after a long hot day, hesitating just above the horizon in District Four, where Hanson was standing in line at Flint's Ribs. He was off duty, wearing jeans and a faded black sweatshirt with the sleeves torn off. It had been two weeks since his concussion, and the headaches were gone. Nobody knew anything about the Muslim whose throat he'd tried to crush. Or a car in the middle of the street. He'd been assaulted by a suspect or suspects unknown. Three months and three weeks and he'd have his POST certificate.

The line snaked out the door and down the broken sidewalk past a paved vacant lot fenced with eight-foot chain link anchored in concrete and topped with spooling razor wire. The asphalt had blistered and split over the years, the cracks erupting with weeds that were mostly dead from the heat now. Someone had spent so much money on paving and fencing that they must have gone broke before they could put up whatever it was they planned to protect so well. The Temple rabbit was over there on the other side of the wire, watching the line at Flint's, scratching his ear.

Hanson, the only white person in line, was so obviously a cop that he was almost as invisible as the black rabbit. If he wasn't a cop, why else would he be there? Some kind of white-boy victim-queer hoping to be beaten up by black people? Probably a common syndrome. Anything you can imagine, they were out there now, doing it, off their meds.

Or was he just another everyday frightened racist who projected his fear wherever he went, enabling—as they say—the latent hostility in what were normally pacific African American citizens? Maybe no one in the line even noticed he was white. He'd known professors and administrators at the university where he'd taught, academic colleagues who certainly were not stupid or insensitive, people with advanced degrees, who never even noticed a student's race and couldn't recall it without consulting a seating chart, if then. Maybe it was just a coincidence that conversation had stopped when he'd walked up the street and gotten in line. Who could know why? He didn't know much of anything anymore. He did know that he was losing weight again, down to one forty. He knew he had a bleeding ulcer but pretended he didn't know. The Pepto-Bismol didn't help anymore.

The sun had begun moving again, slowly, easing itself down into the horizon. Three teenage boys behind him were glaring at the back of his neck, grumbling about po-lice.

Felix's pearly white Rolls rose up out of the sun and down onto the street, coming their way.

"You know who that is? Officer?" One of the boys behind him asked, tentative, semi-friendly, feeling him out.

Hanson shrugged, shook his head without turning around. "A drug dealer?"

"*The* drug dealer..."

"Yeah. Uh-huh," the others agreed.

"So smart, an' proud, so *bad*..."

"Tha's a fac'."

"My *man*."

"He *beyond* the reach of the law."

The heads of everyone in line turned to follow the Rolls as it passed.

"Look here," one of the boys said, almost aggressive now, emboldened by Felix's appearance, "what you doin' out here anyway?"

"On assignment to arrest some ribs."

The sun slid out of sight, the glare gone. The line moved on.

Hanson got two slabs of pork ribs. He smiled and nodded at the three boys as he passed them on the way out, shook the bag of ribs. "In custody."

Felix, in a tan linen suit, was standing on the curb just up the street from the Travelall, waiting for him. His driver was hugging the steering wheel, his head tilted sideways, watching Felix through the open window. The rear door opened, just slightly, then shut again, its tinted window flashing fiery blue-black from the last of the sunset, one of Felix's security guys checking things out.

"Why don't you just come over and work for me?" Felix said, falling into step alongside him.

"I'd be a terrible criminal."

The Rolls followed just behind them on the street. Hanson told himself to relax. Watching them from the bus stop across the street, one of five or six people, was a skinny old man in work pants and a grimy white wife-beater, bent over with age, his shoulder blades folding open like wings. The bus pulled up, its doors hissing open, blocking him from view. The Rolls kept pace with them as they walked, tires grinding and popping over potholes and trash and broken glass.

"There's something I want you to see."

Hanson nodded, looked over at Felix, curious what would happen next.

Across the street the bus hissed, shuddered, and pulled away, the old man gone now.

"Take a walk with me," Felix said, glancing at the sky.

"Lemme throw these ribs in my vehicle," Hanson said.

Felix walked back to the Rolls. "You're making me nervous back here," he told the driver. "We're gonna walk across the cemetery. Wait for us on the other side."

"Levon will have my ass if something happens to you," the driver said.

Felix walked alongside the Rolls for half a block, then stepped back on the sidewalk and under the awning of a shoe shop, where he waved the driver off, telling him, "*I'll* worry about Levon."

Hanson slammed the door to his Travelall and caught up to Felix.

"You drove that all the way from Idaho?" Felix asked him. "Wherever Idaho is."

"It's not pretty," Hanson said. "It's what they call a high-mileage vehicle, but it runs okay."

"You worked for me," Felix said, slipping into a slightly more black accent, "you could buy yourself a *fine* ride."

"Pimpin' ho's an' slammin' Cadillac doors," Hanson said.

They walked into the cemetery on the one-lane blacktop road that wound through the grounds, raised six inches above the grass, like a strip of volcanic lava. So that people could drive to graveside funerals and visit the dead.

"Let's sit down over there," Hanson said, indicating a cluster of Hell's Angels tombstones, a little Stonehenge of black marble, winged skulls on each stone.

"Ruin my suit."

"Well," Hanson said, a little annoyed, adjusting his bag so he'd be able to pull the Hi Power out in a hurry. "You can remain standing or buy a new suit or take that one to the cleaners. It's not that dirty here."

Felix remained standing, watching the sky.

"What did you want to show me?" Hanson said.

"Be patient."

The cemetery was on a hill. Hanson looked north to where, beyond the MacArthur Freeway, the Oakland Hills rose suddenly up, green and affluent. Chabot Park and million-dollar houses. "From East Oakland," he said, thinking out loud, "to the cemetery. Then ascent into the Oakland Hills. Maybe that's heaven in Oakland."

"Just another cemetery," Felix said. "The Muslim you chased the other night, who knocked you out but nobody else saw him?"

"Yeah?"

"He's up there in the park now. With a couple of his bow-tie pals. Why would anybody wear a bow tie?"

"He's dead?"

"I think that's why he stayed in the garbage bag when we rolled him down the hill."

"You know, Felix," Hanson said. "You should just dump people in the bay, or better yet, take 'em out in the desert somewhere and bury 'em there. You're gonna piss off the OPD, dumping bodies in the hills. They don't care about dead black dope dealers, but dumping the bodies in upscale white neighborhoods—it looks bad. It's like jaywalking in front of a police car. Purposely disrespecting them."

Felix laughed. "Time runnin' out. Could this be the end of Felix?" He pulled out his diamond chip hourglass, tipped it, and watched the chips glittering, pulsing, hissing through the neck and spilling out below. When the chips had filled the bottom bulb, he felt his chest, feeling for the beat of his heart, as if he was looking for something in a pocket. "Felix still alive."

"Why didn't anybody see him that night?" Hanson asked. "The Muslim in the hat."

"OPD looks the other way when they catch Muslims in the shit. That's how it is. Because they're *religious,* which they aren't. The city council, the governor, the president, the Rockefellers, all of 'em, made the decision to use the Muslims to be *their* niggers in Oakland. So now the motherfuckers taking over my corners. If I get rid of two or three of them, they recruit replacements out of prison. Give 'em a bow tie and a cheap-ass suit and tell 'em they're the Sons of Allah, Masters of the Earth. And the cops come after *me.* The lieutenant I own—thought I owned—tells me, 'It's just business. Don't worry about it.'

"Look at that," Felix said, pointing up at the sky.

Two stars, suddenly there, bright in the darkening sky.

"Venus and Jupiter," Hanson said. "You can see Jupiter's moons through binoculars, and sometimes, like now, you can sort of see four of them with the naked eye. Looks like they're attached to the planet with wires. Sometimes the two planets look like they're coming head-on from different directions."

"You sure that's what they are?"

"As sure as I am about anything," Hanson said, laughing. "That's what the books say, and I had a telescope in Idaho."

"Okay. But there's something else, besides the planets."

"I like it here," Hanson said. "In the cemetery. Quiet. How come more people don't come up here from the flatlands just to hang out?"

"A cemetery?"

"Some sort of cultural phobia, I guess, huh?"

Felix looked at him and saw that he was smiling. "Yeah," he said. "It's a black thing."

Hanson decided that Felix wasn't going to kill him today. They were talking like normal human beings, something that neither of them ran into very often. Felix had Levon to talk to, Hanson thought. He could see just about where Libya's house was down below.

He smiled at Felix, laughed, settled back against a Hell's Angel tombstone, the evening coming on, considered the rows of tombstones, and thought about Doc, buried in the VA cemetery down in LA. The others? Sergeant Major and Krause probably rotted away in Cambodia, long ago now. He was the one stuck with still being alive. Here he was, sitting in the cemetery with Oakland's major dope dealer, who drove a Rolls-Royce.

"I was fine in the war," he said aloud. "Everybody was afraid of me, and maybe I was crazy, but the whole place was crazy, so if you were *more* crazy, well, that was good. The crazier you acted, the more they were afraid of you. *You* know how that works. If you're crazy and mean, and don't care if you live or die, nobody fucks with you. I could do anything I wanted to over there. I was special. I knew the secret handshake. And I wasn't crazy at all. I wasn't even confused after a while. I was absolutely, utterly sane in that place."

An airliner headed east glinted at thirty thousand feet, catching the last of the sun from over the horizon.

"After that night in front of the liquor store," Felix said, watching the sky, "where you fucked up Lemon and laughed about it, all those people just getting out of your way, I couldn't figure you out. Levon did, but not me. I tried out all kind of, you know, scenarios. Like you were some kind of federal cop."

Hanson laughed.

"Maybe the OPD hired you out of some secret agent school. Or prison."

"I'm scared of prison. Life with morons and retards, the prisoners and the guards, no thank *you*."

"That's what I wanted to show you," Felix said, pointing toward the dark eastern horizon. "It stays in one spot, then moves to another spot, and it's got flashing red and green and blue lights on it, so it looks like it's twinkling."

"One of those phony stars," Hanson said. "It looks like it's twinkling, like stars do, coming up through from the horizon, all that atmosphere reflecting and refracting and distorting them. But that's no twinkling star. In Idaho I took photographs of phony stars through the telescope. And that's no twinkling star."

"The counterfeit stars. They follow me everywhere. Tap my phone, listen in on everything right through walls wherever I go," he said, looking up. "I don't talk about them even to Levon."

"They're sure as shit up there," Hanson said. "And who knows what they can do. But I don't think they're surveilling *you*. Whatever it is, the military puts it up there."

A black Ford jumped up the curb off Camden, skidded on the grass, fishtailed, and straightened out through the arched entrance to the cemetery and up the little one-lane asphalt road, accelerating toward Hanson and Felix, its headlights off. Hanson was already on his feet, recognizing the Ford right away as the Muslims' car from the neighborhood dispute on Monroe Street. There was still enough glow in the west to make out the driver and the two guys in the backseat, who seemed to be arguing, fighting maybe, confused, quick and erratic, really scared, two guys who didn't know what they were doing.

"Well," Hanson said, reaching into his bag, his eyes on the Ford. "Look who's coming here."

The Ford braked, jerked to a stop, rolled a car length closer, stopped again.

Hanson raised the Hi Power free of the bag, shrugging the strap off his shoulder, and ran toward the car, the bag falling to the ground, as the Ford lurched forward again. The rear door flung open and the passenger stumbled out, a pistol in his hand. Flame and smoke filled the car behind him, an automatic weapon, blowing holes up through the roof. Hanson put his front sight on the shooter as he got to his feet, holding the pistol sideways with one hand, like he must have seen in the movies, pointed at Hanson. It bucked silently in his hand each time he jerked the trigger, again and again, not having released the safety. He stood there, looking at Hanson, knowing he was dead. Hanson squeezed two rounds off, into the center of his chest, knocking him back against the car as it squealed off the asphalt, onto the grass across the road. The other shooter up on one knee, trying to get to his feet and swap hands on the smoking Uzi, holding it like somebody who'd never shot one before. He grabbed the barrel, red-hot from the burst of fire he'd put through the roof of the car. It burnt his hand and he dropped it.

Hanson ran past the first shooter, kicked his pistol away and put a round in his head. *Dead.* Then he shot the guy reaching for the Uzi in the forehead and neck, from four feet away. *Dead.*

Skidding on the grass, shifting his stance, he brought the Hi Power up and around, putting one, two, three, four, five, six rounds through the back window and trunk of the Ford, spinning it into an eight-foot marble obelisk. Hanson ran to the driver's window, shielded his face with his left hand, and shot the already dying driver in the head as he tried to reach a pistol with his unbroken arm. *Dead.*

A little out of breath, Hanson stepped back, looked at the holes in the trunk, and lowered the hammer of the Hi Power. Nobody would be coming out of the trunk, but he watched it, anyway, backing away from the car, then spinning around, bringing the pistol up again at the sound of shots from behind him.

Felix stood over the two dead shooters, both sprawled half on the asphalt and half on the grass, shooting them, speckling his suit pants with blood and dirt and bits of asphalt. Hanson watched Felix empty his pistol, then stuck his Hi Power into the back pocket of his jeans and walked over to him. His ears rang from the gunshots and he was all but deaf, but he could hear Felix shouting down at the bodies, "Fuck you and your stars. Fuck the stars. Spy on *this*."

Down in East Oakland the first tiny whirlwinds of red and blue lights appeared, formed into clusters, and spun silently up toward the cemetery.

Hanson still had the Hi Power in his hip pocket when the headlights of the unmarked car lit him up. Too late to set it down on the grass and back away. *Not mine.* They must have been watching Felix. The unmarked car stopped fifty yards away, its spotlight sweeping up into his face. The doors opened and slammed shut, but the car was invisible behind the glare. He felt a web of crosshairs brush his leg, pause, then crawl up his hip and stop in the center of his chest.

"Fuckin' stars," Felix said, behind him. "They what set this all up."

Red and blue emergency lights flared up out of the dark flatlands below—little fires in the night—converging and burning toward the cemetery. Behind him patrol cars were already screaming down from the MacArthur Freeway, their sirens drowning out whatever it was Felix said next. Somebody must have declared a Code 33 emergency, sending every patrol car in the city. An opportunity for patrol car collisions and accidental officer-involved shootings. Chinese fire drill. Whoever was holding the rifle sight on his chest should have just shot him, then shot Felix. Problem solved. Send all the other cars back to work.

A patrol car jumped the curb down by the maintenance building, and another one came through the trees behind it. The next one blew beneath the arched entrance going way too fast, off the asphalt onto the grass, the rear end coming around, hammering down a row of tombstones.

He didn't want to get killed in a clown circus like this, or participate at all. He focused his eyes on a genuine star, light years away from the cemetery in Oakland, and watched it all from there as cops piled out of their patrol cars, guns drawn and held in sloppy two-handed grips, crouched and kneeling, duckwalking, waiting for somebody to issue commands louder than the shrieking sirens.

Hanson knew they'd want him to interlace his fingers behind his head, then turn around—so they could check him for weapons—keep turning—then stop, get on his knees, then down on his belly in a prone position, but he wouldn't do anything until he was told to do it. He didn't want to confuse anybody. No accidental discharges. Wanted the sequence of commands and responses to go off exactly like it was supposed to, like it did in training drills.

Felix didn't have his hands up. He looked pissed off, but he was keeping his hands out from his body while the cops formed a circle around him, weapons aimed across the circle. If anyone popped off a shot now, half the Department would be killed by friendly fire. My friends, Hanson thought. Felix Maxwell the drug kingpin and half the OPD wiped out in circular cross fire. He felt the crosshairs scurry up his cheek to his forehead. Four or five cops were shouting at him to clasp his hands behind his head, and so he did.

"Now, turn *around*..."

"Turn around until I *tell* you to *stop*...

"Do it *now*..."

He turned around, hands behind his head, ignoring a female patrol officer shouting, "Freeze, motherfucker." Hanson silently sang a star song: *Star of wonder, star of light, star of roy-al beauty bright, westward leading, still proceeding...*

Then he was down on his knees, watching himself assume the prone position, textbook perfect, probably the best prone position any of them had ever witnessed. On his belly, arms out like a snow angel, legs scissored as wide as his jeans would permit, his cheek in the grass, the red and blue lights washing over his face and the cops' boots. He listened to footsteps approaching him. Someone removed the pistol. He was cuffed and lifted to his feet, dragged to a patrol car, his head shoved to his chest, and then pushed into the backseat. Still alive.

Sergeant Jackson, he noticed, was standing by the car, watching him.

CHAPTER FORTY

EVERYTHING'S FINE

It was almost midnight when Internal Affairs told Hanson he could go home but they'd want to see him first thing in the morning. He'd done a good job, which was easy since he told the truth every time, except when he said that he'd feared for his life, and since almost anyone else would have feared for their life, it was an easy, almost foolproof lie. The most difficult part of the endless interview was not losing his temper, but that had been a big part of his everyday life since he'd come back from the war. But he'd described what happened exactly the same way each time and answered the individual, specific questions the same way, almost word for word, though that made them suspicious at first. On the trick questions he'd contradicted himself a few times, but that was what he should have done, what they wanted, it was built into the process. He might have been, well, friendlier, or tried to be friendlier, even though they'd have used that as a way to trip him up. They were sons of bitches.

They'd offered to let him use the phone, like any criminal, but he knew they'd record everything he said. The only person he

304

wanted to call was Libya, and he didn't want them to know any-thing about Libya, though they probably already did. Still, he didn't want to just hand them her phone number.

They'd towed his Travelall and searched it, and left it for him in Transportation with all the patrol cars, comical looking, but no one made fun of it or so much as spoke to him, coming from IA like he was carrying a disease.

The safest thing would be to go home and get drunk. No surprises there.

Driving home, he saw that the little Korean grocery store, where he usually stopped on the way to work for a half pint of vodka, was still open. They might let him use the phone. Or they might not. Why should they? They didn't know him, who he was, other than the fact that he bought half a pint of their cheapest vodka five days a week. Fuckin' Koreans anyway. They were good soldiers, though, brutal motherfuckers. Good luck on finding a pay phone that wasn't destroyed. If he went home, he could call from there, but IA probably had a tap on his phone. He pulled into the seedy little strip mall, broken glass all over the asphalt. Usually it was crawling with winos, junkies, fuckers trying to work up enough nerve to rob the place. You couldn't blame the Koreans for facing the world hard-ass, he'd never really considered that before. But no one was hanging around tonight.

He'd have to beg to use the phone, then beg Libya to…what? Talk to him? Say "Poor baby"? Tell him he was on his own? Get it over with, he thought. Then you can buy a whole fifth of liquor to take home. Anyway, what did he think? What did he expect?

He sat in the van, looking at the junk for sale in the barred window of the store. He turned the ignition off and sat there looking through the window. Fuck it, he thought. There's no good news to report here. He started up the Travelall to drive home, then killed the engine trying to jam it into first gear. It wouldn't start again.

The lights in the grocery began to click off. He got out of the van and walked to the door. Bars on the windows. Little blinking red lights that may or may not be connected to alarms. Pole-mounted cameras that might or might not be real. The armored door was locked, it always was. The owner had to buzz you in. He rang the bell. Most of the lights were off now. He rang again, looked through the window, spoke into the speakerphone grille.

"Hello," he said, not expecting anything good to come of it. "Hello?"

"We close now," a woman said from somewhere in the back of the store.

"Ma'am?"

"Close now. Too bad. Come back in morning."

"I apologize, ma'am, for bothering you so late…" He took a breath and finished his sentence. "Could I use your phone, please? For just a minute. I'll pay you. My car won't start."

When the door buzzed open, he jumped like he'd been electrocuted. He walked inside, closed the door behind him. "Hello?" The only person he saw was himself, in the convex mirrors mounted all over the store.

"I know you," the voice said. "You come every day to buy small vodka. Okay. Police officer, I know. Use phone, okay. On top of counter. You use."

The voice from the back of the store.

"Thank you," Hanson said.

The old black phone must have weighed five pounds. He dialed Libya's number that he'd written down on a piece of an assignment card he had in his wallet.

When she answered the phone, he began, "Hi…"

"That was you, wasn't it?"

"Libya?"

"The shooting. In the cemetery. It was you."

"Yeah. I probably woke you and Weegee up, didn't I? I'm sorry."

"We're awake, we're fine. Are you okay?"

Another light went out in the store.

"Are you okay?" she asked again. "We saw it on TV. Are you okay?"

Only a single light was still burning at the back of the store now.

"I'm okay," he said. "Yes, yes, I'm okay. I'm okay. I have to go, though. This place is closing up. Tell Weegee I said hello. Tell him about us. Tell him... You two get some sleep now, and I'll call in the morning. Everything's fine. Talk to you when the sun comes up. I miss you."

He hung up the phone in the dim light from way back in the store. "Thank you. Thank you very much," he said. "I'm very grateful for your help. Good night," he said.

He'd walk home, it was only a few miles, and dawn would be something to see. "Good night," he said and went out the door. When he saw the Temple rabbit watching him from the trash-strewn strip of grass and weeds between the parking lot and the street he wasn't surprised.

CHAPTER FORTY-ONE

SECRET GOVERNMENT

Felix limps as he walks down the hallway, angry and brooding, a cut on his jaw, one eye swollen half shut. Injuries from the beating he took in the graveyard, from cops who didn't know who he was, and didn't care. The OPD lieutenant he's paying off told him it was "just the cost of doing business."

In the background he hears a police scanner jumping from call to call, the TV is turned up for *Wheel of Fortune*. A helicopter clatters over the project.

When Tyree comes up the hall, Felix gestures to him, and they both go into the bunker. Felix closes the heavy, steel-clad door and it's absolutely quiet, deathly quiet.

Felix sits on the sofa. "You know," he begins, then stands in the middle of the bombproof, fireproof, windowless room, studying the recessed light fixture in the ceiling above him. Tyree starts to say something, but Felix silences him with a raised hand, shaking his head. *Not now.*

He seems to be listening to the silent room as he slowly turns, looking at the molding between the wall and ceiling. In a moment he walks to the bookcase, stands there, pulls a book partly out, and another, looks behind them, pushes them back into place. He picks up a telephone that's on the desk by the bookcase and holds it to his ear, listens, puts it back down, still looking at it. He picks it up again, jerks the cord out, and holds it to his ear, listens, then carefully puts it back and sits down on the sofa again. The swelling under his eye is worse than it appeared at first, the white of his eye bloodshot when he looks at the reading lamp next to him.

He turns it on, then off, looks up beneath the lampshade, pats the leather cushion next to him, studying the lamp while Tyree walks over. He pats the cushion again, impatiently, until Tyree sits next to him. He points up into the lamp and nods, looks at Tyree, and screws the bulb out of the lamp.

"Listen," he whispers, cutting his eyes toward Tyree, turning the light bulb next to his ear, one way, then the other. "They…"

He touches his swollen eye with the bulb, swallows, gets his breath back. He raises his other hand to the silent room, shakes his head. They're everywhere.

CHAPTER FORTY-TWO

THE LION

The lion's golden eyes were quiet and calm as night, considering Hanson as he walked through the door of the lion house and stopped at the brass railing, close enough to lean over, reach through the bars, and touch him if he felt like risking it.

The lion was looking beyond him now, into the distance, as if he might have imagined himself out of the lion house, back now in the heat and tall yellow grass of the savannah. Maybe he could come and go as he wished, Hanson thought. Even locked up, the lion owned everything.

This wasn't the first time Hanson had come to watch the lion, who had no fear of death, certainly not his own. He hadn't chosen to be born a lion and fearless, a killer with neither mercy nor regret, but that's what he was.

Hanson had been born afraid, and it was only later—it had taken a war—that he became who he was. He was brave on his first combat operations, pretending to ignore the fear that followed him everywhere, stepping on his heels, complaining, second-guessing each decision he made. He knew that he couldn't be brave for another year if he stayed in Vietnam. Two or three months, maybe, but not a year. He was running out of courage, not knowing how much longer it would last or what he'd do when it was gone. Then early one morning, after surviving another ambush, while calling in medivacs for the wounded and dead, it came to him like a miracle: he was dead too. His name was on the books, the to-die list, and nothing more was required of him, he would be served in his turn. He no longer had to be afraid and brave. Fear had left him to deal directly with Death.

The lion was back in his cage, waiting. All the big cats had come inside, restless, turning, showing their teeth. The clatter of locks and bars echoed through the lion house, the screech of steel hinges. An attendant came out through the wall, from a service door, brushing vitamin powder and horse blood off his hands and from the legs of his white uniform, looking at Hanson.

"I see it now," Hanson said. "It's a lot of responsibility."

The attendant nodded, then Hanson had to go, all the cats were pacing their cages. Feeding time.

Hanson didn't have a TV. He had to buy one at a shopping center to watch the nightly news about the shootings. Police officers standing behind yellow crime scene tape at the end of the block. Keeping reporters and cameras at a distance, they announced, in order to preserve the integrity of the crime scene. Three armed men, one with an assault rifle, all of them on parole, had been killed in a shoot-out with an undercover police officer. The officer was on an administrative leave with pay—standard procedure after an officer-involved shooting.

*   *   *

Hanson is sleeping.

It's late. The lion purrs beside him. Hyenas whisper in the brush. In the distance, traffic rumbles and groans above the black water, over the Bay Bridge. East Oakland is deserted. The attendant glides past, ghostlike, in his white uniform.

CHAPTER FORTY-THREE

MEDAL OF VALOR

He was running through Piedmont, into the second week of his paid leave. He'd find out the next day what the Department had decided to do with him. He'd done what he did and he'd do the same thing again, and worrying wouldn't help. The worst they could do was fire him. But all cops are afraid of Internal Affairs, the largest detective unit on the OPD by far, with four times as many officers as the homicide bureau. When they hired you it was as if Internal Affairs implanted a fear chip in your brain. They could do anything they wanted to.

In all the interviews with Internal Affairs he'd made himself say "I feared for my life." The magic words that justified almost any shooting. It was his only lie. But lying is the one thing they'll fire you for, even if you haven't done anything else wrong.

No OPD officer had ever been fired for killing a citizen, on duty or undercover, much less prosecuted. One or two, over the years, had been terminated, briefly, before the police union lawyers reversed the decision and put them back on the job with back pay. How would the Department find anyone to work the streets of East Oakland if they knew they'd be second-guessed for shooting somebody in an instant of panic, confusion, poor judgment? You only had to say you feared for your life. He'd done everything perfectly, but he'd lied.

Nothing to do for it but run a little harder.

He was running down Fairview Avenue when he saw Knox's Piedmont PD patrol car cruising uphill toward him. He turned, hunched his shoulders, and walked briskly in the opposite direction. When he heard the *blip* of the patrol car's loudspeaker, he walked even faster, the patrol car getting closer until, from just behind him, in an amplified whisper, "Go ahead, punk. Make my day." He stopped walking and held his hands high in the air.

"How you doin', Hanson? I heard about it. You killing those three Black Muslims."

Hanson clasped his hands behind his head, took a wider stance.

"Witnesses said they'd never seen anything like it. They said you executed them."

Hanson turned around, looking at Knox. "What else did you hear?"

"A lot of guys don't like you."

"True. What do they say?"

"You name it. Rumor has you moonlighting as Felix's bodyguard."

"What do you think?"

Knox snorted. "You're a good cop. Those fuckers would have killed you if you hadn't killed them first. Three fuckin' thugs, two pistols, and an *Uzi?* Christ. Somebody needed to kill them—who cares why? You did an excellent job."

"Well," Hanson said, lowering his hands, walking to the patrol car, "thank you very much, Officer Knox. Thanks, man."

"Probably, though, you shouldn't hang around with Felix

Maxwell. Not because it looks bad, which it does, but…I've worked the Bay Area pushing twenty years now, most of it on a real police department."

Hanson nodded.

"There was a time, in fact, when I was a real hot dog over there. A real son of a bitch, working narcotics and gangs, a special unit," Knox said, thinking about it, shaking his head at the memory. "I know all about Felix Maxwell. He's smart and he's slick. They think he's Robin Hood in East Oakland." He looked at Hanson. "A sociopath and a treacherous motherfucker. Crazy too. He knows it but doesn't believe it. Don't trust him. Do me a favor and watch your ass."

That night he was still awake at 2 a.m., looking at the dark ceiling. He hadn't drunk enough to go to sleep, not wanting to be hung-over in the morning for his meeting with Sergeant Jackson.

He worked on his breathing. Just as he was going to sleep, he thought about Mickey and Champagne. Lone Pine, up there in the mountains where it was green, the air was clear, and birds danced through the trees.

Across town, Felix was still awake too, watching the stars. That afternoon a couple of OPD motorcycle cops had pulled him over, just to fuck with him, as if they *could*. They wrote him a warning ticket, laughing when they handed it to him. "Have a nice day, *Mr. Maxwell*." When he drove off, he was so angry that he hit a parked car with the Rolls. He'd driven away and told Levon to take care of it.

Levon had just looked at him. "Okay." He said maybe Felix should take some time off, relax a little bit. The cops were touchy about that graveyard shooting. Patronizing him. Relax? There's no relaxing in this world. You relax and they'll kill you.

They're just *waiting* for you to relax. That's exactly what they want.

At 9:50 the next morning Hanson pushed through the main entrance of the Justice Center on his way to the elevators. He stopped for a moment at the black marble End of Watch memorial wall, the names of all the OPD officers killed in the line of duty and the date they died, forty names and dates cut into the polished stone. It seemed small and cobbled together and a little shabby, individual names poorly aligned with the others, some done in a slightly different font where it was obvious that one engraver had been replaced by another over the years, some doing better work than others. As if the budget had been used for something else, and then another cop was killed and they had to find the money somewhere else to pay the lowest bidder. The lettering was too small, the names overwhelmed by the gleaming wall. Half a dozen leafy potted plants had been pushed against the base of the wall. A guest register was chained to a wooden podium flanked by the American flag and the State Flag of California.

The dead had been killed by gunfire and in traffic, pursuit, and motorcycle accidents, most of them victims of bad luck, inexperience, carelessness, and confusion. The street wasn't like the war, where if you lasted a couple of months you had a good chance of surviving your tour because you knew what to expect, what to look for. Where you paid attention all the time because people got killed every day, not every few years. It was war all the time, without marriage problems or money problems, no traffic jams, supermarket lines, or bills in the mailbox. The cops got careless because they'd go insane if they tried to remain alert all the time like you did in a war.

Hanson heard them talking behind the wall, dead but still bitching about how fucked up things were: the out-of-touch

316

Department brass, who were politicians instead of cops, the *citizens* out there, the self-righteous liberals who, with all their education, knew nothing about the real world. And Tyrone out in East and West Oakland, of course. Who could ever know what went on inside his head. You might as well try to reason with a fuckin' mailbox, and if you tried, he'd see it as weakness. And Tyrone *would* kill you if you gave him a chance. The same conversations Hanson heard in the locker room every day.

He crossed the lobby, checking the big clock that was a giant OPD badge, seeing his reflection in the locked glass door of a bulletin board. Anywhere but on the street, when he was in uniform, he felt like he was wearing a costume.

Waiting for the elevator, he relaxed his shoulders, slowed his breathing, told himself to expect nothing, good or bad. Whatever happened was the correct outcome. Don't think too much. Don't react. Don't get angry. You have no friends in this place.

The elevator doors closed behind him when he stepped out onto the fifth floor, a bleak corridor of gray walls, acoustic tile ceiling, recycled air, and solid core doors. The hallway was silent, deserted, dust motes barely moving in the dead air. His ears clicked and whined. For just an instant he thought he might have gotten off on some wrong, off-limits floor, but the numbers on the doors were right. Sergeant Jackson's office was at the end of the hall. Every other office on the fifth floor—those that had names on the doors—were assigned to captains and above.

He knocked, and Sergeant Jackson told him to come in, "and close the door behind you." Hanson went in and closed the door, not knowing what the protocol was. He stood at attention.

He'd stepped out of the grim hallway into another dimension. The light was softer and the air fresher. The Persian carpet had a simple but elegant design in blacks and dark reds. A leather sofa against one wall was dark cinnamon, a big brooding Hudson River

School landscape, sunset in the mountains, on the wall above it. What he'd heard about Sergeant Jackson having a rich wife must be true.

He was sitting behind a solid oak desk, the desktop bare except for a single personnel folder, which Hanson assumed was his. Sergeant Jackson watched him taking it all in. He reminded Hanson of his relatives in North Carolina, the cheekbones and hard green eyes.

"At ease, Hanson," he said. "Relax. Take off your hat if you want to. In one afternoon you killed three citizens. Sit down."

Hanson went to the sofa, and Sergeant Jackson swiveled his chair, following him around.

"A couple of witnesses said it looked like an execution. Three in one day," he said. "You only killed one suspect in Portland, now you're out here doing it in batches."

"They'd have killed me if I'd waited for them to figure out how their guns worked."

"They were there to kill Felix Maxwell. They'd been following him around for a couple of days, waiting for a chance. They picked a bad time."

If the OPD had been following the Muslims around, Hanson thought, they must have watched the whole thing.

"What is your relationship with Felix Maxwell?" Sergeant Jackson said, looking at him.

"A year ago, I hadn't heard of him. The biggest drug dealer in the state, maybe the country, and I'd never heard of him."

"Our unit knew you'd been talking to him."

"I gave him a warning about double-parking in front of Raylene's Discount Liquor. It was pretty obvious that he was a drug dealer. Though maybe I just jumped to a racist conclusion because of the Rolls-Royce."

Sergeant Jackson didn't smile.

"After that I ran into him once in a while. I like him."

"Felix Maxwell doesn't run into anybody unless he plans to run into him. What were you doing with him the afternoon when you shot the three suspects?"

IA had already asked the same questions. Many times. Sergeant Jackson must have read the reports.

Hanson thought about it. "I'd just gotten some ribs at Flint's Ribs and was going back to my car when he came walking up to me. He wanted me to work for him. I said I couldn't. We went to the cemetery and talked about the counterfeit stars he's been seeing."

Sergeant Jackson leaned back in his chair. "We were watching you," he said. "We checked everything out. Nobody believed you. Who would believe a story like that?" He paused. "The Department is going to give you a Medal of Valor."

Hanson glanced back at the painting. It wasn't a sunset. The mountains were on fire.

"Back in the Academy, when I was hitting you with those focus gloves? I saw it in your eyes then. If we fought I'd have to kill you. I talked to the lieutenant about it. I want you on The Unit."

Hanson didn't say anything. The mountains were in flames. Elk and deer were running for a river far below.

"Well?"

"Thank you, Sergeant Jackson. I appreciate that. Working with you. Can I think about it for a few days?"

Sergeant Jackson looked surprised, then annoyed, then he said, "Why not? Take another week off, the award ceremony can wait. Let me know."

"Thank you," Hanson said, and Sergeant Jackson nodded, giving him permission to leave.

Hanson was opening the door when Sergeant Jackson said, "Don't fuck up. The city council's not happy about this. The Black

Muslims are their houseboys. Me, I think it was a good thing you killed those thugs. Keep the others in line. But I'm not the boss."

Hanson turned the handle.

"I know you don't get along with Barnes and Durham, but just testify for them on that case. They think it's a big deal. Call the DA and set it up."

Hanson nodded, stepped out into the hall and closed the door.

He didn't want to be on The Unit. He didn't want to be a cop at all, but that's what he was, and he wasn't a quitter. He'd never quit anything before. If you quit, that first time, then you'd quit again the next time, and the next, till you got so you couldn't handle anything you were given, even the easy stuff, and you might as well put a gun to your head and quit everything.

He thought about Lone Pine. You can get there from Oakland, through the mountains, but you have to leave before winter closes the road. Drive east over Tioga Pass, across Yosemite, and down to Mammoth Mountain, then follow the road south, past the ghost towns and hot springs and bottomless lakes, till you see Mount Whitney.

CHAPTER FORTY-FOUR

RED PORSCHE

Hanson is sleeping.

It's late but still hours yet until the garbage trucks will appear on the empty streets, groaning and banging as the new day begins. For now it's quiet and the air is still as Hanson sleeps. A pair of silvery possums waddle down the hill behind his flat, toward the Safeway Dumpsters.

Across town, on the far border of District Five, the wind is blowing through the alleys, dead ends, and vacant lots that the OPD has crosshatched out of their beat map, where the street signs are gone, faded to white, or pointing the wrong way. Where the old women Weegee said were witches live and die alone in California bungalows on Bleeker Court.

Out there in the wind a red Porsche 911 has backed into a graveyard of broken boxcars, hundreds of them, their wheels and axles gone, stacked two high. It sits low to the ground, the windows tinted black, all but hidden from the dirt road it drove in on. The passenger-side door opens, as far as it can so close to one of the boxcars, and Felix Maxwell pulls himself out of the low-slung sports car. He shuts the door, hears the click-thud of the latch, stands up straight and taps on the window. When it slides down he raises a pistol to his waist, shooting three times into the car, illuminating the interior. The windshield glows pink for an instant, then goes dark again.

Felix puts the gun back in the waistband of his tailored slacks, bends down to look inside the Porsche. He pushes the sleeve of his shirt up to the elbow and gingerly reaches into the car. He takes hold of something, twists and jerks, then he pulls his arm back out, a gold star held between his bloody index finger and his thumb.

He edges between the Porsche and the side of the railroad car, about to work his way through the rows of boxcars to another road. He pauses before stepping out into the next row, takes half a step back, listening, or trying to, his ears must ring and whine from the gunshots, and he's night-blind from the muzzle flashes. He squints to focus his eyes. Something is watching him. What? Against the side of a sagging boxcar, so close Felix almost didn't see him, a boy with a bicycle is standing absolutely still, the way an animal will freeze when it's in danger. Felix is able to make out his features now, recognizes him as he raises the pistol. Even half blind he can't miss.

A shadow leaps up from the grass at his feet and races away. Felix fires wildly at it, fires again, trying to track it through the weeds and scattered junk. Fires again at nothing. The boy and the bike are gone. Three boxcars down, the black rabbit nibbles a few blades of grass, keeping a pearly black eye on Felix.

CHAPTER FORTY-FIVE

WEEGEE IN PERIL

It was late in the afternoon and Hanson had just finished running his miles around Lake Merritt for the second time that day. He was catching his breath, a little dizzy, as he walked beneath the three-story neon marquee of the Grand Lake Theatre where *Jaws 3-D* was playing.

He'd outrun his craziness, left it back at Lake Merritt, looking for him, like an alcoholic stepfather. He was feeling a little out of his body, trying to catch up with himself now before anyone on Grand Avenue noticed. Part of it, he knew, was from being off the street for almost two weeks on paid leave after the shootings. Thinking too much. Life was simpler working the street, in the moment, expecting the worst but relaxed at the same time. It was easier to keep up with yourself working the street with a gun, and you could act pretty weird out there too, before anybody even noticed it.

He passed a *Tribune* newspaper box and the headline stopped him:

OPD LIEUTENANT SLAIN ON SPECIAL UNIT SURVEILLANCE

He felt in his pockets for a quarter, but all he could find was a four-inch folding knife, so he crouched down, then knelt on one knee, legs aching from the run, and read what he could through the warped plastic box cover, as far as the center fold.

The lieutenant must not have been surveilling in an alert and appropriate manner to get shot through the window of his car. Another special unit op gone bad…and found out, this time. But there wouldn't be anything more about it in tomorrow's paper, whatever it really was—a meet, a buy, a trade, a snitch, a threat, a bad look or wrong word—that got the lieutenant killed. That's all it took, Hanson thought, limping up Grand toward the Safeway. The Department would be kicking in doors, and so would some members of the armed Oakland drug community, he thought, stealing each other's dope stashes…

An OPD patrol car turned onto Grand, coming Hanson's way, the cop behind the wheel looking at him hard. Some day-shift guy Hanson had never even seen before. Cops always noticed him right away, since he'd come back from the war. It had taken work, but now he usually talked himself out of making eye contact with them. The way he was feeling today, though, stupid as he knew it was, he locked eyes with him, the car slowing, then going on past and through the intersection.

And then, Hanson thought, if the cops decided to kick ass because of the dead lieutenant, after a mini drug war and a spike in drive-by shootings, everything would all be just the same as it had been before except for a few dead mean-ass black kids—who were gonna die eventually anyway—and maybe another seventeen-year-old quadriplegic watching daytime TV for the rest of his useless life, from a piss-soaked mattress in East Oakland. But then, so what? His life would have been shit even if he could still use his arms and legs. Fuckin' cops, Hanson thought, shifting his shoulders like a boxer. Fuck 'em, he thought, dancing the pain from one leg to the other as he passed the coffee shop on the corner of Grand and Elwood, loosening up to run the last half uphill mile of switchback streets to his house. He took the left on Elwood and leaned into an angry, punishing sprint, working the anger for two long steep blocks before turning right on Mira Vista which was even steeper, up the section of steps built into the broken sidewalk, past the cars parked with their wheels turned and wedged into the curb. Another left onto Alta Vista, snarling, daring his heart to blow up and kill him. Yeah. Do it fucker, do it. At Jean Street, though, he stopped, sobbing for air, sweating tequila, sneering at his weak, gutless heart. Then he heard the slow *tick, tick, tick* of Weegee's bike coming up the hill behind him.

"Weegee," he said, straightening up, turning. "Good. To see you. Amigo."

Weegee was walking the bike, leaning against it, wobbly with exhaustion, but he managed a genuine smile. "Hi, Officer Hanson. How come you not at work again today?"

"I'm on my paid vacation."

"For shooting those guys?"

"Yes, sir. But it's not really a vacation. They're trying to decide what to do with me."

"Did you really shoot all three of those Muslims, by yourself, to protect Felix?"

"Not *for* Felix. They were shooting at me too."

"I heard that maybe you were working for Felix."

"No, sir," Hanson said, and Weegee looked relieved.

"You're different from the other cops," he said, "but I didn't know you was so *bad*. Three to one."

"I'm not that bad, just had a lot of practice learning to shoot. You practice enough at anything, keep practicing, and you get good at it. Whatever it is. Riding a bike, recognizing birds, or shooting people. And those poor guys, they were scared and didn't even know how to use their weapons."

"Weren't you scared?"

"Not exactly. It's complicated. I don't really understand it myself. Come on inside," Hanson said, cutting across his front yard, untying the door key from his shoelace. "Bring your bike in. What've you been up to?"

"Oh, you know, just ridin'."

"Well, come on inside," Hanson said, taking the bike from him, carrying it up the stairs, unlocking and opening the door. "You okay?"

"Okay," he said, "doin' okay." But he wasn't doing okay, and he wasn't just tired, he was scared too. Hanson knew what scared looked like, and he'd never seen it in Weegee. He reached down and touched his shoulder.

"Looks like we could both use some water. You want a glass of water, man?"

"With some ice?"

"Coming up," Hanson said, wheeling the bike into the kitchen. "Don't got Coke or soda pop or anything else in that refrigerator, but hell yeah, I got ice like you wouldn't believe, all the ice you can handle," he said, beginning to laugh at himself. "Just close the door behind you, and we'll be *on* that ice." He ran some water into a glass, put in ice cubes, and took it into the living room. "Have a seat," he said, gesturing to the sofa. "Here you go. Be right back." He returned with a pillow on top of a folded blanket, setting them both down on the couch, saying, "Just in case."

"You gotta go to work today?"

"No, sir. Still on vacation."

"That's what I was hopin', cause I'll tell you what, I didn't get much sleep last night."

"Saw it right away. Police training. Which is why I went and got this take-a-nap equipment, which I think you should utilize, in conjunction with that sofa, in a timely manner, and get some rest."

Weegee smiled. "You so funny sometimes, talkin' like that," he said, and Hanson, his eyes stinging, had to look at the ceiling for a second, thinking that his heart might be what would kill him after all, his own heart.

"You okay?" he asked again.

"Yes, sir. Just tired."

"Make yourself comfortable," Hanson said. "I'll be out on the porch reading if you need anything. At your service. You just holler, okay?"

Weegee pulled off his Nikes, fixed the pillow, and pulled the blanket over himself. "Back there, on *that* porch?" he asked, half sitting up and nodding toward the back of the house.

"That's where I'll be, señor, the only porch they'd rent me back when I moved to Oakland."

"Not going anywhere?"

"No, sir."

Hanson sat down on the porch and looked out at the darkening sky. The birds were gone for the day, their feeder almost empty. He wondered why Weegee was so tired. He should have tried harder to find out. No, he thought, he shouldn't have. He'd find out later. Even worried about him, it felt good to have Weegee in the house. He wondered if he should call Libya, let her know Weegee was with him. The house was always empty, and sad. Haunted maybe. Someone who had lived in the place when it was new and beautiful, before it had been cut into apartments, disrespected, ruined, and for some reason had been left a ghost, all alone now.

He picked up a book he'd gotten the day before at Walden Pond Books and thumbed through it, a new book, about the

Special Forces raid on the Son Tay prison camp back in 1970, including a lot of recently declassified material. Sixty Special Forces troops in six helicopters had crossed the border and continued deep into North Vietnam to assault the prison camp and rescue fifty American POWs. The camp was empty. The POWs had been moved the month before, there was nobody left to rescue.

If he'd come back from Vietnam a few months later, he'd have probably been on one of those helicopters. He looked through the photos in the middle of the book, wondering if he'd recognize anyone he knew, guys like him, their faces blackened, already exhausted and expecting to die. Guys like him. He wondered how they were doing these days, back in the world. One of the photos stopped him, five guys looking at the camera from inside a helicopter. He thought he recognized one of them. He tipped the glossy page with the grainy black-and-white photo into the light.

The phone rang.

He looked hard at the phone, as if he could stare it down, but it just rang again as it always did. He picked it up and said hello.

"Felix gonna kill that kid Weegee. Has to do it hisself, 'cause nobody else will." Then the voice was gone in an electronic wind, before the phone stuttered into a dial tone.

Thank you, Tyree, Hanson thought.

Hanson put the book down, picked his Hi Power up, and checked to be sure the front door was locked. And the windows. And the door to the basement. Then he went into the living room, where Weegee was asleep on the sofa. He sat down across the room from Weegee, put the pistol beneath one leg, and watched him sleep. Weegee needed to be rescued—not just from Felix, from everything. Weegee was worth saving. He was worth everything. He was worth living for.

The phone rang again. He picked it up and said, "Hello."

328

It was Libya. "Felix Maxwell is looking for Weegee. He came here…His eyes are crazy and he's looking for Weegee. Tyree called after he left…"

"I talked to Tyree," Hanson said. "Weegee is safe. He's with me. We're all safe."

"Not while Felix is alive."

The OPD could keep their Medal of Valor and their special units. If he really couldn't be killed, why not use his life for someone else instead of just dragging it around with him, whining about the unfairness of the world. And if he could be killed, why not trade the life he'd already written off for something worth dying for?

"I saw something I shouldn't have," Weegee said, when Hanson woke him. "But I can't tell anybody about it."

"And they know you saw it?"

Weegee nodded.

"Don't worry. Nothing bad is going to happen to you. Libya will be here soon."

Across town the headlights of a gleaming Rolls-Royce on the hunt flare and recede through the streets of District Five.

He didn't have to show Libya how to handle the shotgun.

CHAPTER FORTY-SIX

I'M DONE

With a very small Beretta .22 caliber pistol in the hip pocket of his jeans, his copy of *Skyguide: A Field Guide to the Heavens* in his left hand, Hanson was buzzed through both gates into the compound. Tyree opened the door for him.

"Is Felix here?" Hanson asked, holding up the book. The planets orbited the sun, their paths diagramed against a midnight-blue sky. "The stars, Tyree," Hanson said, "maybe it's all up there in the stars, simple and clear, if only we could read what they've written to us."

Tyree met his eyes, nodded, pointed down a hallway that led to the bunker. "Talking to Levon," he said, "he'll let you in," watching Hanson turn and walk down the hall. A police scanner was on in the next room, but radio traffic was slow.

At the end of the hall Hanson knocked on the steel-sheathed door. "Hi, Felix," he said, speaking into the intercom box by the side of the door.

Felix opened the door and Hanson shot him three times, the pistol cracking like small firecrackers, the muzzle almost touching his face. Three black dots appeared across the bridge of his nose, and his forehead speckled with powder burns. Felix fell dead and Hanson stepped around him into the bunker, closing the heavy door behind him. Levon looked up at Hanson from where he was sitting in his La-Z-Boy recliner, waiting to be shot, a book about Costa Rica open in his lap. *Choose Costa Rica for Retirement: Retirement, Travel & Business Opportunities for a New Beginning.*

Hanson clicked the safety on the little pistol and sat down on the leather couch. He put the astronomy book on the floor. The peppery smell of gunpowder floated in the air between them like smoke from a cigarette.

"I'm sorry, Levon."

Levon closed his book, set it on the lamp table. Outside in the hall they were pounding on the door, the intercom was chirping.

"If the OPD hasn't figured out it was Felix already, they will in another day or two. You can't get away with shooting a police lieutenant no matter how corrupt he might have been. Felix would have been dead soon one way or another," Hanson said, "but I'm sorry it was me."

"I'm going to tell them to leave us be for now," Levon said, asking permission, with his eyes, to stand up. Hanson nodded and Levon got up, walked to the door, and spoke through the intercom. "We'll be out shortly. Please stop pounding on the door so we can talk in here."

"What do you want?" he asked Hanson.

"I'm done," Hanson said, looking down at Felix's body, dark blood spider-webbing his face, pooling beneath his head, and seeping up into the fabric of his suit coat.

"But what now?"

"That's as far as I've planned," he said, looking at the little pistol in his hand, only four rounds left in the clip. "I don't want to shoot anybody else, I really don't, but I'll kill as many as I can before you kill me. The OPD will take a couple of days to put together a SWAT team or a task force to come in here and burn the place down."

"What would you *like* to do now?"

"Walk out that door and leave this town forever. But there's no reason for me to leave here alive unless I know that you won't come looking for us. The police might, but I doubt it. Anything I say will only make things more complicated for them. So I'd like to have your promise that you won't come after me, or send anyone else after me—or Weegee or his sister—once I'm gone. Otherwise, adios. I may as well shoot you and open the door and get it over with."

"You won't have to shoot anyone else."

Levon kneeled down by the body. "Felix," he said, as though some part of Felix was alive to hear him. "I'm sorry, son, but you knew time was running out. You were smart and brave and fought who you were as long as you could. Sleep now. I'll take care of things." He reached inside the front of Felix's shirt, snapped the hourglass free from its delicate gold chain, and stood up. He tipped it over and watched the diamond chips roil and hiss their way to the bottom, put it in his own pocket, walked to the door, and pressed the intercom button.

"Tyree," he said, "Officer Hanson and I are coming out. Things are as they should be. He's going to leave, and then we have to talk. I promised him he could leave. So when we come out I don't want to see any guns."

He unlocked the door and they stepped out into the hall. "Tyree," he said, "would you please see Officer Hanson out. Then come back here, if you would. I don't think we have much time to make plans."

Tyree took him to the door, opened it for him, and walked with him across the compound.

"Thank you, Tyree," Hanson said, "for calling. I'm sorry…"

"Had to happen," Tyree said. "Better you than somebody else. Better than him going to prison and getting murdered on the yard."

Outside the compound they shook hands.

"Good luck, Tyree. Levon too."

Tyree nodded. "I tell him."

Sunday morning. Early for Hanson…or late. It was going to be a nice day, he thought as he started up the Travelall and clattered away from the curb, out of The Ville, and onto East 14th Street. Looking into his rearview mirror, he saw that he could turn around in the street—if he did it right now—and drive back into his past, stopping wherever he wished to begin his life again from there. But he didn't know what he'd do differently, he hadn't made any notes to himself on what he'd done wrong the first time, so he drove on into East Oakland, the familiar streets crossing and intersecting, the future continuing to invent itself up ahead.

CHAPTER FORTY-SEVEN

LONE PINE

It's midnight in Lone Pine. Snow pinwheels in the headlights coming up the unplowed road below Mount Whitney. The lights sweep through the trees and down a long driveway, where they go dark next to a house all but hidden back there. Inyo County sheriff's deputy. Hanson steps out of the patrol car into ankle-deep snow and quietly closes the door with a *click*. He looks good in the khaki uniform, like he's been eating better, getting more sleep, his cheeks rosy in the cold.

Candlelight from a window in the otherwise dark house carries him flickering through the falling snow to the barn beyond the house, where he pulls the heavy-timbered door open, carving an angel's wing in the snow. Inside it feels like September, as if all the grass hay and sweet alfalfa stacked there had been cut and baled only that afternoon, still warm from the autumn sun and scented with purple clover. The hay door is closed and latched against the weather, the windows are opaque with age, but somehow the barn is pearly with light.

Champagne nickers to see him and her silver-gray foal, who

was born late in the summer, rises from the hay. Hanson gives her an apple from his coat pocket and reaches down with a sugar cube for the foal. "See you when the sun comes up."

When he turns to go a small, furious commotion stops him, and the Temple rabbit bursts from a broken bale of alfalfa and, trailing hay, fixes Hanson with a fearless eye. Hanson smiles. "You bet." He gives him the carrot he's brought, turns again, and touches his own forehead, as if he's trying to remember something, and the warmth of the barn rushes to surround him—Champagne and her foal, the Temple rabbit, mice in the hayloft, the family of skunks sleeping out the winter beneath the floor, spiders in their webs, doves cooing from the rafters. They're all safe. He's kept them safe, he tells himself, taking a last look before pushing the door closed. The snow has picked up, and the barn glows in the soft sourceless light.

When he opens the door of his patrol car the light inside comes on and we see something on the seat wrapped in a cone of old-fashioned brown paper which he lifts out, pushing the door closed with his elbow. He pulls the paper open and looks at the bunch of yellow tulips for Libya. Spring, he thinks. It's April again.

Snow has covered the roof and the hood of the car, drifted up over the hubcaps. He stands there a moment, snow in his hair, on his lips, the flowers in the crook of his arm, watching the candle in the window, and we can see that he's not wearing a pistol, he's unarmed. He goes inside with the yellow tulips, past Weegee's snowboard, propped up next to the back door and behind him snow covers the patrol car.

We can hear Libya in the bedroom, where the candle flutters in the window.

"Well, Deputy Hanson. Aren't you something."

"Yes, ma'am, but lookit you."

"Come on to bed," she says.

"Look," he says.

"They're just beautiful," she tells him.

A minute later the candle goes out.

Hanson is sleeping, his arm across the perfect curve of Libya's back, while the snow piles up against the house, drifting higher, deeper, until even the house is gone.

ACKNOWLEDGMENTS

My wonderful mother, Jane Anderson
Judith Root, who I'll always love
Jerry "The Professor" Schofield
Emily Giglierano, my editor at Mulholland Books, who asked the all-important question
My agent, Lukas Ortiz. Hakuna Matata.
Karen Landry, thank you for all the extra work
Dianna Stirpe, the copyeditor who made it a better book
Ken Khatain and Pat Neeser, who kept me alive and out of prison
Dennis McMillan—old friend and publisher
Chas Hansen, up in rainy Longview
James Patterson, for his kindness and generosity
Eric Vieljeux—publisher of *Pas de saison pour l'enfer*
Lieutenant James "Bomber" Alexander
Kevin and Tina Frostad, who supported me from the beginning
Andy Tillman, out in Oregon
Thierry Pitel, trusted friend in Paris
Meridee Mandio, for her invaluable advice

Johnny Jozwiak
Corey Perry
Chase Hamilton

ACKNOWLEDGMENTS

The Mayordomo Dennis Santistevan and his wife, Mariquita

Command Sergeant Major Forrest K. Foreman
Gustav Hasford
Jim Crumley

ABOUT THE AUTHOR

Kent Anderson is a U.S. Special Forces veteran who served in Vietnam and a former police officer in Portland, Oregon, and Oakland, California. He was an assistant professor in the English Department at Boise State University, and, as a protégé of John Milius, he wrote screenplays for New Line Cinema for five years. His previous novels are *Sympathy for the Devil* and the *New York Times* Notable Book *Night Dogs*. He may be the only person in U.S. history to have been awarded two NEA grants as well as two Combat Bronze Stars. He lives in New Mexico.

MULHOLLAND BOOKS

You won't be able to put down these Mulholland books.

BLUEBIRD, BLUEBIRD *by Attica Locke*

RIGHTEOUS *by Joe Ide*

A MAP OF THE DARK *by Karen Ellis*

THE GIRL ON THE VELVET SWING *by Simon Baatz*

THE TAKE *by Christopher Reich*

DOWN THE RIVER UNTO THE SEA *by Walter Mosley*

GREEN SUN *by Kent Anderson*

Visit mulhollandbooks.com for
your daily suspense fix.